APPLE CRUSH

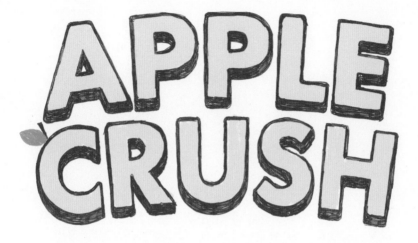

Also by Lucy Knisley

French Milk

Relish

An Age of License

Displacement

Something New

Kid Gloves

Stepping Stones

Picture Books

You Are New

APPLE CRUSH

By Lucy Knisley

Colored by Whitney Cogar

RH GRAPHIC

New York

Apple Crush was drawn and colored digitally.

Text, cover art, and interior illustrations copyright © 2022 by Lucy Knisley

All rights reserved. Published in the United States by RH Graphic, an imprint of Random House Children's Books, a division of Penguin Random House LLC, New York.

RH Graphic with the book design is a trademark of Penguin Random House LLC.

Visit us on the web and sign up for our newsletter! RHKidsGraphic.com • @RHKidsGraphic

Educators and librarians, for a variety of teaching tools, visit us at RHTeachersLibrarians.com

Library of Congress Cataloging-in-Publication Data is available upon request.
ISBN 978-0-593-12538-0 (hardcover) — ISBN 978-1-9848-9688-9 (lib. bdg.)
ISBN 978-1-9848-9687-2 (paperback) — ISBN 978-1-9848-9689-6 (ebook)

Designed by Patrick Crotty
Colored by Whitney Cogar

MANUFACTURED IN CHINA
10 9 8 7 6 5 4 3 2 1
First Edition

A comic on every bookshelf.

APPLE CRUSH

By Lucy Knisley

FOR
Marie King ♡
and all the teachers
& librarians who have
known "Just the book for you."

Chapter One

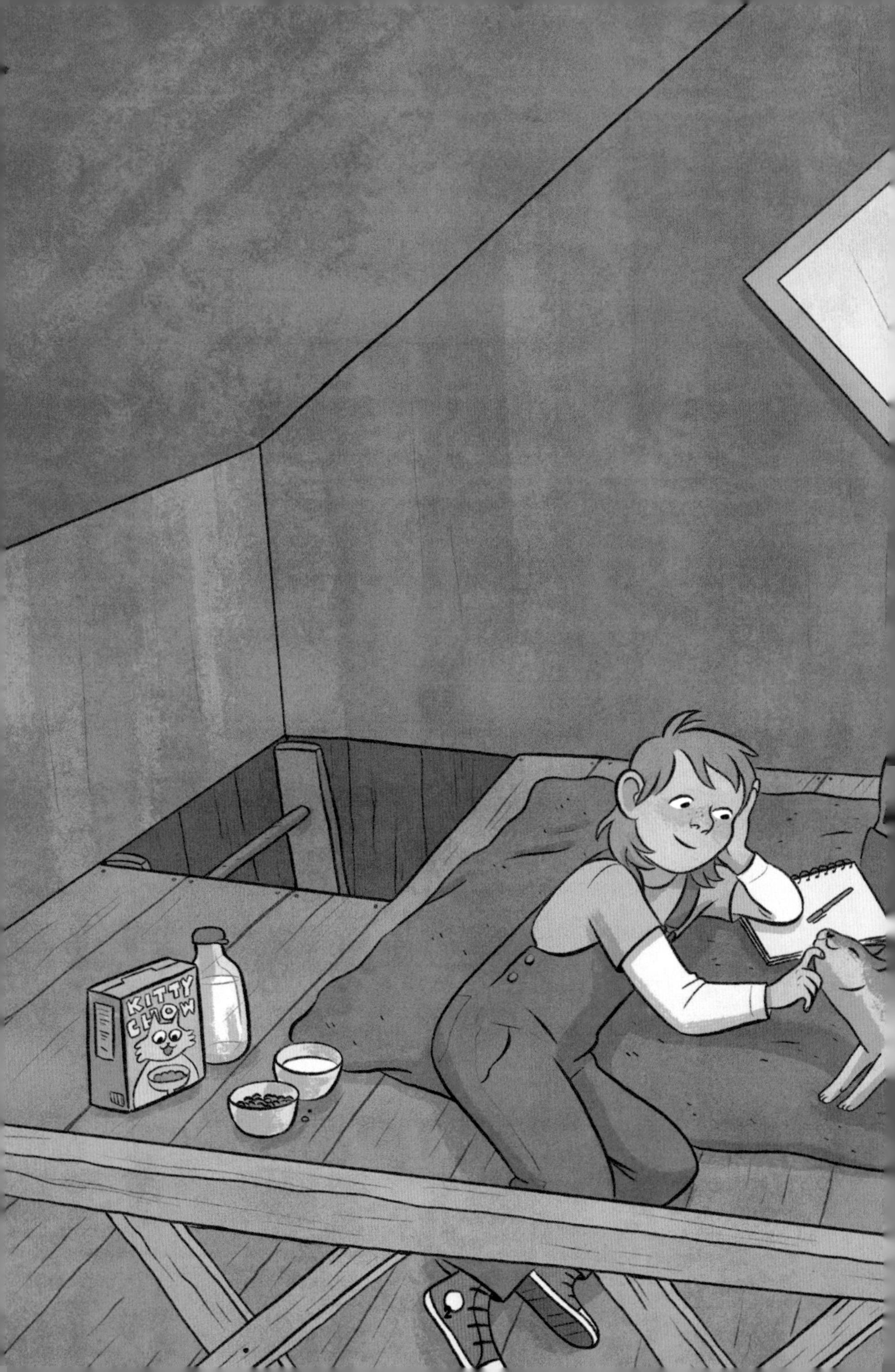
KITTY CHOW

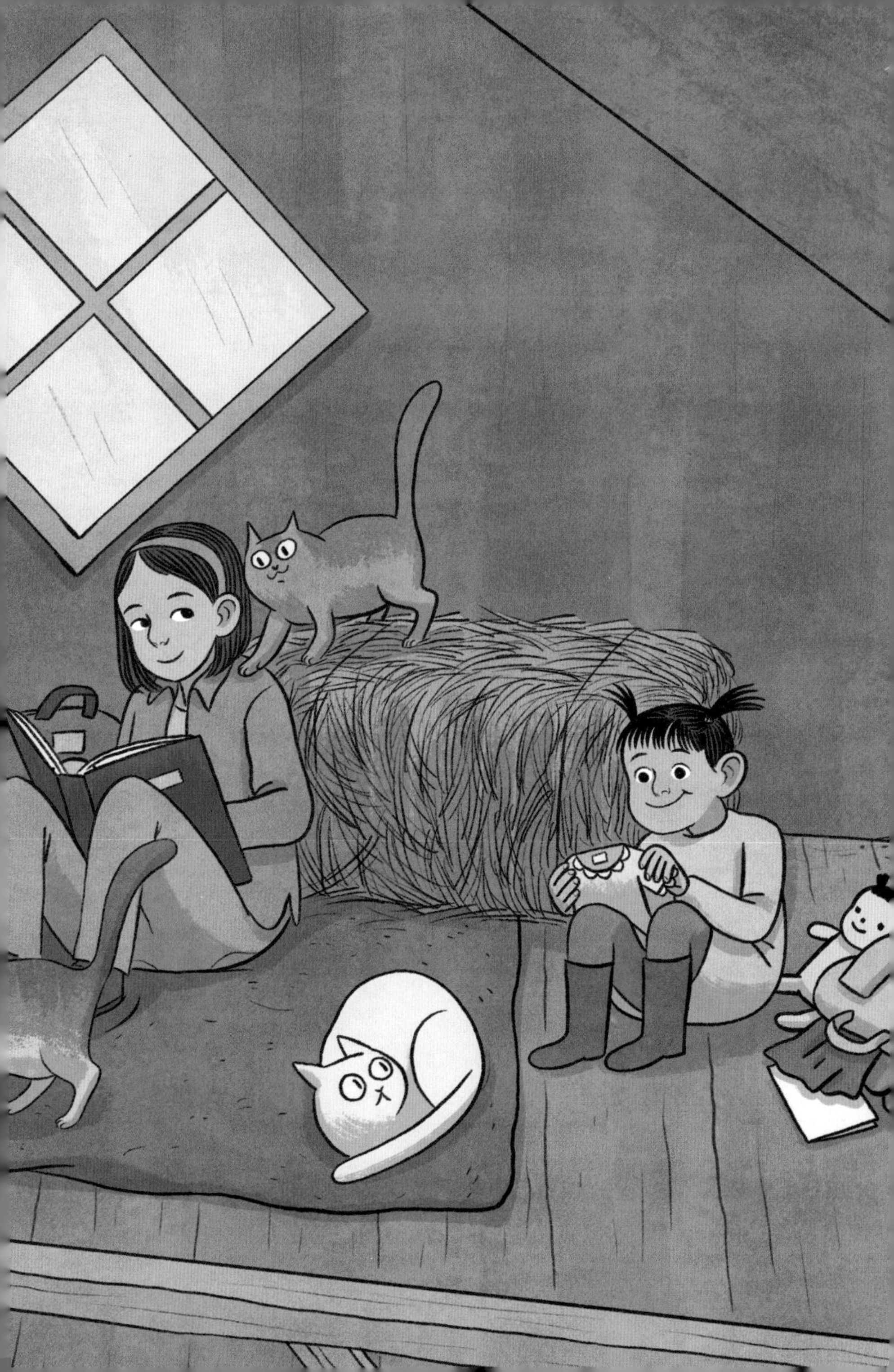

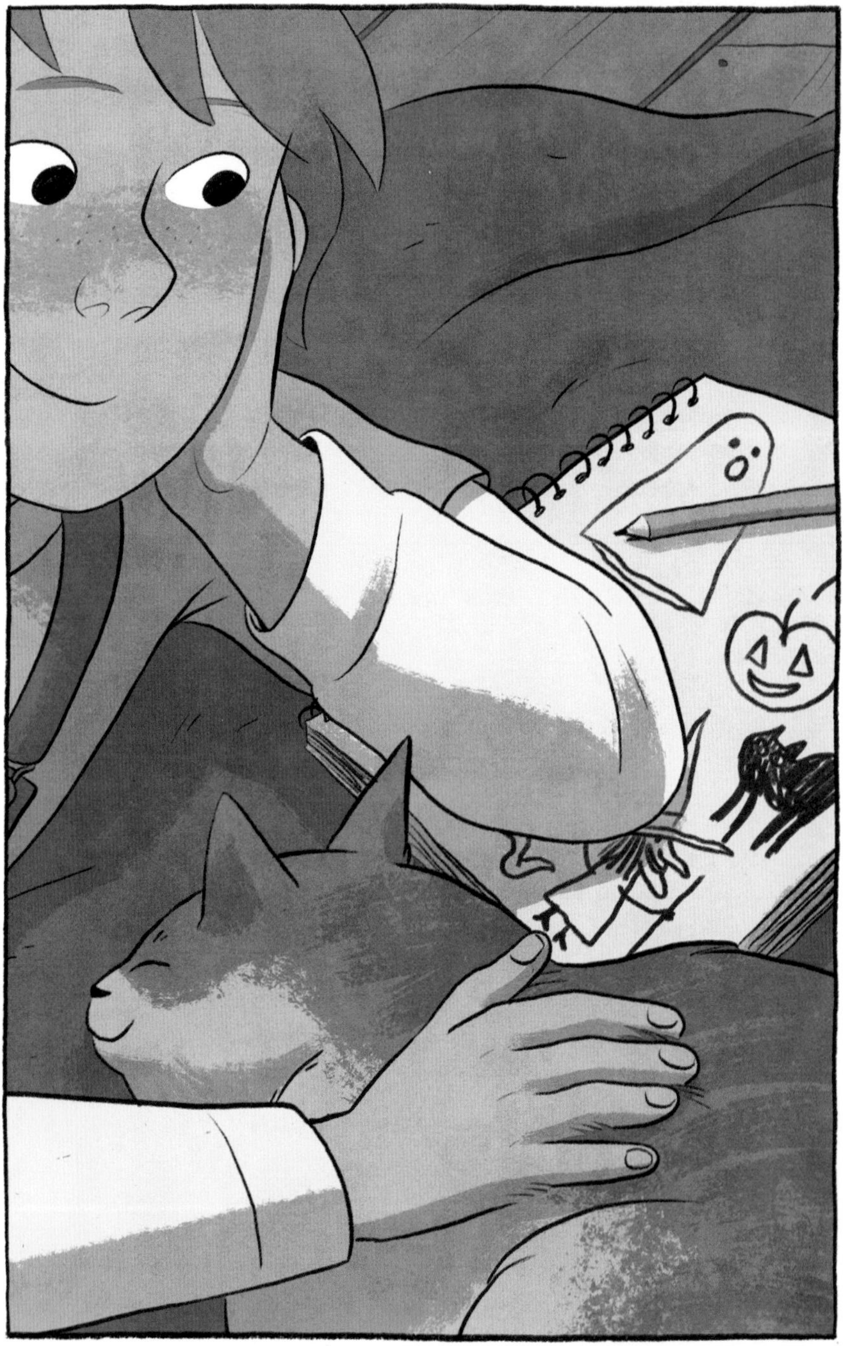

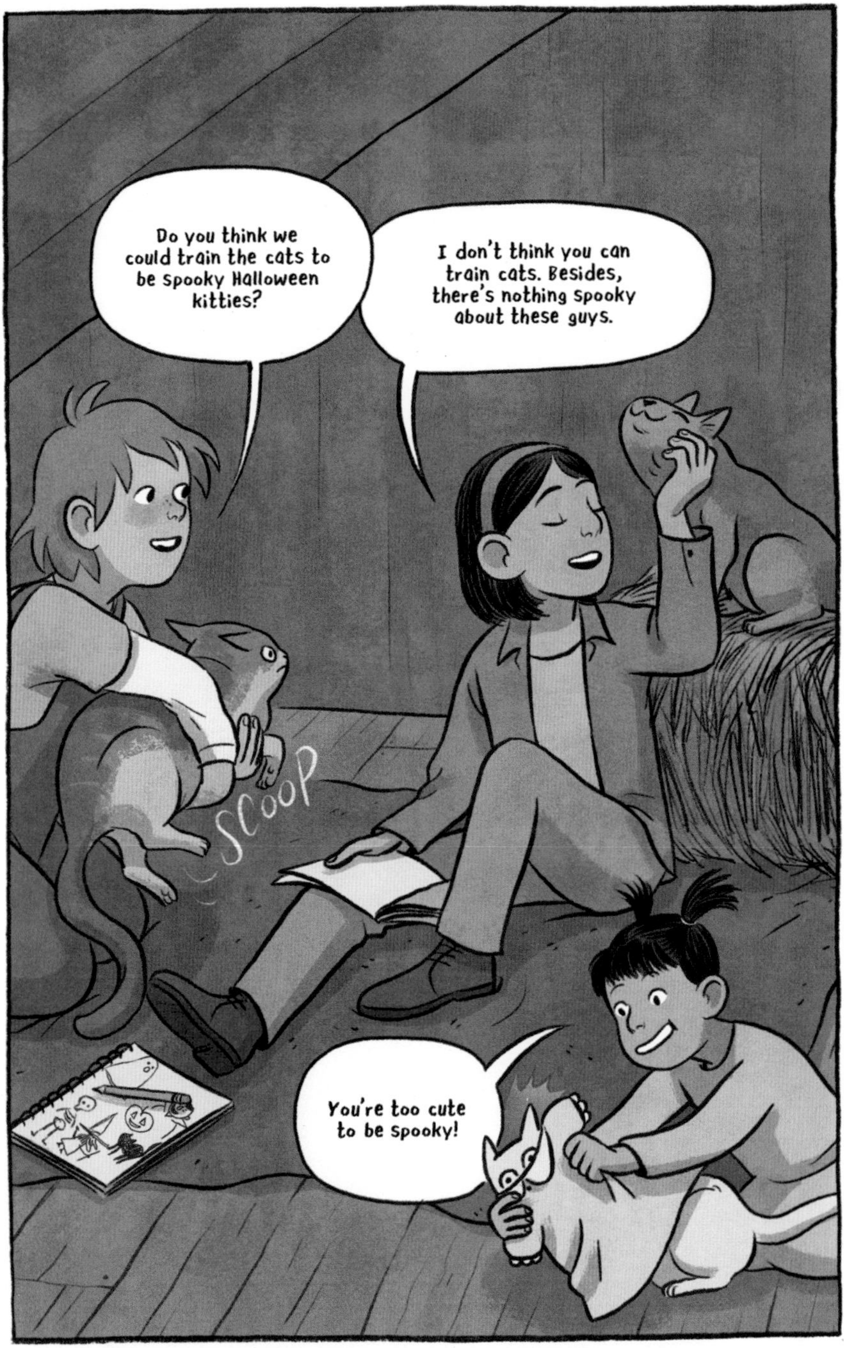
Do you think we could train the cats to be spooky Halloween kitties?
I don't think you can train cats. Besides, there's nothing spooky about these guys.
SCOOP
You're too cute to be spooky!

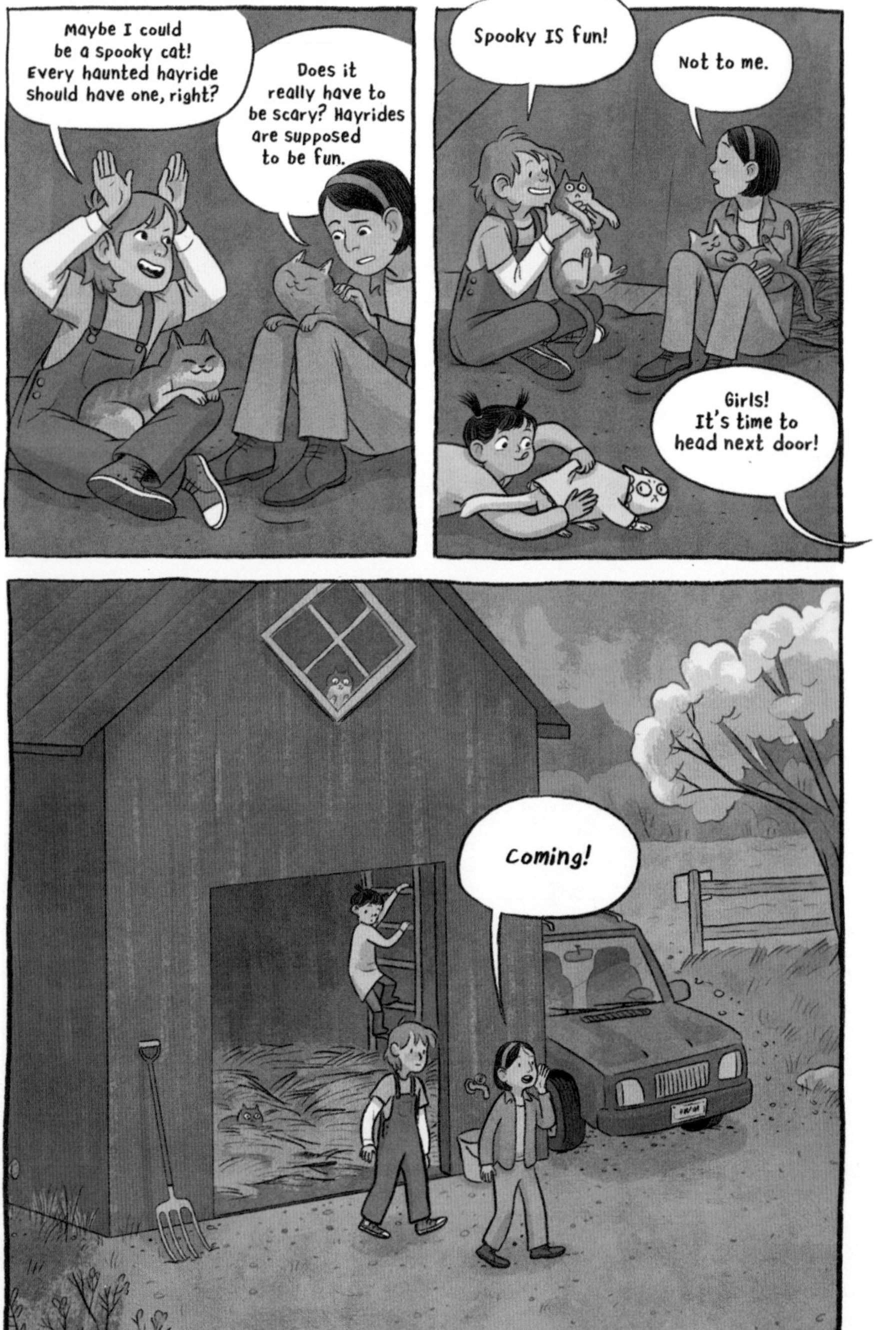
Maybe I could be a spooky cat! Every haunted hayride should have one, right?
Does it really have to be scary? Hayrides are supposed to be fun.
Spooky IS fun!
Not to me.
Girls! It's time to head next door!
Coming!

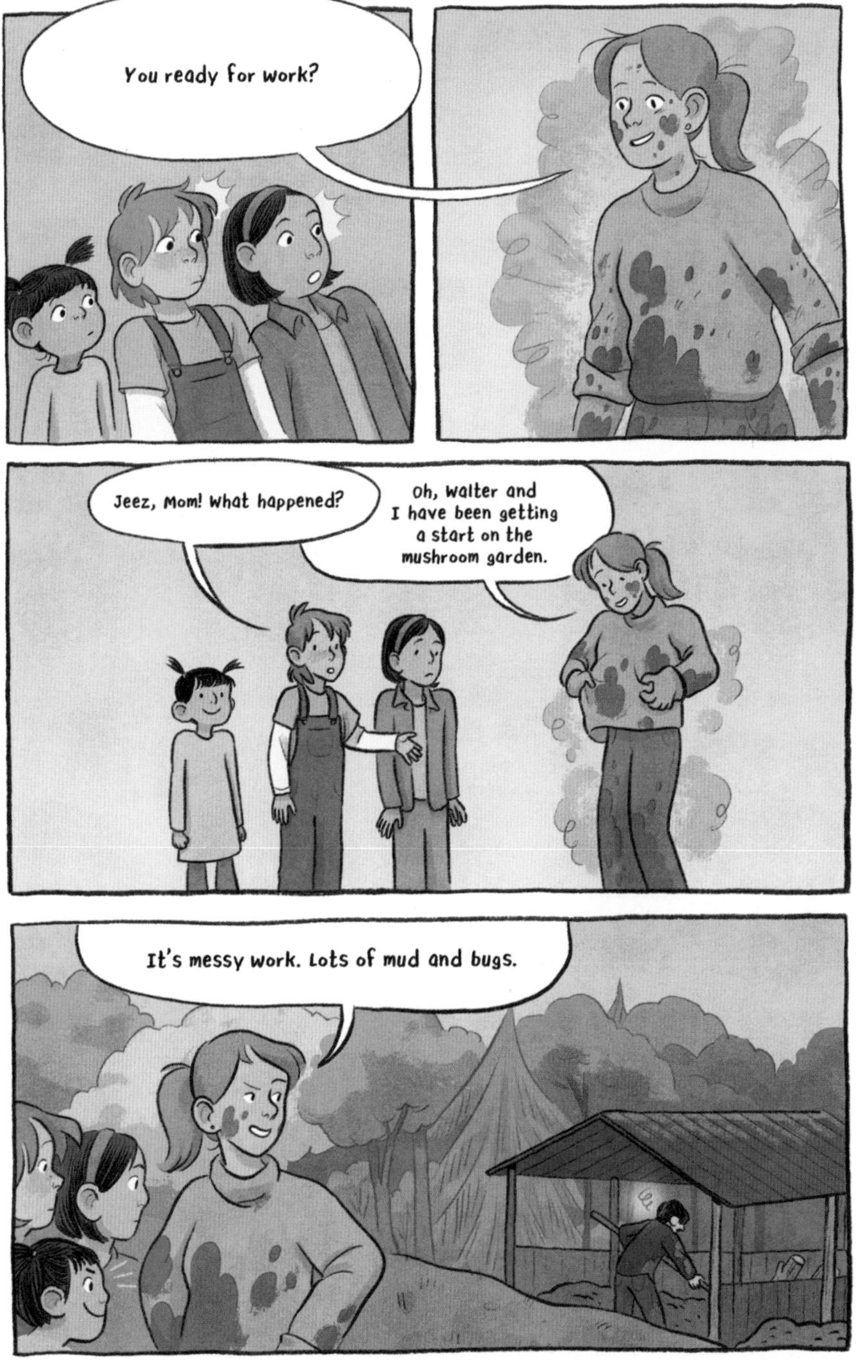
You ready for work?
Jeez, Mom! What happened?
Oh, Walter and I have been getting a start on the mushroom garden.
It's messy work. Lots of mud and bugs.

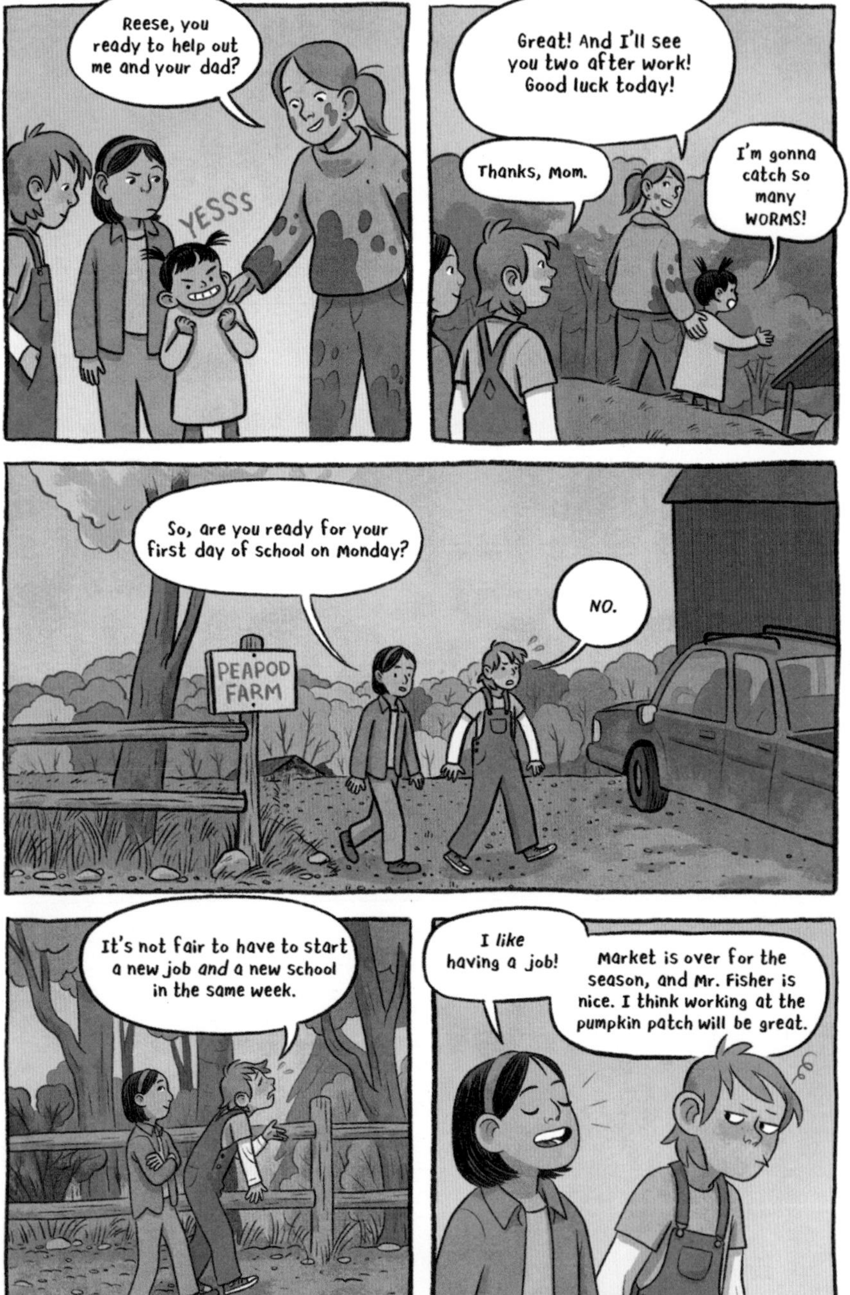
Reese, you ready to help out me and your dad?
YESSS
Great! And I'll see you two after work! Good luck today!
Thanks, Mom.
I'm gonna catch so many WORMS!
So, are you ready for your first day of school on Monday?
PEAPOD FARM
NO.
It's not fair to have to start a new job *and* a new school in the same week.
I *like* having a job!
Market is over for the season, and Mr. Fisher is nice. I think working at the pumpkin patch will be great.

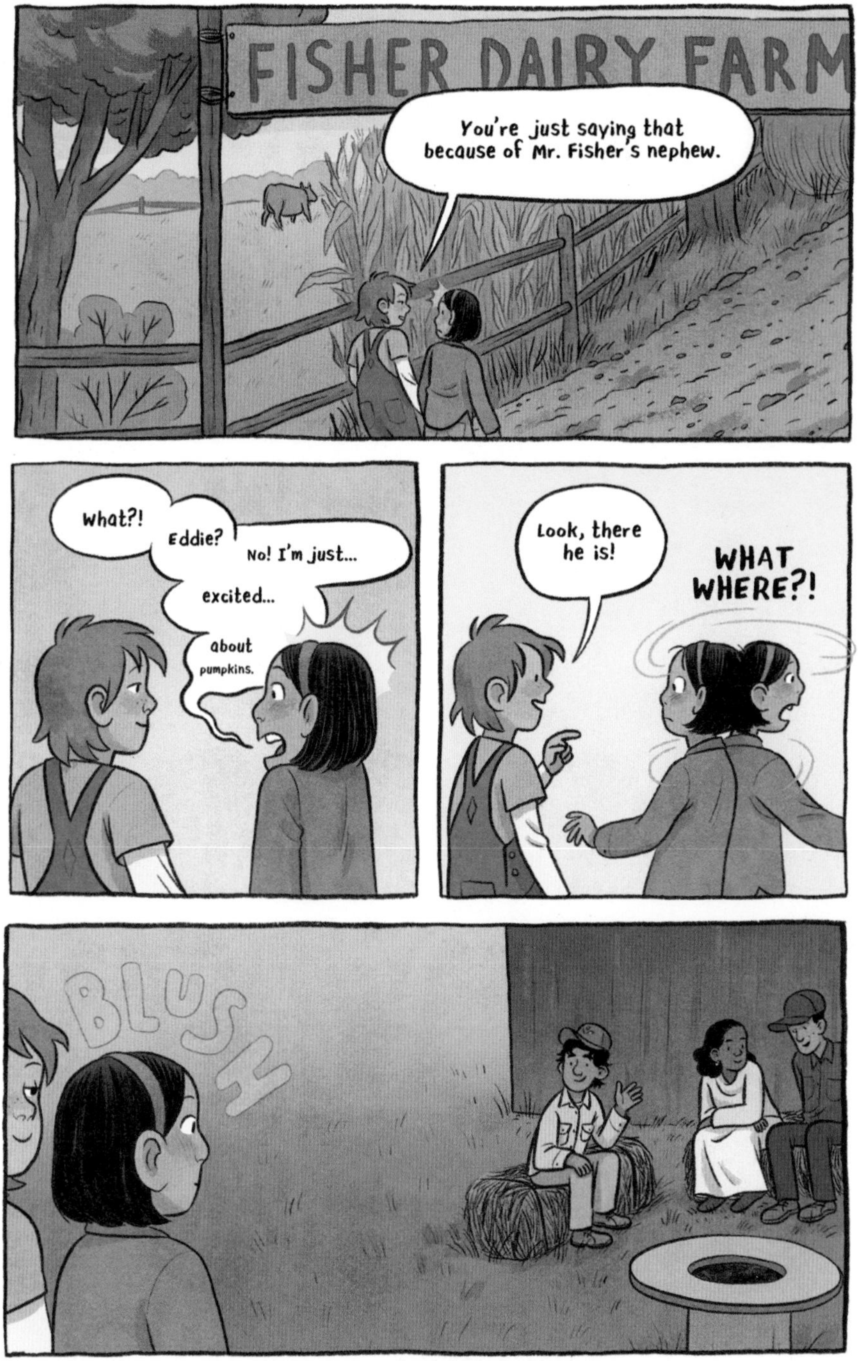
FISHER DAIRY FARM
You're just saying that because of Mr. Fisher's nephew.
What?!
Eddie?
No! I'm just...
excited...
about
pumpkins.
Look, there he is!
WHAT WHERE?!
BLUSH

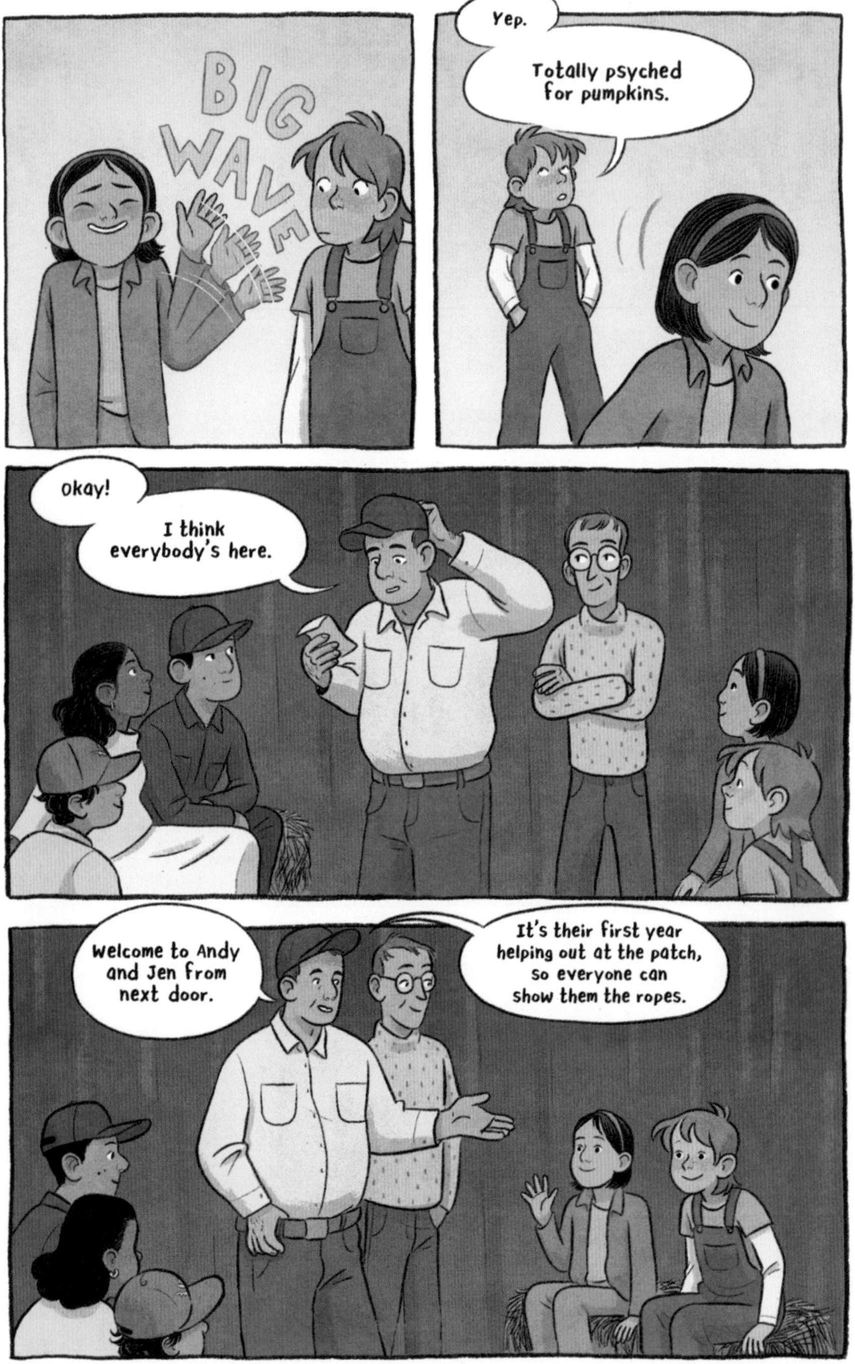
BIG WAVE
Yep.
Totally psyched for pumpkins.
Okay!
I think everybody's here.
Welcome to Andy and Jen from next door.
It's their first year helping out at the patch, so everyone can show them the ropes.

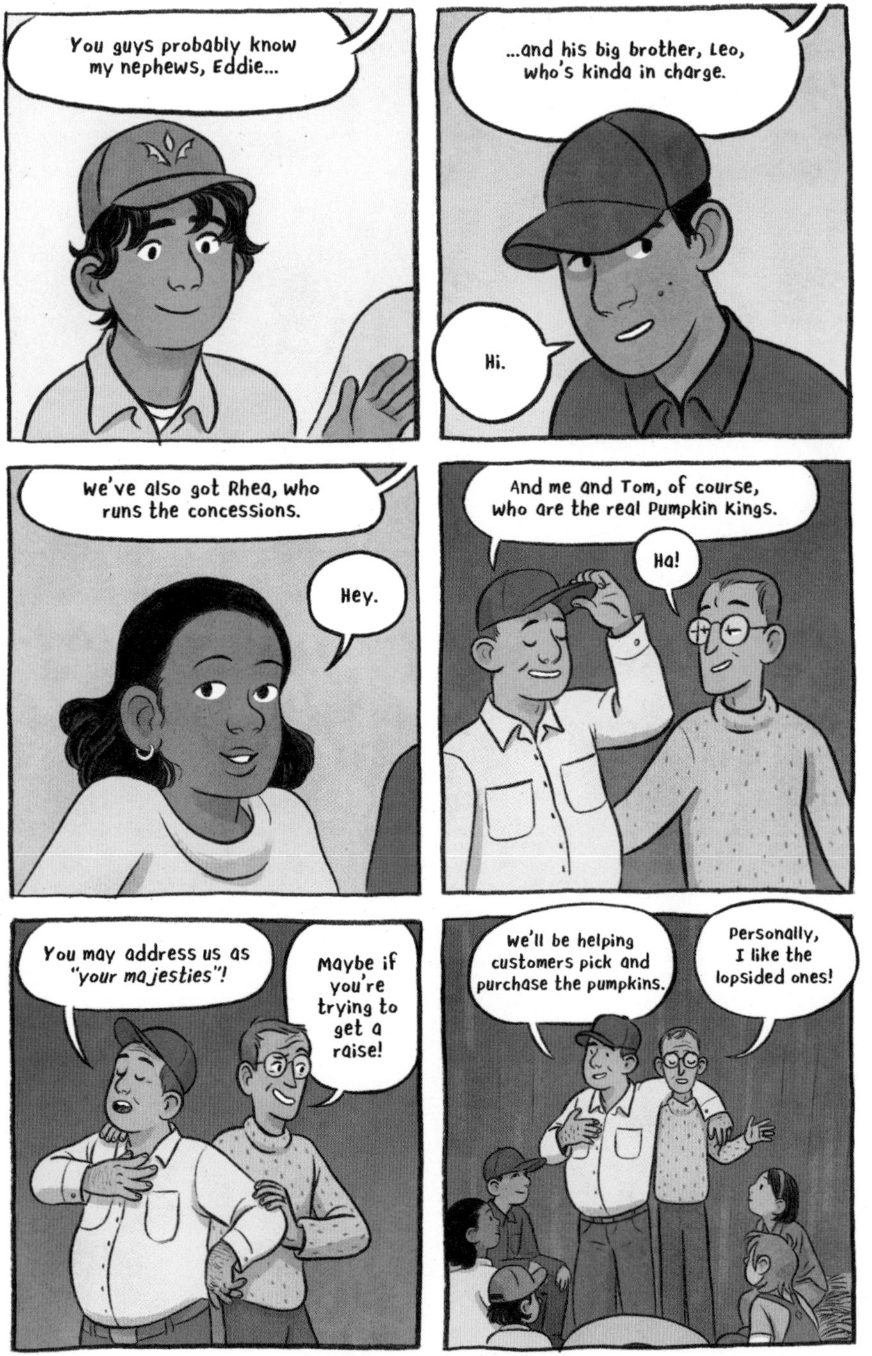

You guys probably know my nephews, Eddie...
...and his big brother, Leo, who's kinda in charge.
Hi.
We've also got Rhea, who runs the concessions.
Hey.
And me and Tom, of course, who are the real Pumpkin Kings.
Ha!
You may address us as "your majesties"!
Maybe if you're trying to get a raise!
We'll be helping customers pick and purchase the pumpkins.
Personally, I like the lopsided ones!

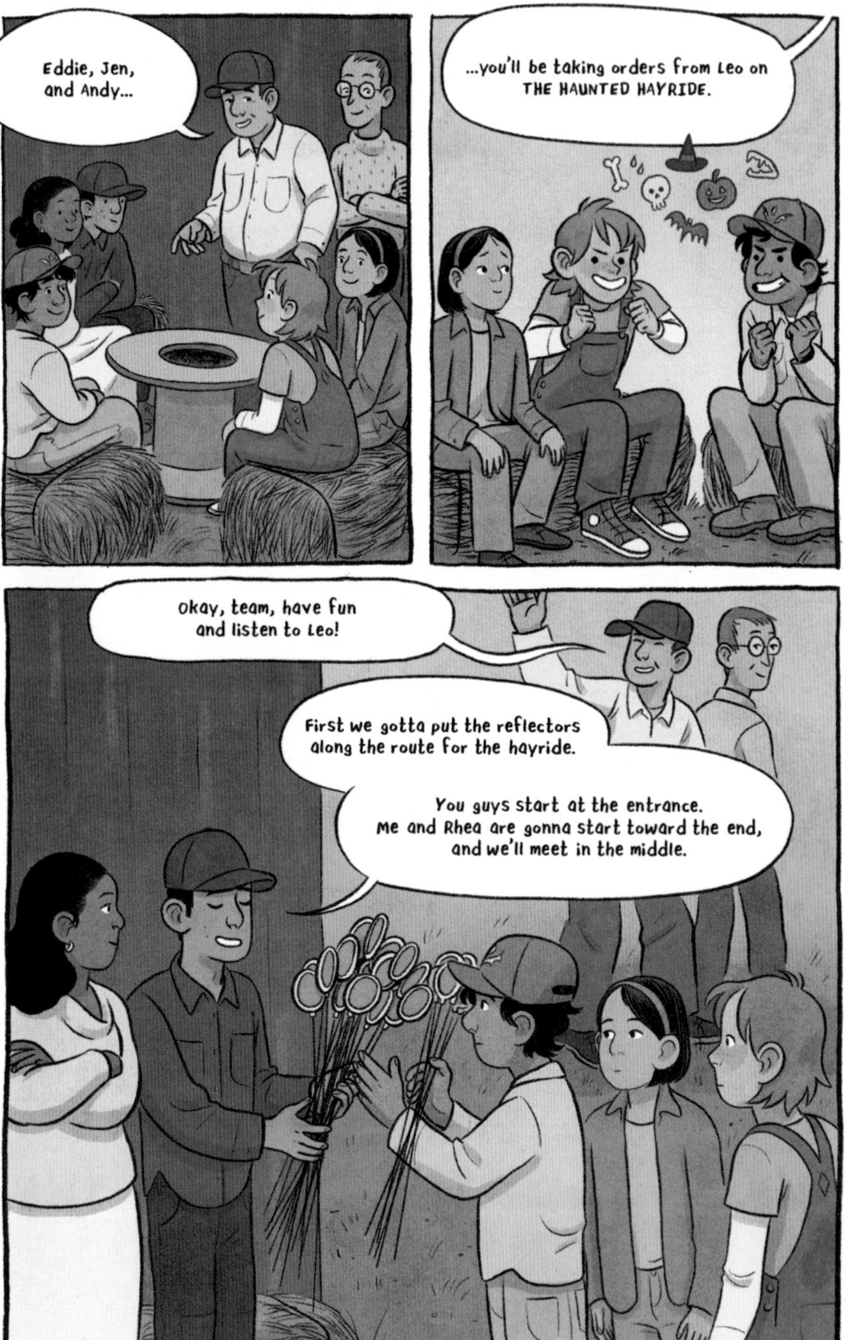
Eddie, Jen, and Andy...
...you'll be taking orders from Leo on THE HAUNTED HAYRIDE.
Okay, team, have fun and listen to Leo!
First we gotta put the reflectors along the route for the hayride.
You guys start at the entrance. Me and Rhea are gonna start toward the end, and we'll meet in the middle.

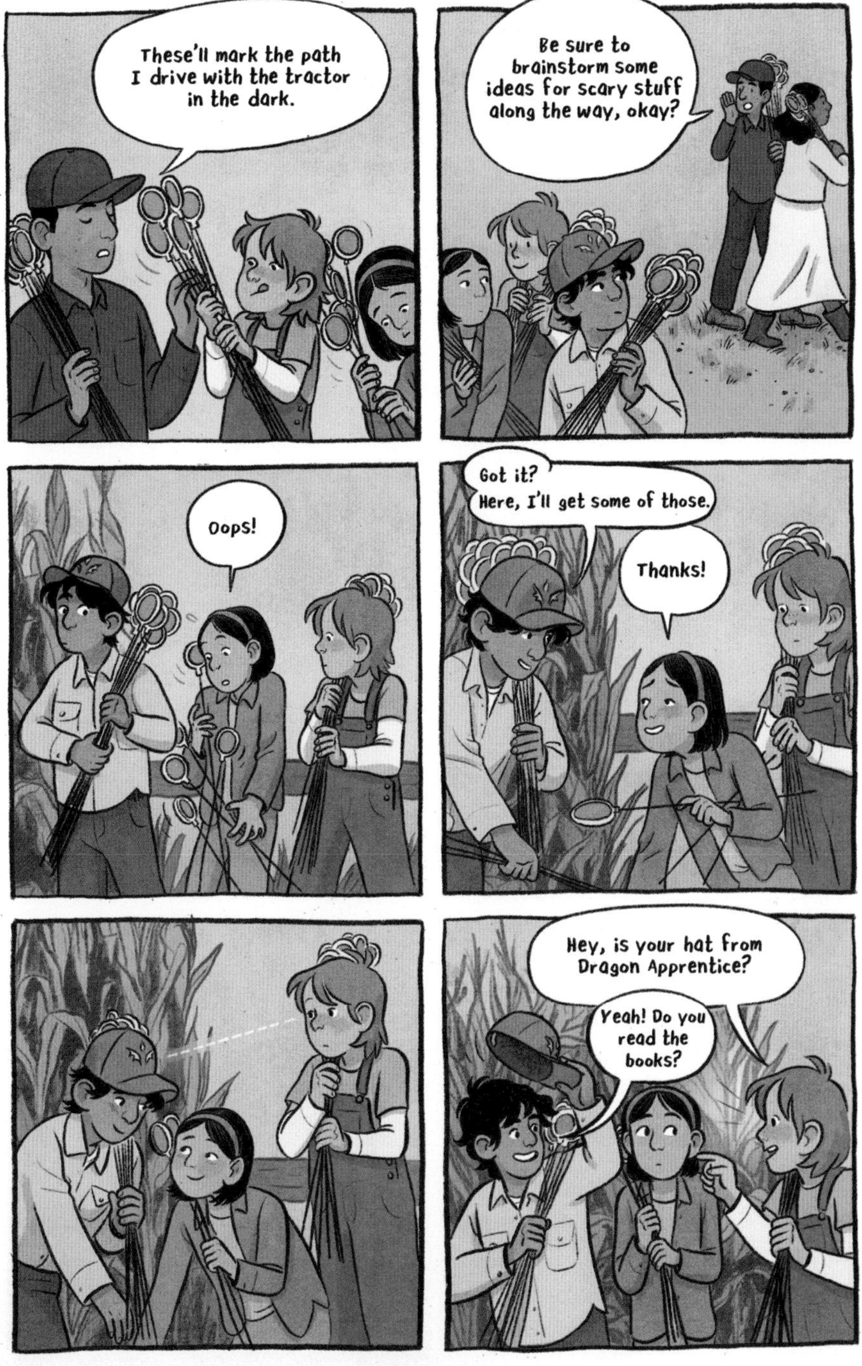
These'll mark the path I drive with the tractor in the dark.
Be sure to brainstorm some ideas for scary stuff along the way, okay?
Oops!
Got it? Here, I'll get some of those.
Thanks!
Hey, is your hat from Dragon Apprentice?
Yeah! Do you read the books?

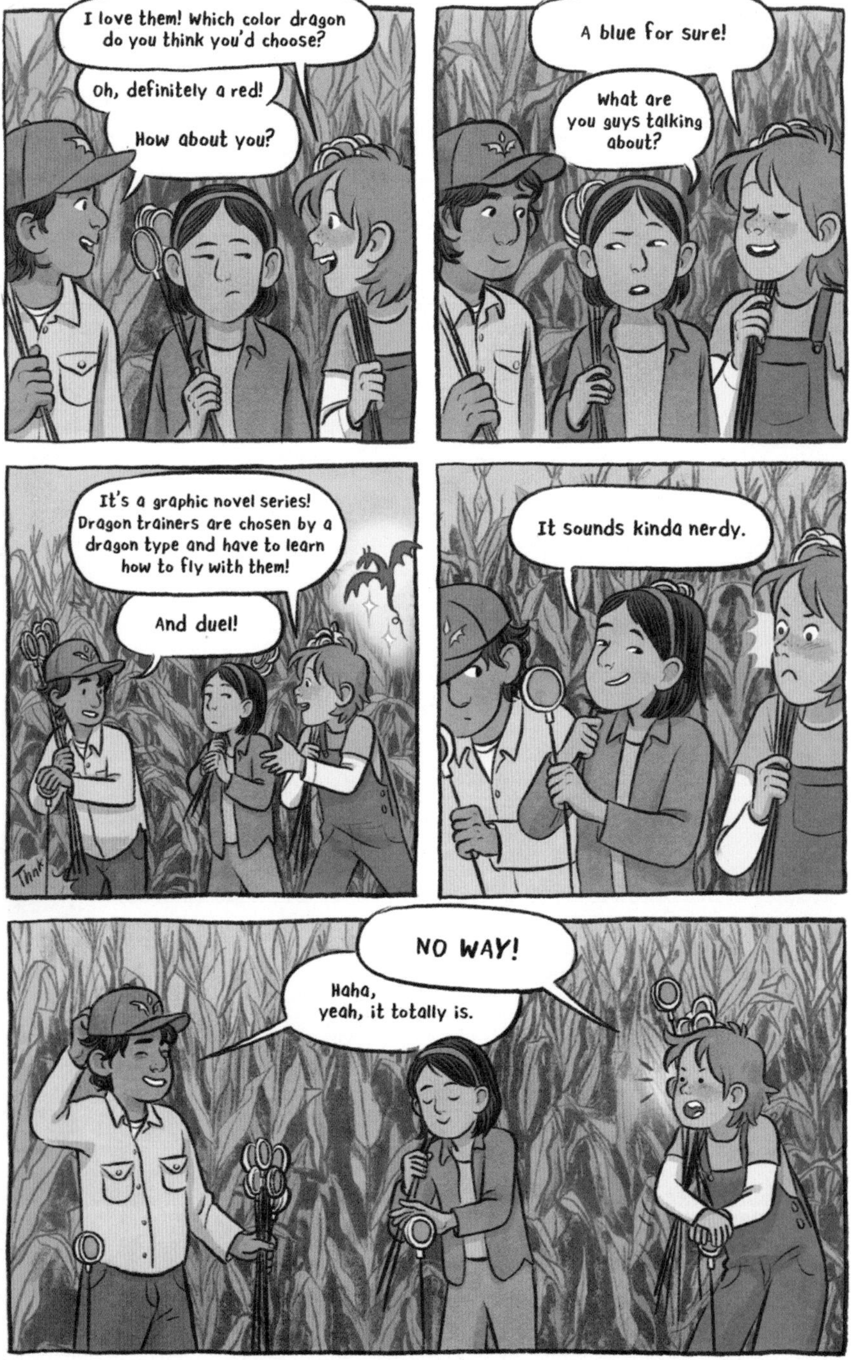

I love them! Which color dragon do you think you'd choose?
Oh, definitely a red!
How about you?
A blue for sure!
What are you guys talking about?
It's a graphic novel series! Dragon trainers are chosen by a dragon type and have to learn how to fly with them!
And duel!
Thnk
It sounds kinda nerdy.
NO WAY!
Haha, yeah, it totally is.

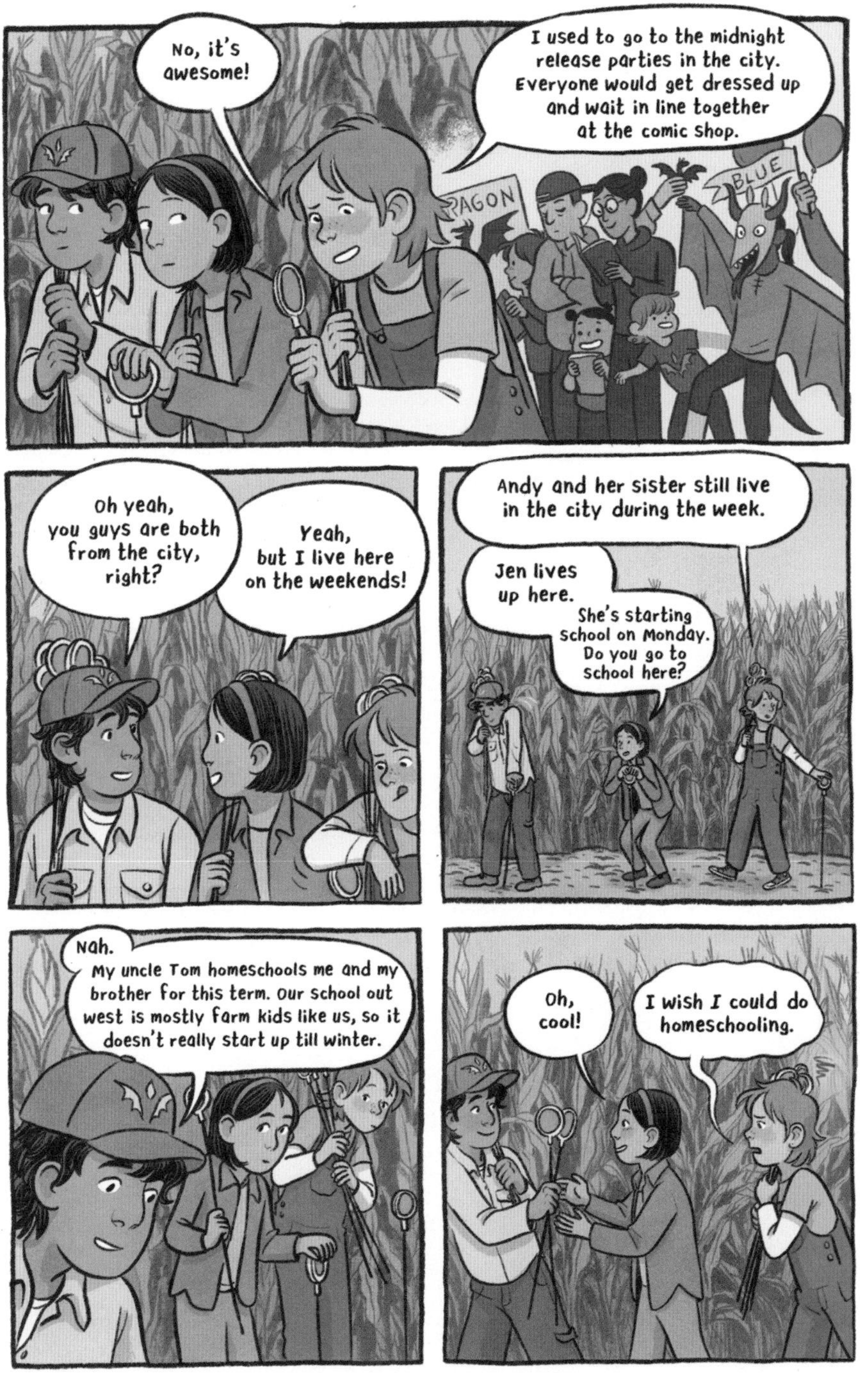
No, it's awesome!
I used to go to the midnight release parties in the city. Everyone would get dressed up and wait in line together at the comic shop.
AGON
BLUE
Oh yeah, you guys are both from the city, right?
Yeah, but I live here on the weekends!
Andy and her sister still live in the city during the week.
Jen lives up here.
She's starting school on Monday. Do you go to school here?
Nah.
My uncle Tom homeschools me and my brother for this term. Our school out west is mostly farm kids like us, so it doesn't really start up till winter.
Oh, cool!
I wish I could do homeschooling.

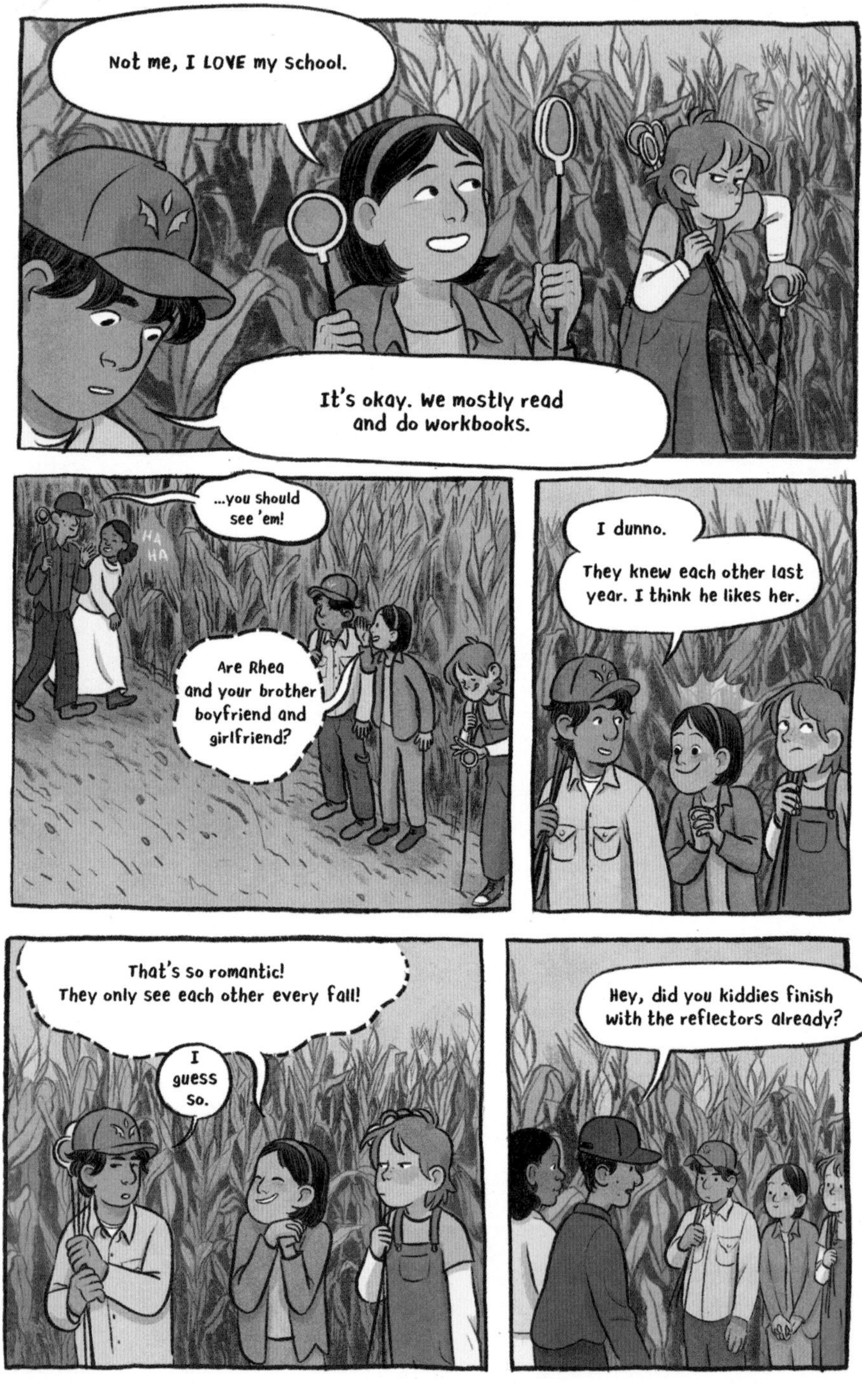
Not me, I LOVE my school.
It's okay. We mostly read and do workbooks.
...you should see 'em!
HA HA
Are Rhea and your brother boyfriend and girlfriend?
I dunno.
They knew each other last year. I think he likes her.
That's so romantic! They only see each other every fall!
I guess so.
Hey, did you kiddies finish with the reflectors already?

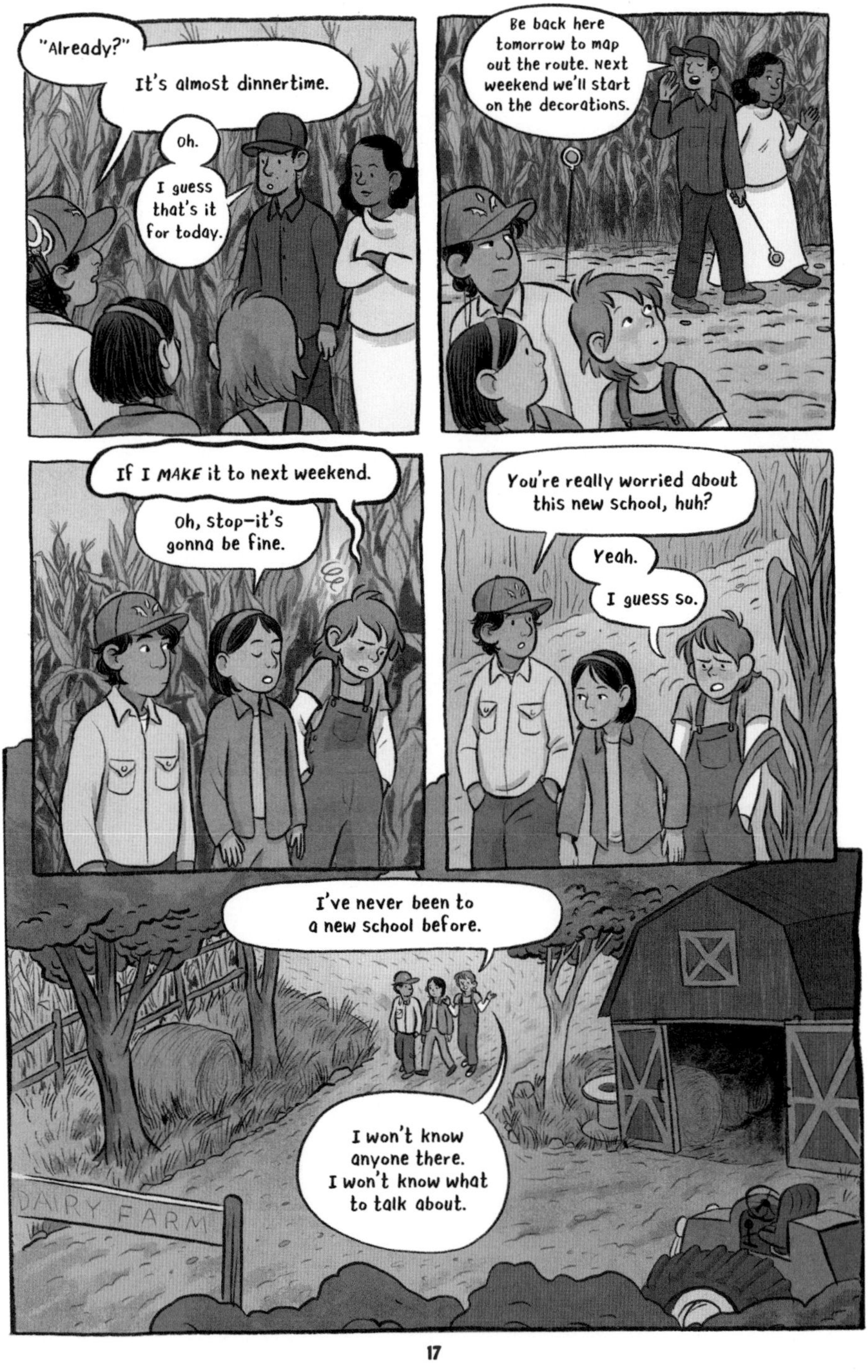
"Already?"
It's almost dinnertime.
Oh.
I guess that's it for today.
Be back here tomorrow to map out the route. Next weekend we'll start on the decorations.
If I MAKE it to next weekend.
Oh, stop—it's gonna be fine.
You're really worried about this new school, huh?
Yeah.
I guess so.
I've never been to a new school before.
I won't know anyone there. I won't know what to talk about.
DAIRY FARM

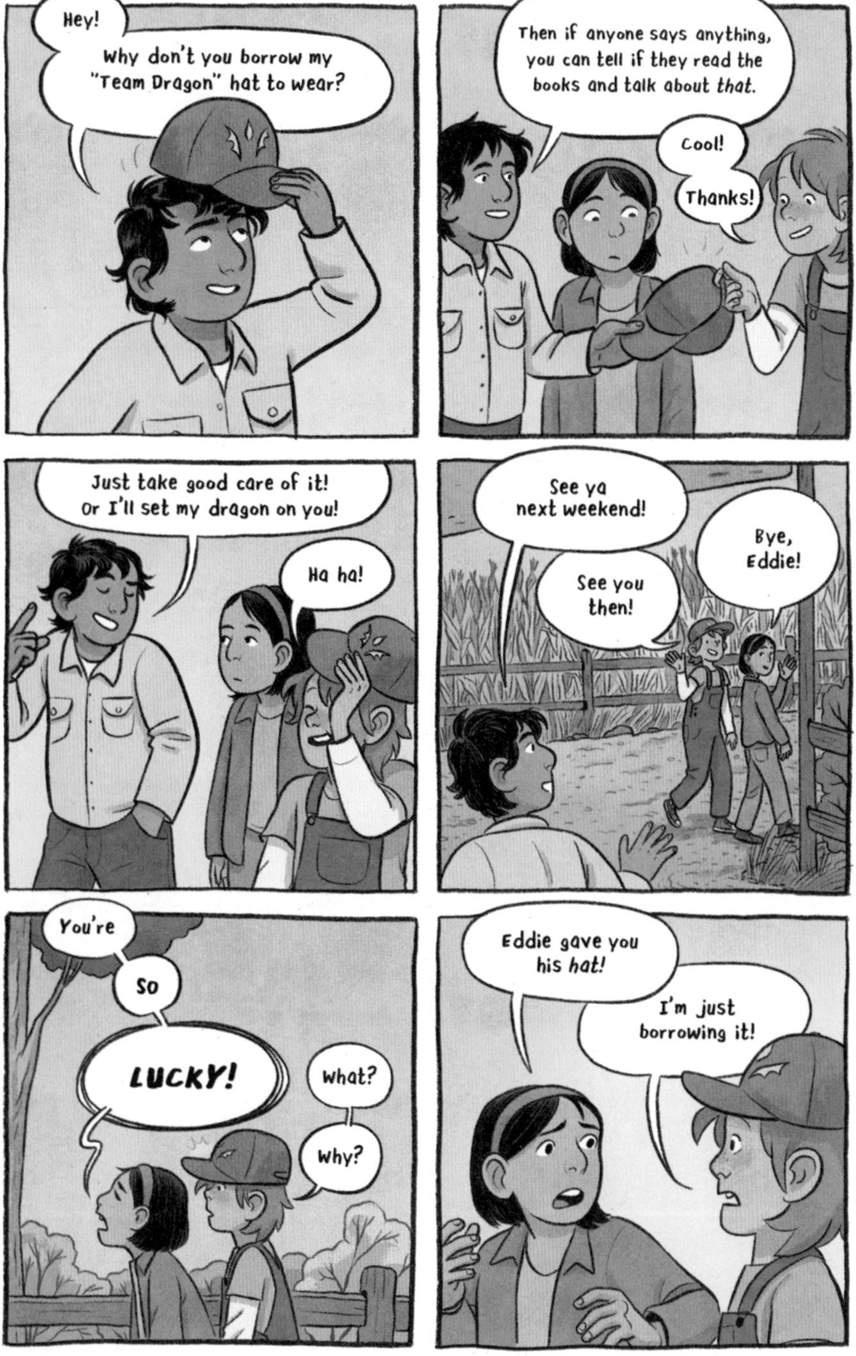
Hey!
Why don't you borrow my "Team Dragon" hat to wear?
Then if anyone says anything, you can tell if they read the books and talk about *that*.
Cool!
Thanks!
Just take good care of it! Or I'll set my dragon on you!
Ha ha!
See ya next weekend!
See you then!
Bye, Eddie!
You're
So
LUCKY!
What?
Why?
Eddie gave you his *hat!*
I'm just borrowing it!

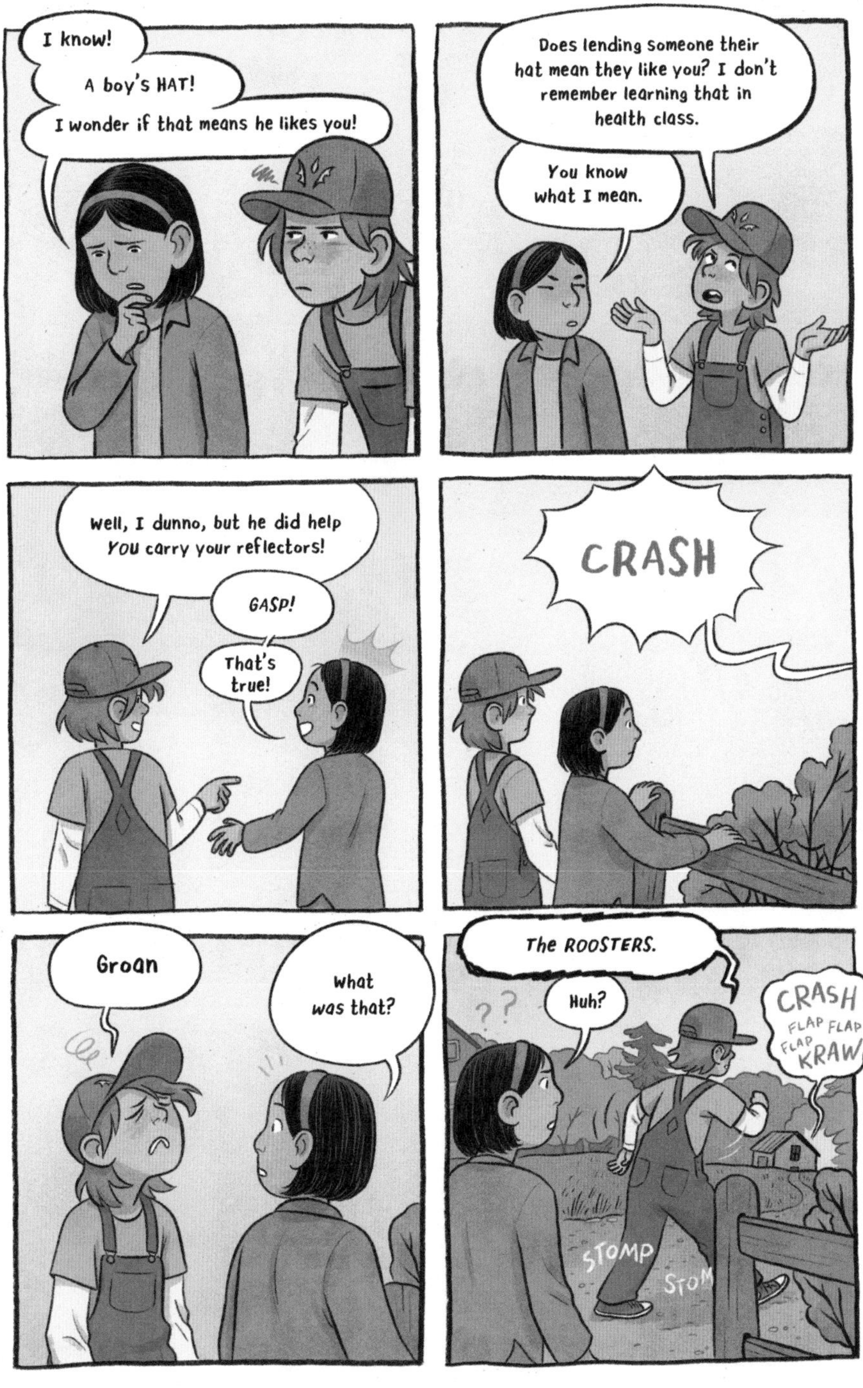
I know!
A boy's HAT!
I wonder if that means he likes you!
Does lending someone their hat mean they like you? I don't remember learning that in health class.
You know what I mean.
Well, I dunno, but he did help YOU carry your reflectors!
GASP!
That's true!
CRASH
Groan
What was that?
The ROOSTERS.
Huh?
? ?
CRASH
FLAP FLAP
FLAP
KRAW
STOMP
STOM

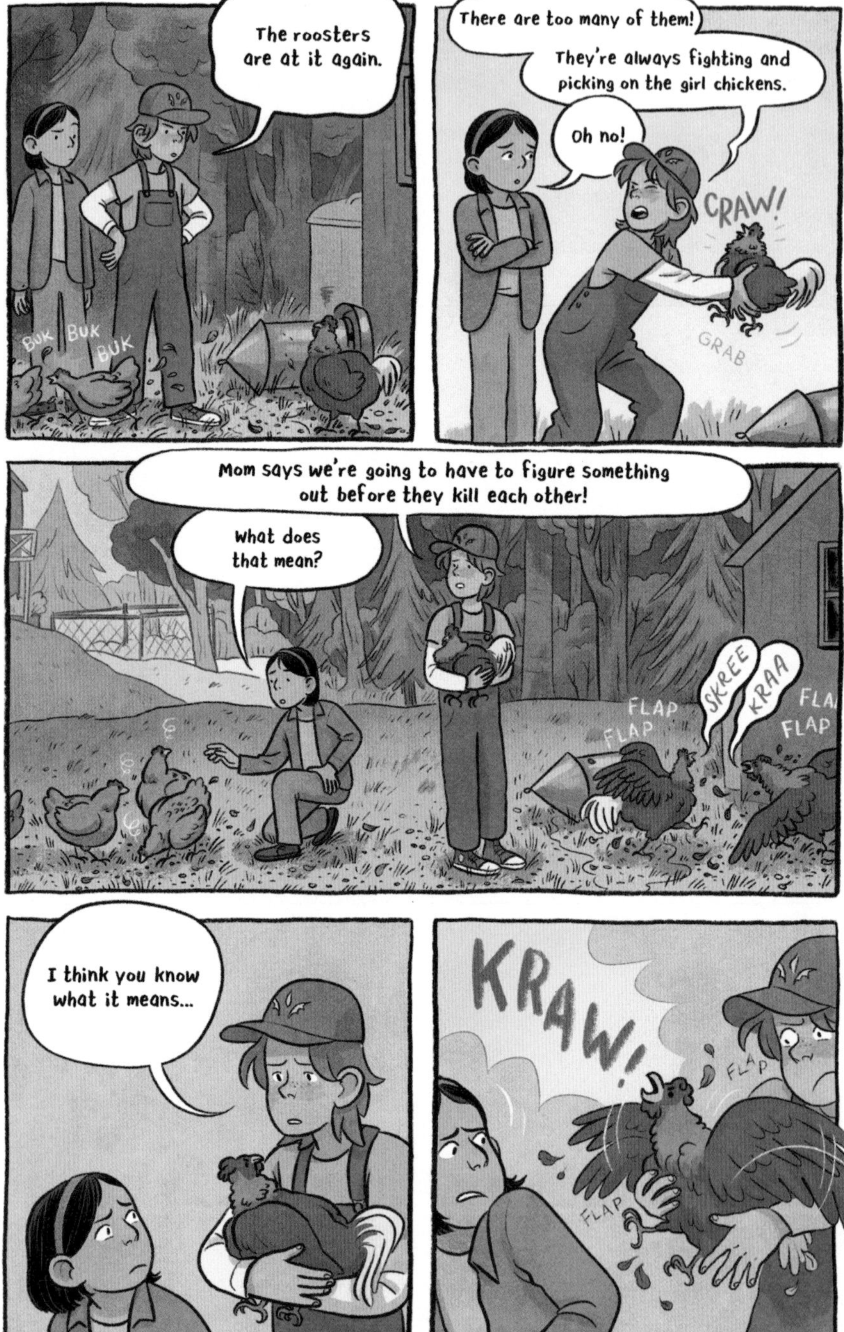
The roosters are at it again.
BUK BUK BUK
There are too many of them!
They're always fighting and picking on the girl chickens.
Oh no!
CRAW!
GRAB
Mom says we're going to have to figure something out before they kill each other!
What does that mean?
FLAP FLAP
SKREE
KRAA
FLAP FLAP
I think you know what it means...
KRAW!
FLAP
FLAP

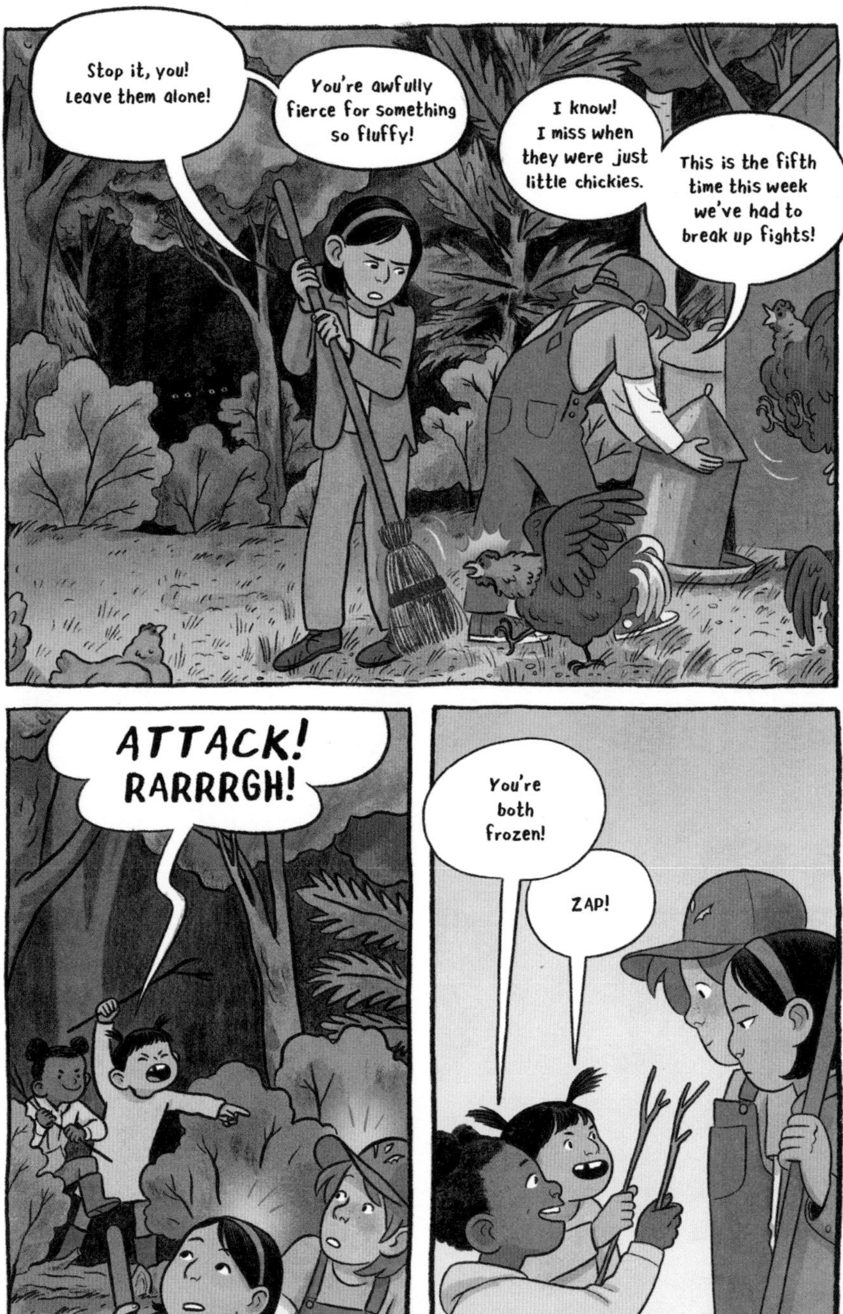
Stop it, you! Leave them alone!
You're awfully fierce for something so fluffy!
I know! I miss when they were just little chickies.
This is the fifth time this week we've had to break up fights!
ATTACK! RARRRGH!
You're both frozen!
ZAP!

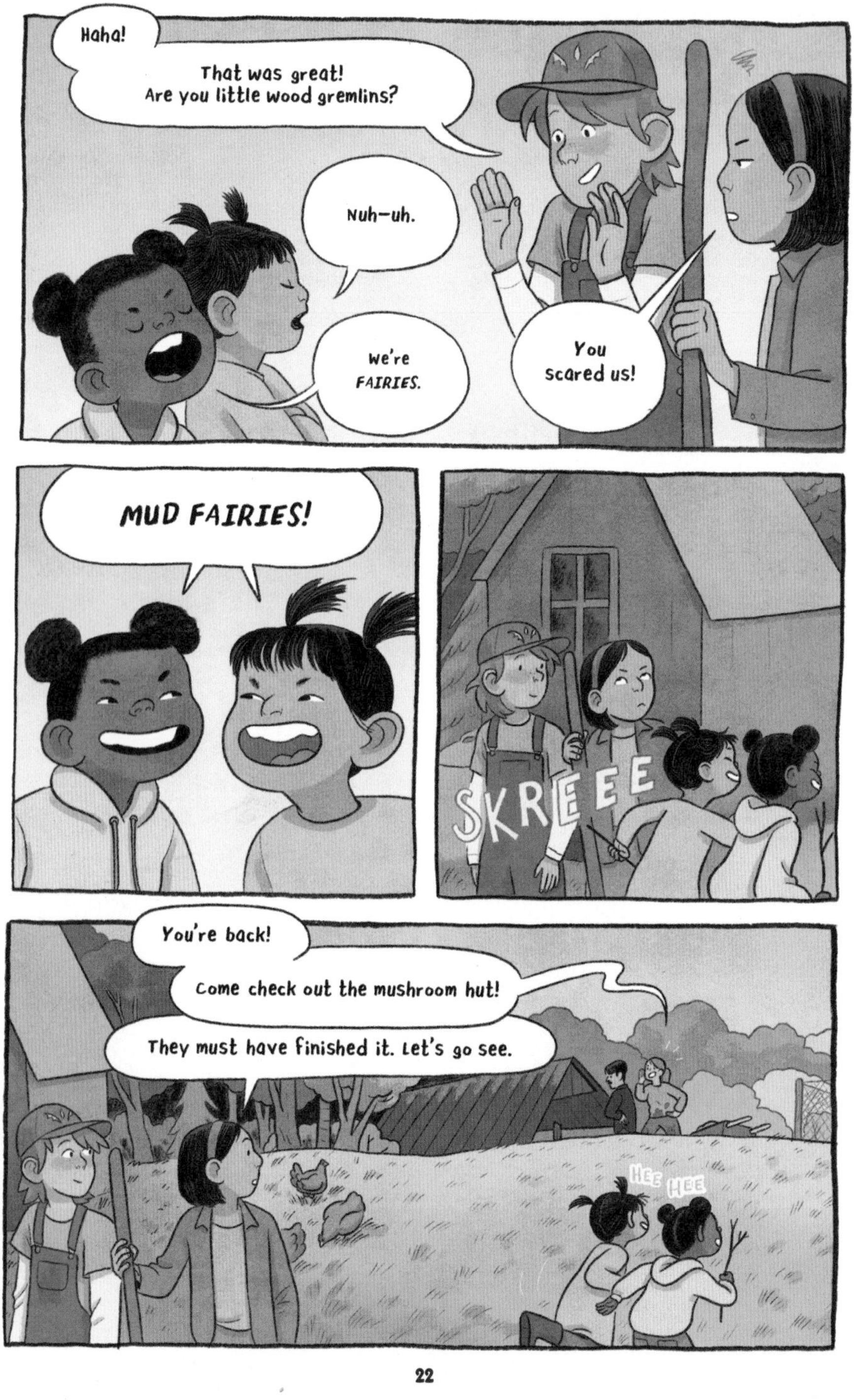

Haha!
That was great! Are you little wood gremlins?
Nuh-uh.
We're FAIRIES.
You scared us!
MUD FAIRIES!
SKREEEE
You're back!
Come check out the mushroom hut!
They must have finished it. Let's go see.
HEE HEE

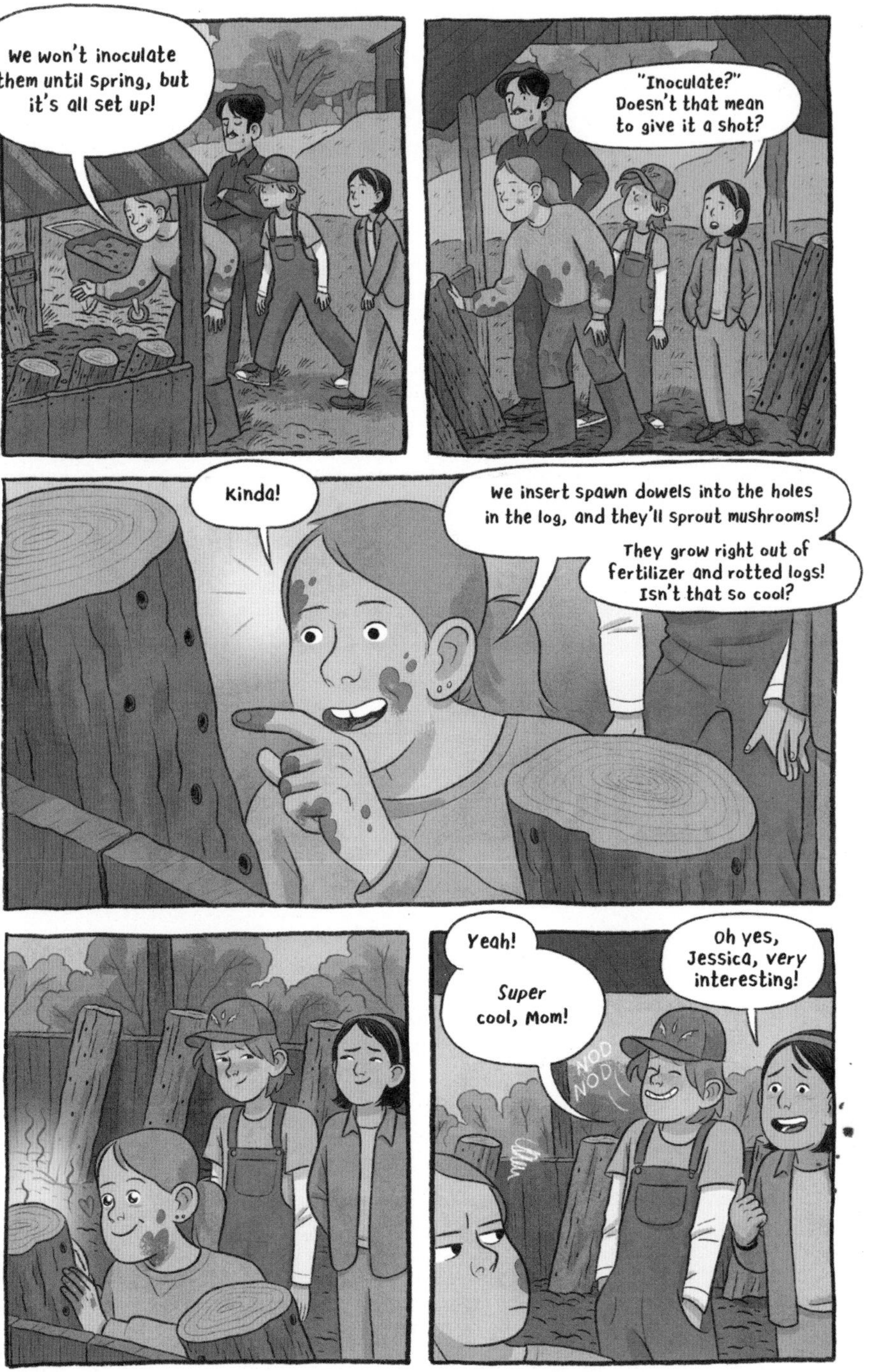
We won't inoculate them until spring, but it's all set up!
"Inoculate?" Doesn't that mean to give it a shot?
Kinda!
We insert spawn dowels into the holes in the log, and they'll sprout mushrooms!
They grow right out of fertilizer and rotted logs! Isn't that so cool?
Yeah!
Super cool, Mom!
NOD NOD
Oh yes, Jessica, very interesting!

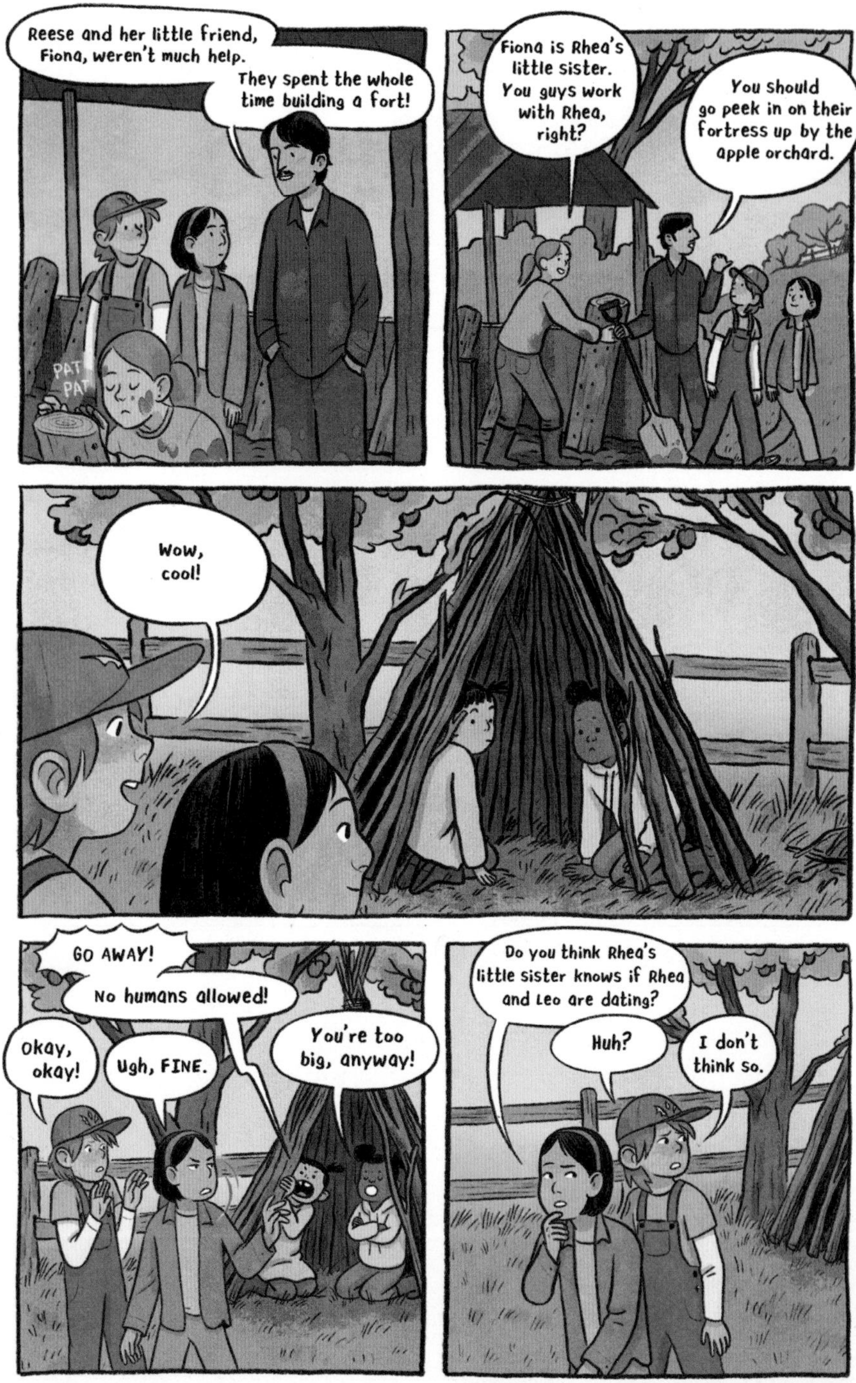
Reese and her little friend, Fiona, weren't much help.
They spent the whole time building a fort!
PAT PAT
Fiona is Rhea's little sister. You guys work with Rhea, right?
You should go peek in on their fortress up by the apple orchard.
Wow, cool!
GO AWAY!
No humans allowed!
Okay, okay!
Ugh, FINE.
You're too big, anyway!
Do you think Rhea's little sister knows if Rhea and Leo are dating?
Huh?
I don't think so.

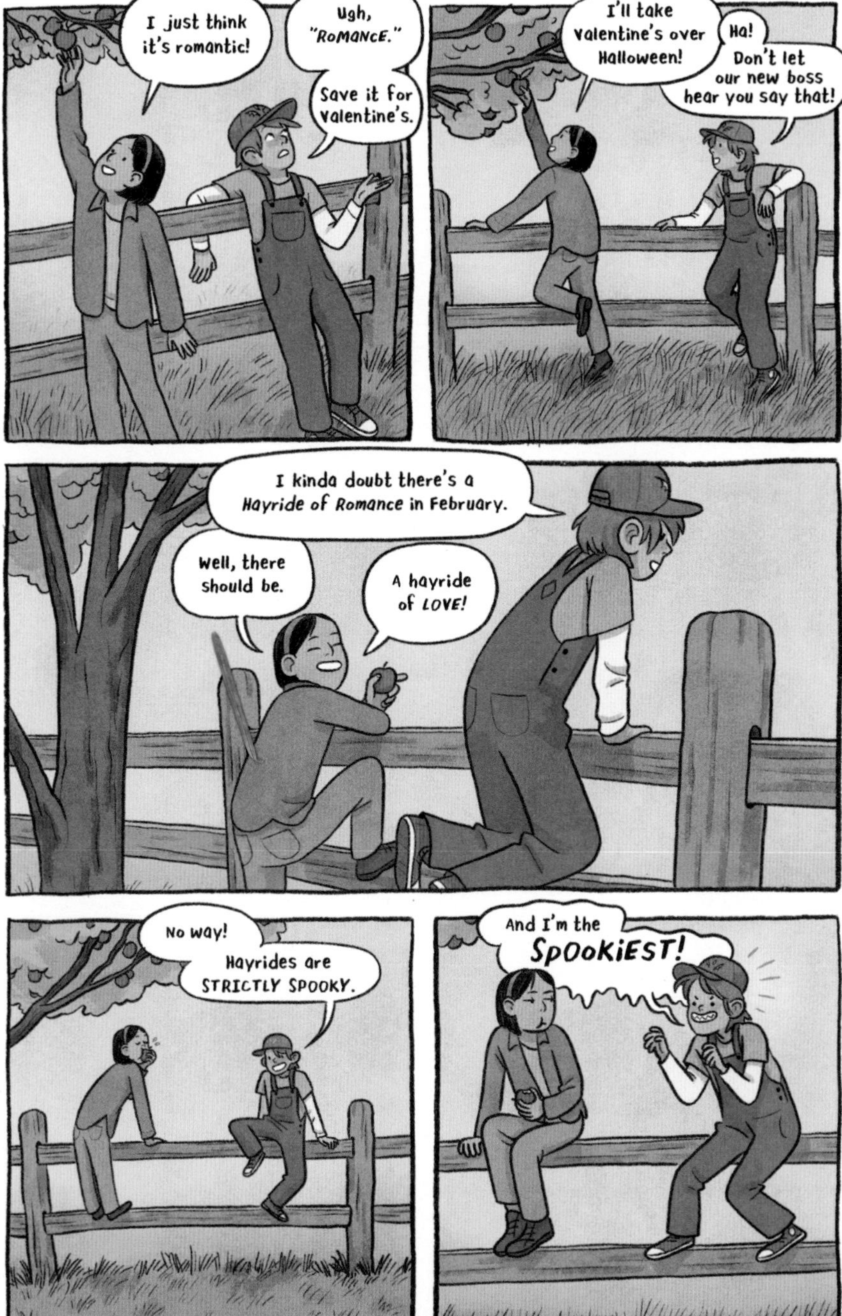
I just think it's romantic!
Ugh, "ROMANCE."
Save it for Valentine's.
I'll take Valentine's over Halloween!
Ha!
Don't let our new boss hear you say that!
I kinda doubt there's a Hayride of Romance in February.
Well, there should be.
A hayride of LOVE!
No way!
Hayrides are STRICTLY SPOOKY.
And I'm the SPOOKIEST!

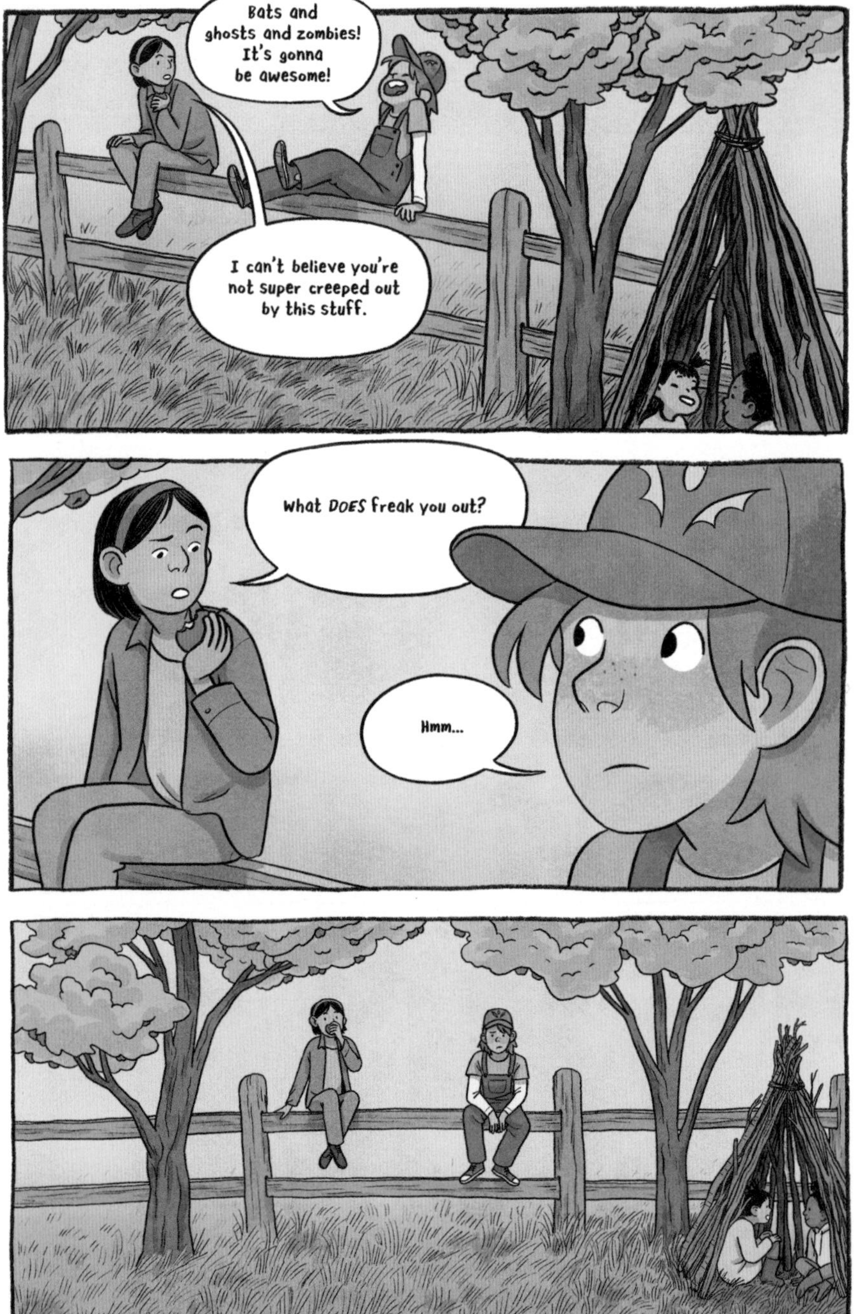
Bats and ghosts and zombies! It's gonna be awesome!
I can't believe you're not super creeped out by this stuff.
What DOES freak you out?
Hmm...

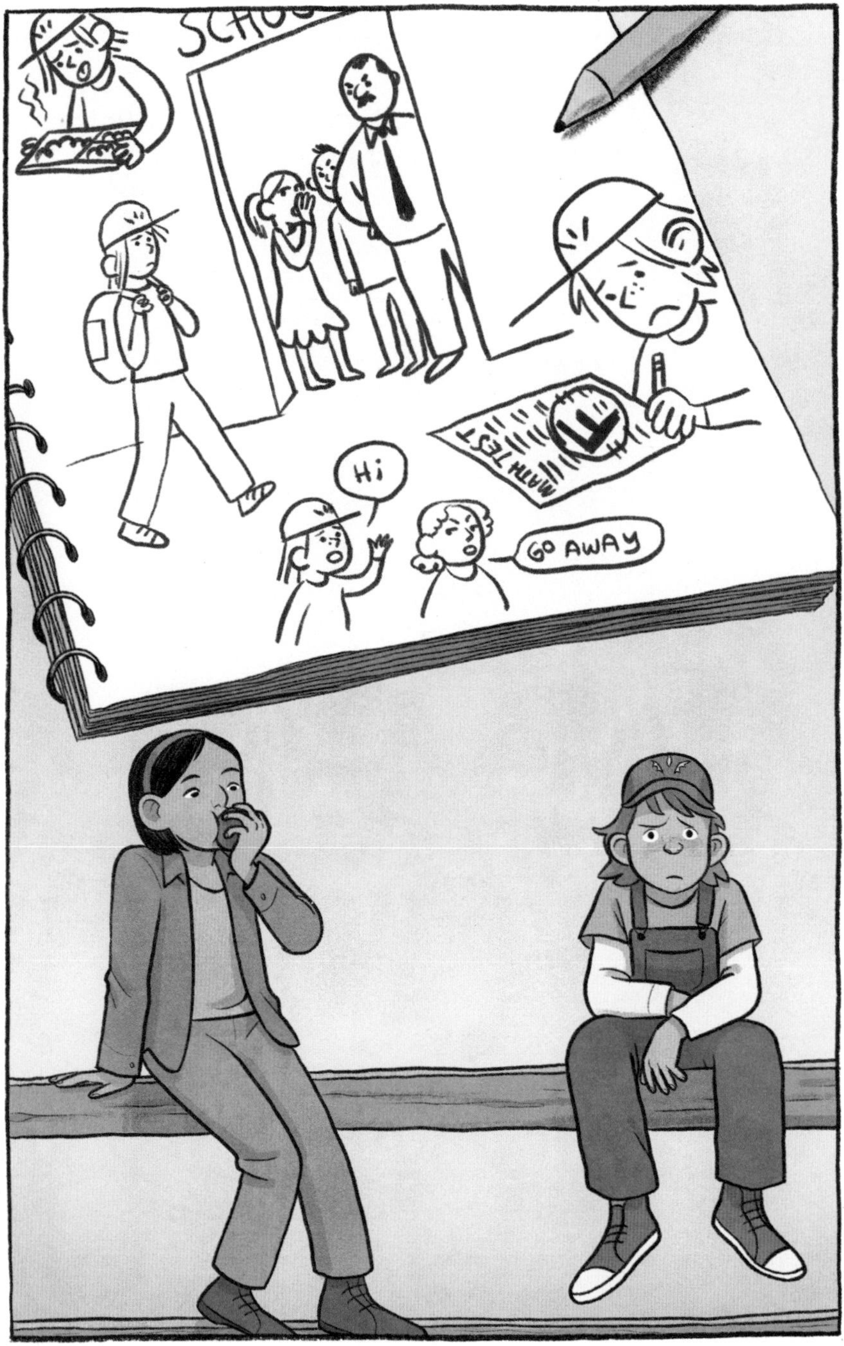
SCHO
MATH TEST
F
HI
GO AWAY

Chapter Two

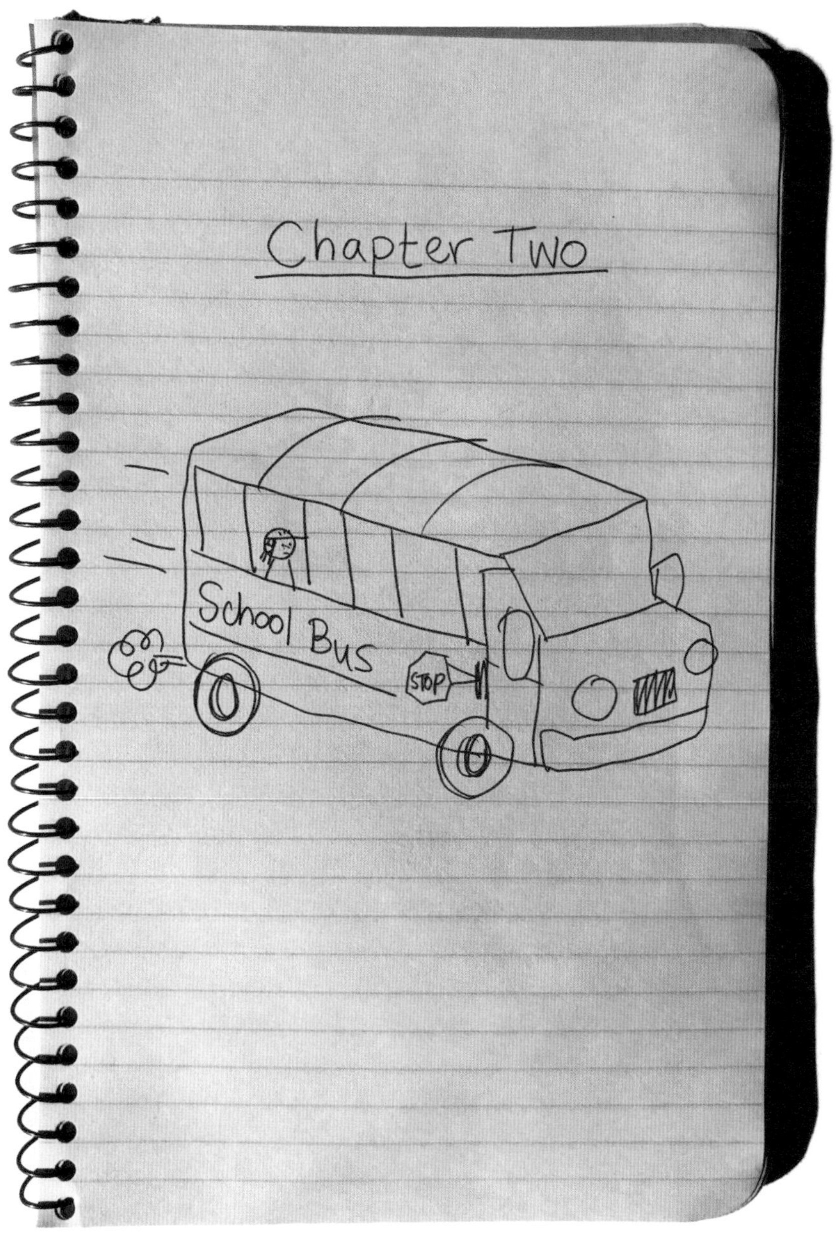
School Bus
STOP

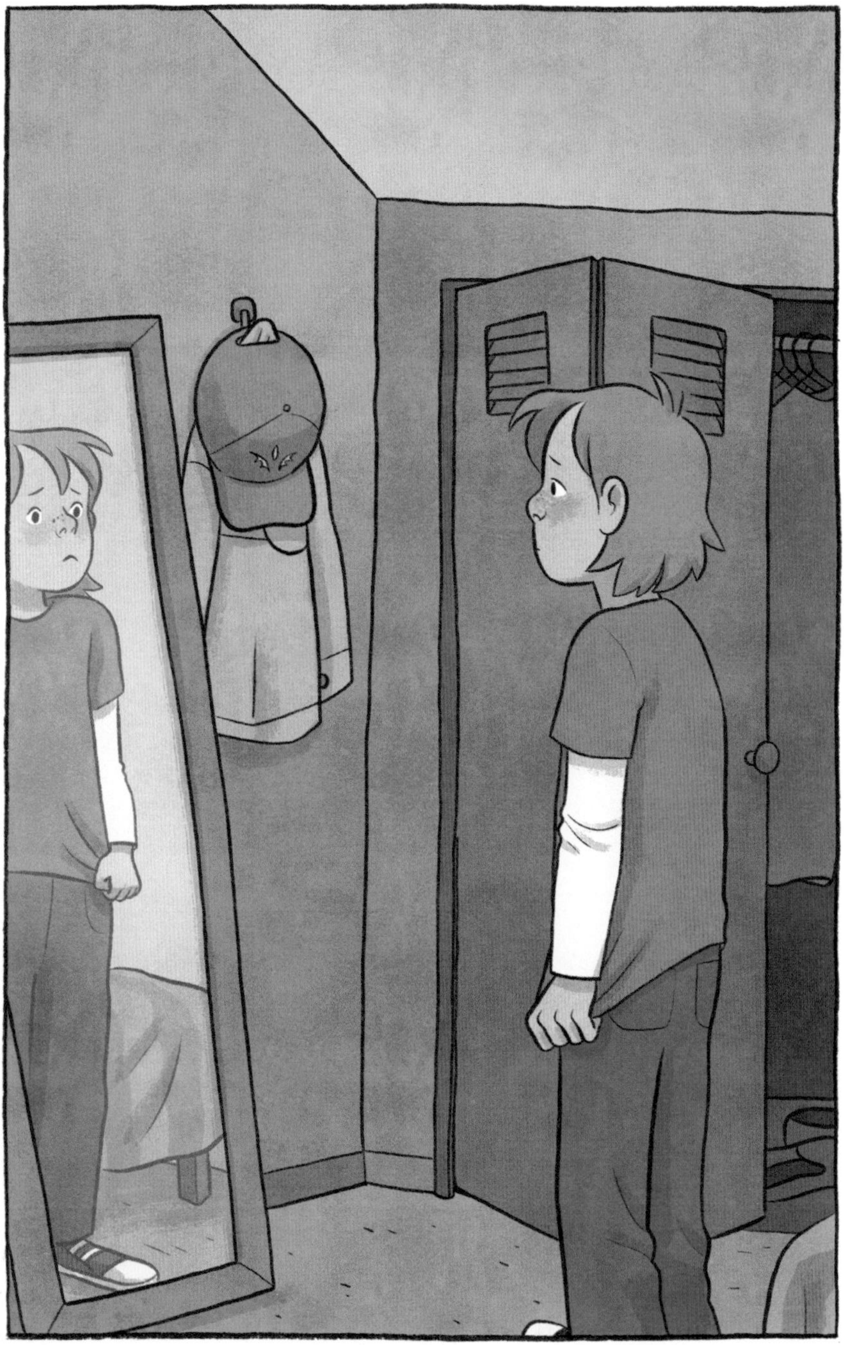

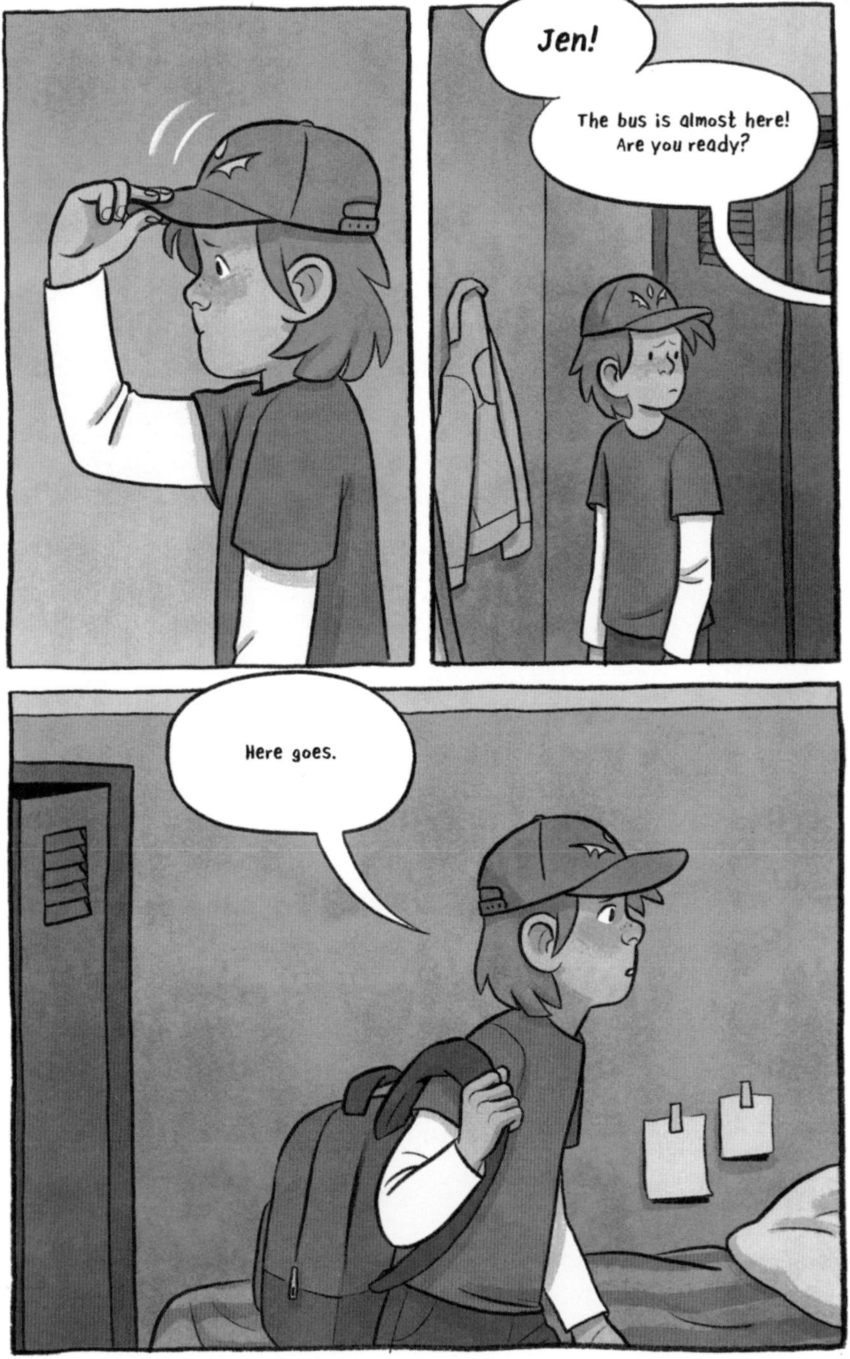
Jen!
The bus is almost here! Are you ready?
Here goes.

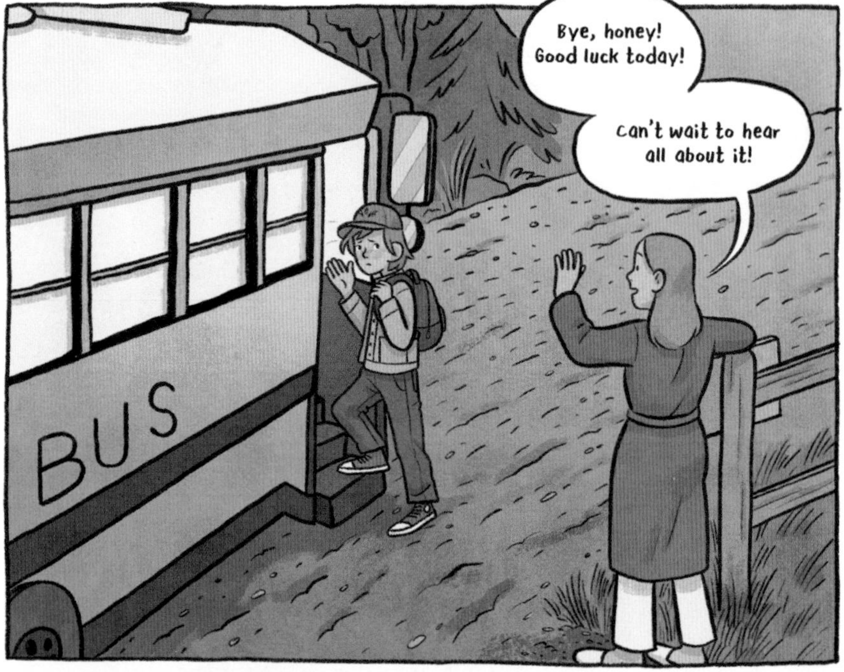
Bye, honey!
Good luck today!
Can't wait to hear
all about it!
BUS

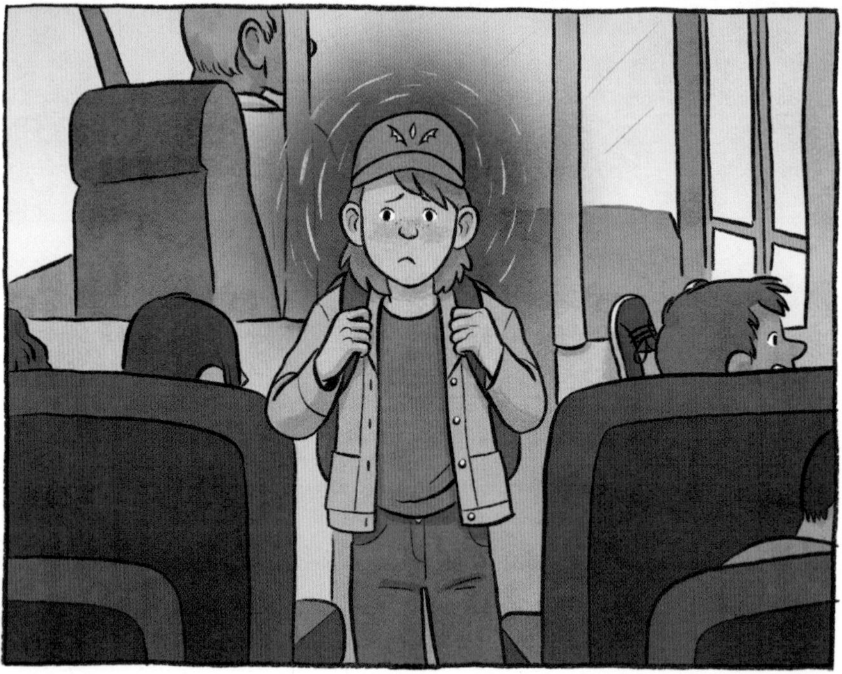

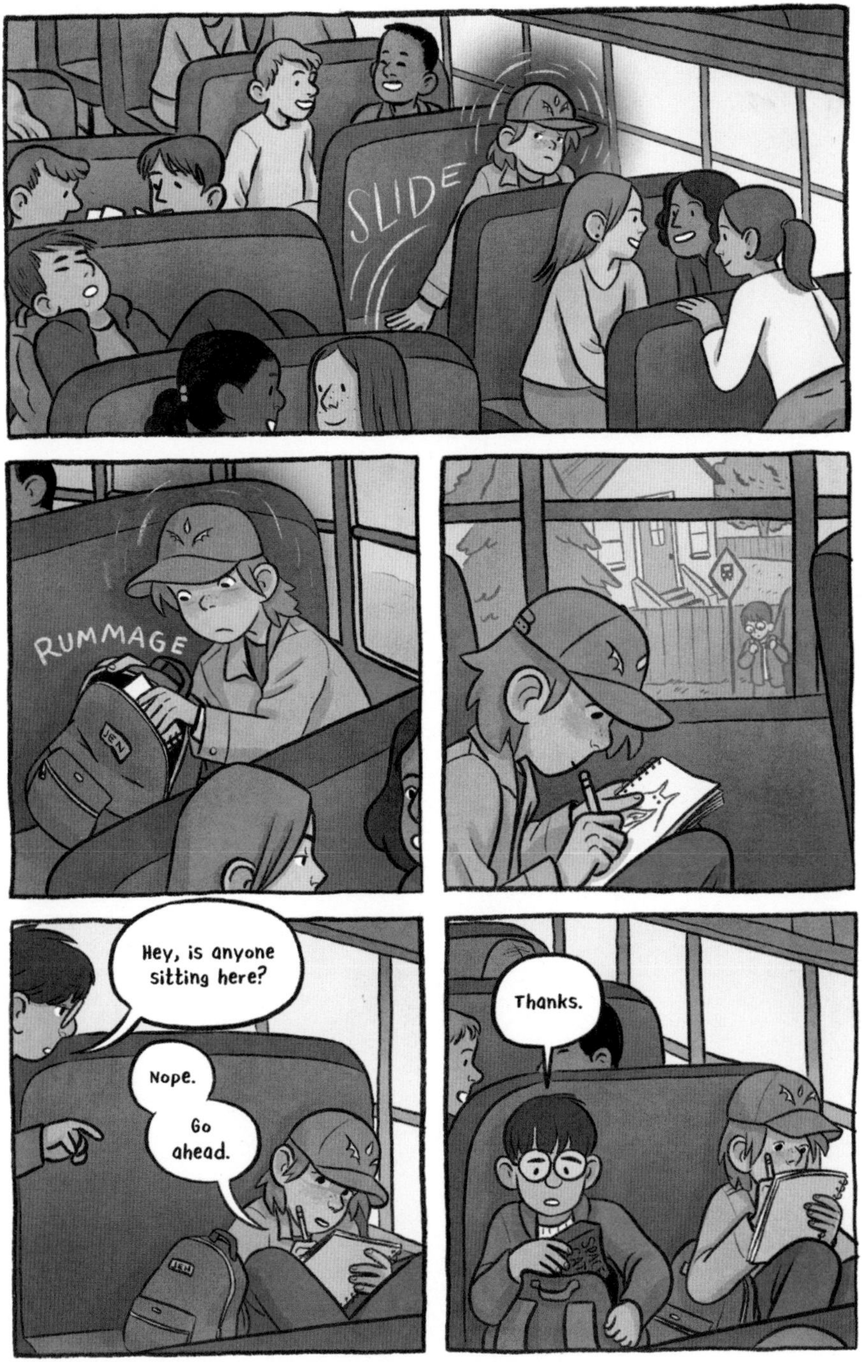
SLIDE
RUMMAGE
JEN
Hey, is anyone sitting here?
Nope.
Go ahead.
Thanks.

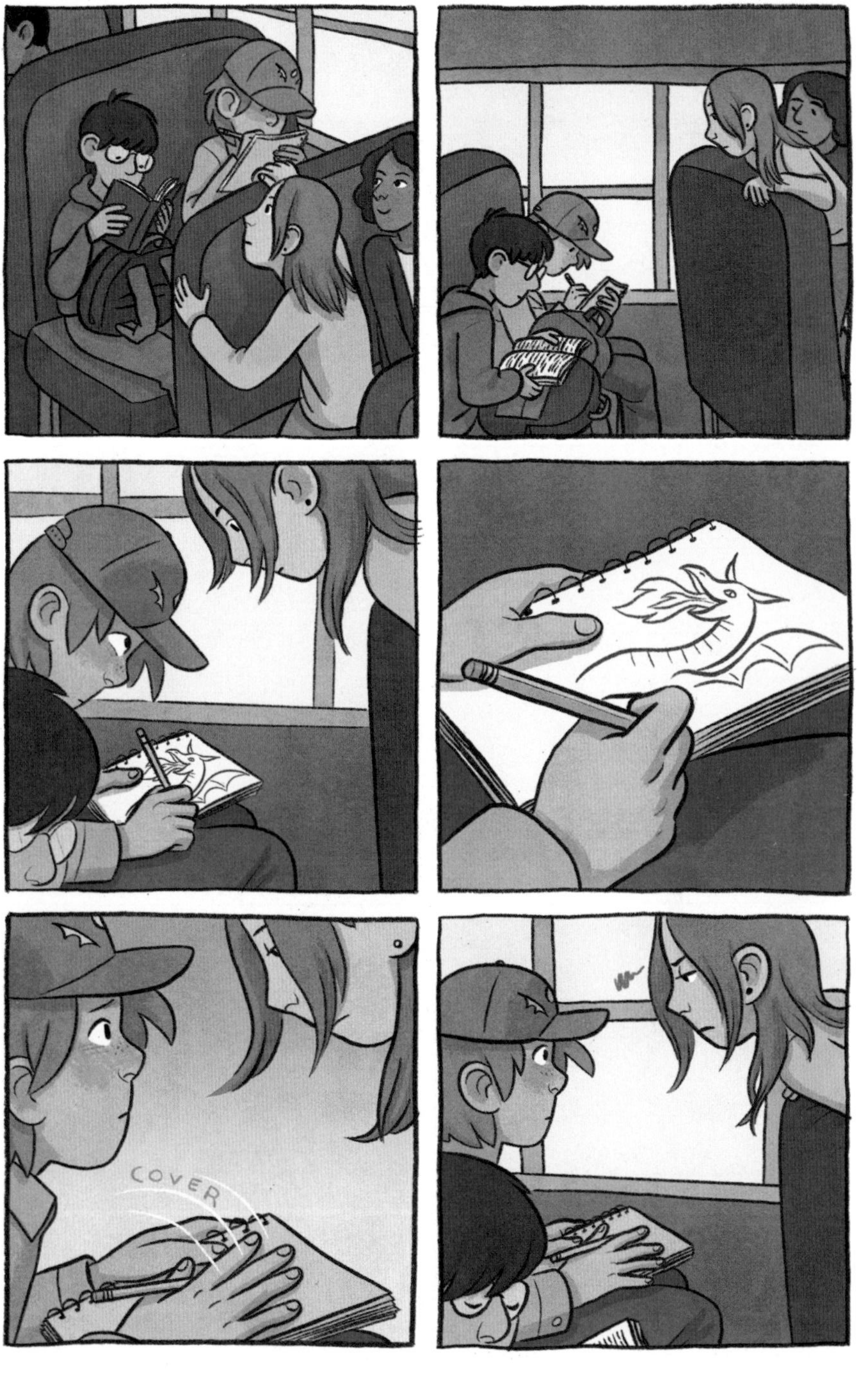
COVER

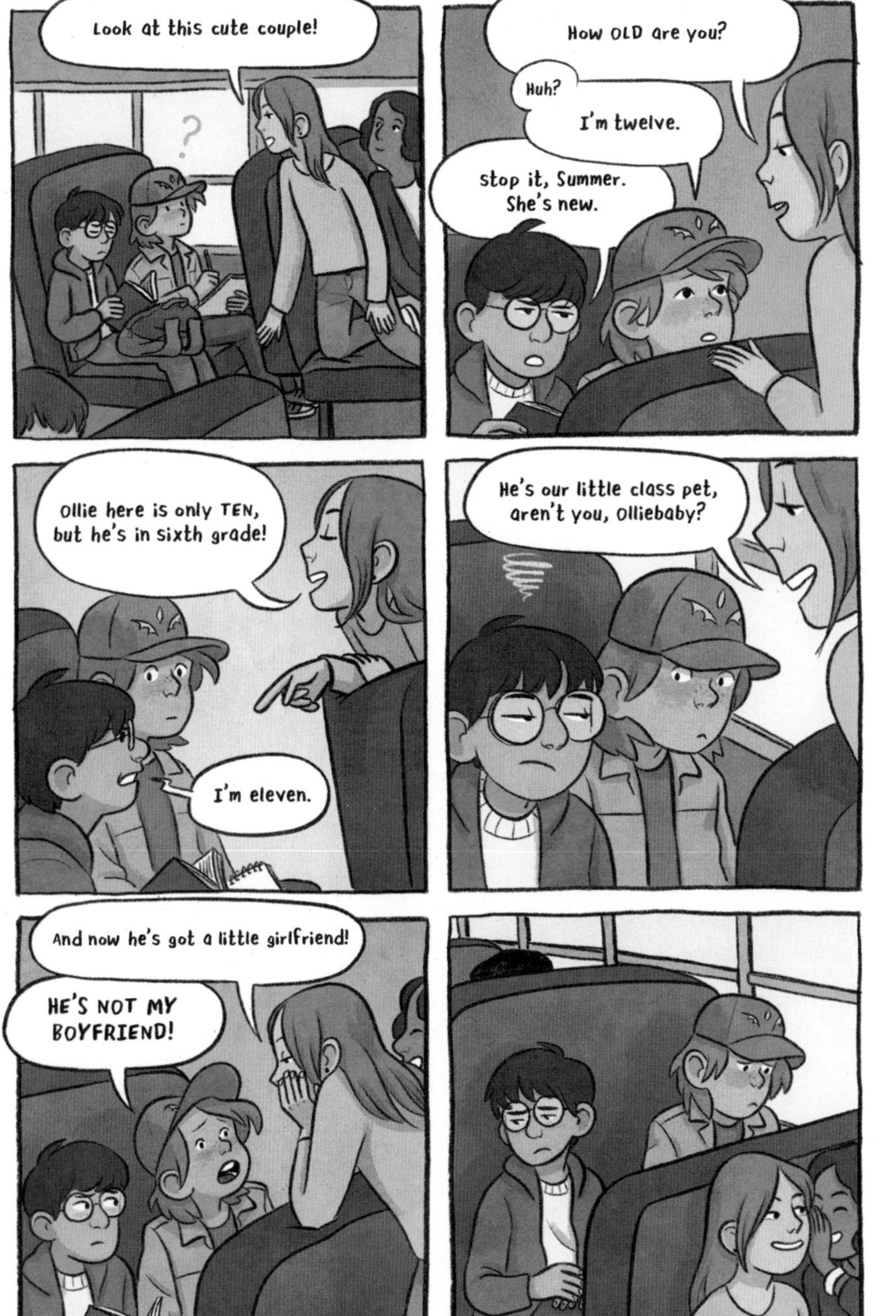
Look at this cute couple!
?
How OLD are you?
Huh?
I'm twelve.
stop it, Summer.
She's new.
Ollie here is only TEN, but he's in sixth grade!
I'm eleven.
He's our little class pet, aren't you, Olliebaby?
And now he's got a little girlfriend!
HE'S NOT MY BOYFRIEND!

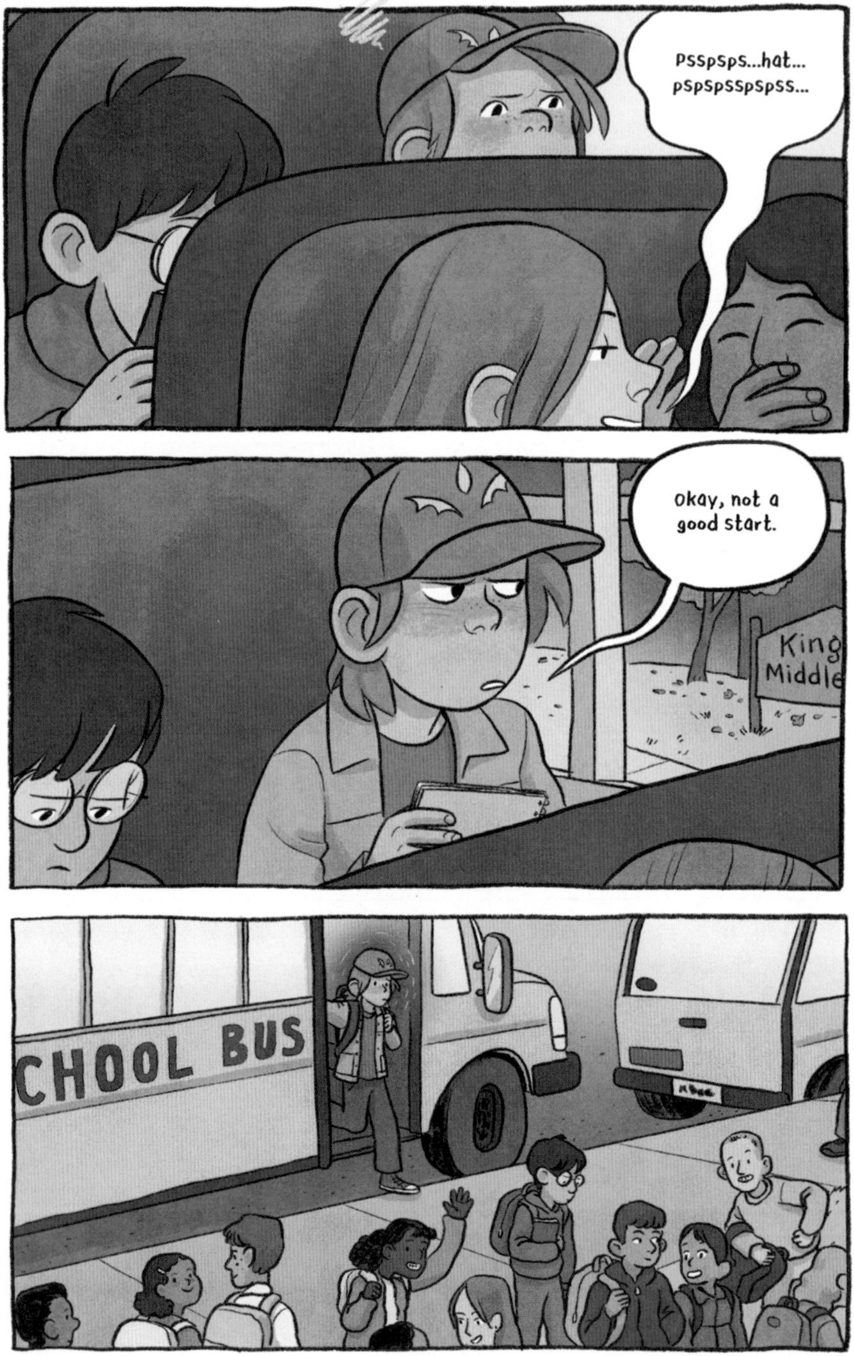
pssspsps...hat...
pspspsspspss...
okay, not a good start.
King
Middle
CHOOL BUS

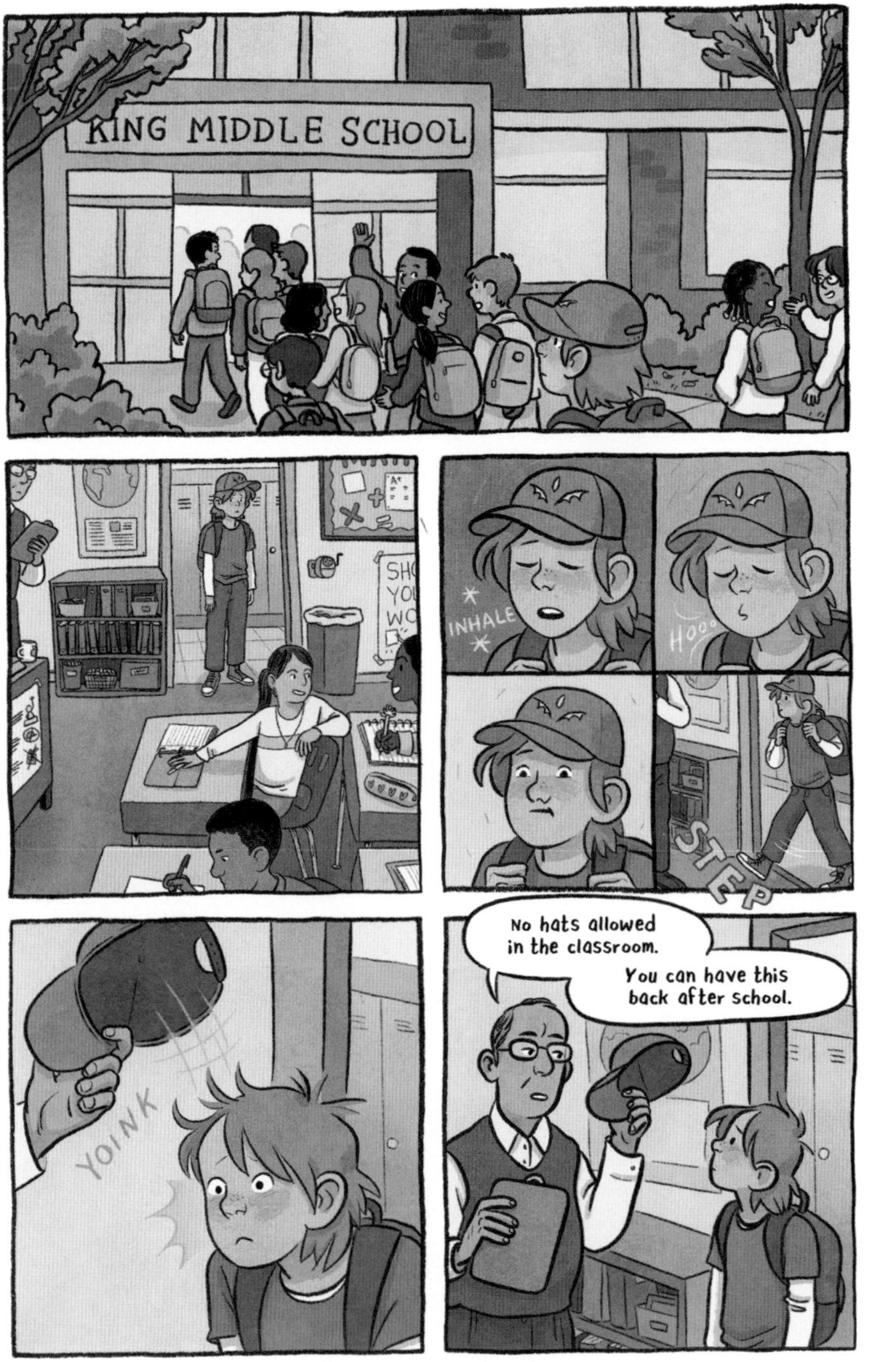
KING MIDDLE SCHOOL
INHALE
Hooo
STEP
YOINK
No hats allowed in the classroom.
You can have this back after school.

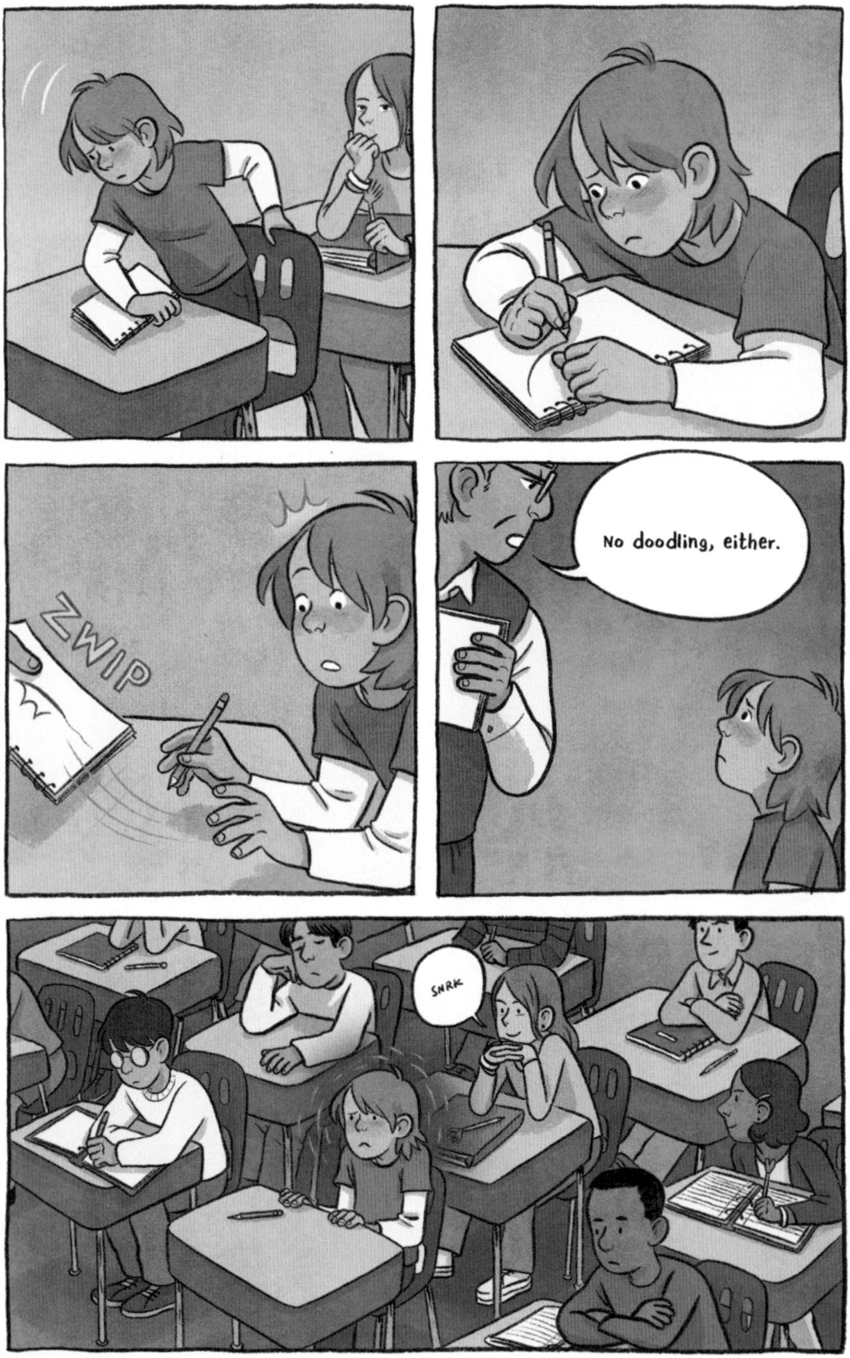
ZWIP
No doodling, either.
SNRK

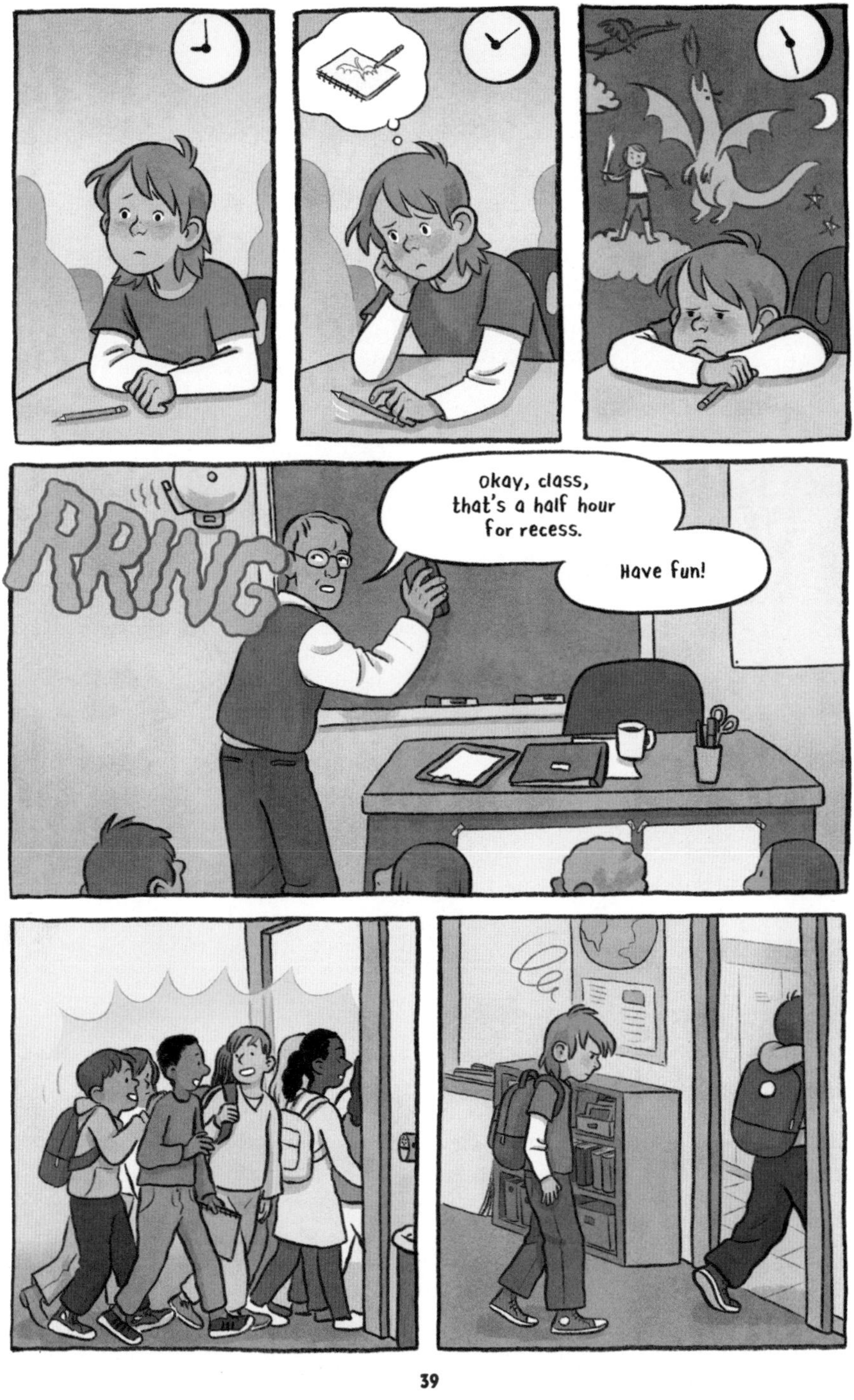
RRING
Okay, class, that's a half hour for recess.
Have fun!

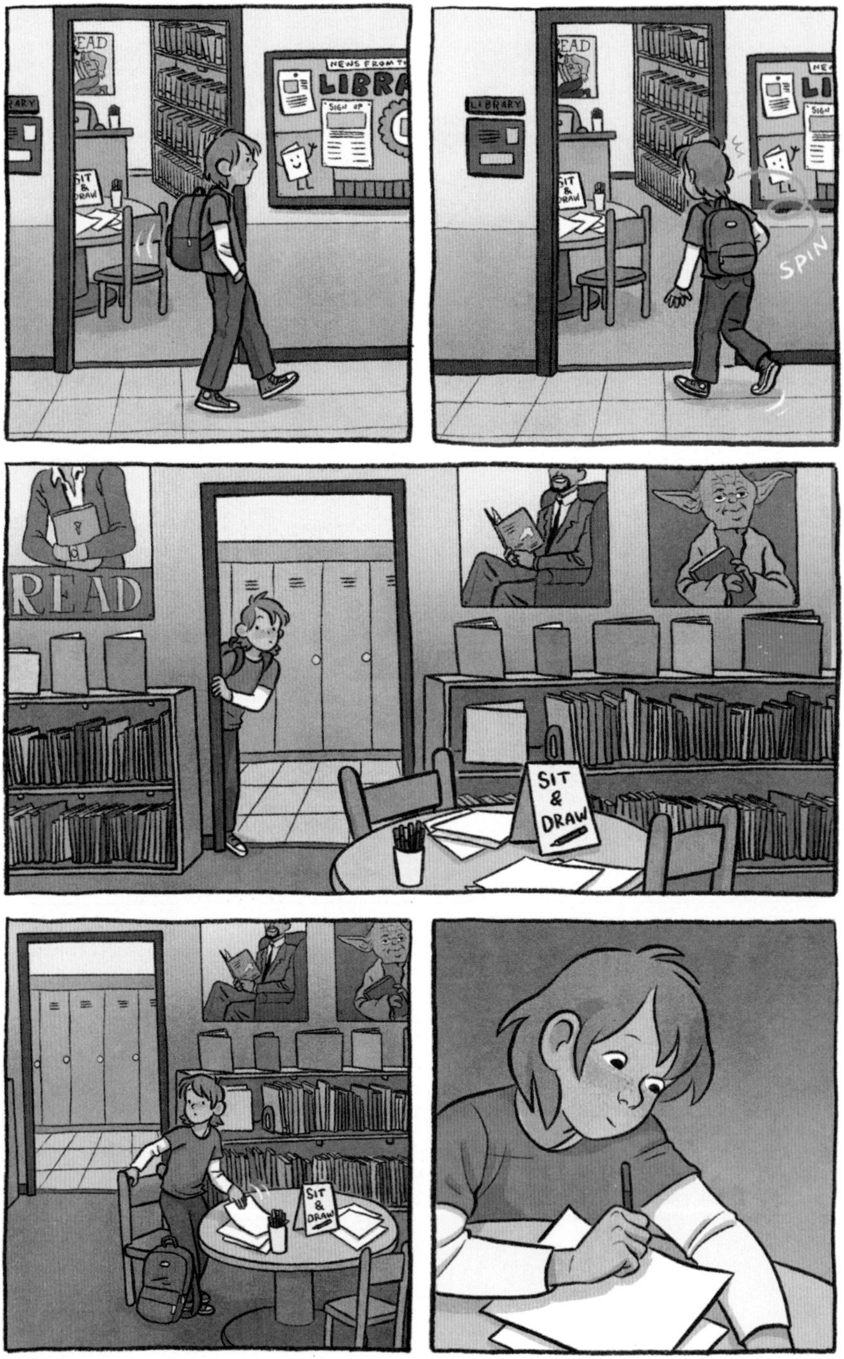
READ
LIBRARY
SIT & DRAW
SIGN UP
SPIN
READ
SIT & DRAW
SIT & DRAW

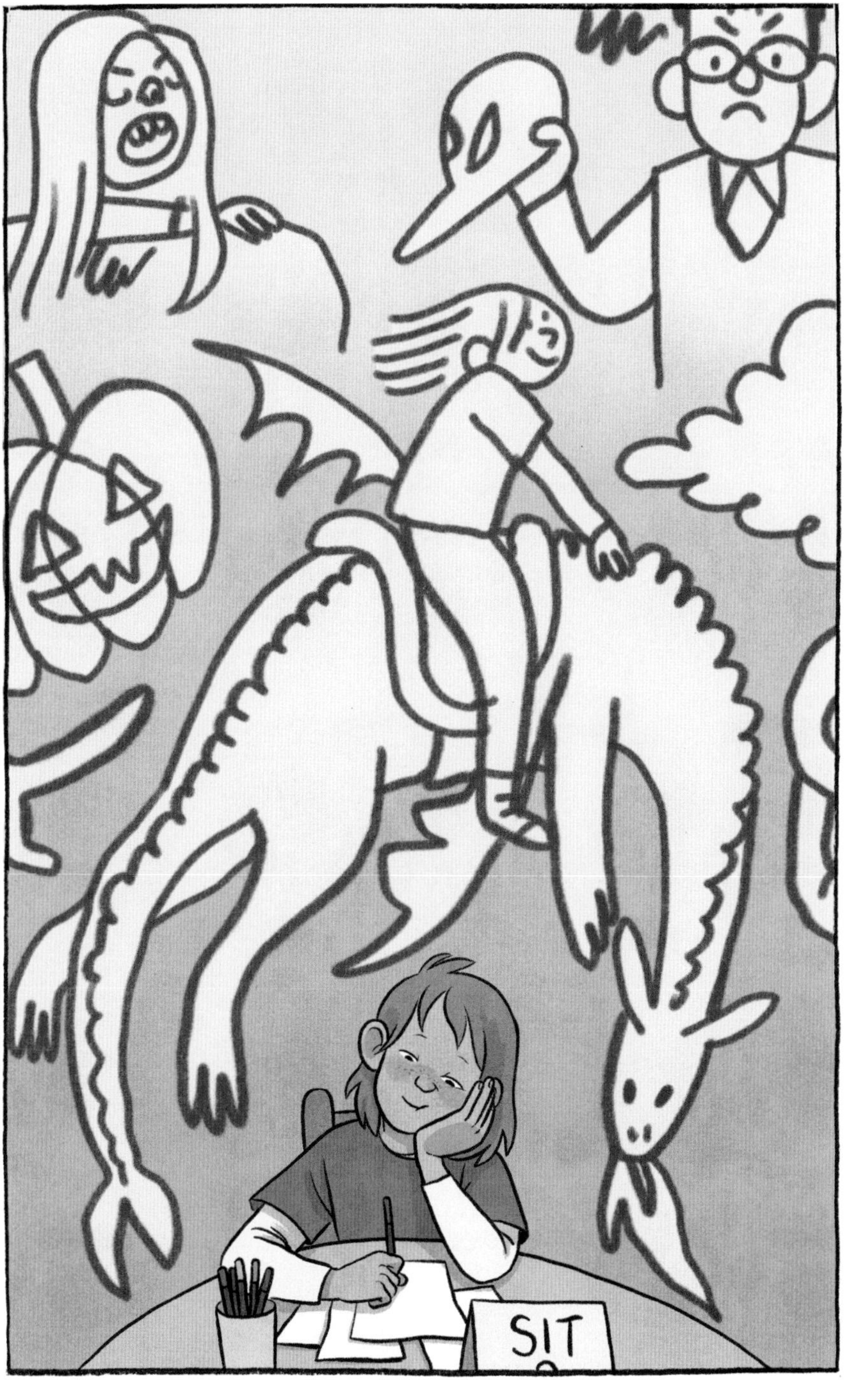
SIT

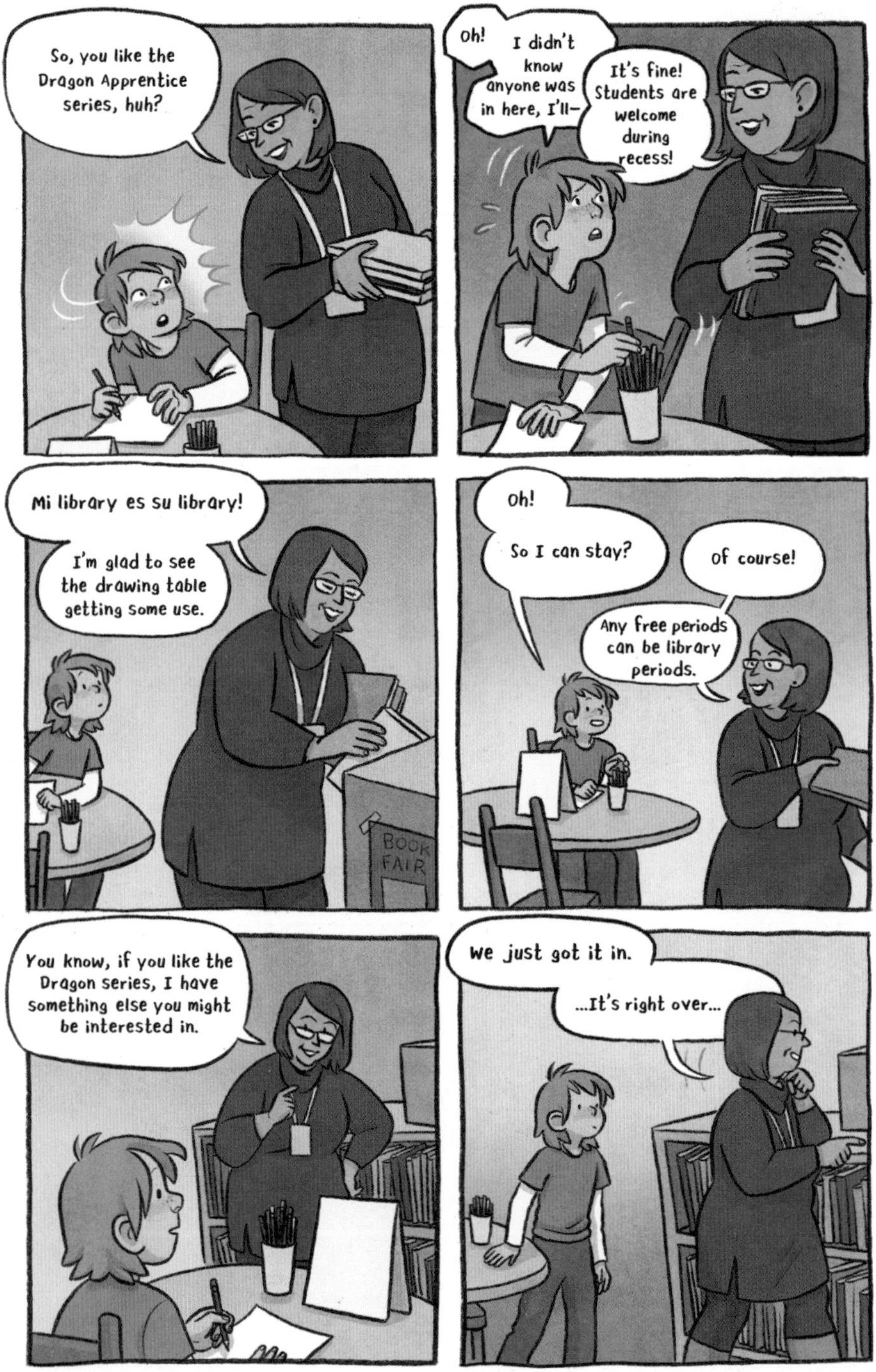
So, you like the Dragon Apprentice series, huh?
Oh!
I didn't know anyone was in here, I'll—
It's fine! Students are welcome during recess!
Mi library es su library!
I'm glad to see the drawing table getting some use.
BOOK FAIR
Oh!
So I can stay?
Of course!
Any free periods can be library periods.
You know, if you like the Dragon series, I have something else you might be interested in.
We just got it in.
...It's right over...

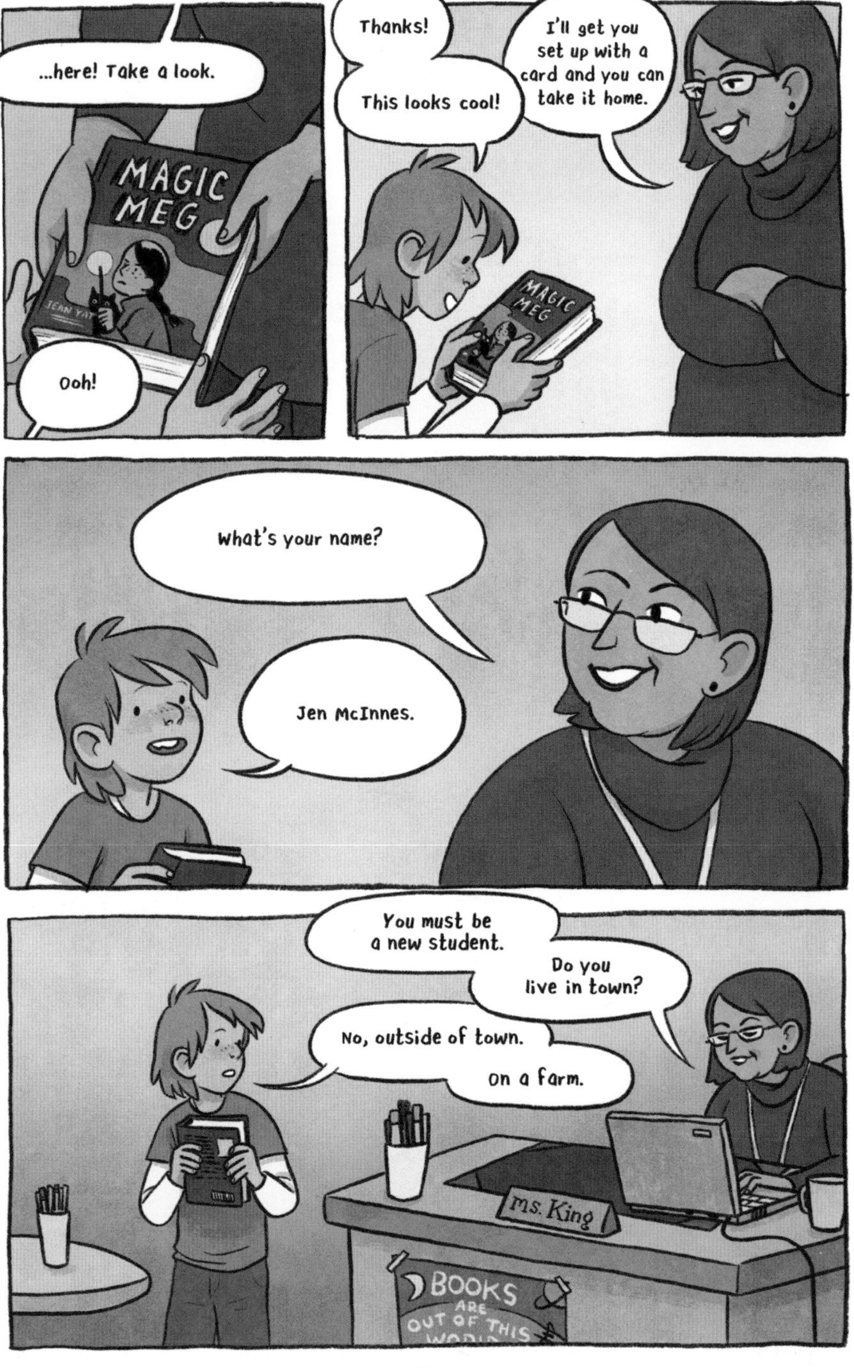
...here! Take a look.
MAGIC MEG
Ooh!
Thanks!
This looks cool!
I'll get you set up with a card and you can take it home.
What's your name?
Jen McInnes.
You must be a new student.
Do you live in town?
No, outside of town.
On a farm.
Ms. King
BOOKS ARE OUT OF THIS

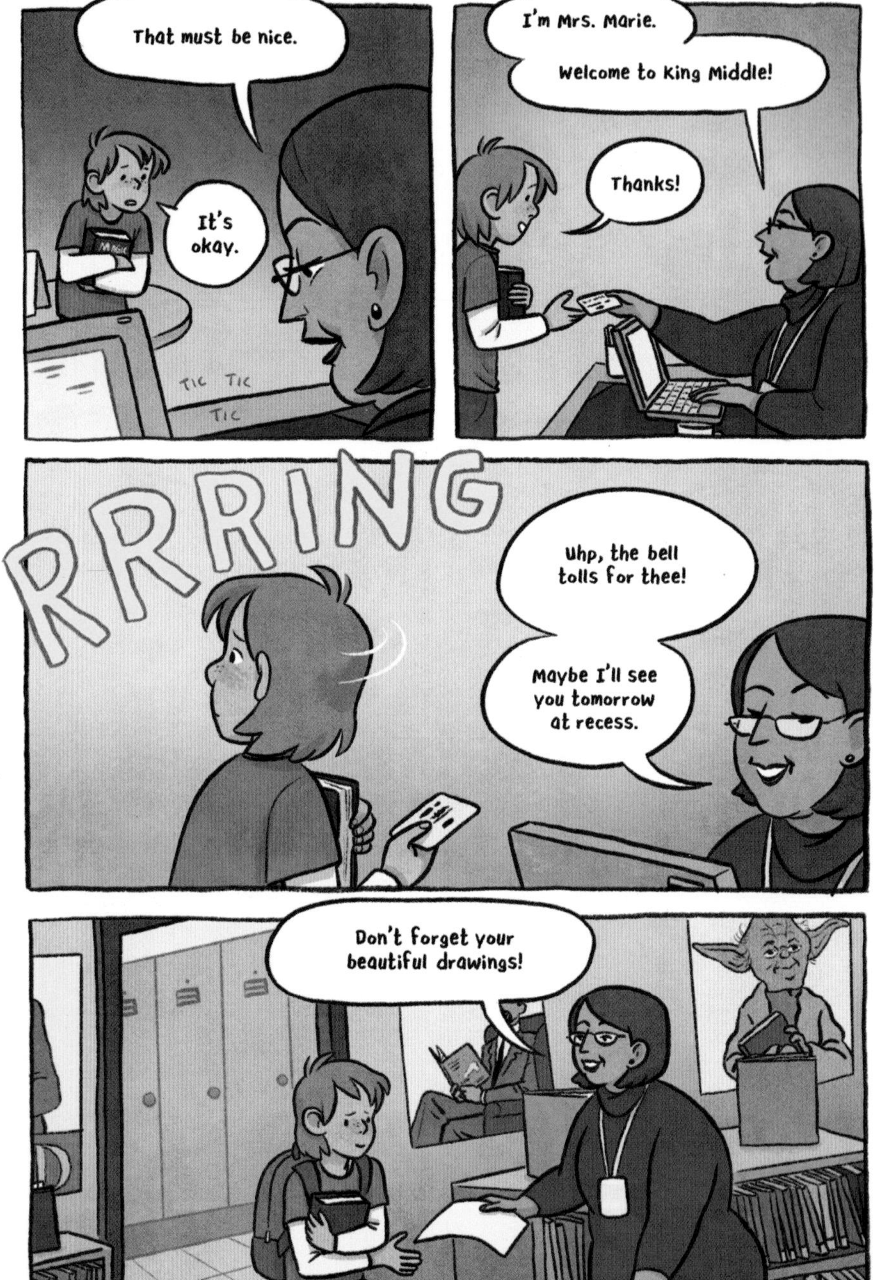

That must be nice.
It's okay.
TIC TIC
TIC
I'm Mrs. Marie.
Welcome to King Middle!
Thanks!
RRRING
Uhp, the bell tolls for thee!
Maybe I'll see you tomorrow at recess.
Don't forget your beautiful drawings!

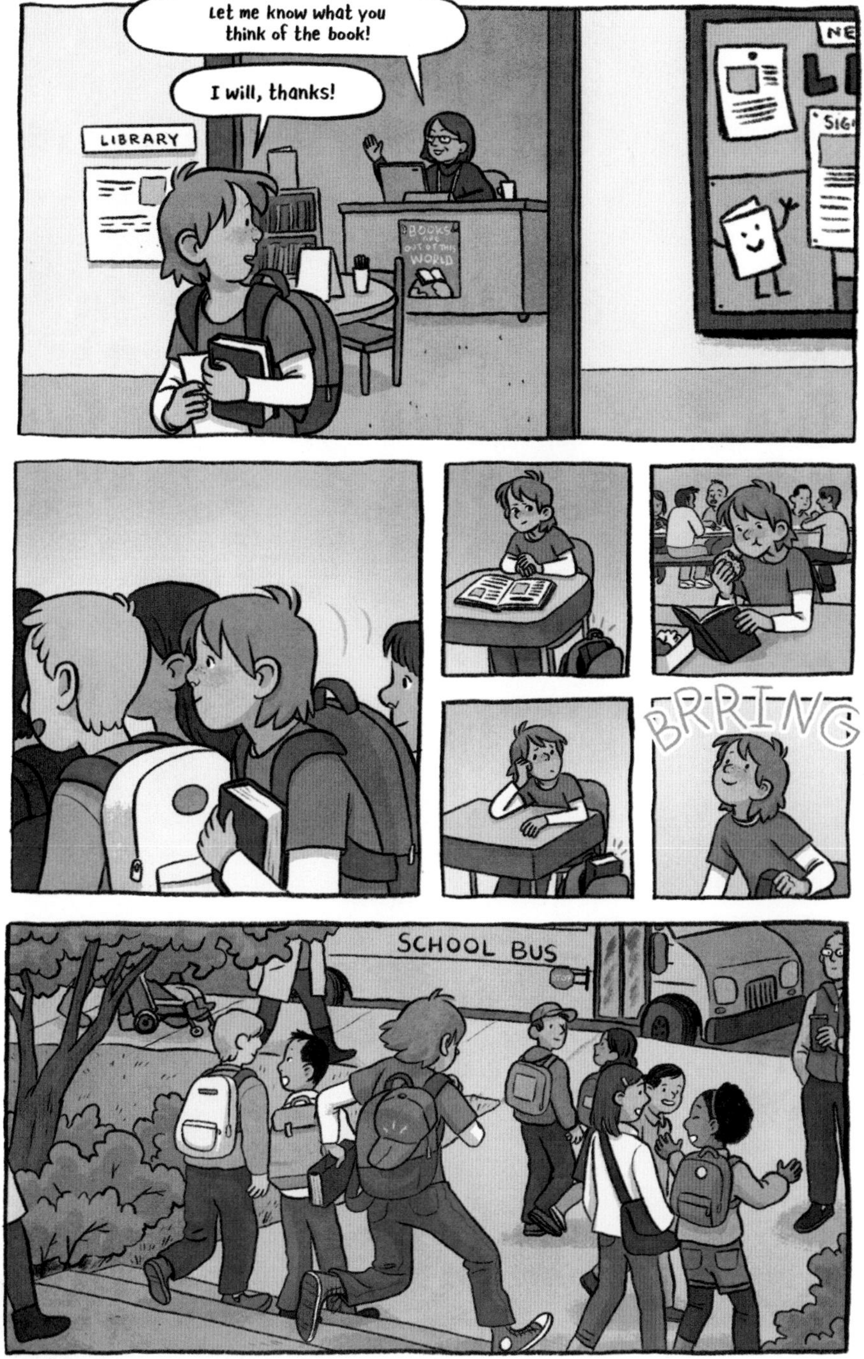
Let me know what you think of the book!
I will, thanks!
LIBRARY
BOOKS ARE OUT OF THIS WORLD
BRRING
SCHOOL BUS

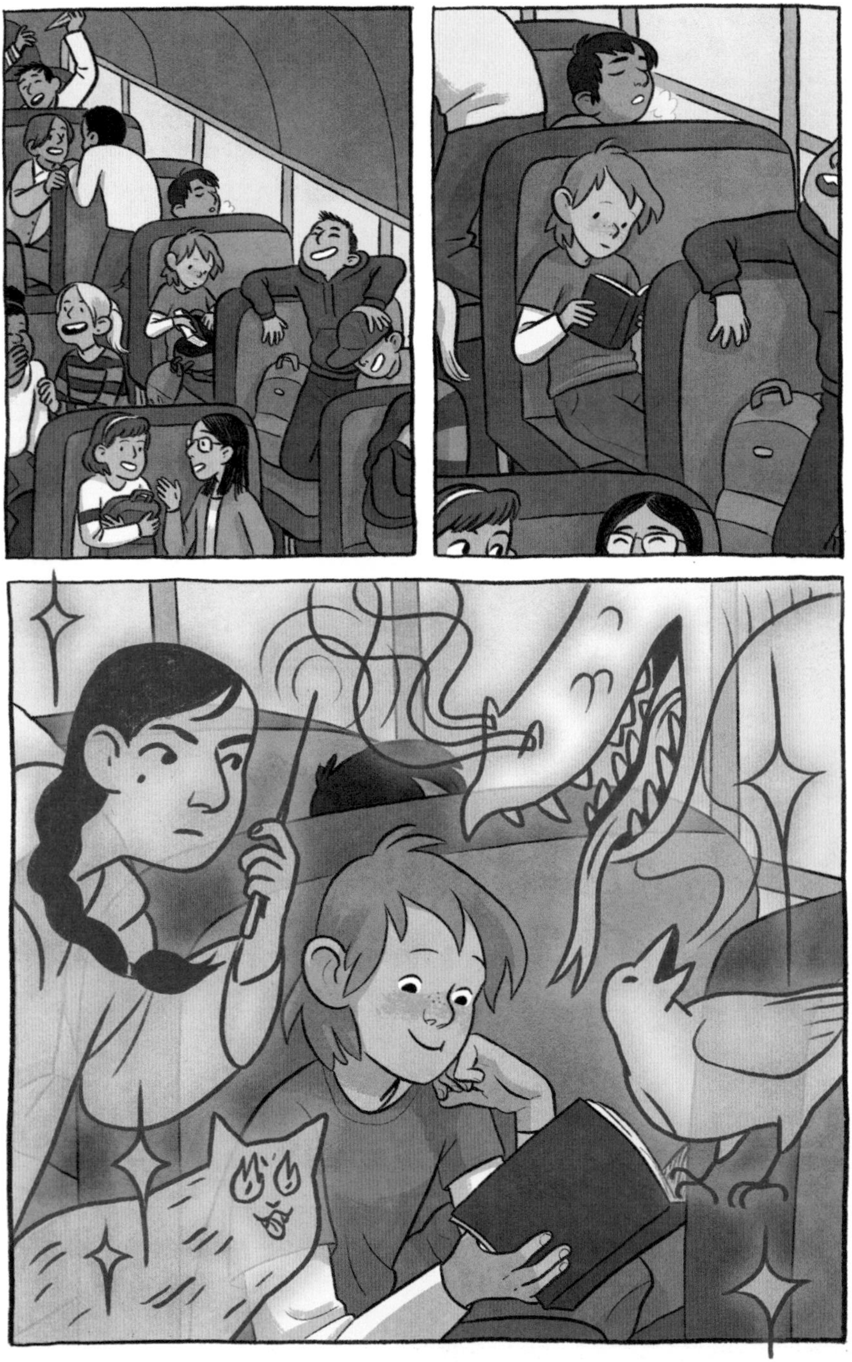

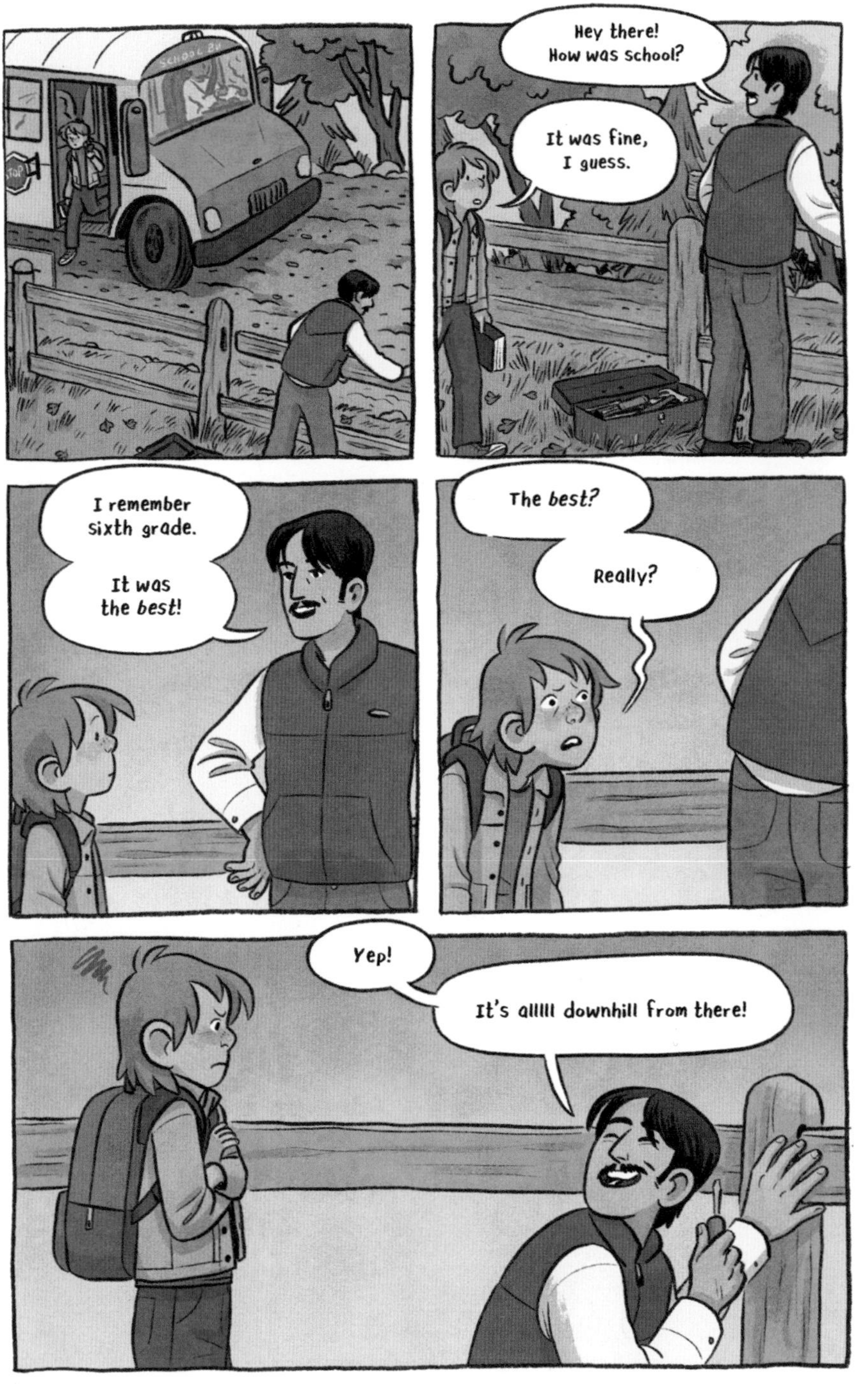

Hey there!
How was school?
It was fine,
I guess.
I remember
sixth grade.
It was
the *best*!
The *best*?
Really?
Yep!
It's alllll downhill from there!

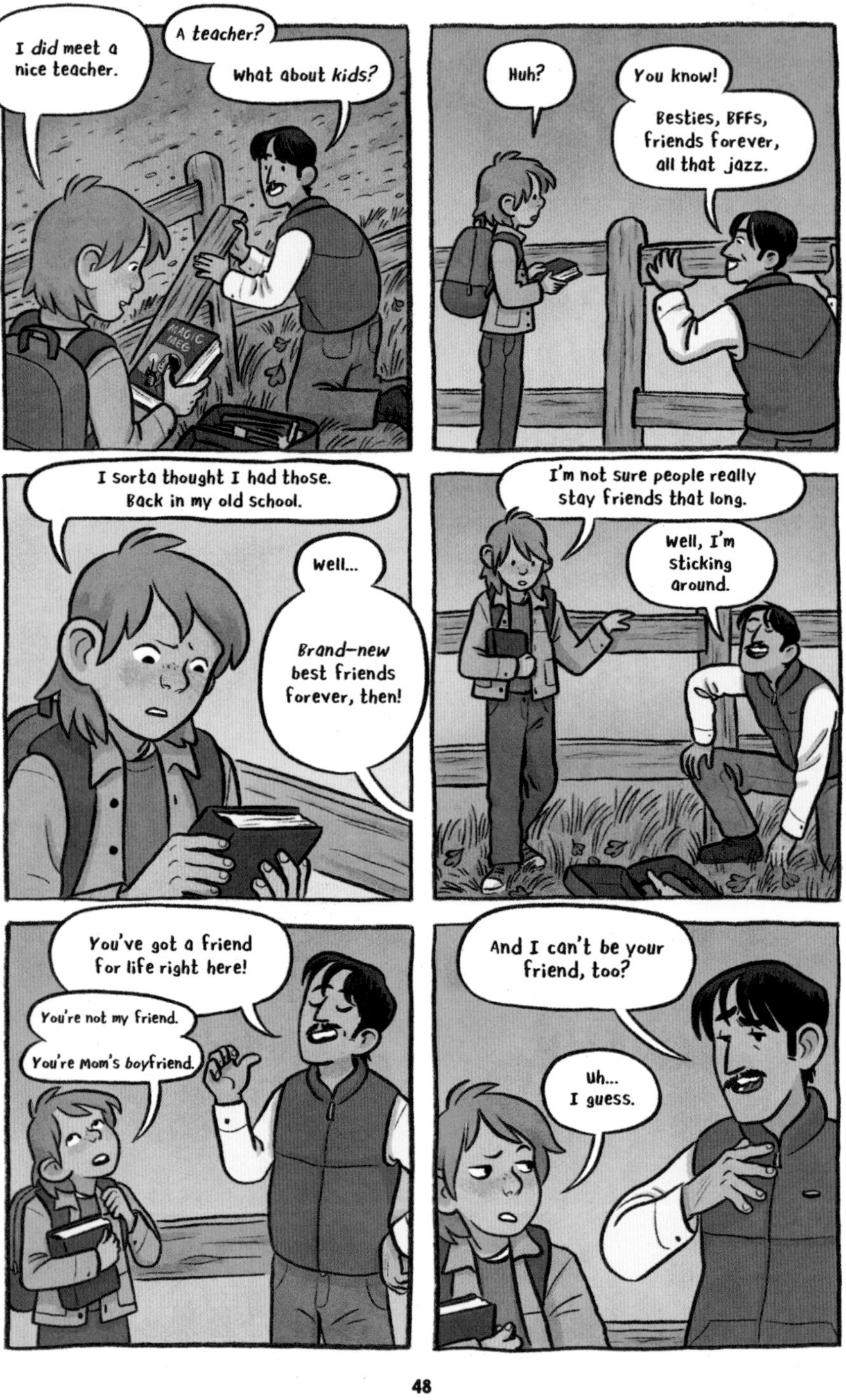
I *did* meet a nice teacher.
A *teacher?*
What about *kids?*
Huh?
You know!
Besties, BFFs, friends forever, all that jazz.
I sorta thought I had those. Back in my old school.
Well...
Brand-new best friends forever, then!
I'm not sure people really stay friends that long.
Well, I'm sticking around.
You've got a friend for life right here!
You're not my friend.
You're Mom's *boy*friend.
And I can't be your friend, too?
Uh... I guess.
MAGIC MEG

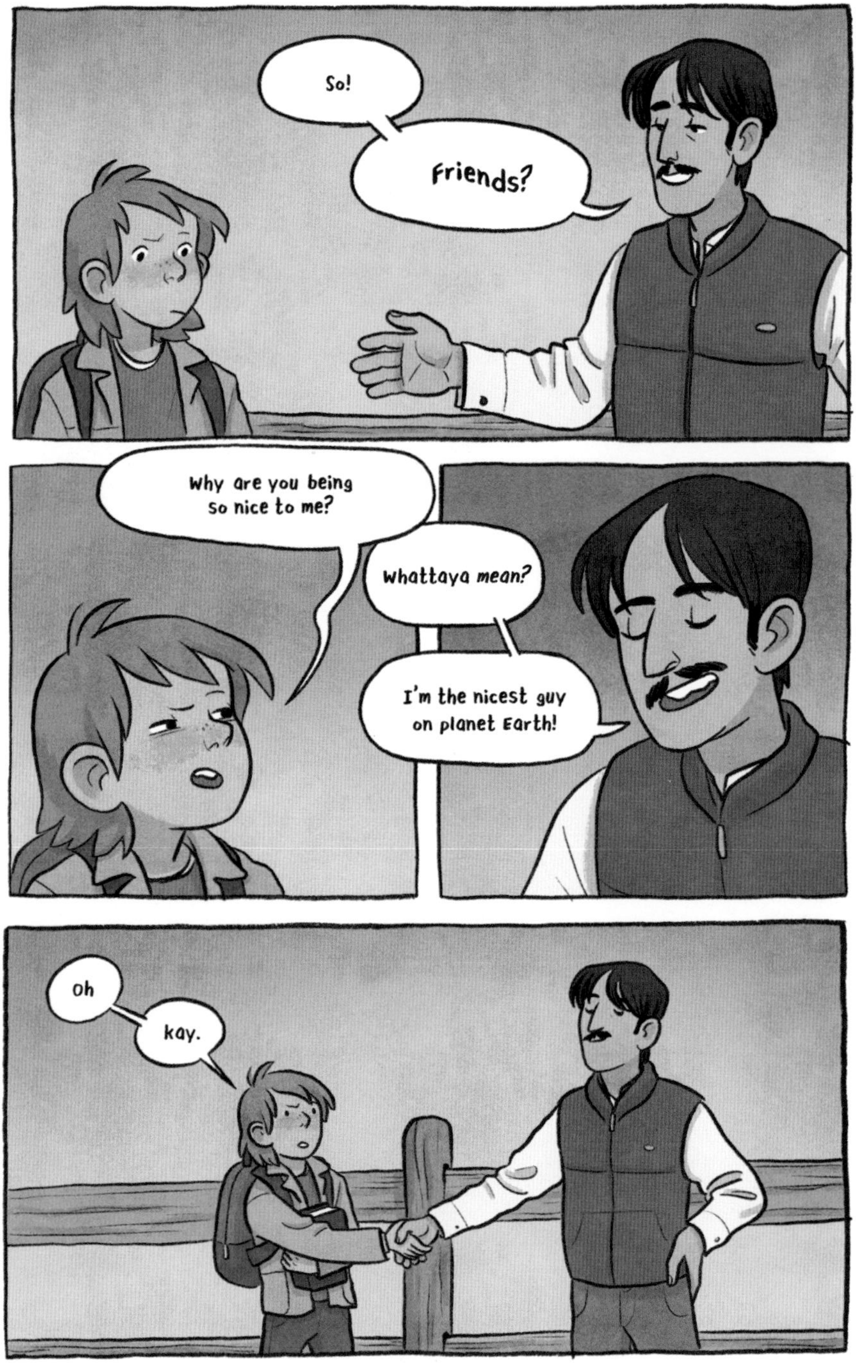
So!
Friends?
Why are you being so nice to me?
Whattaya mean?
I'm the nicest guy on planet Earth!
Oh
kay.

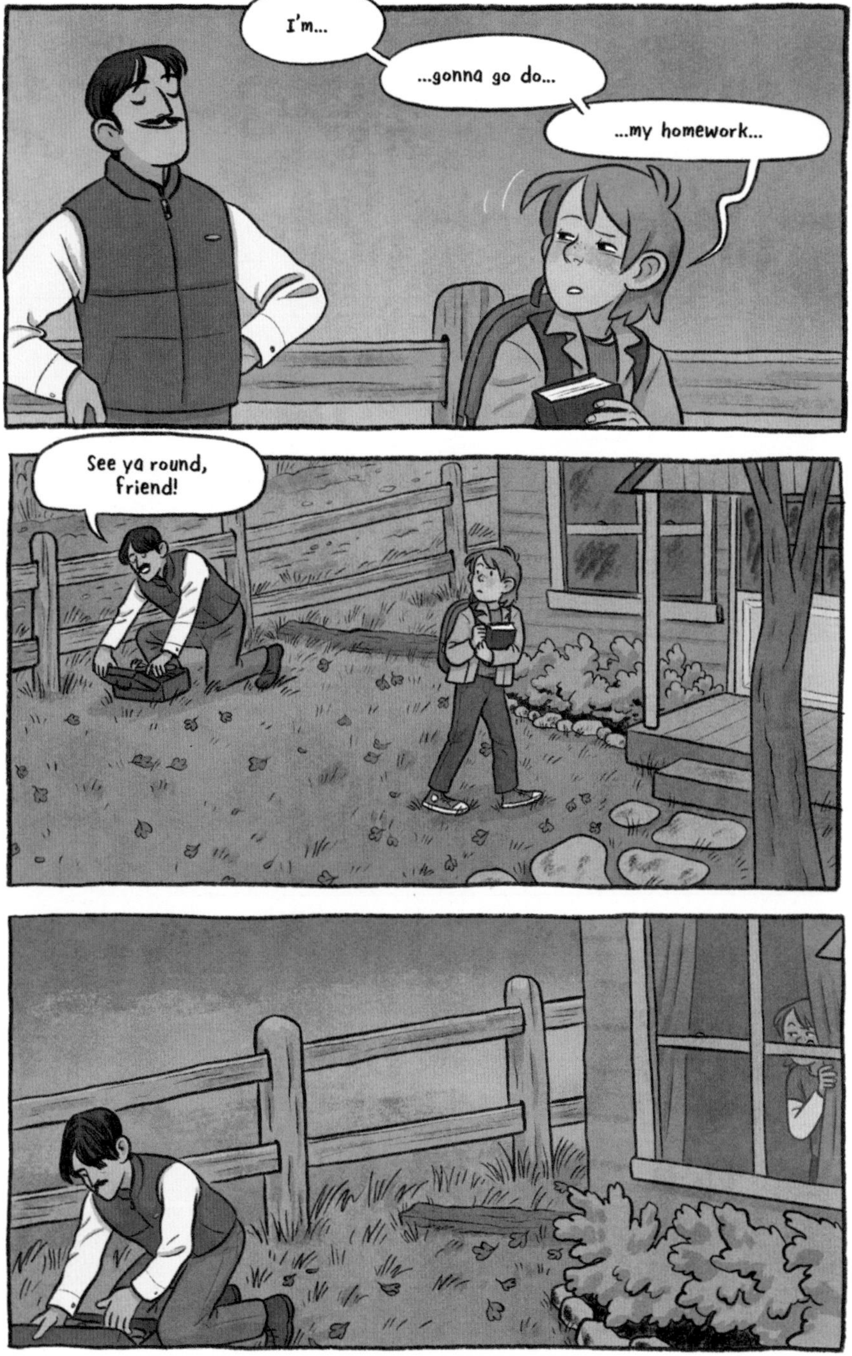

I'm...
...gonna go do...
...my homework...
See ya round, friend!

Chapter Three

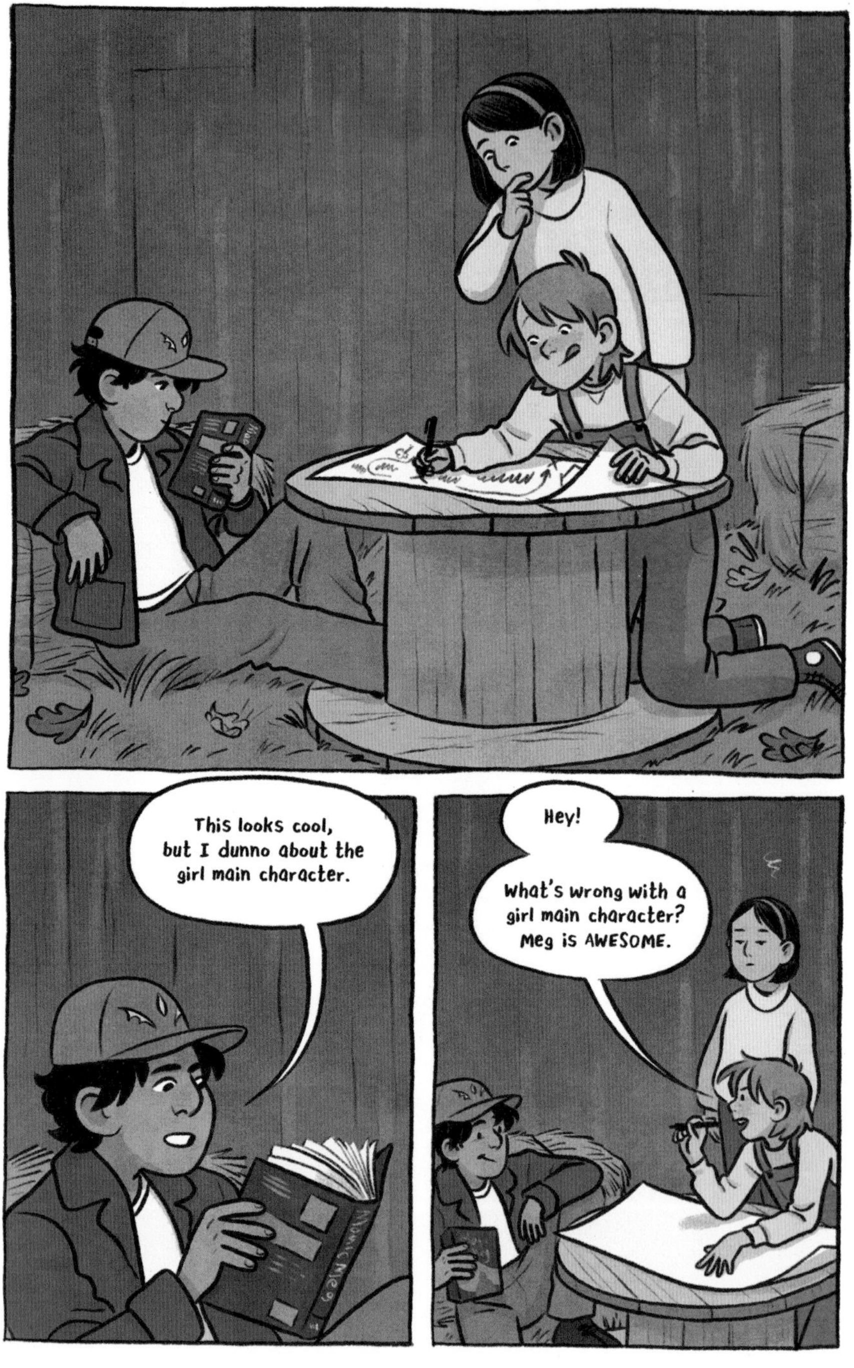
This looks cool, but I dunno about the girl main character.
Hey!
What's wrong with a girl main character? Meg is AWESOME.

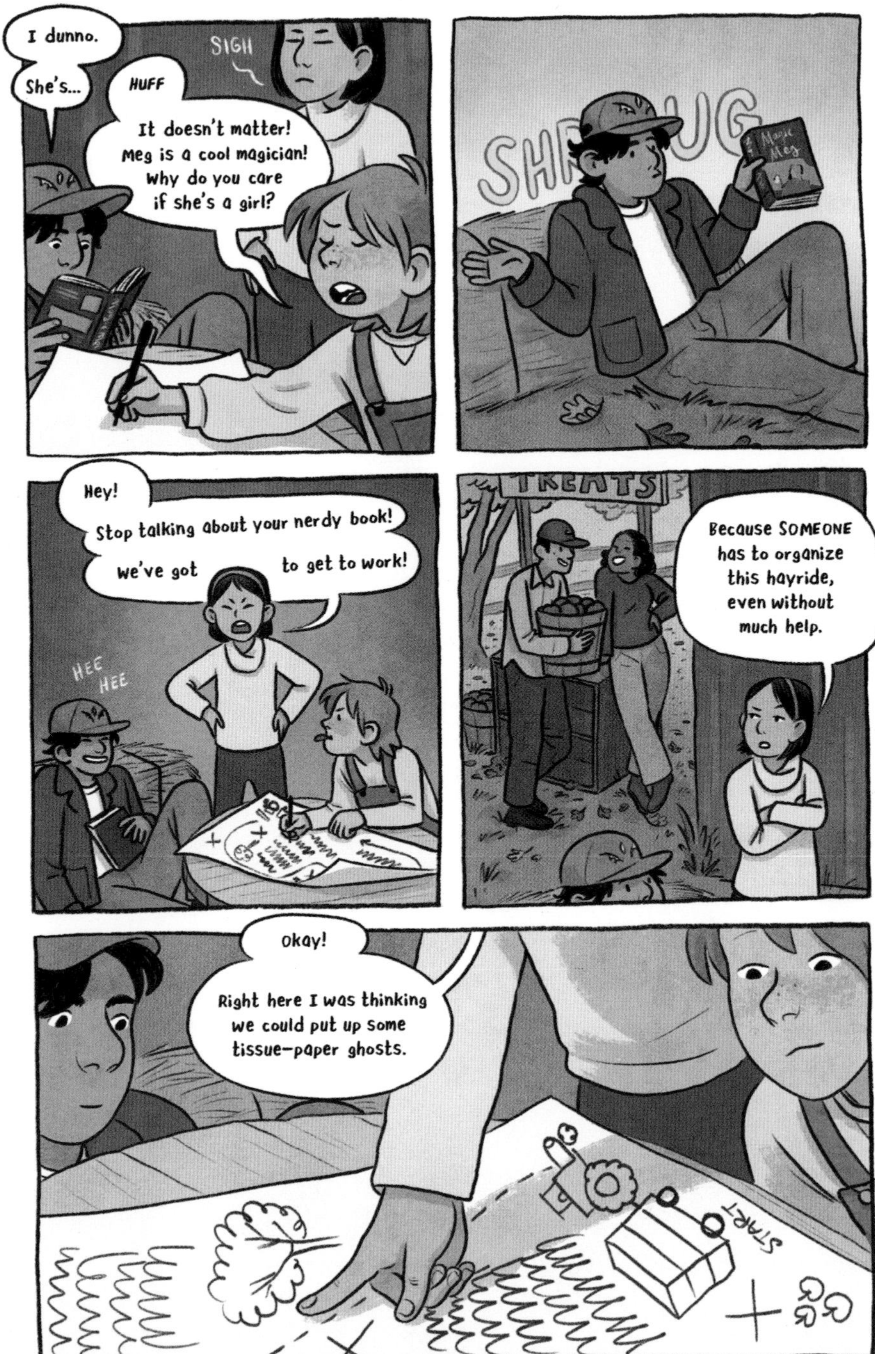
I dunno.
She's...
SIGH
HUFF
It doesn't matter! Meg is a cool magician! Why do you care if she's a girl?
SHRUG
Hey!
Stop talking about your nerdy book!
We've got to get to work!
HEE HEE
TREATS
Because SOMEONE has to organize this hayride, even without much help.
Okay!
Right here I was thinking we could put up some tissue-paper ghosts.
START

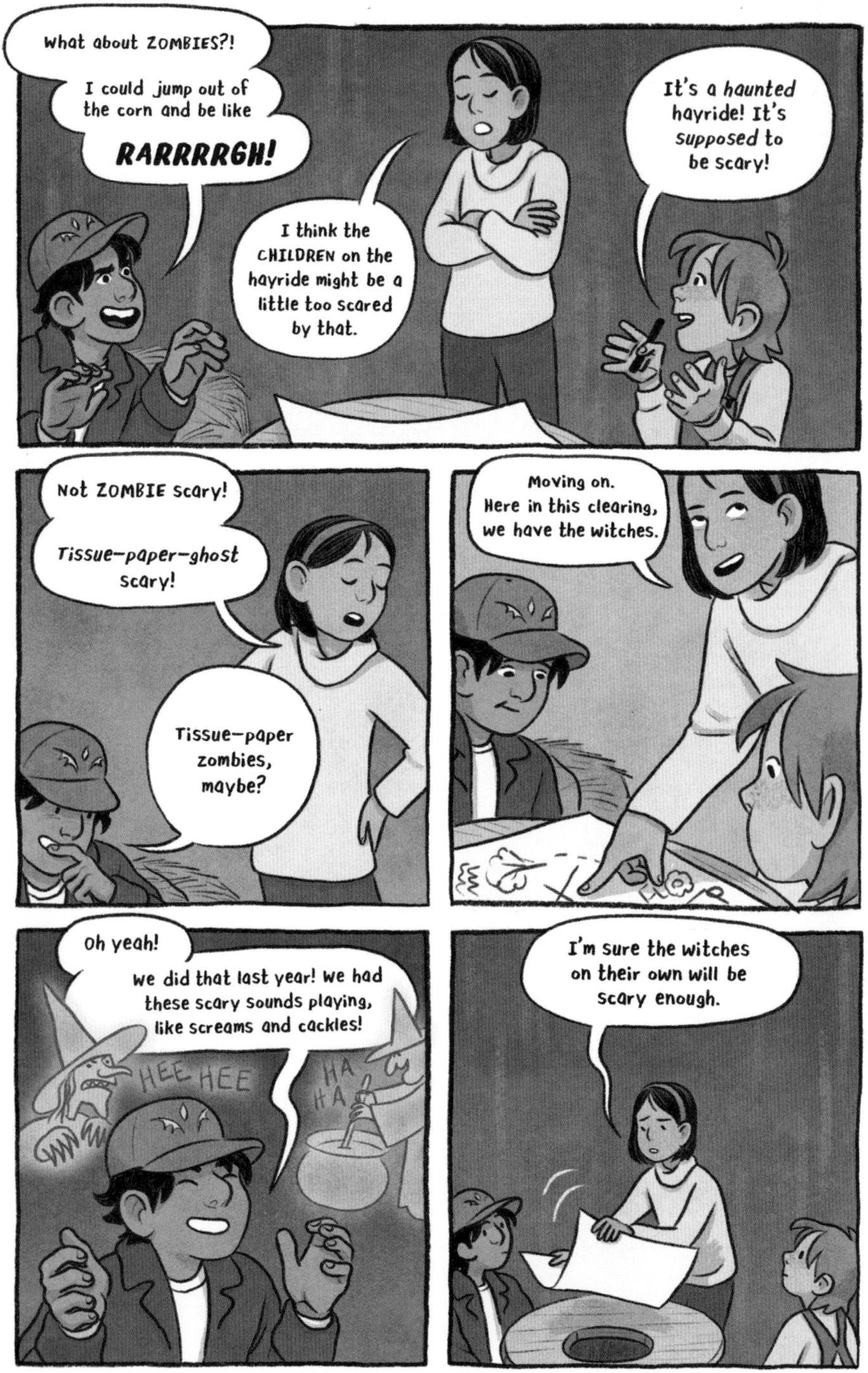
What about ZOMBIES?!
I could jump out of the corn and be like
RARRRRGH!
I think the CHILDREN on the hayride might be a little too scared by that.
It's a *haunted* hayride! It's *supposed* to be scary!
Not ZOMBIE scary!
Tissue-paper-ghost scary!
Tissue-paper zombies, maybe?
Moving on. Here in this clearing, we have the witches.
Oh yeah!
We did that last year! We had these scary sounds playing, like screams and cackles!
HEE HEE
HA HA
I'm sure the witches on their own will be scary enough.

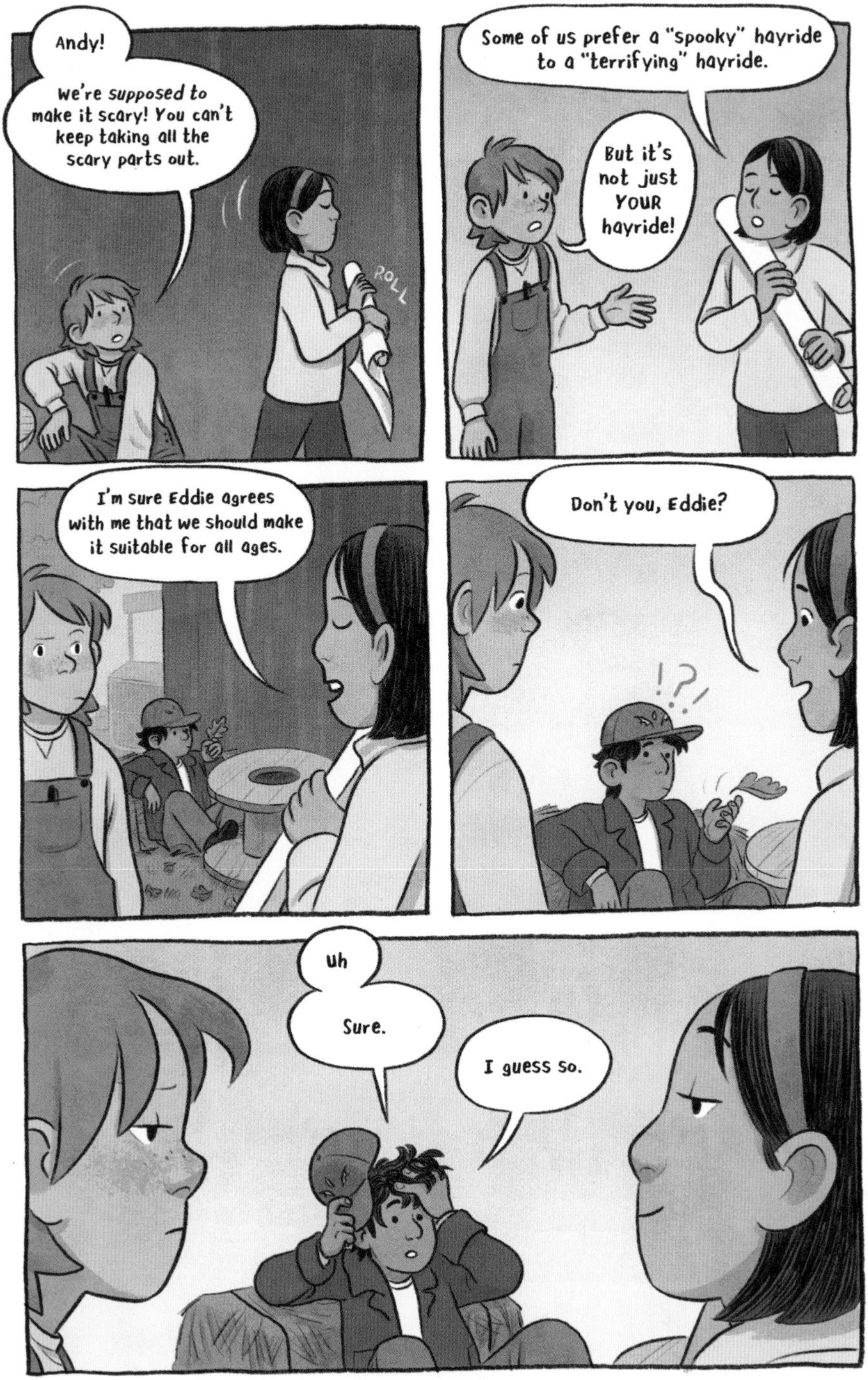
Andy!
We're supposed to make it scary! You can't keep taking all the scary parts out.
ROLL
Some of us prefer a "spooky" hayride to a "terrifying" hayride.
But it's not just YOUR hayride!
I'm sure Eddie agrees with me that we should make it suitable for all ages.
Don't you, Eddie?
!?!
Uh
Sure.
I guess so.

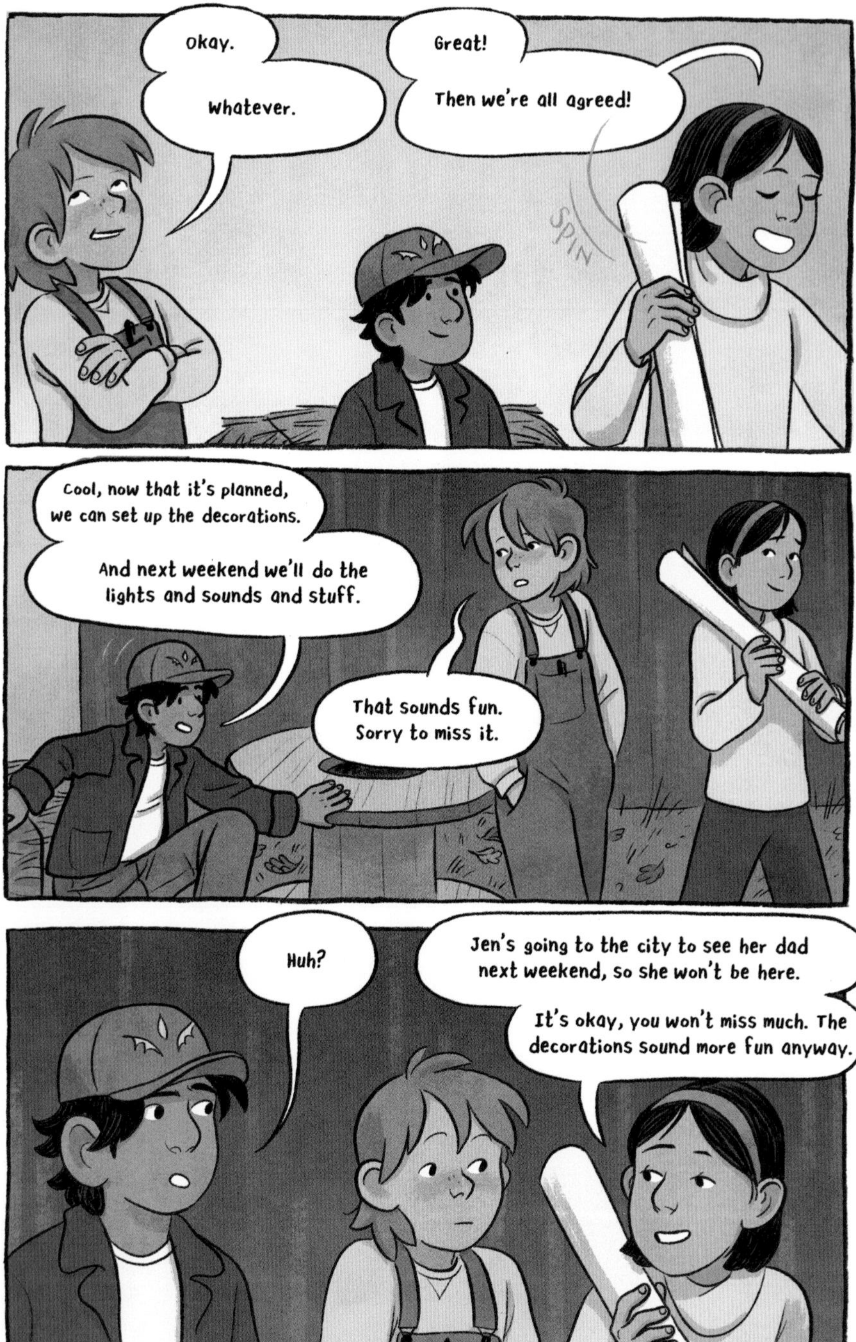

Okay.
Whatever.
Great!
Then we're all agreed!
SPIN
Cool, now that it's planned, we can set up the decorations.
And next weekend we'll do the lights and sounds and stuff.
That sounds fun. Sorry to miss it.
Huh?
Jen's going to the city to see her dad next weekend, so she won't be here.
It's okay, you won't miss much. The decorations sound more fun anyway.

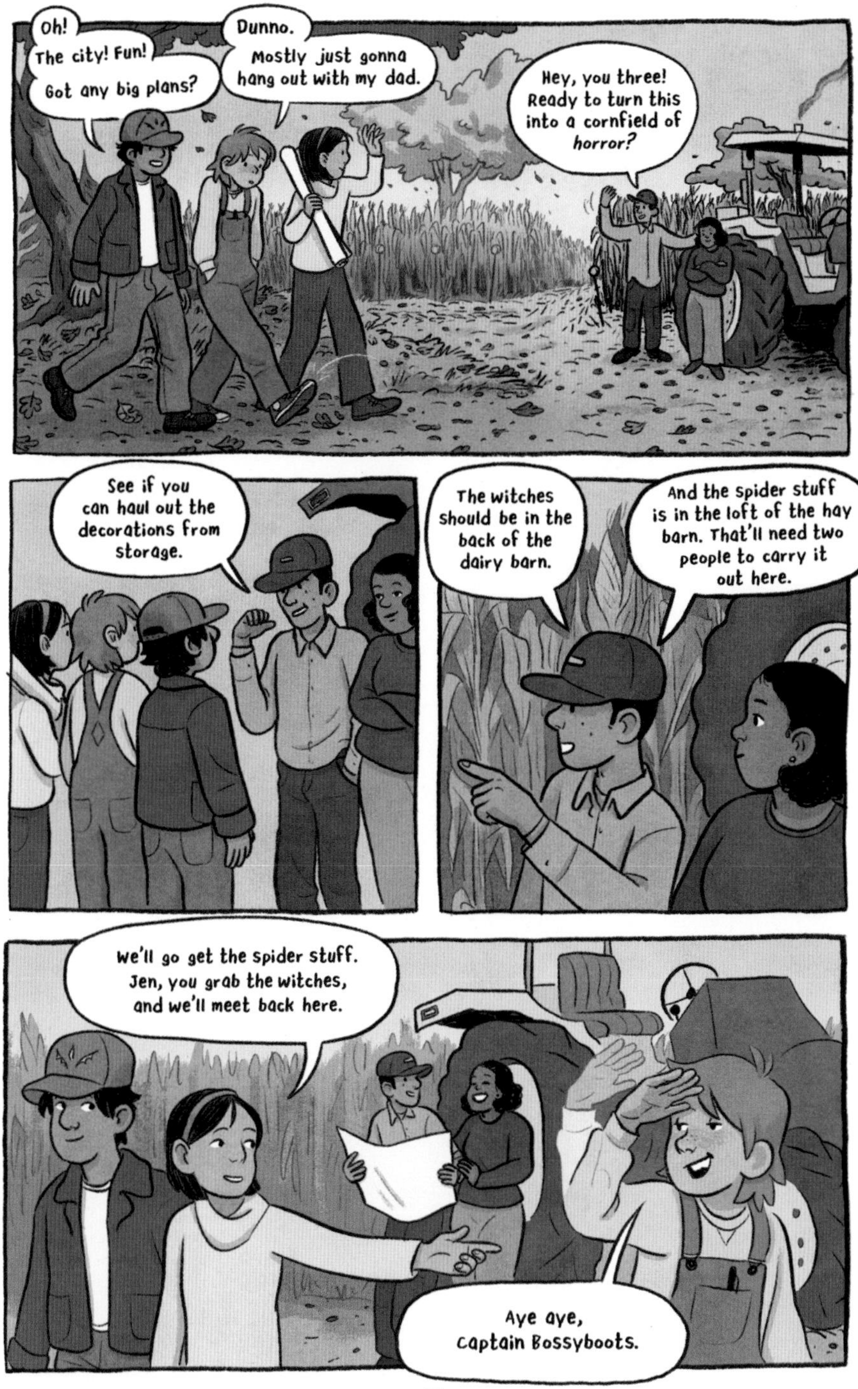
Oh!
The city! Fun!
Got any big plans?
Dunno.
Mostly just gonna hang out with my dad.
Hey, you three! Ready to turn this into a cornfield of *horror?*
See if you can haul out the decorations from storage.
The witches should be in the back of the dairy barn.
And the spider stuff is in the loft of the hay barn. That'll need two people to carry it out here.
We'll go get the spider stuff. Jen, you grab the witches, and we'll meet back here.
Aye aye, Captain Bossyboots.

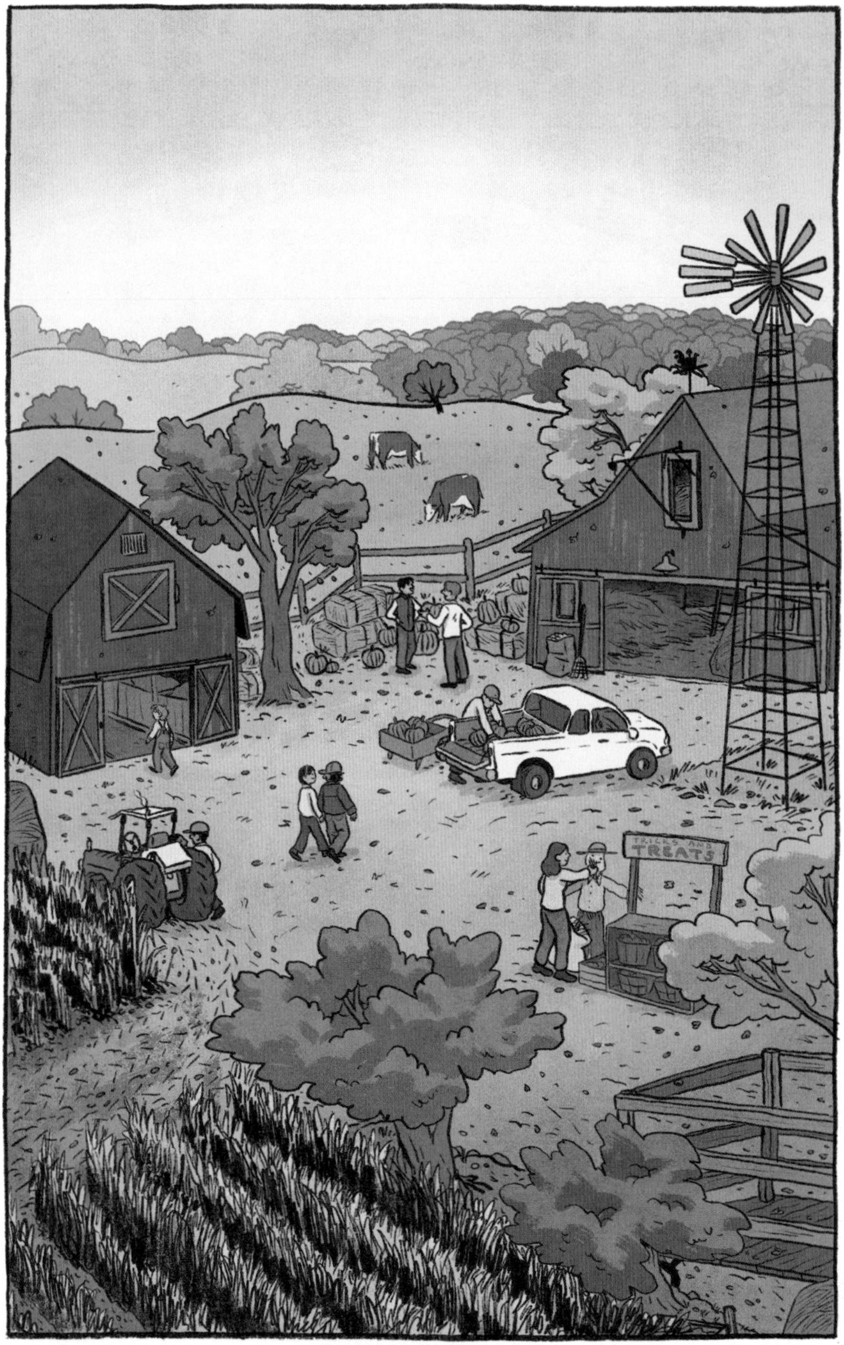
TRICKS AND
TREATS

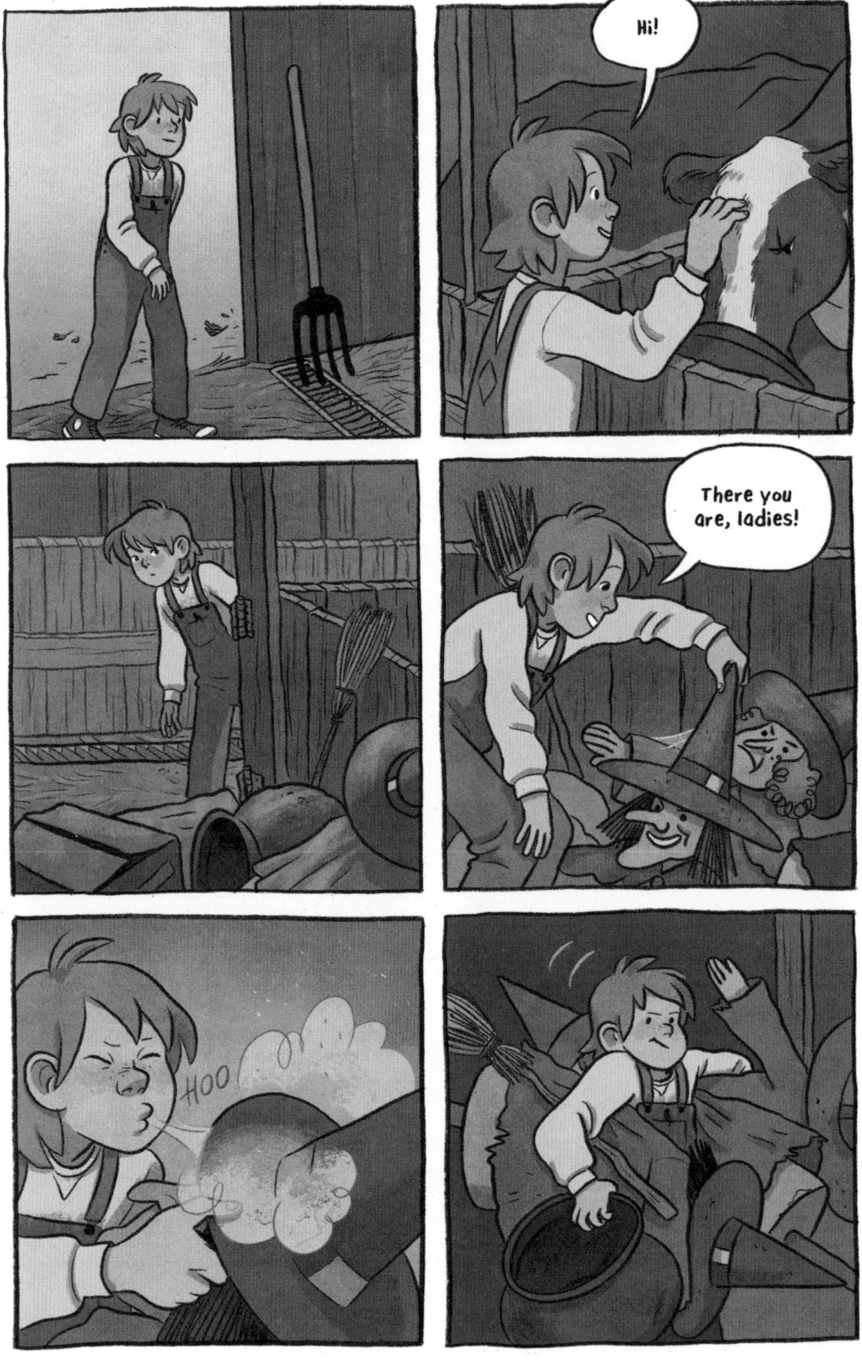
Hi!
There you are, ladies!
HOO

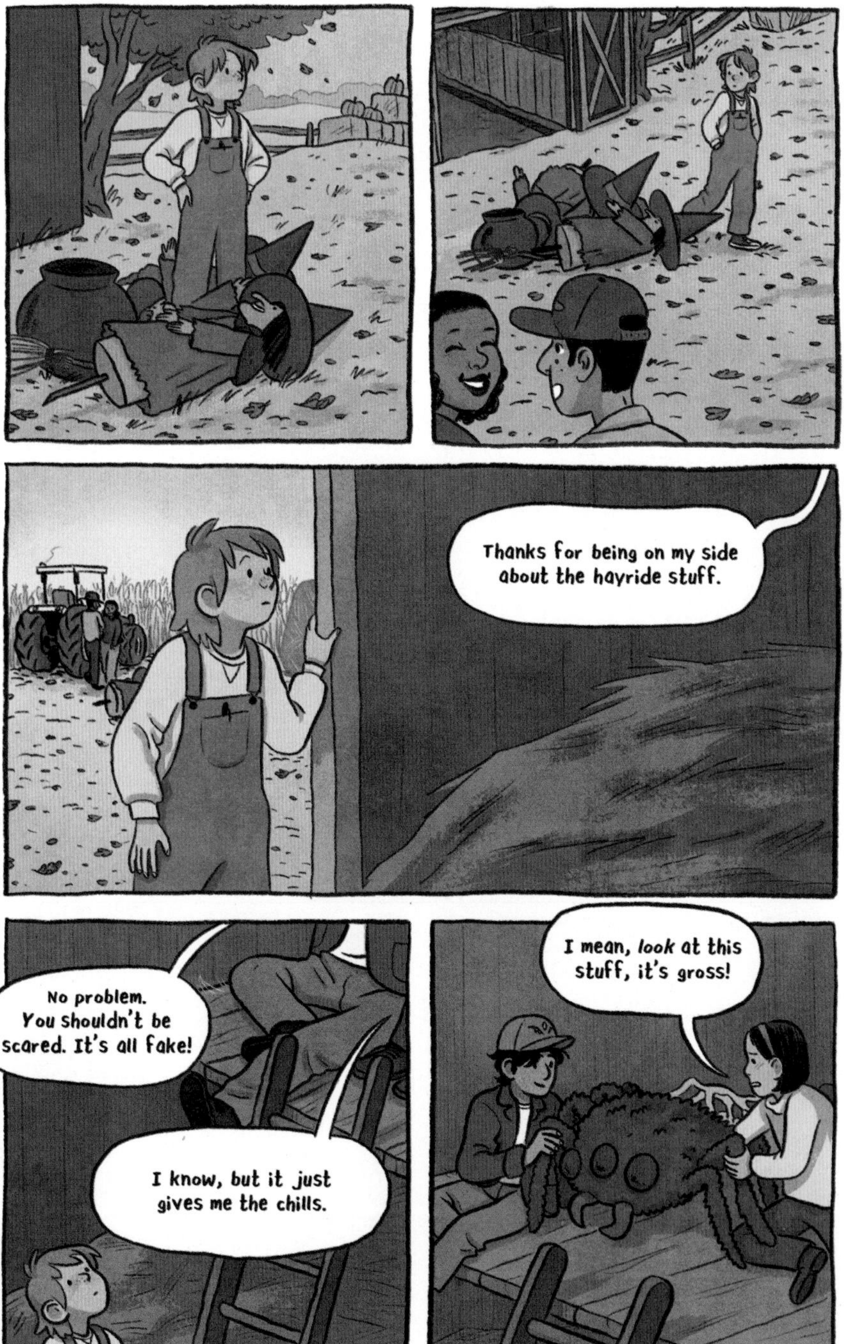
Thanks for being on my side
about the hayride stuff.
No problem.
You shouldn't be
scared. It's all fake!
I know, but it just
gives me the chills.
I mean, *look* at this
stuff, it's gross!

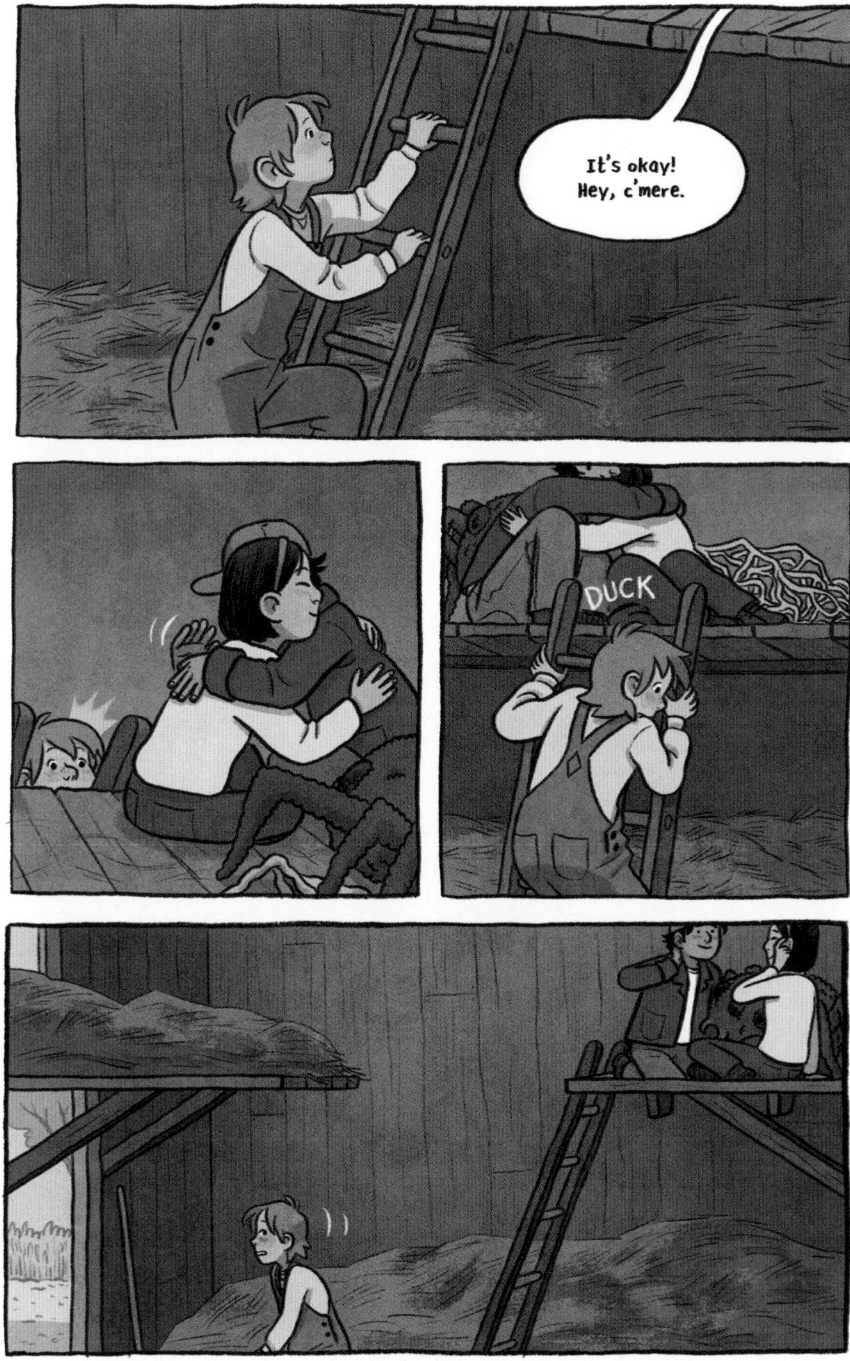
It's okay!
Hey, c'mere.
DUCK

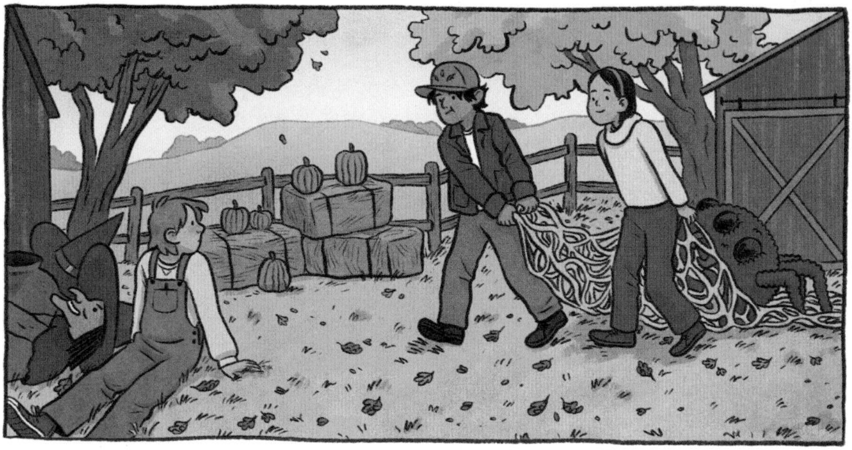

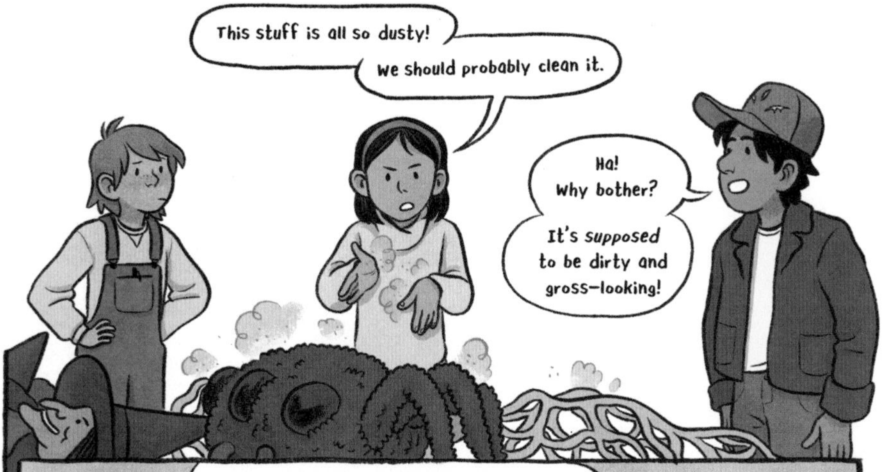
This stuff is all so dusty!
We should probably clean it.
Ha! Why bother?
It's *supposed* to be dirty and gross-looking!

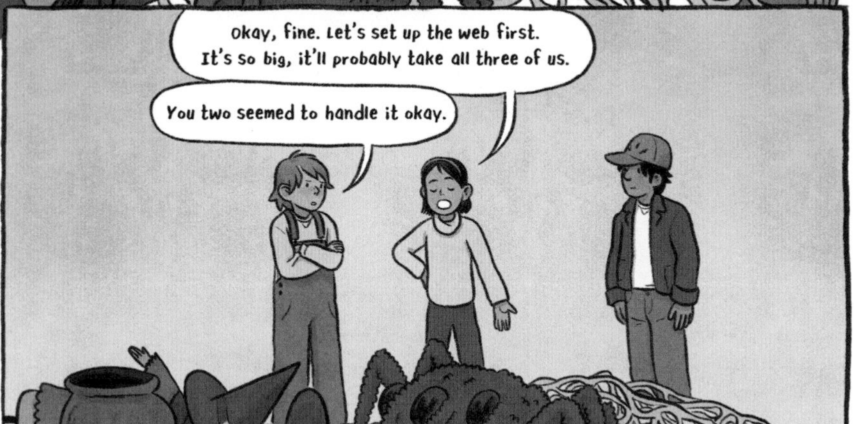
Okay, fine. Let's set up the web first. It's so big, it'll probably take all three of us.
You two seemed to handle it okay.

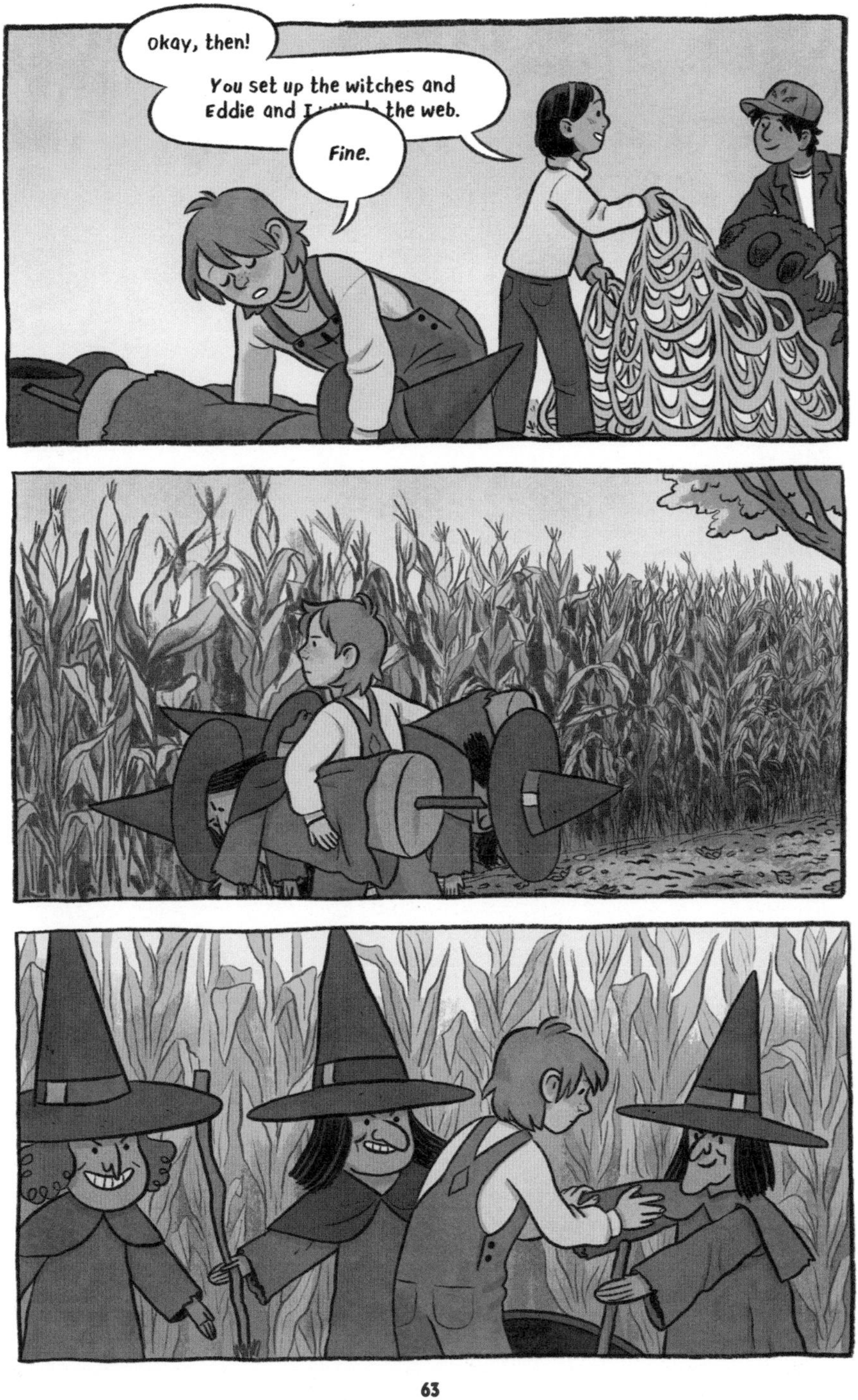
Okay, then!
You set up the witches and
Eddie and I the web.
Fine.

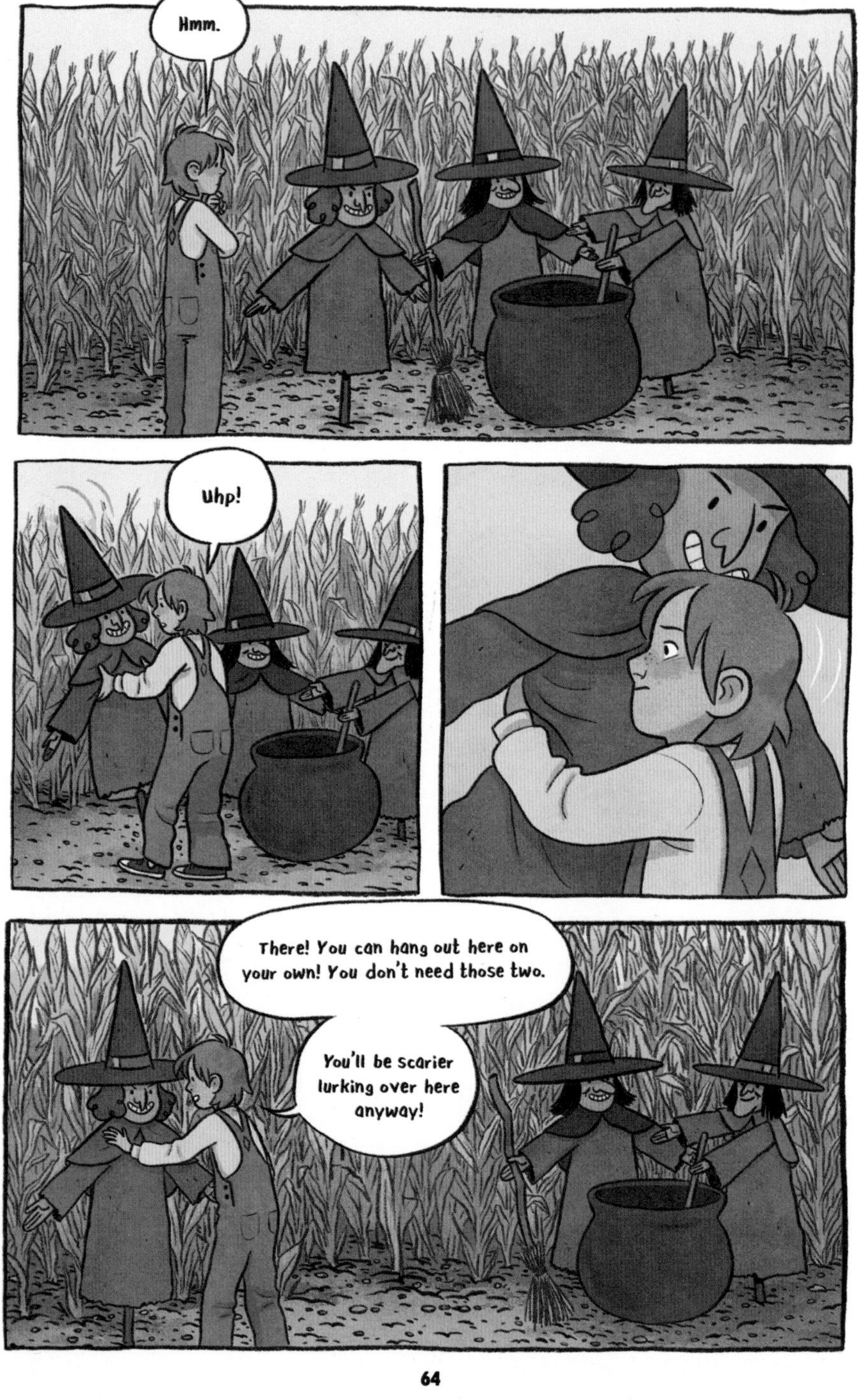

Hmm.
Uhp!
There! You can hang out here on your own! You don't need those two.
You'll be scarier lurking over here anyway!

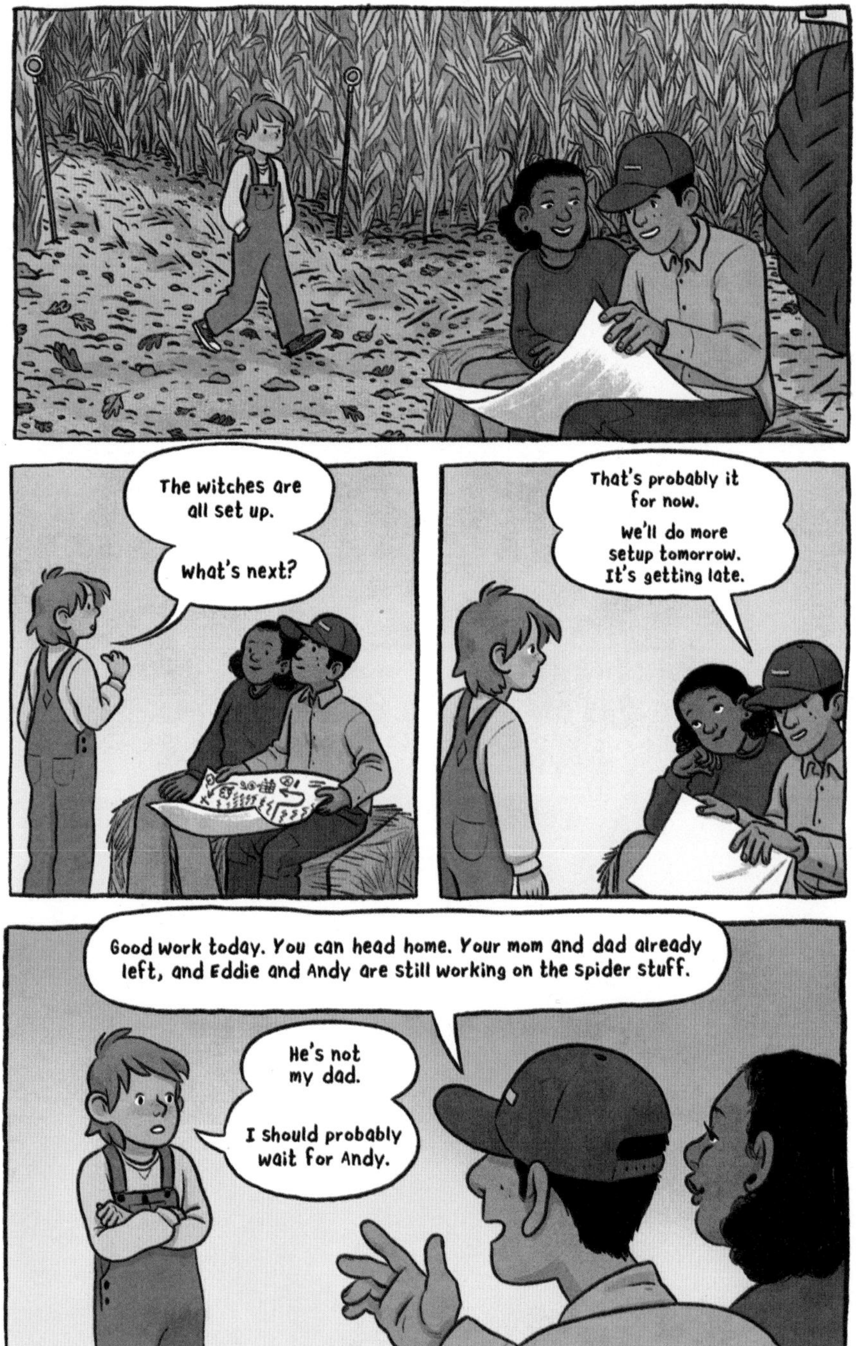
The witches are all set up.
What's next?
That's probably it for now.
We'll do more setup tomorrow. It's getting late.
Good work today. You can head home. Your mom and dad already left, and Eddie and Andy are still working on the spider stuff.
He's not my dad.
I should probably wait for Andy.

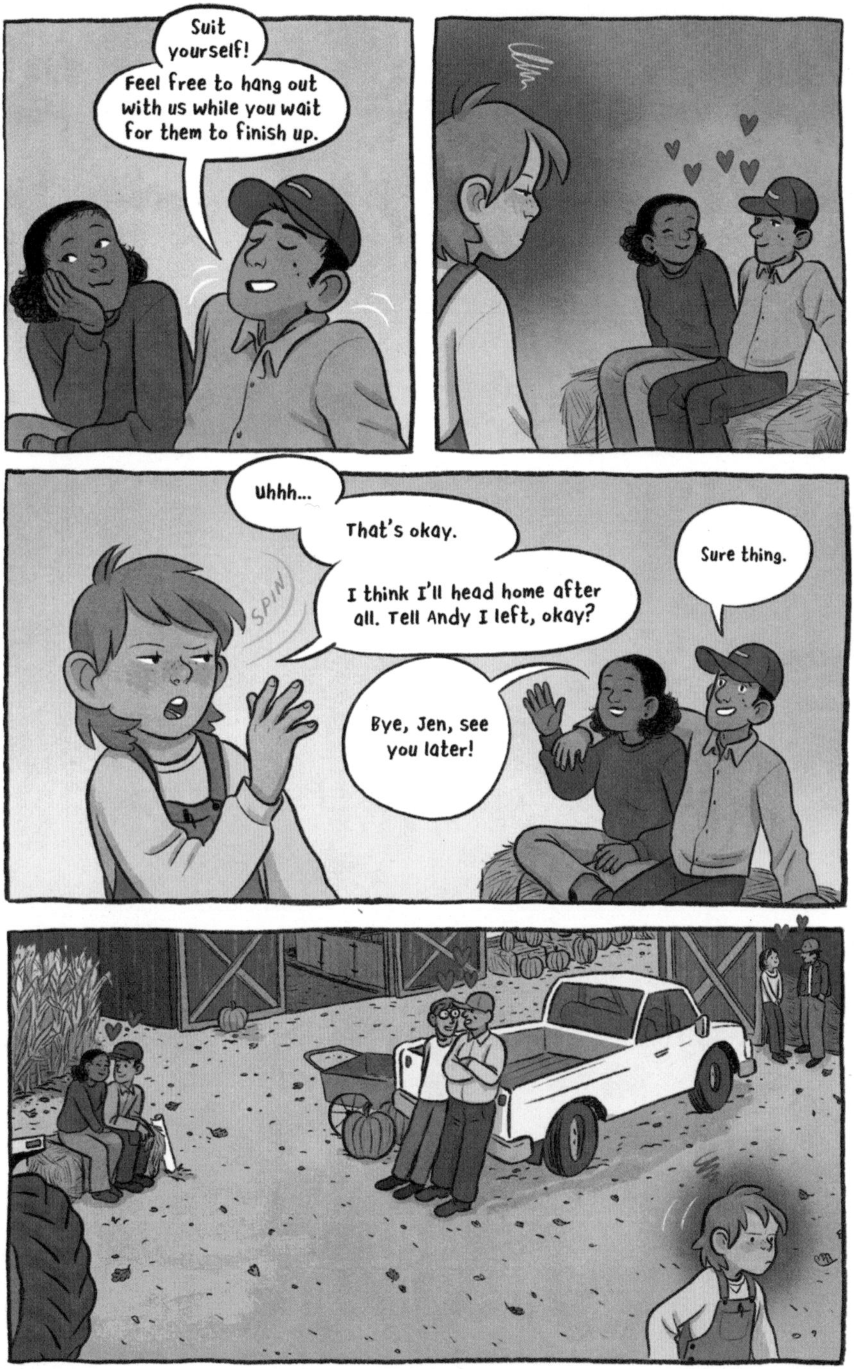
Suit yourself!
Feel free to hang out with us while you wait for them to finish up.
Uhhh...
That's okay.
I think I'll head home after all. Tell Andy I left, okay?
SPIN
Sure thing.
Bye, Jen, see you later!

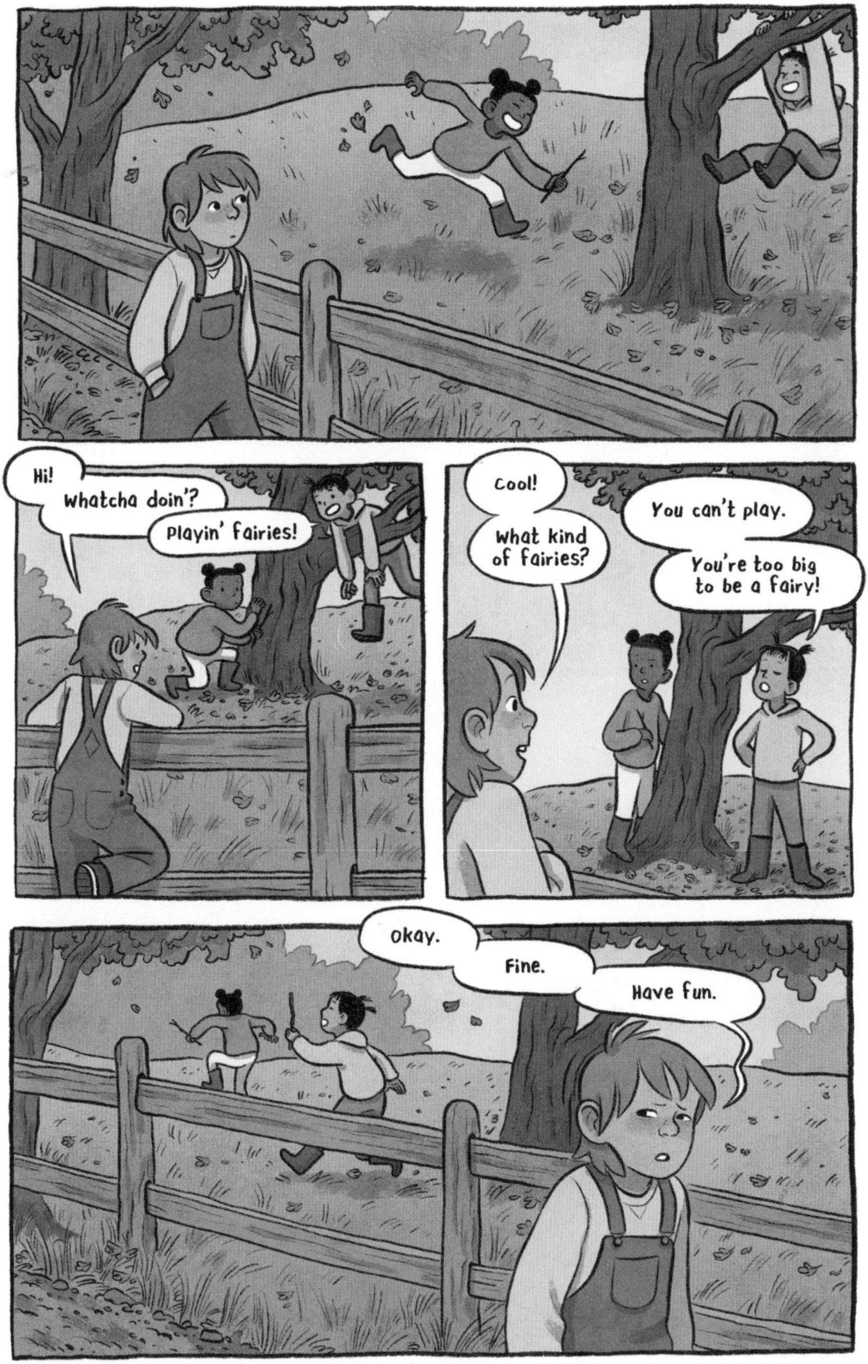
Hi!
Whatcha doin'?
Playin' fairies!
Cool!
What kind of fairies?
You can't play.
You're too big to be a fairy!
Okay.
Fine.
Have fun.

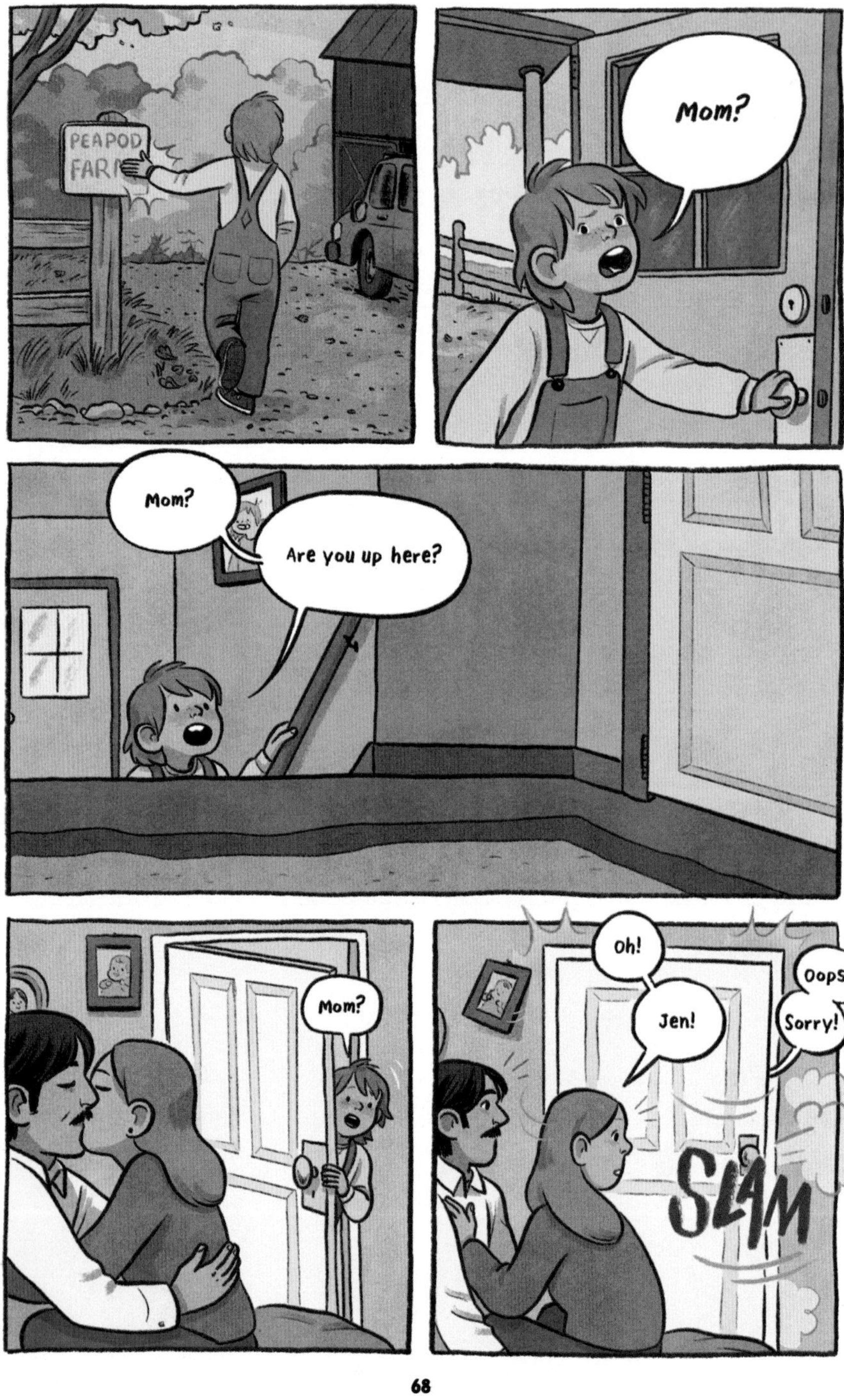
PEAPOD FAR
Mom?
Mom?
Are you up here?
Mom?
Oh!
Jen!
Oops!
Sorry!
SLAM

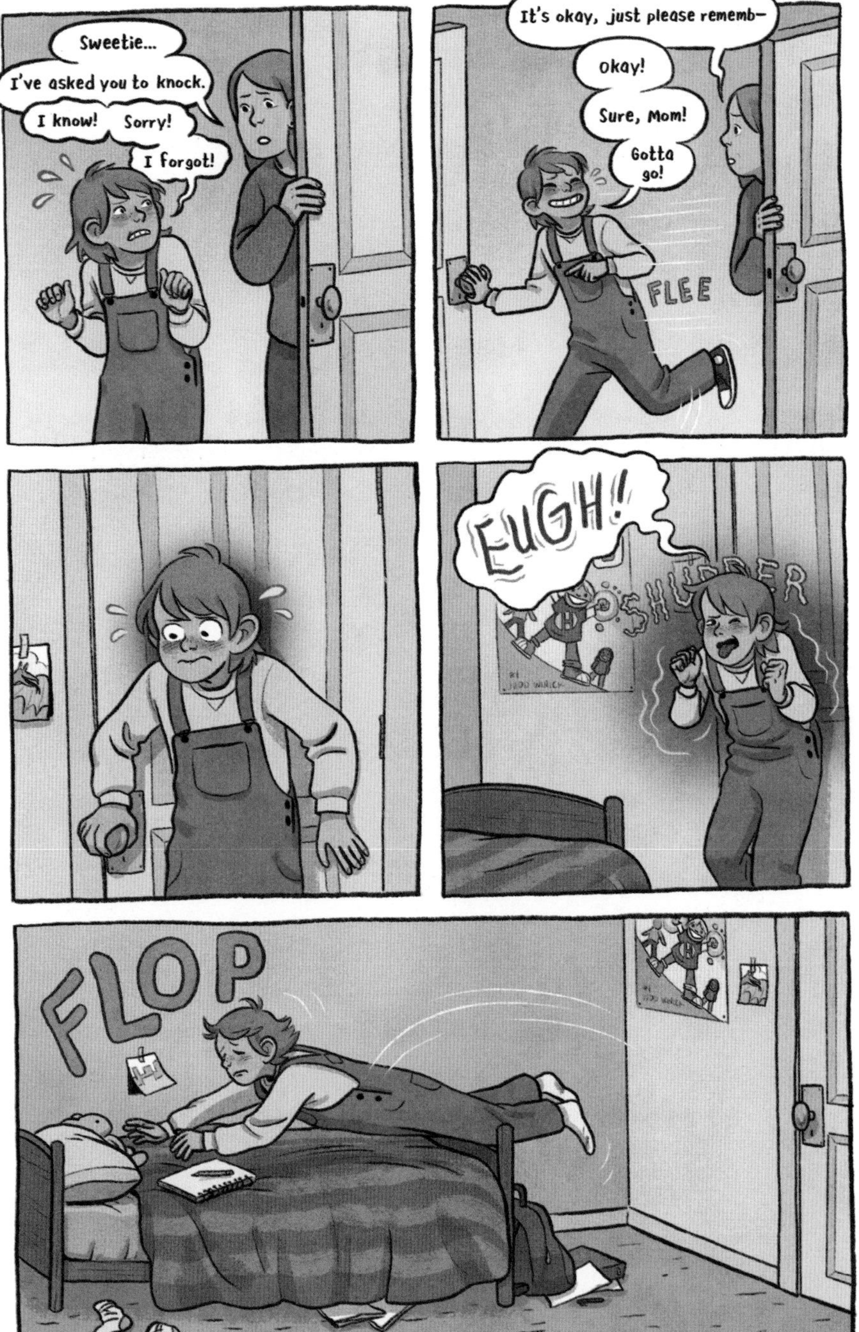
Sweetie...
I've asked you to knock.
I know!
Sorry!
I forgot!
It's okay, just please rememb—
Okay!
Sure, Mom!
Gotta go!
FLEE
EUGH!!
FLOP

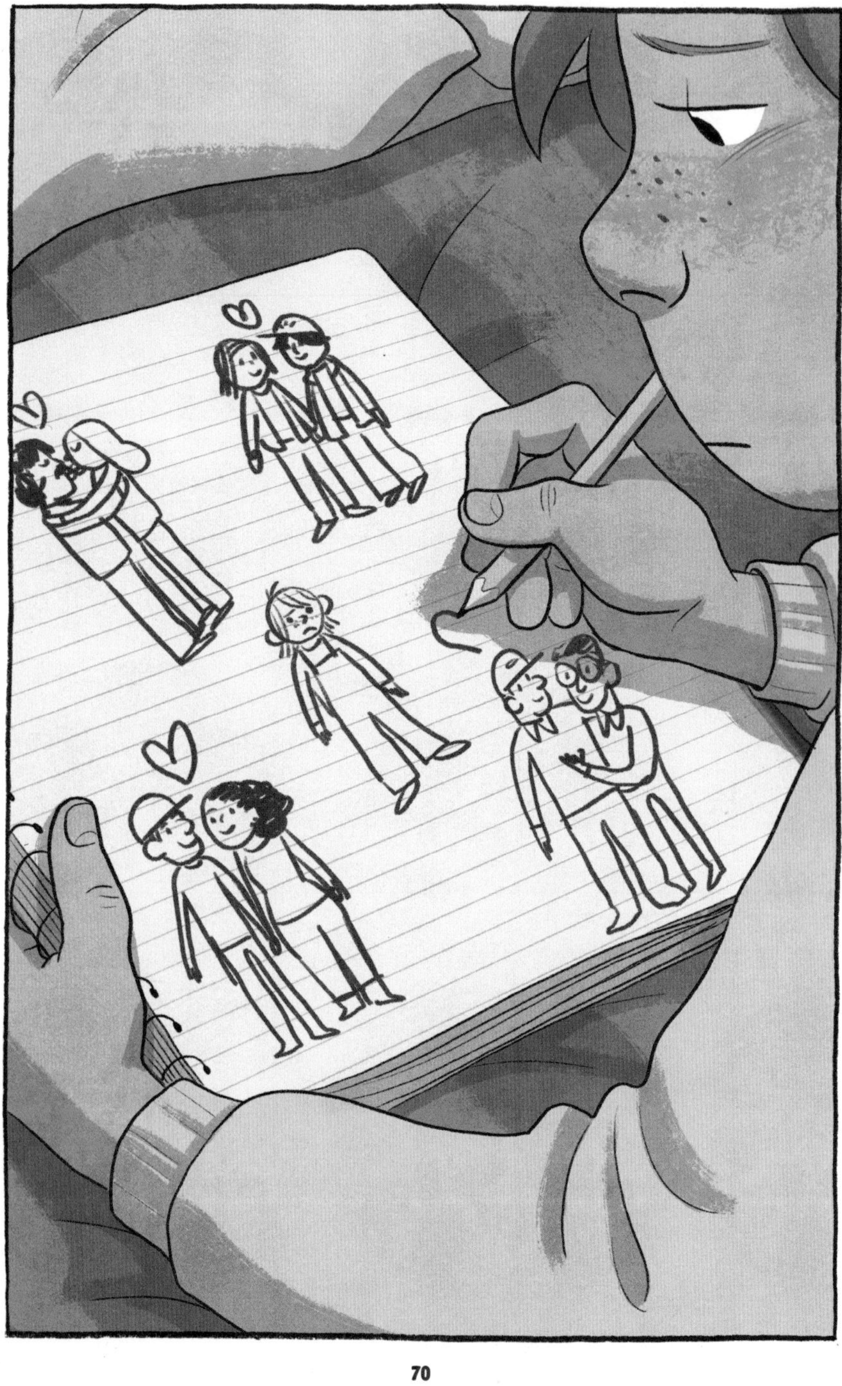

Chapter Four

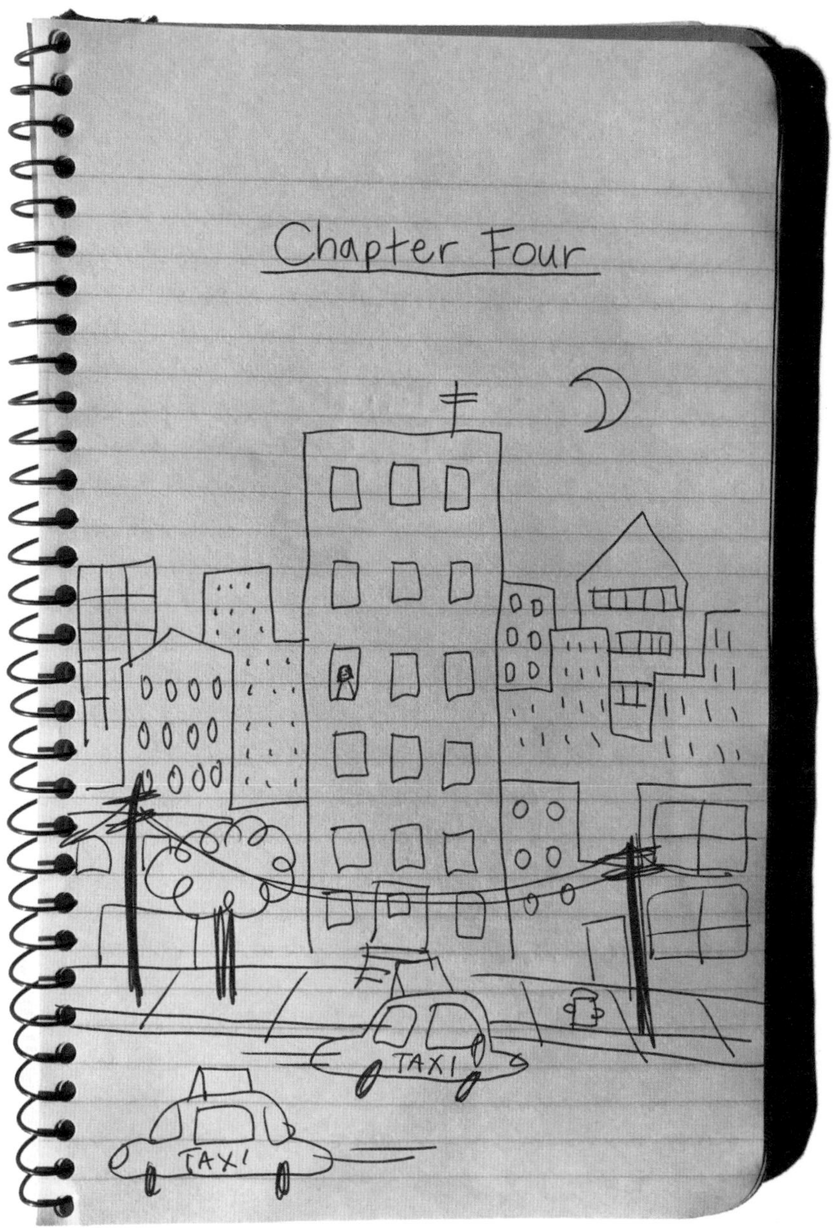
TAXI
TAXI

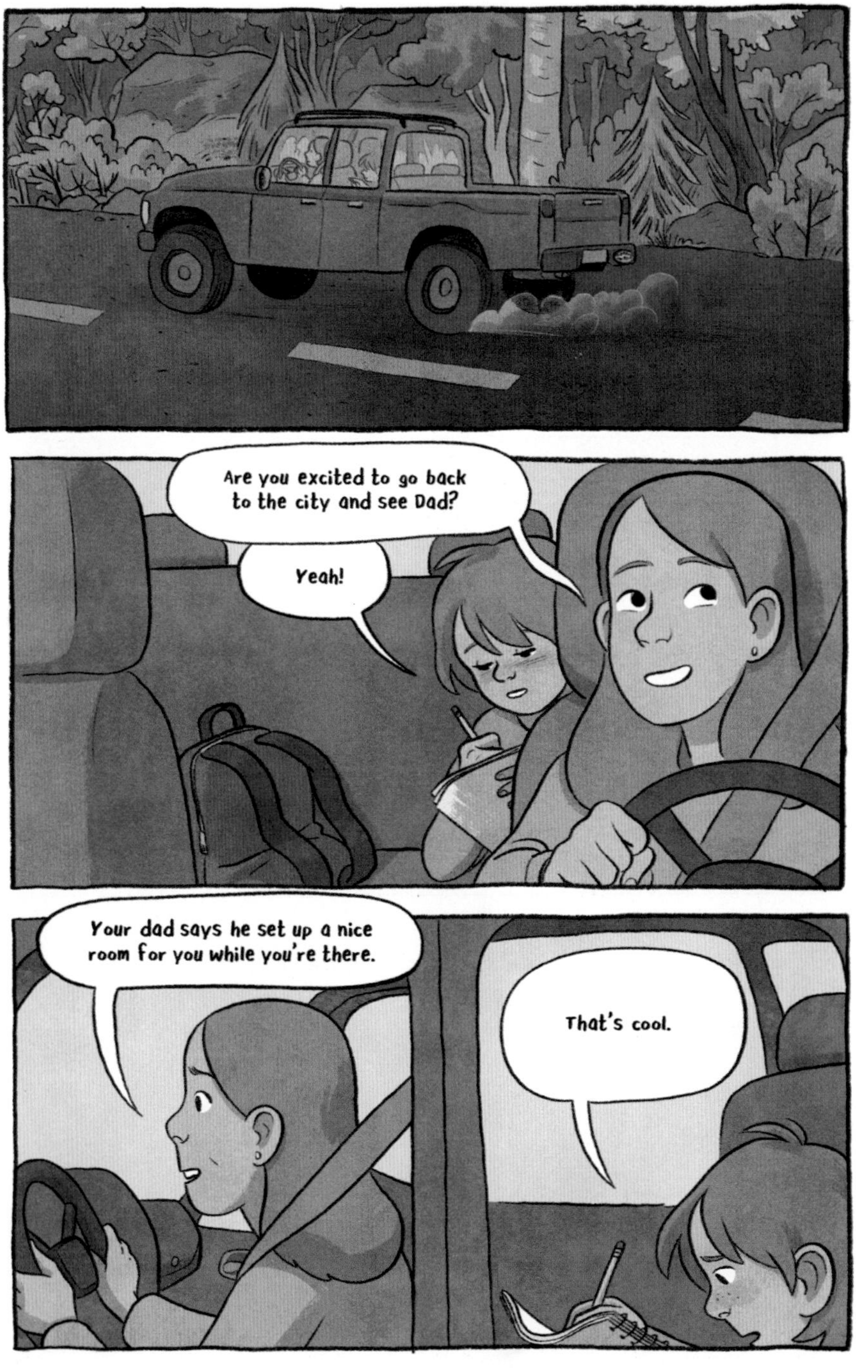
Are you excited to go back to the city and see Dad?
Yeah!
Your dad says he set up a nice room for you while you're there.
That's cool.

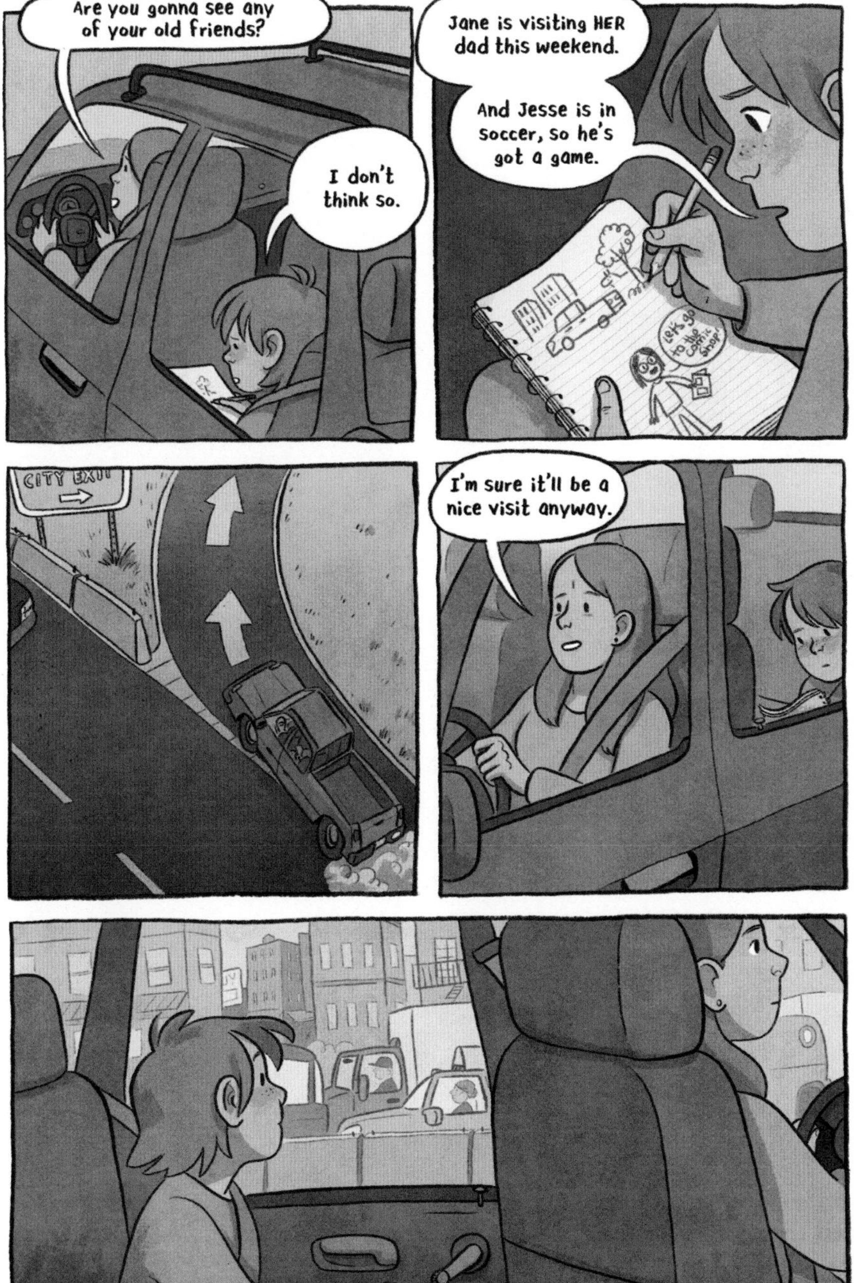

Are you gonna see any of your old friends?
I don't think so.
Jane is visiting HER dad this weekend.
And Jesse is in soccer, so he's got a game.
Let's go to the comic shop!
CITY EXIT
I'm sure it'll be a nice visit anyway.

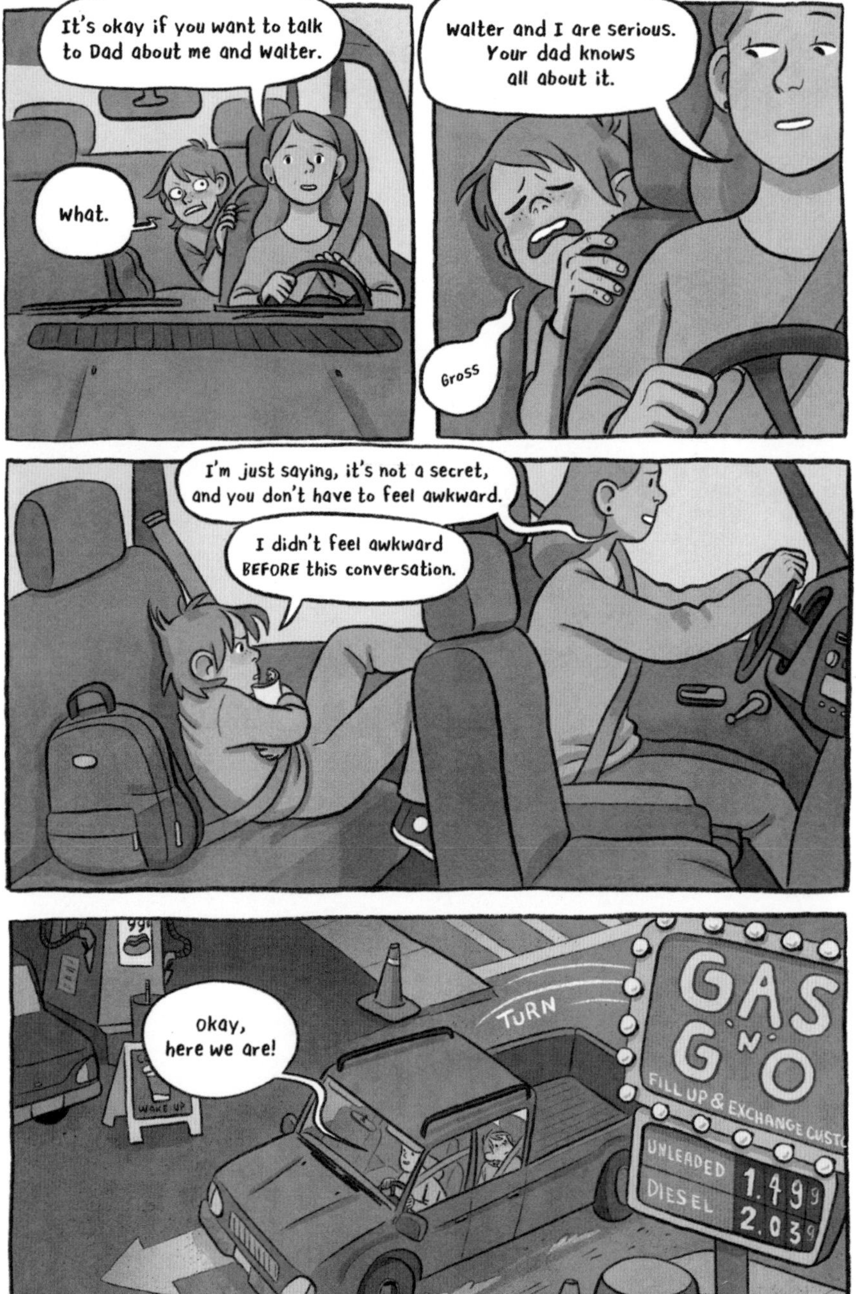
It's okay if you want to talk to Dad about me and Walter.
What.
Walter and I are serious. Your dad knows all about it.
Gross
I'm just saying, it's not a secret, and you don't have to feel awkward.
I didn't feel awkward BEFORE this conversation.
TURN
GAS 'N' GO
FILL UP & EXCHANGE
UNLEADED 1.49
DIESEL 2.03
Okay, here we are!

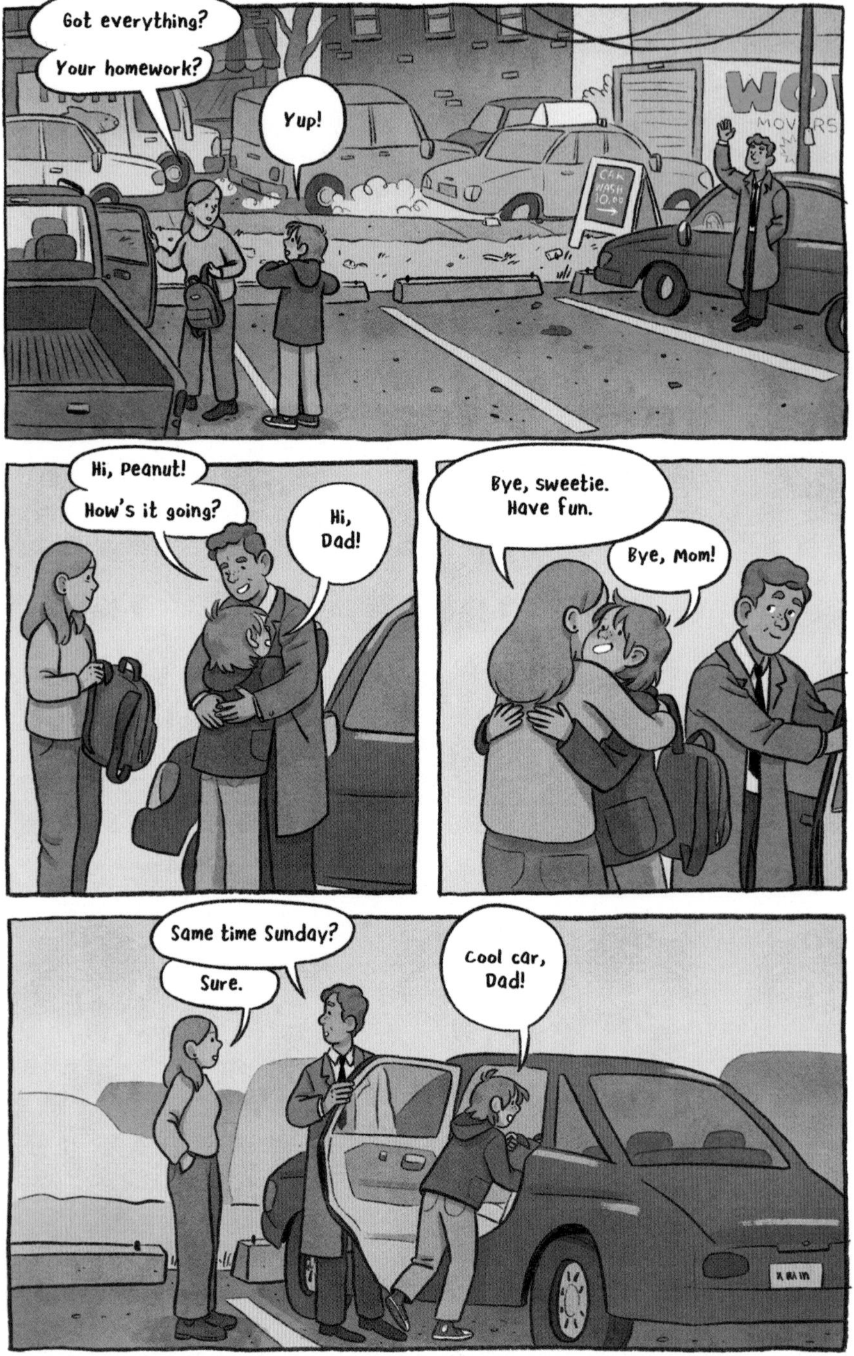
Got everything?
Your homework?
Yup!
Hi, Peanut!
How's it going?
Hi, Dad!
Bye, sweetie. Have fun.
Bye, Mom!
Same time Sunday?
Sure.
Cool car, Dad!

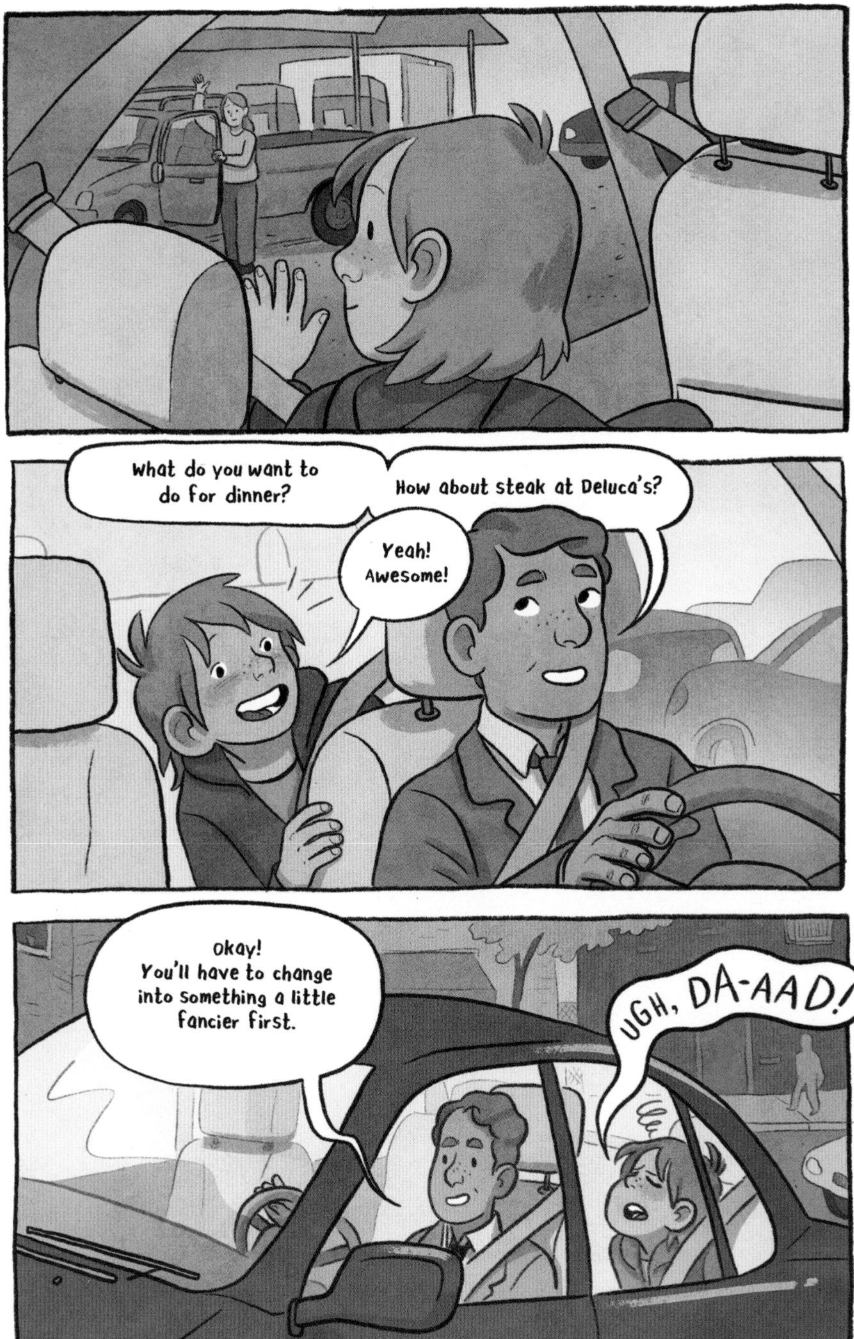
What do you want to
do for dinner?
How about steak at Deluca's?
Yeah!
Awesome!
Okay!
You'll have to change
into something a little
fancier first.
UGH, DA-AAD!

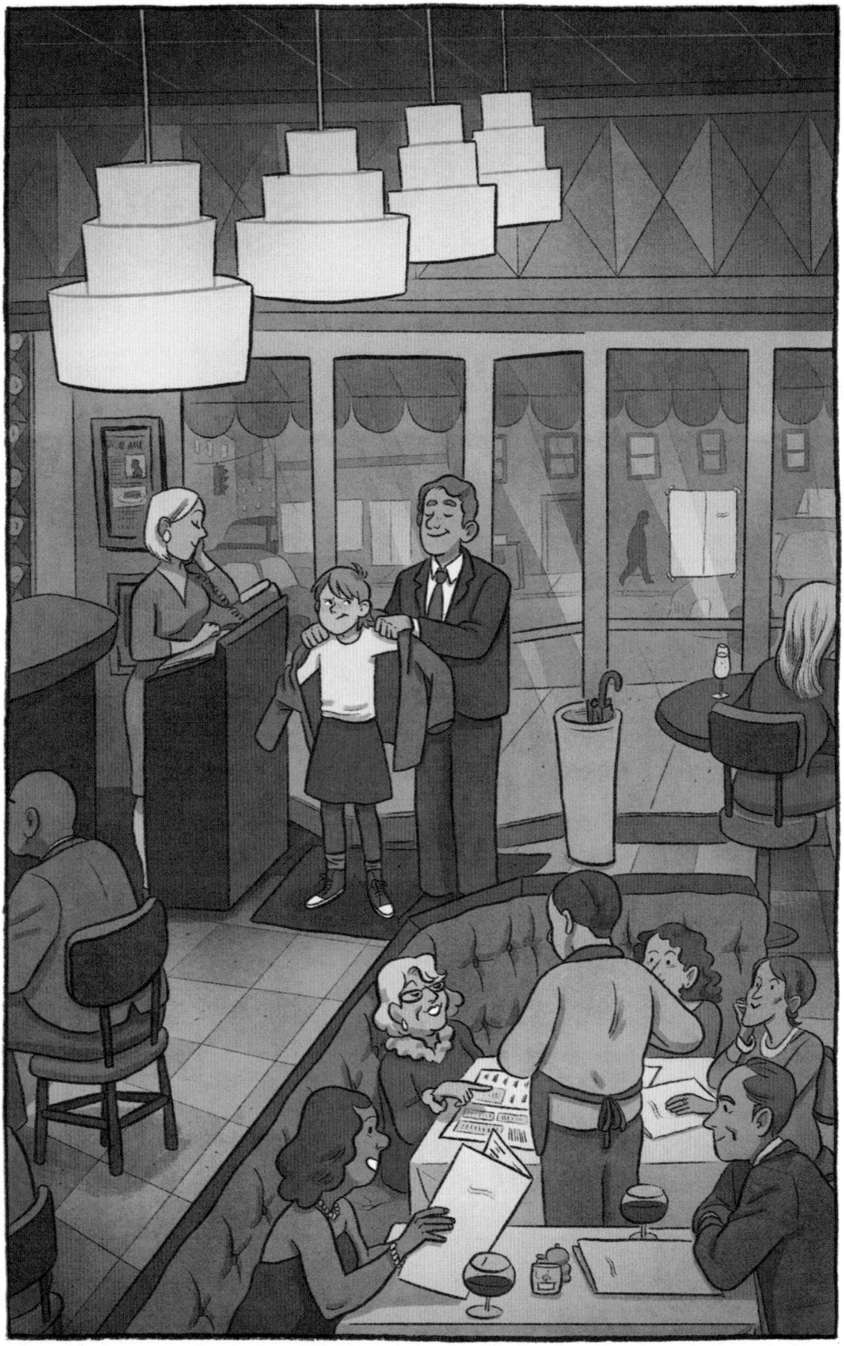

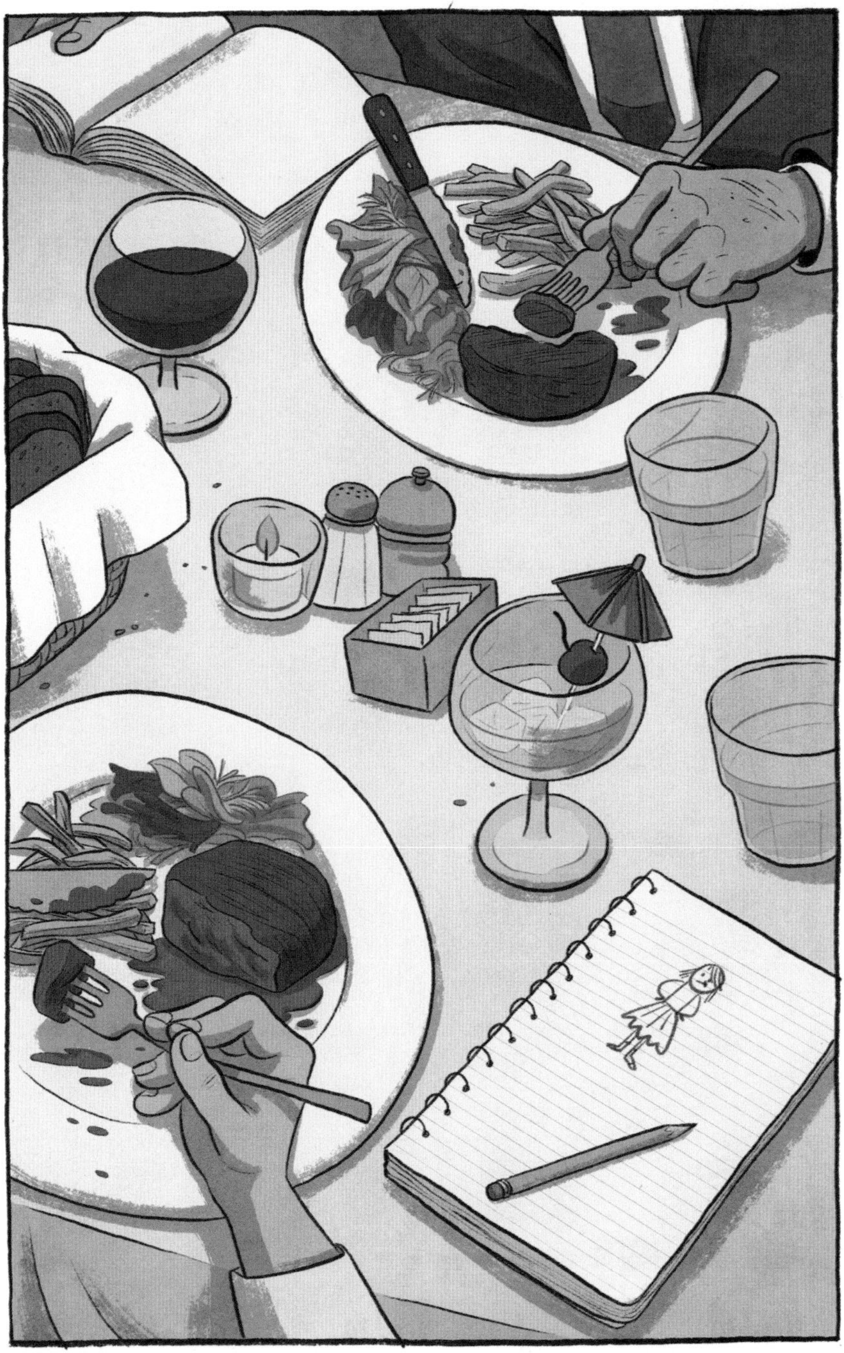

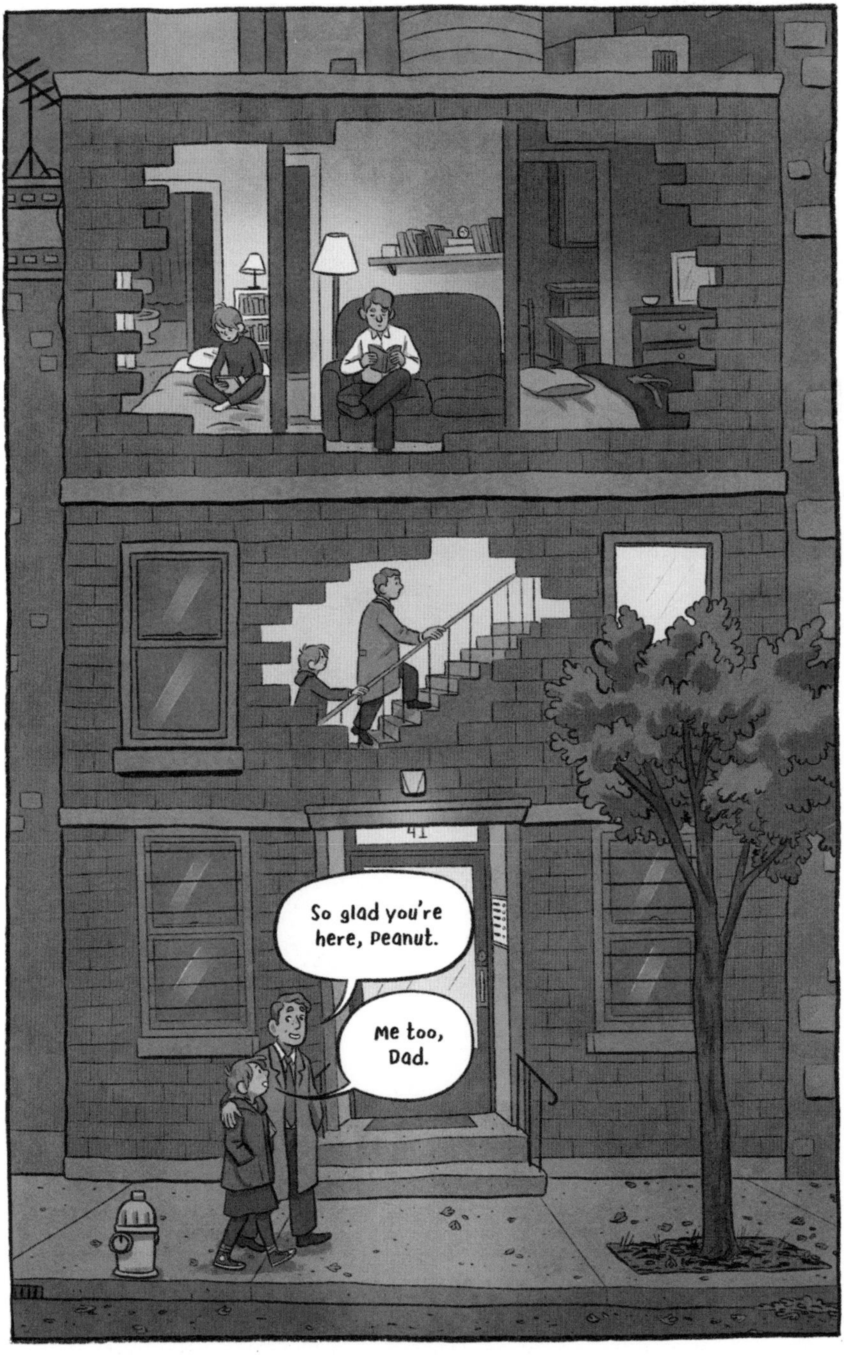
41
So glad you're here, Peanut.
Me too, Dad.

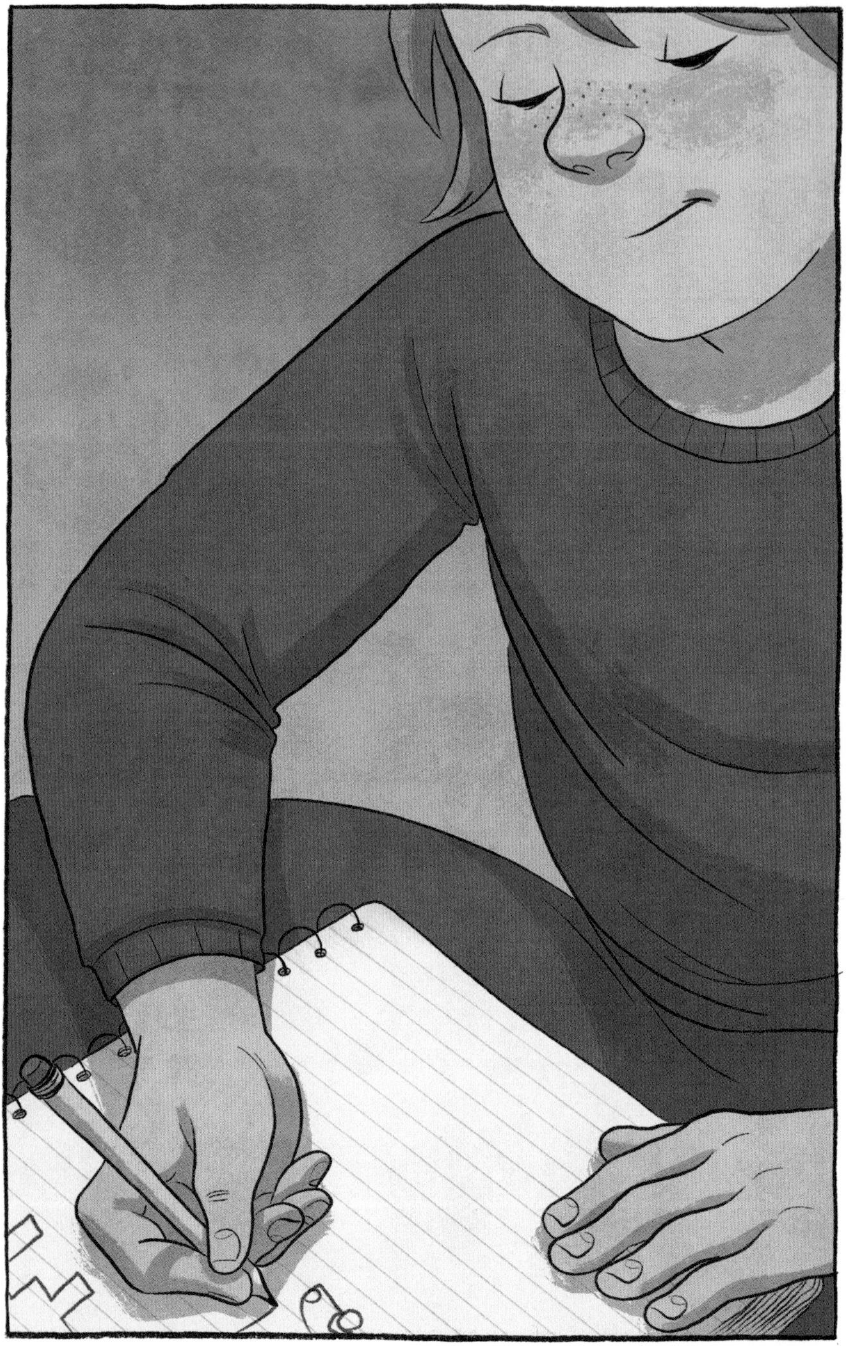

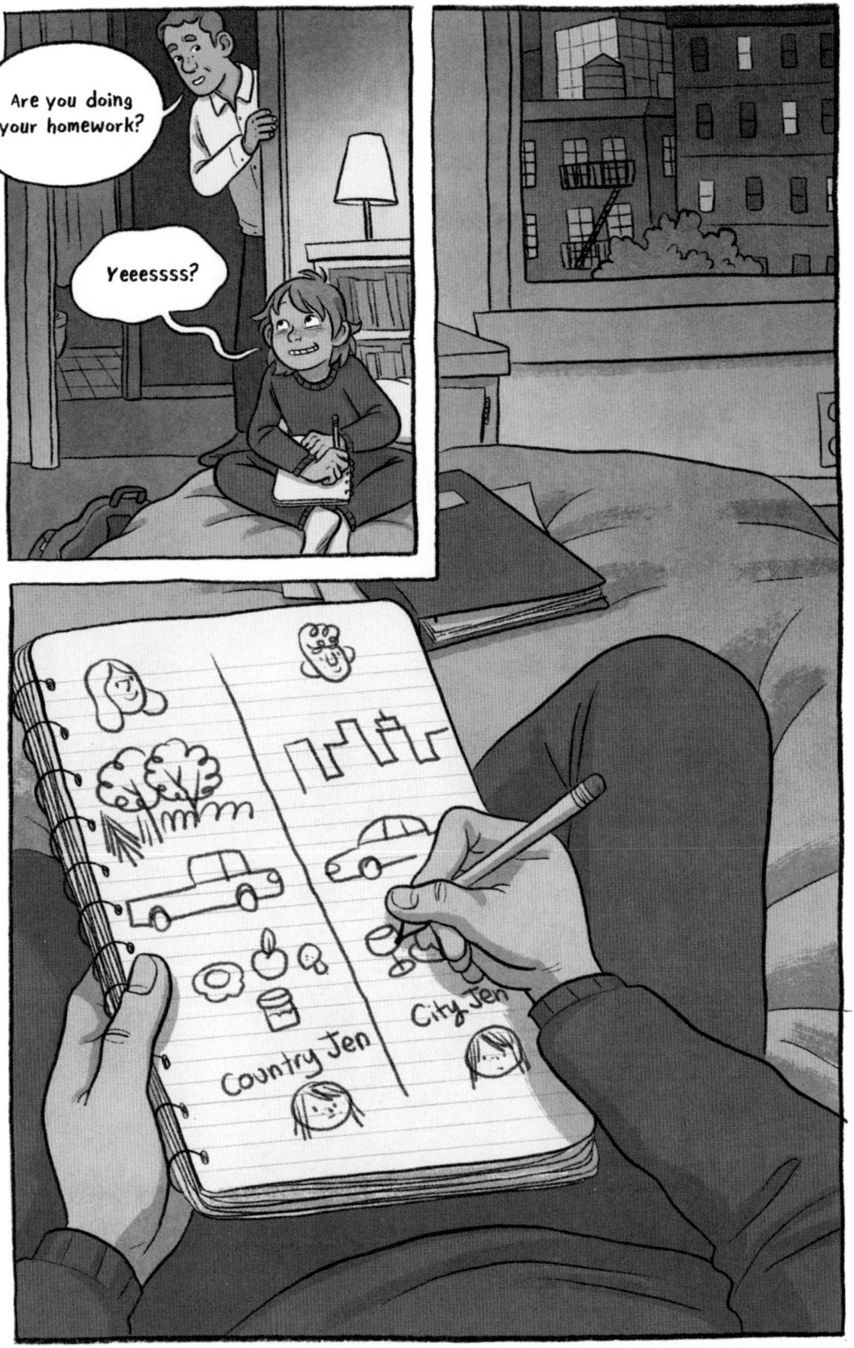
Are you doing your homework?
Yeeessss?
Country Jen
City Jen

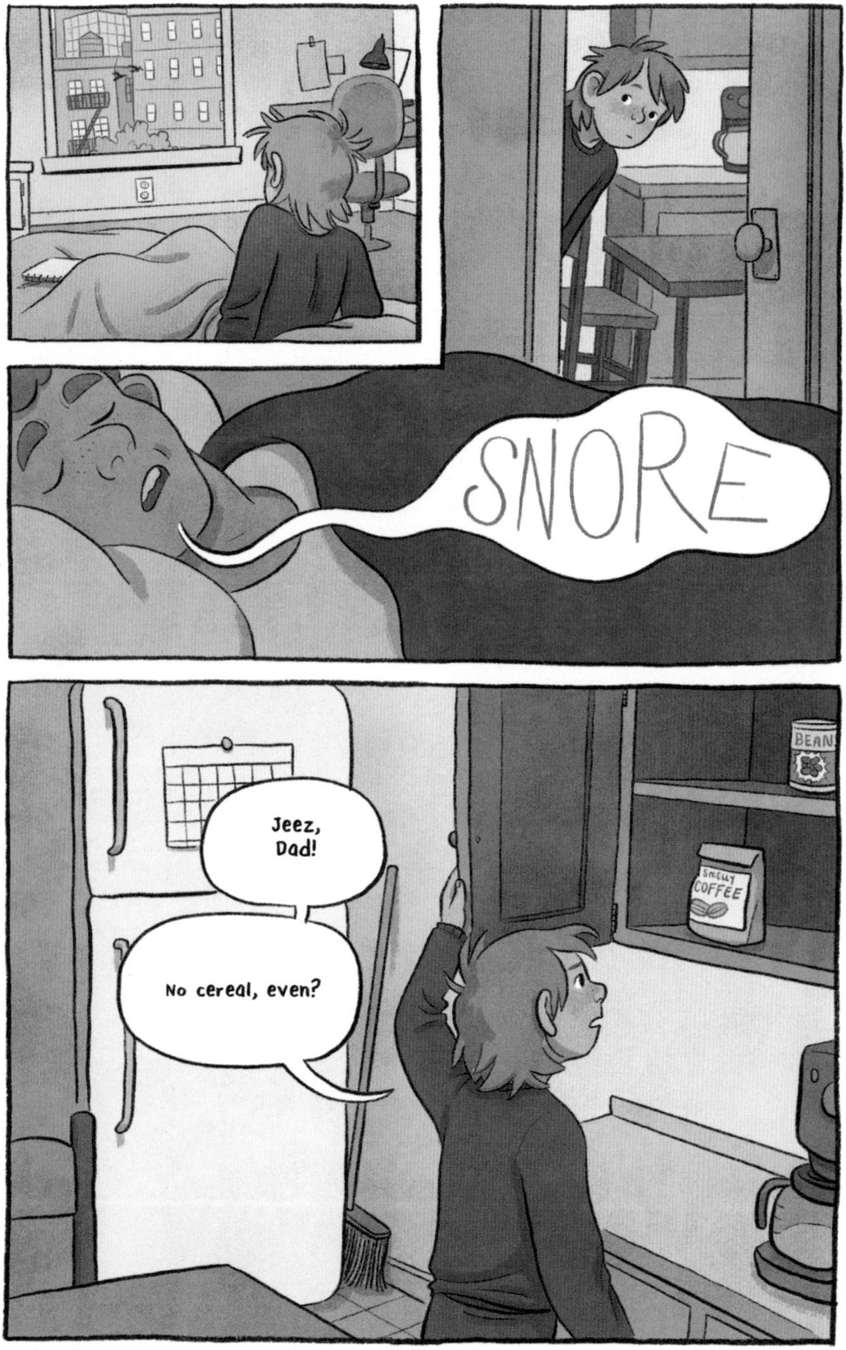
SNORE
BEANS
SMELLY COFFEE
Jeez, Dad!
No cereal, even?

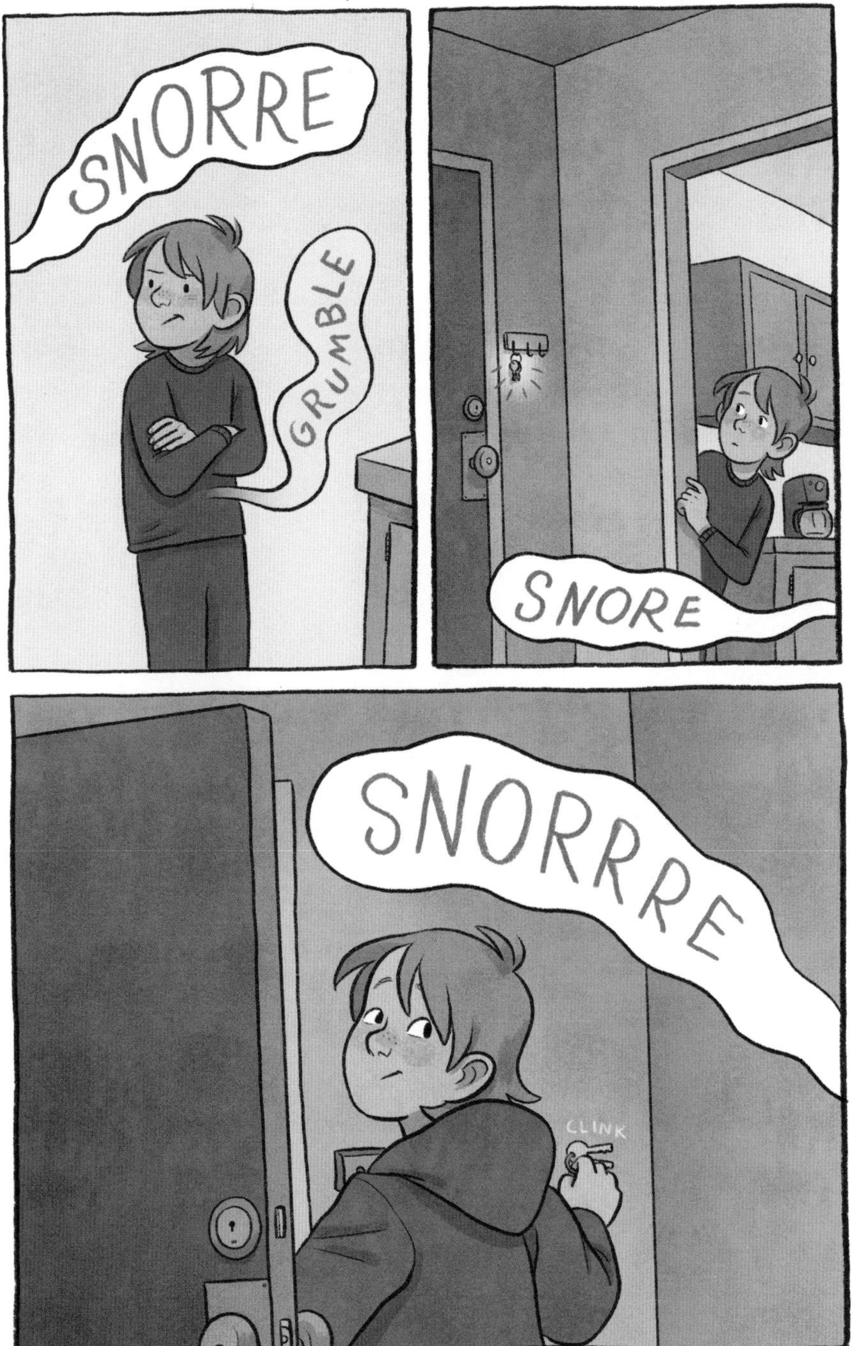
SNORRE
GRUMBLE
SNORE
SNORRRE
CLINK

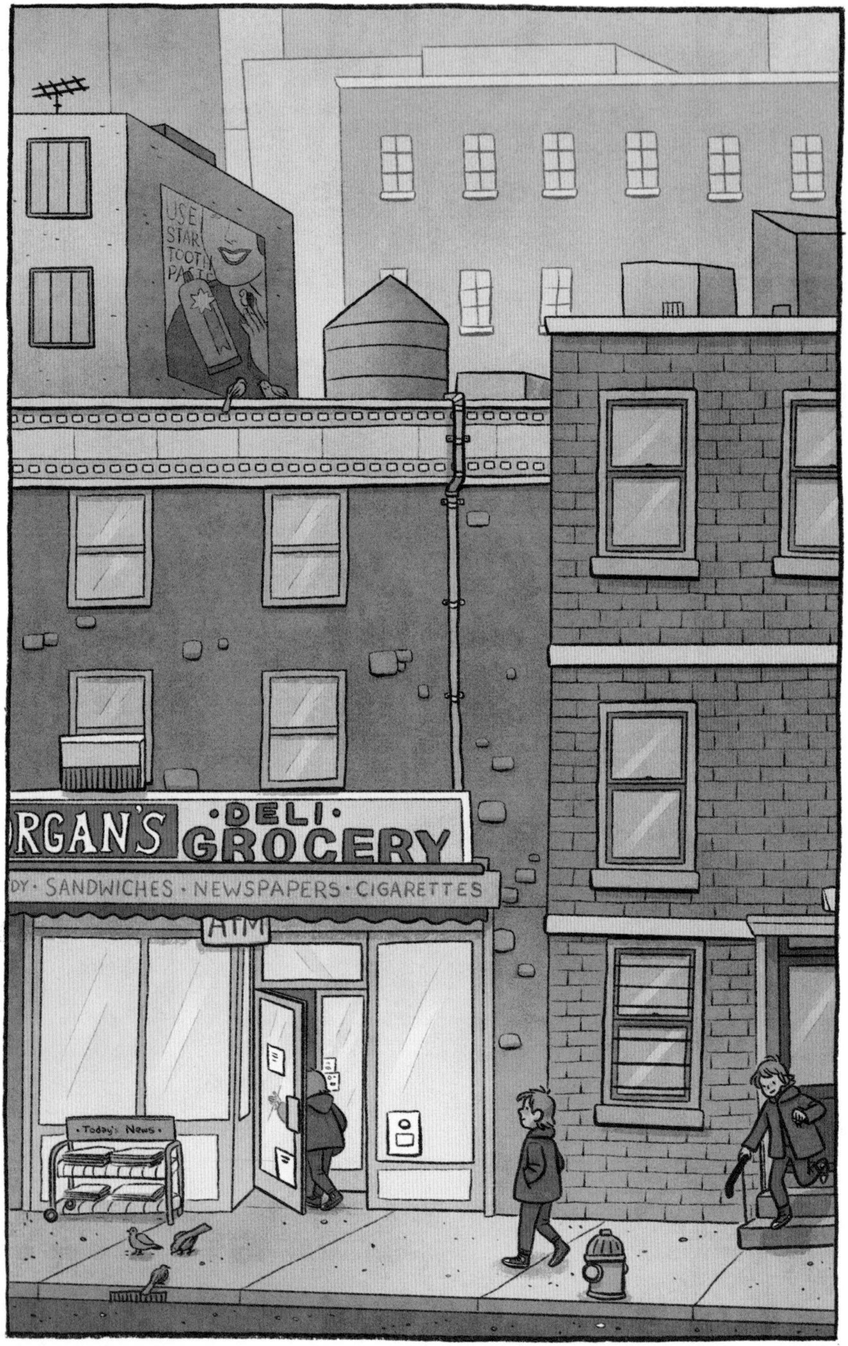
RGAN'S
·DELI·
GROCERY
DY · SANDWICHES · NEWSPAPERS · CIGARETTES
ATM
Today's News

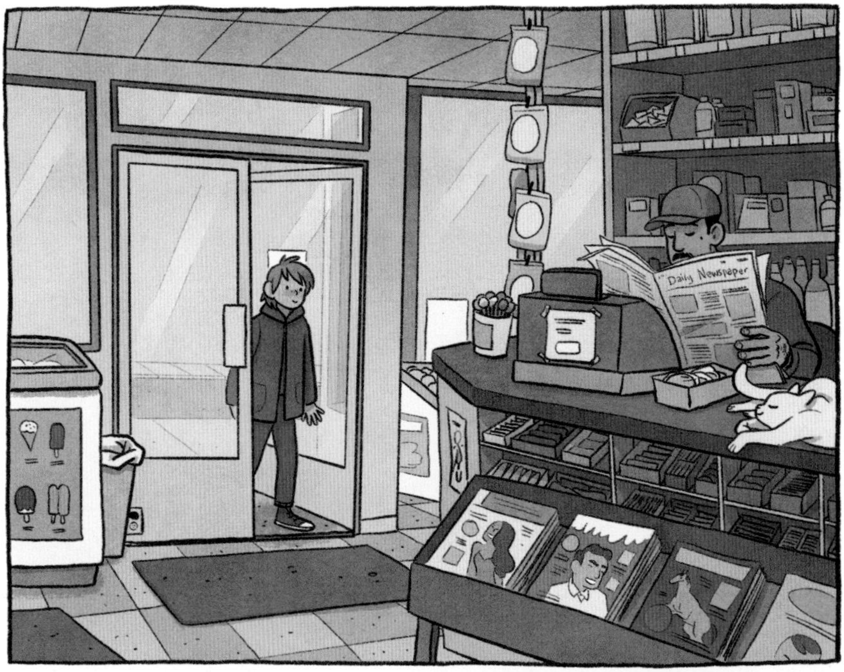
Daily Newspaper

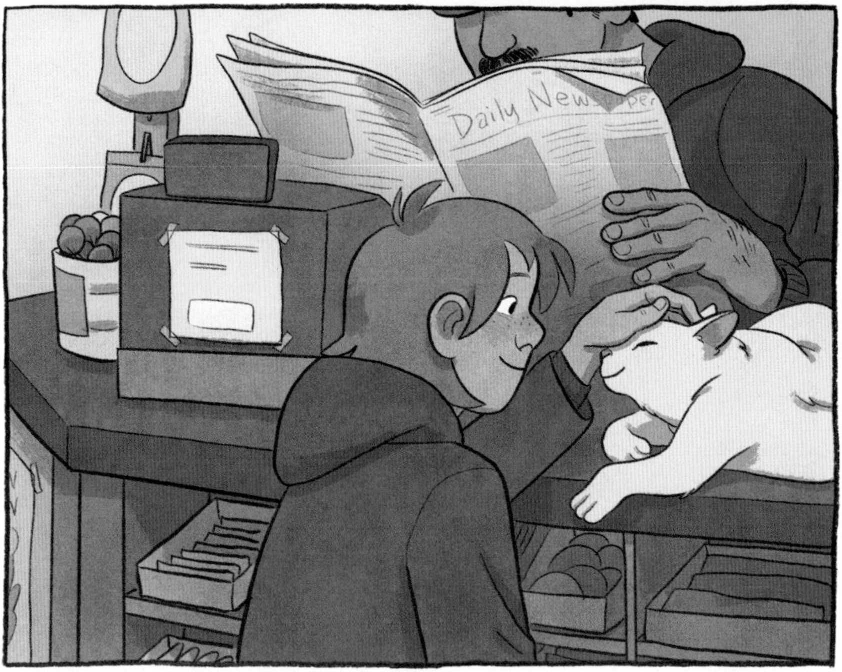
Daily News

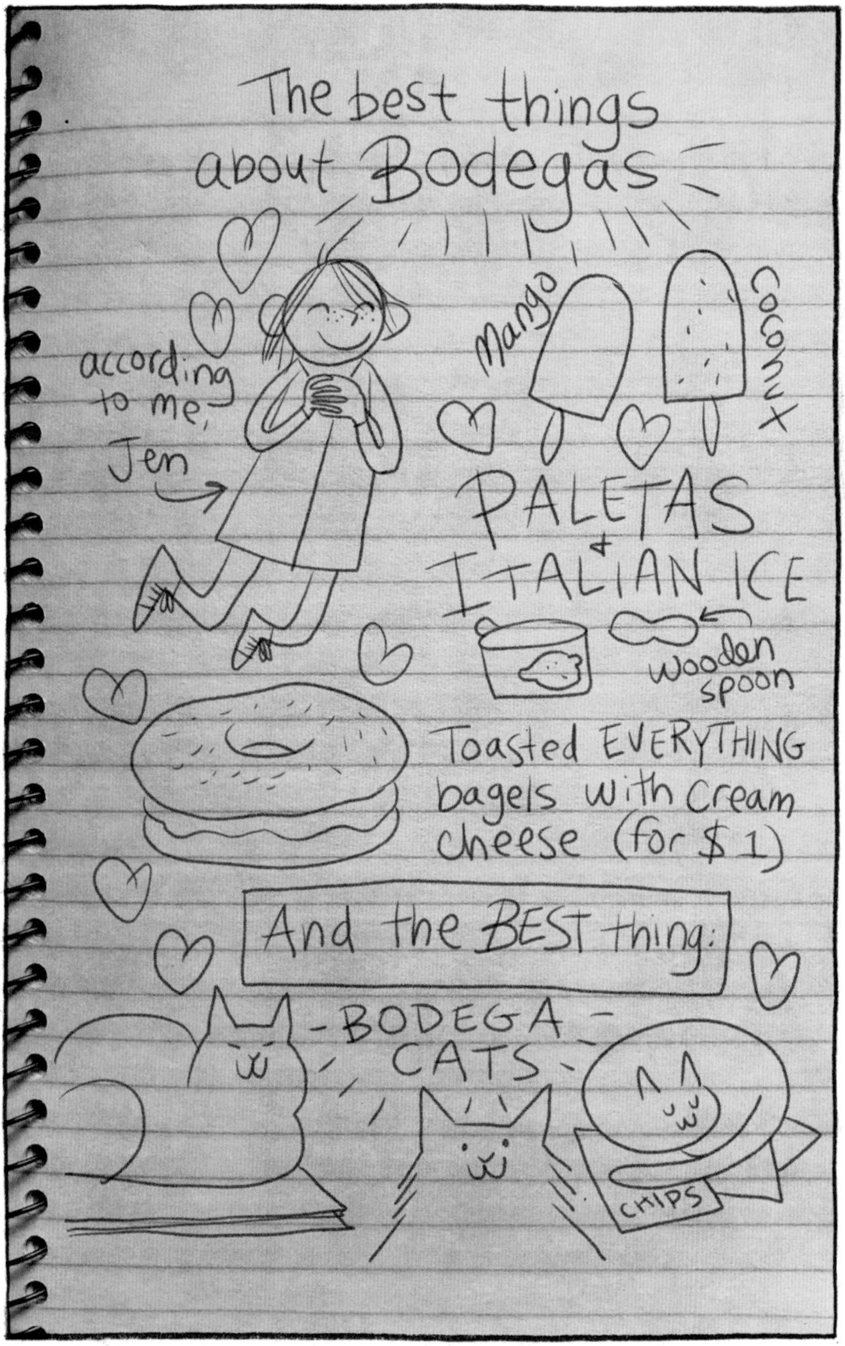
The best things about Bodegas
according to me, Jen
Mango
Coconut
PALETAS & ITALIAN ICE
wooden spoon
Toasted EVERYTHING bagels with cream cheese (for $1)
And the BEST thing:
- BODEGA - CATS -
CHIPS

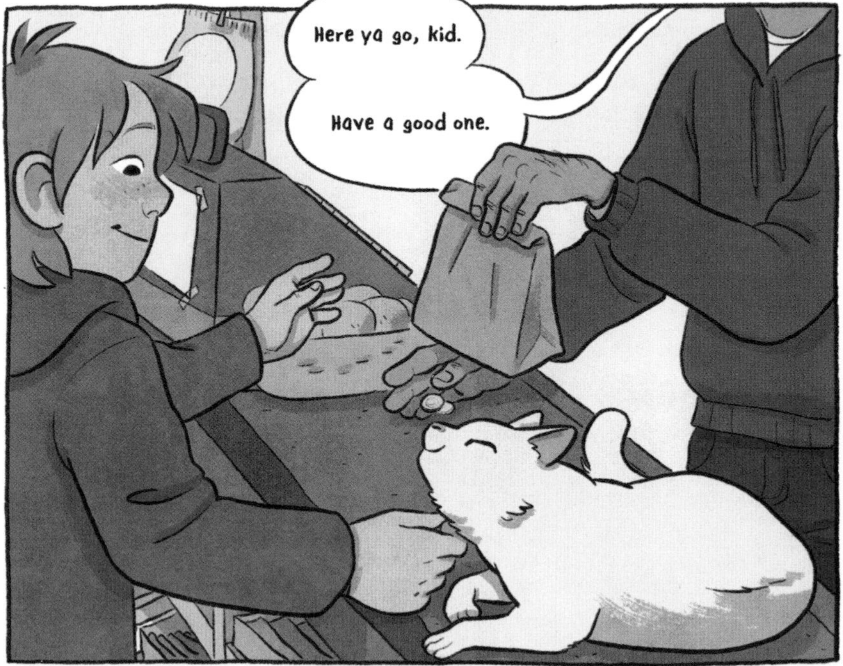
Here ya go, kid.
Have a good one.

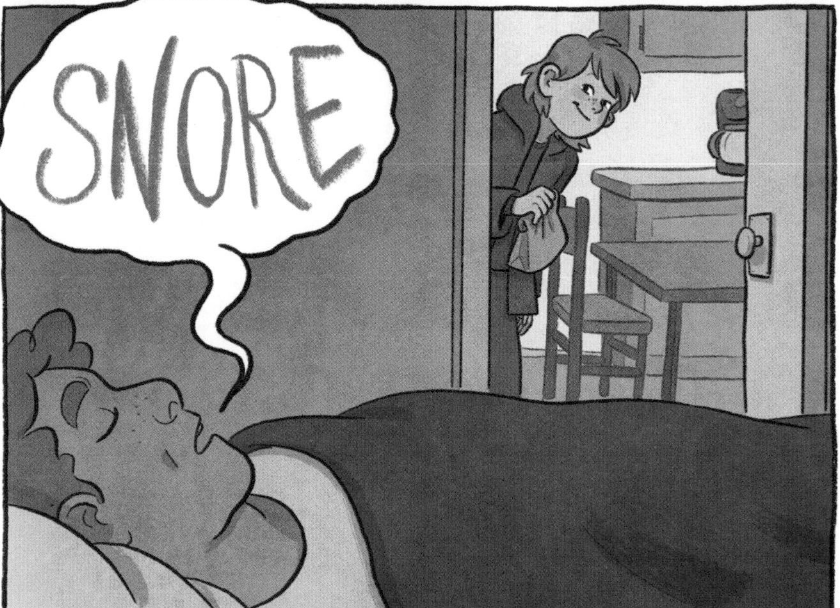
SNORE

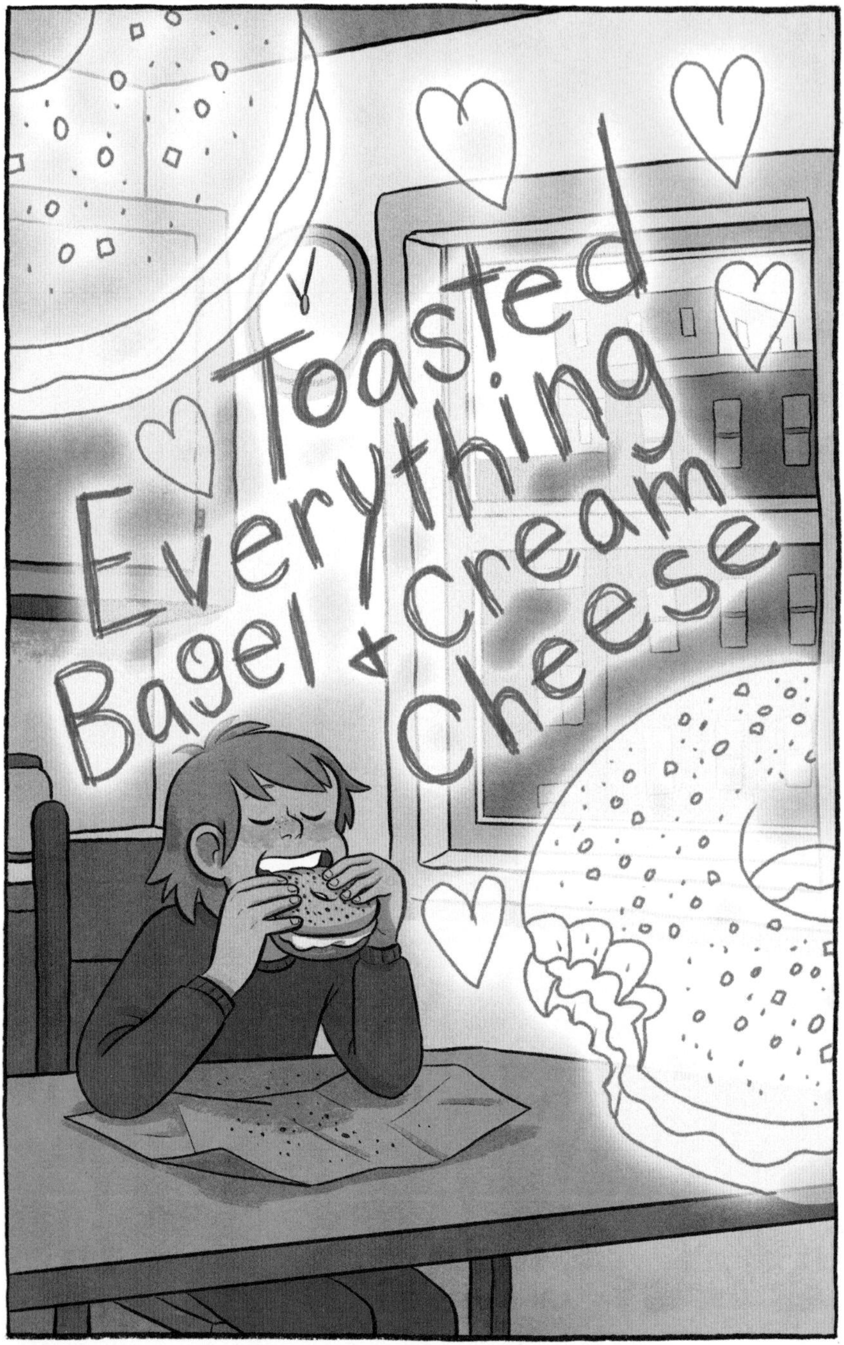
Toasted Everything Bagel + Cream Cheese

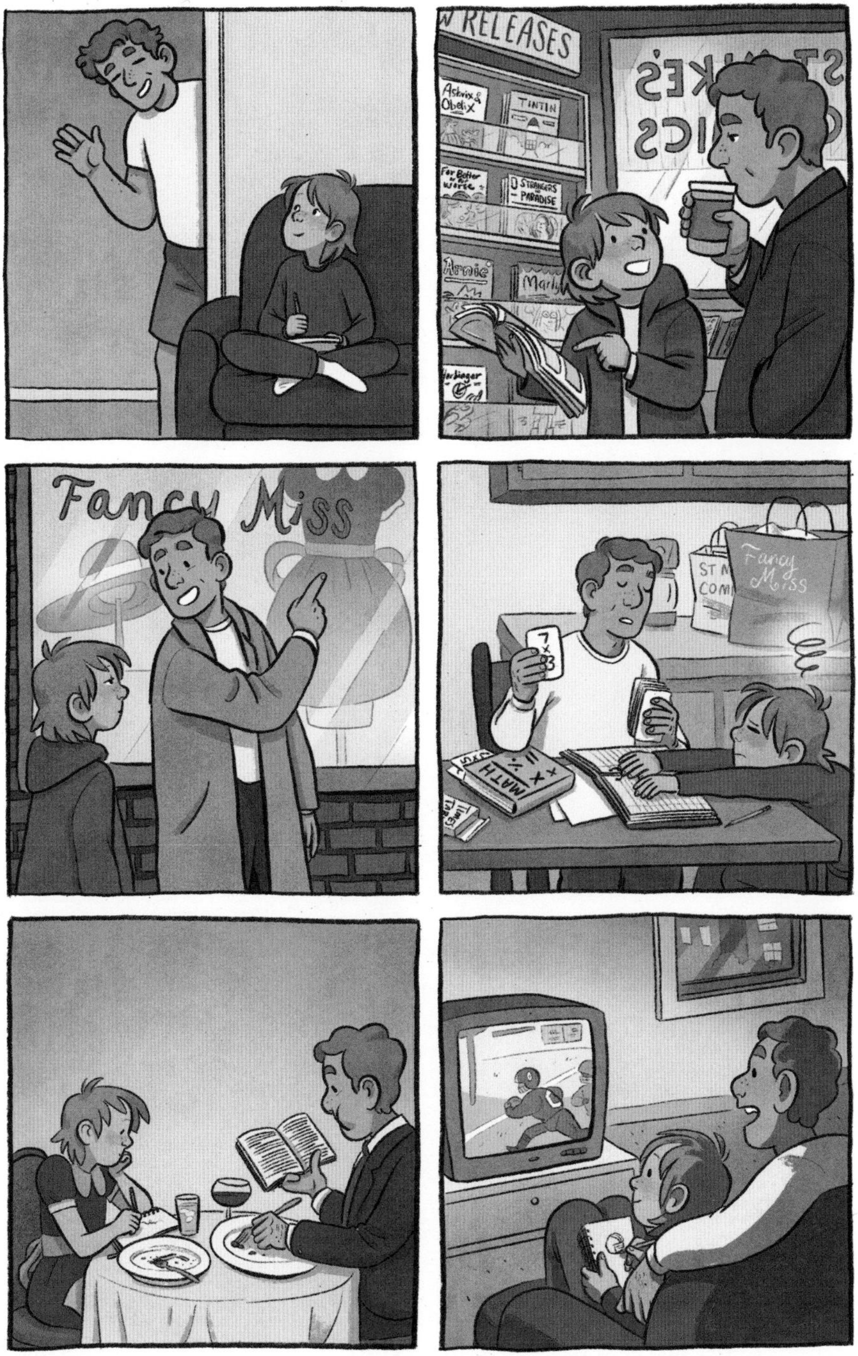
RELEASES
Asterix & Obelix
TINTIN
STRANGERS IN PARADISE
Fancy Miss
Fancy Miss
7 x 3
MATH

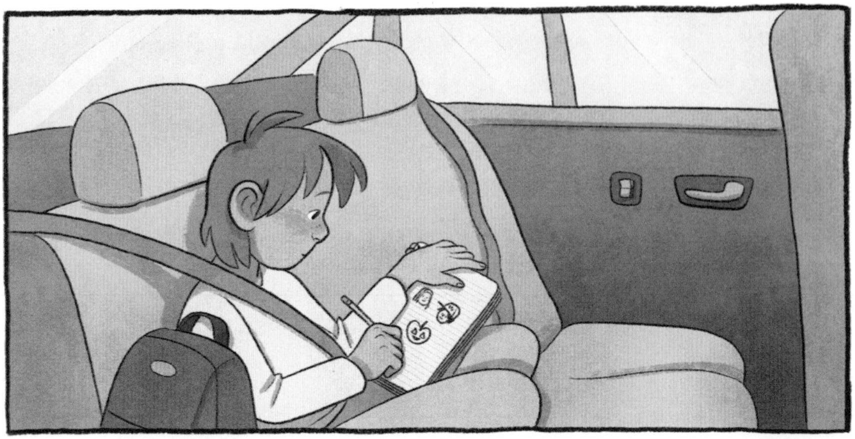

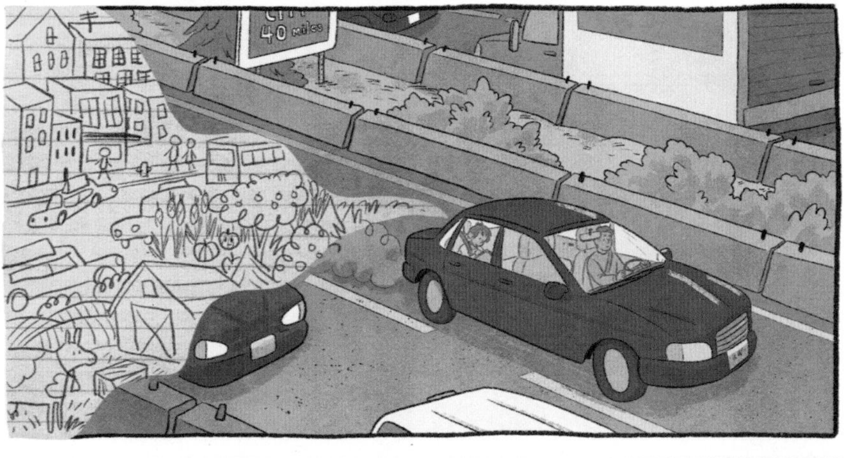
40 miles

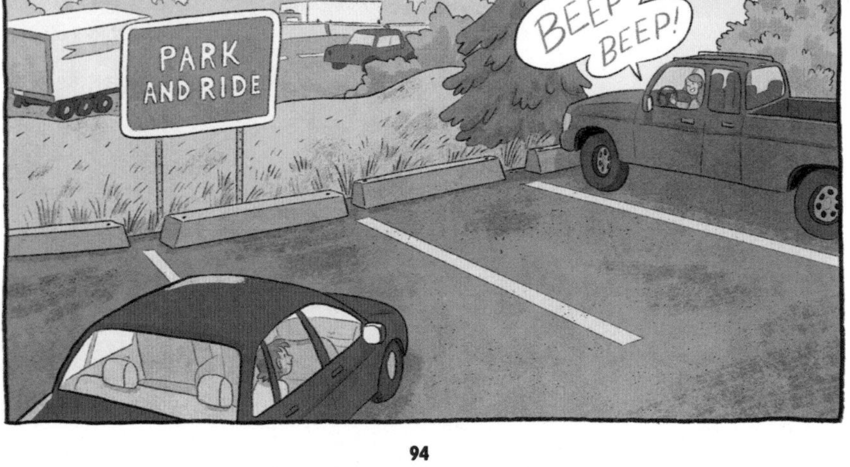
PARK
AND RIDE
BEEP
BEEP!

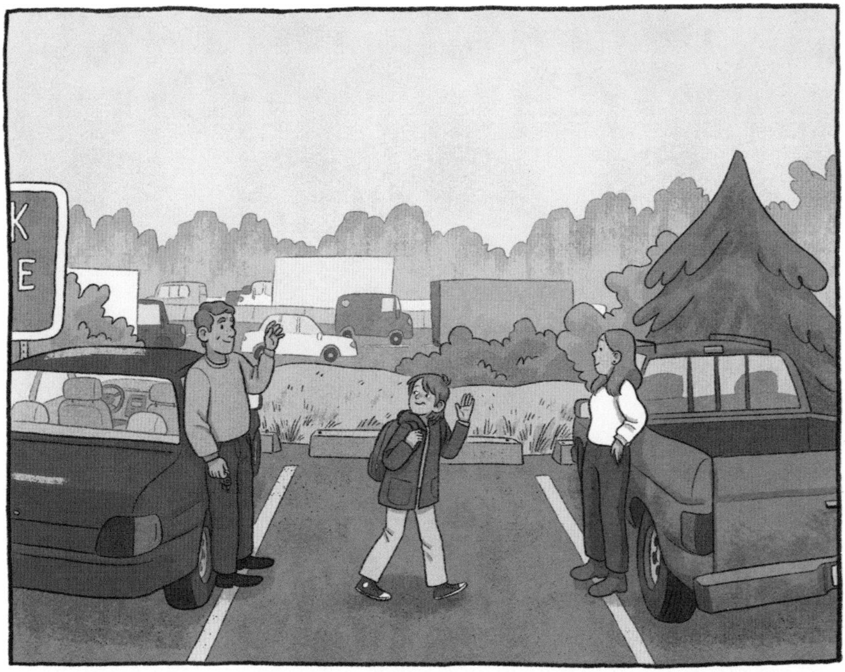

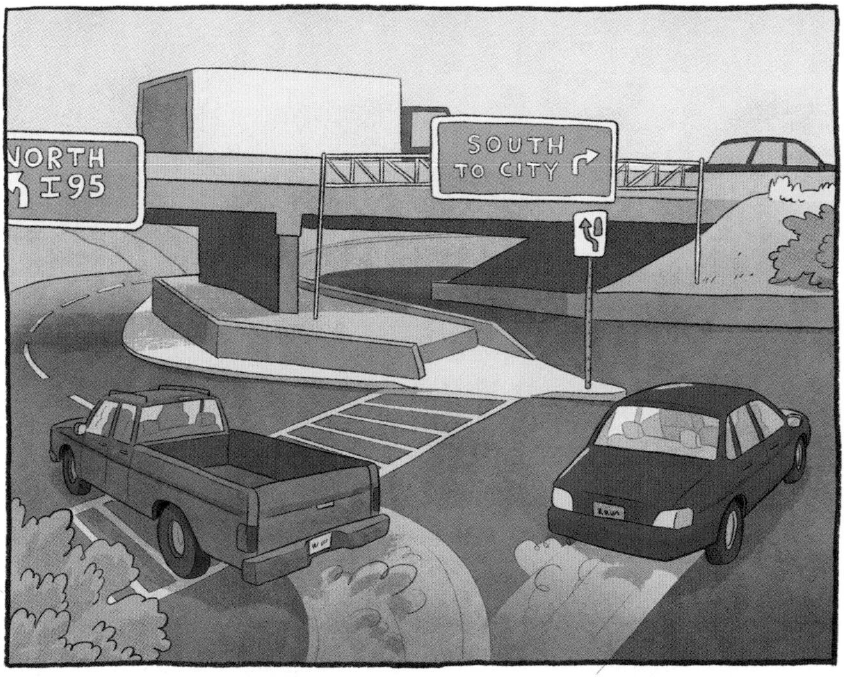
NORTH I95
SOUTH TO CITY

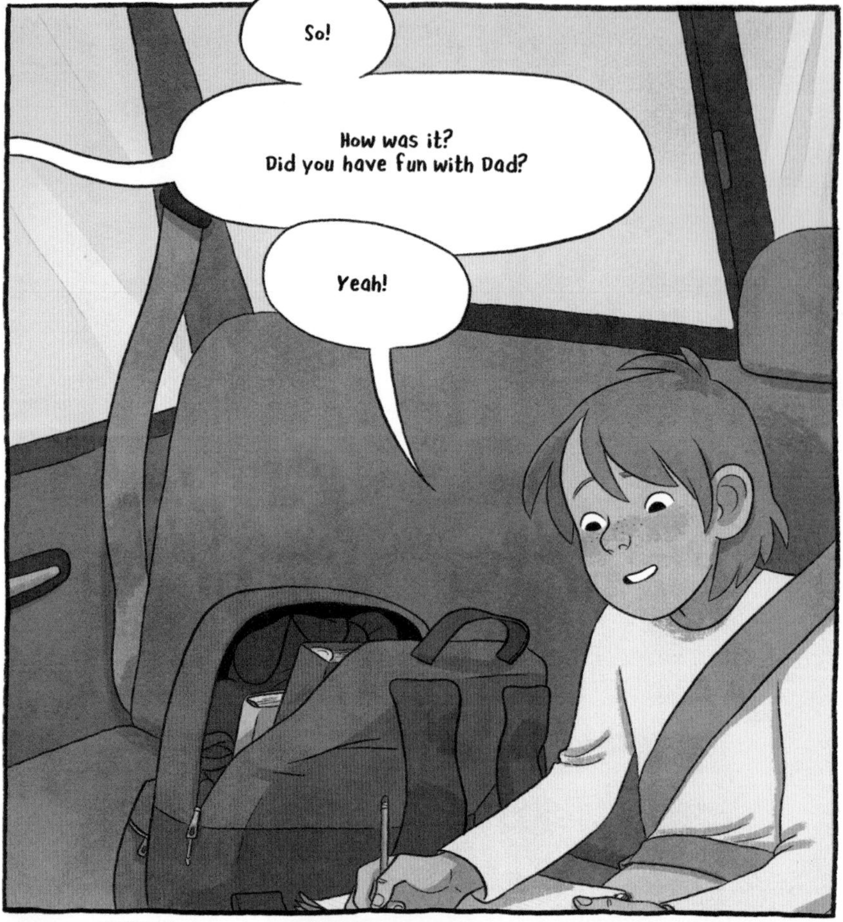
So!
How was it? Did you have fun with Dad?
Yeah!

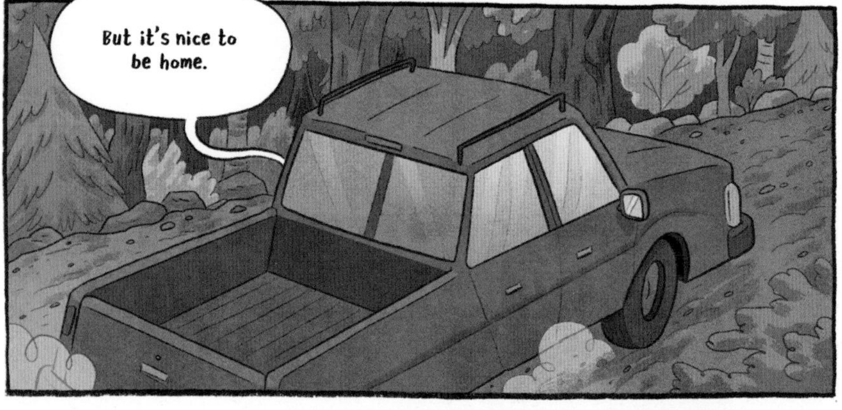
But it's nice to be home.

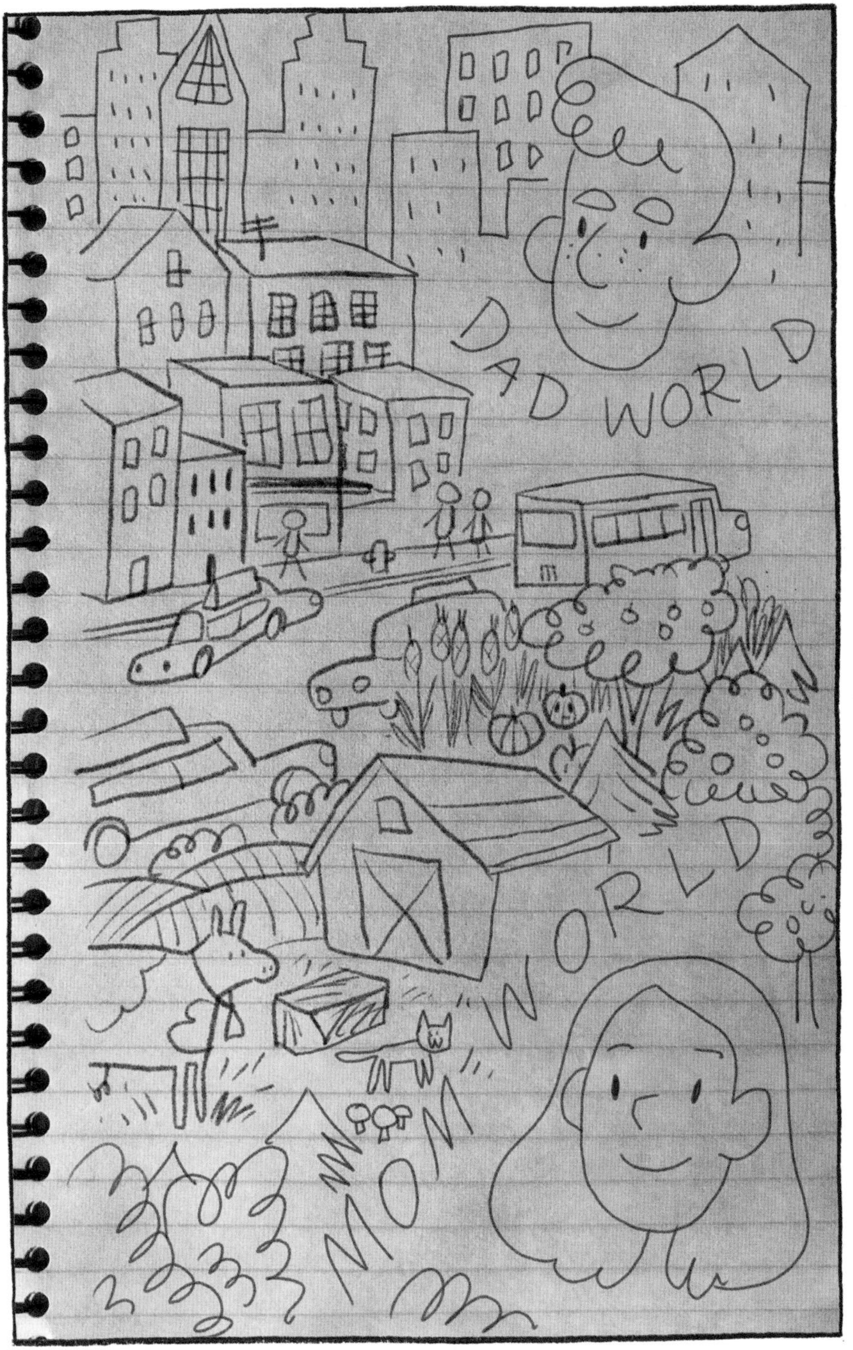
DAD WORLD
MOM WORLD

Chapter Five

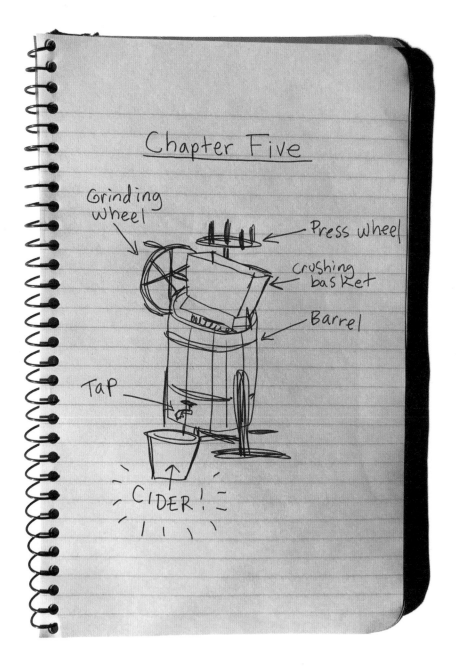

Grinding wheel

Press wheel

crushing basket

Barrel

Tap

CIDER!

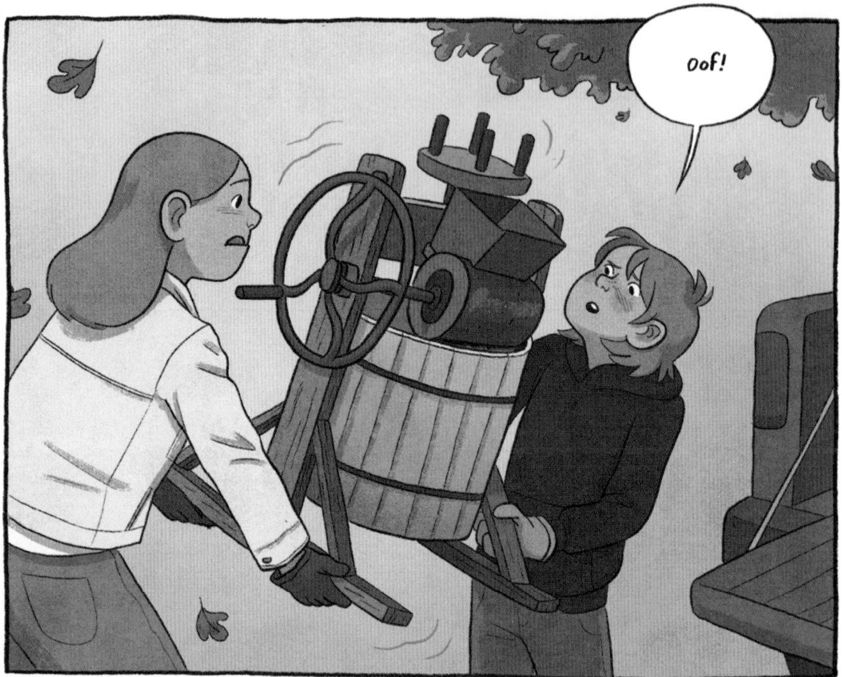
Oof!

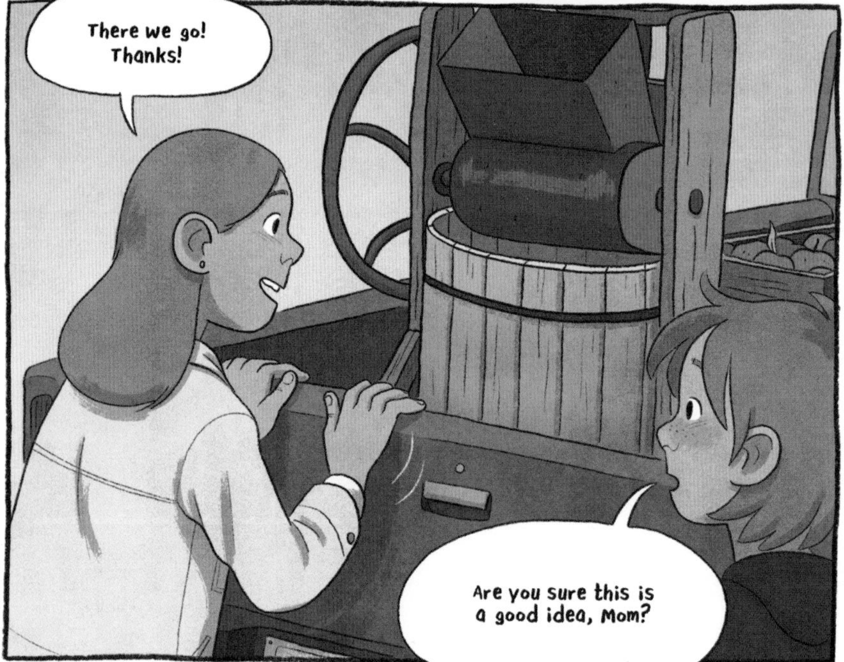
There we go!
Thanks!
Are you sure this is
a good idea, Mom?

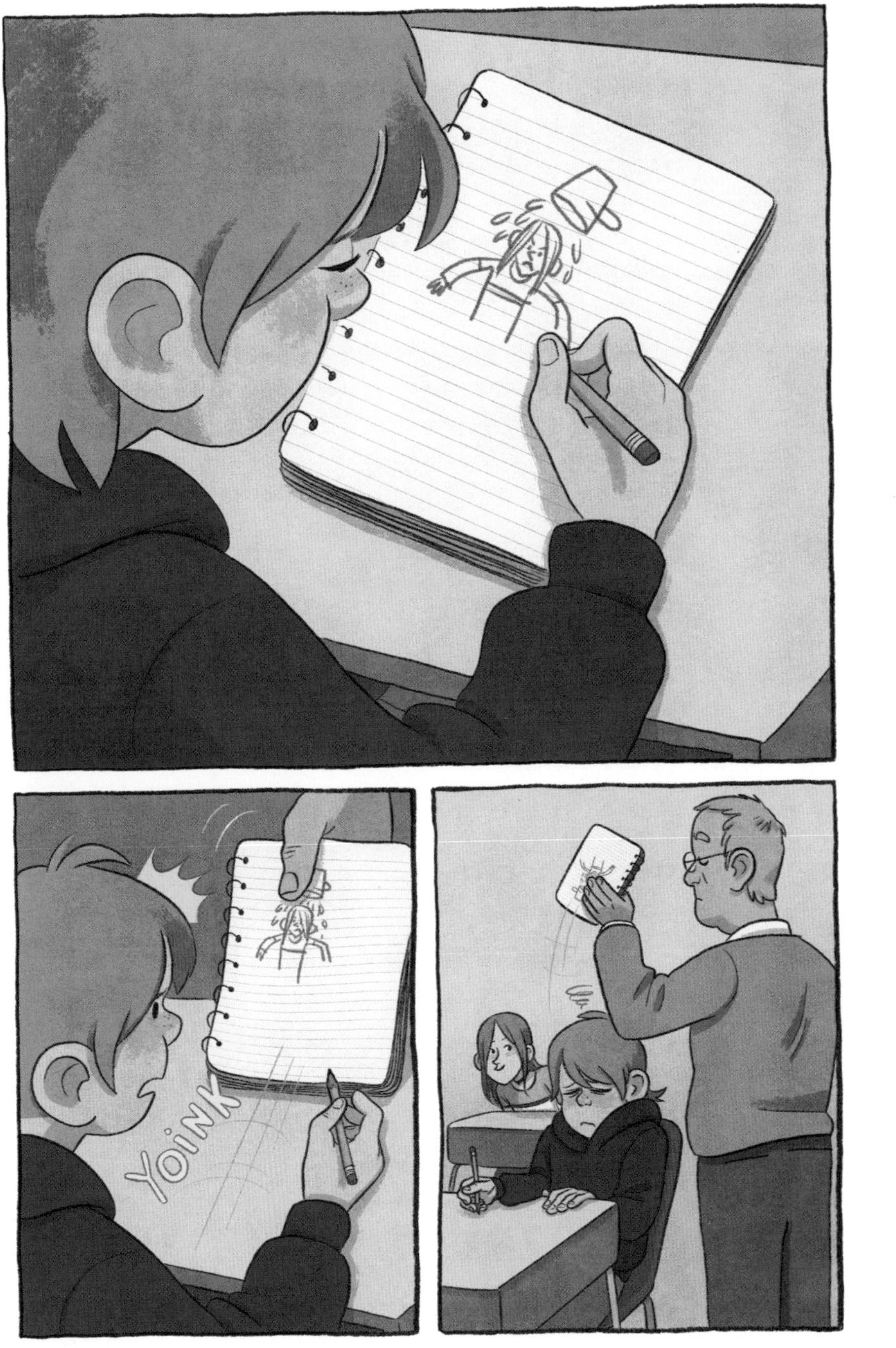
YOINK

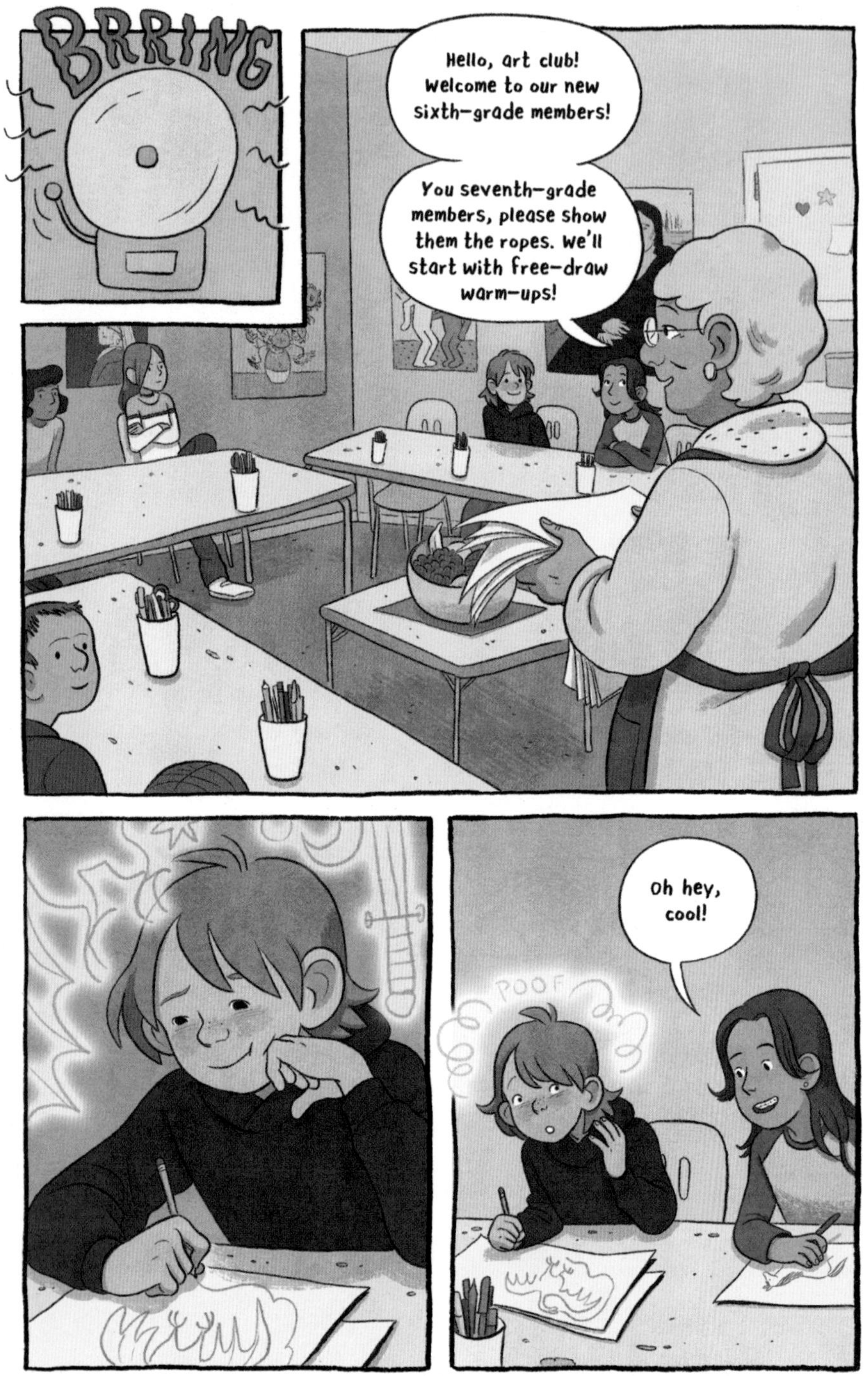
BRRING
Hello, art club! Welcome to our new sixth-grade members!
You seventh-grade members, please show them the ropes. We'll start with free-draw warm-ups!
POOF
Oh hey, cool!

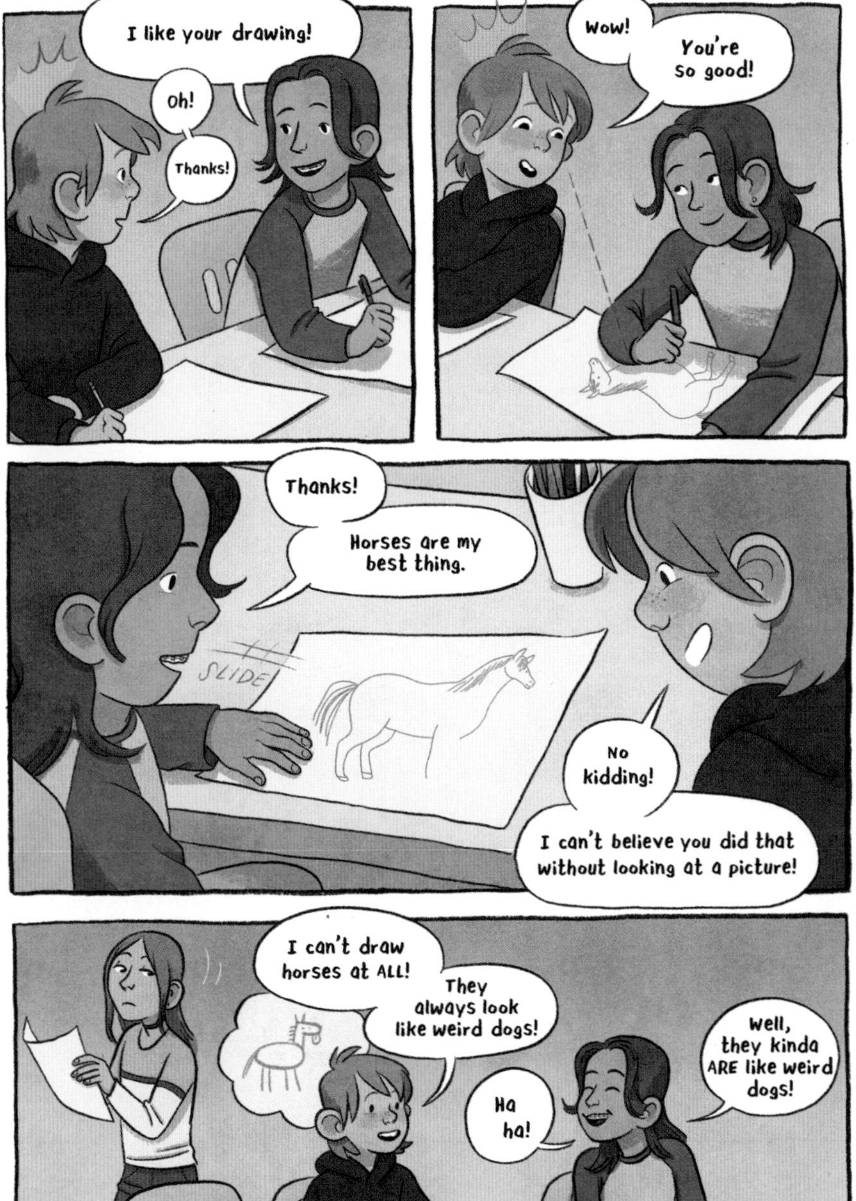
I like your drawing!
Oh!
Thanks!
Wow!
You're so good!
Thanks!
Horses are my best thing.
SLIDE
No kidding!
I can't believe you did that without looking at a picture!
I can't draw horses at ALL!
They always look like weird dogs!
Ha ha!
Well, they kinda ARE like weird dogs!

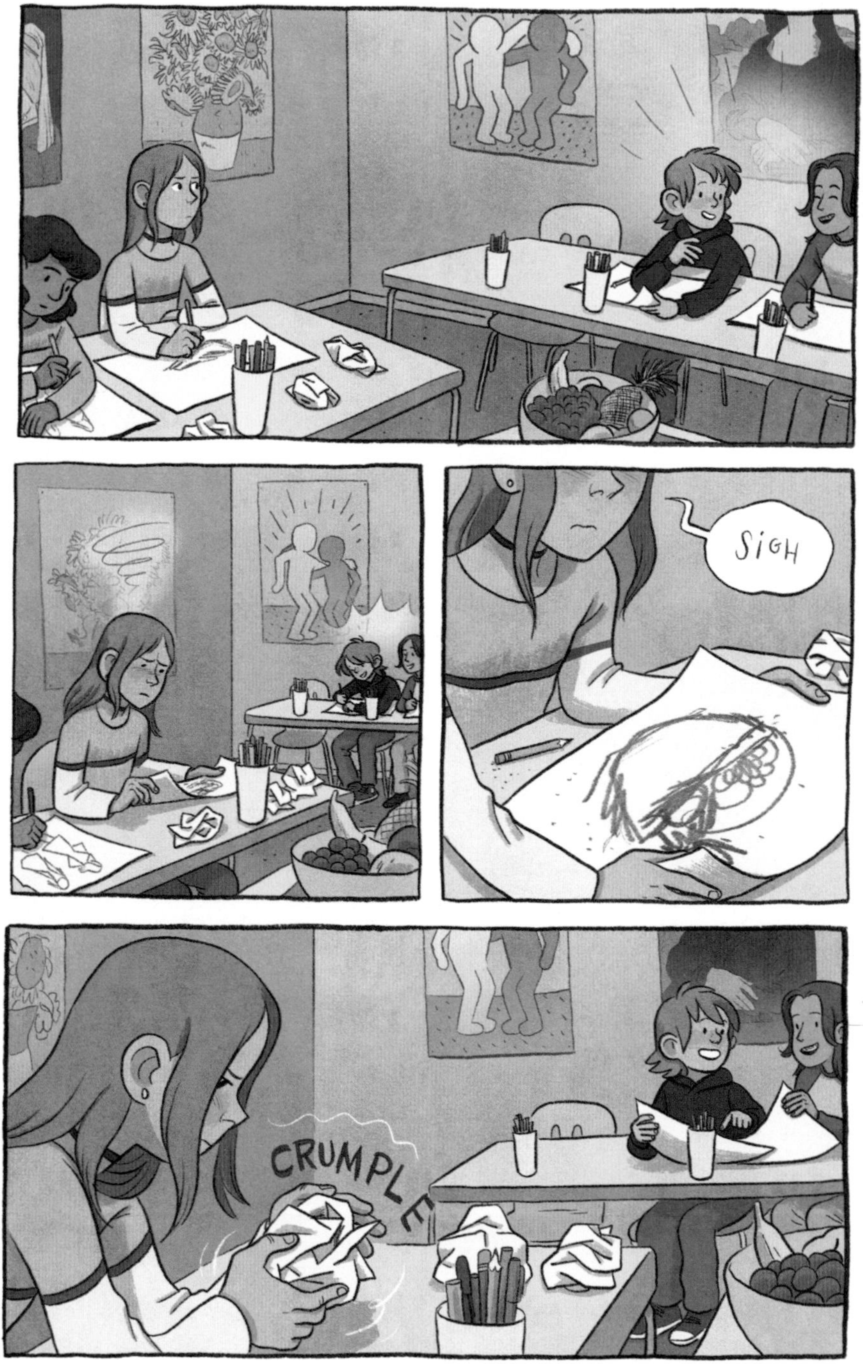
SIGH
CRUMPLE

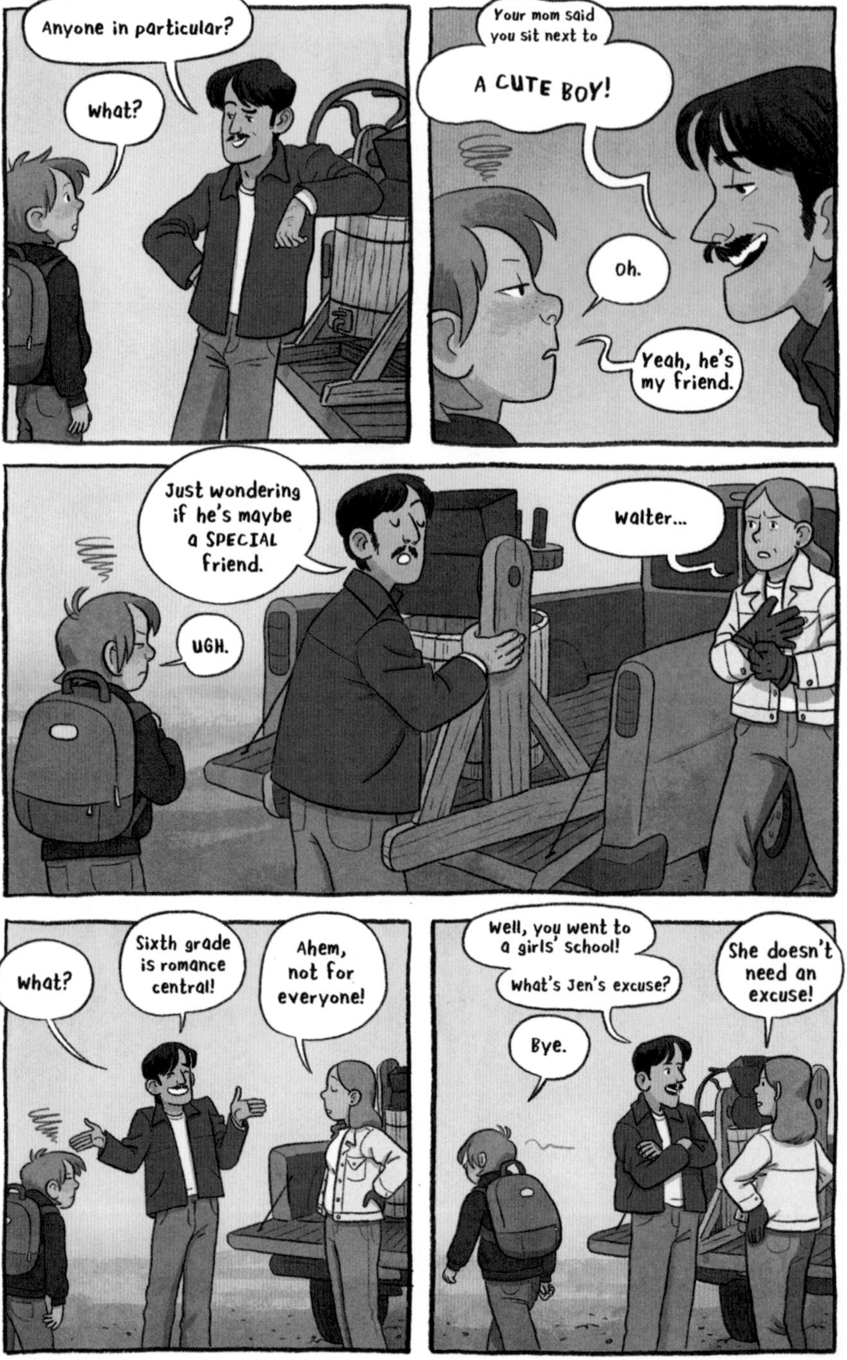
Anyone in particular?
What?
Your mom said you sit next to
A CUTE BOY!
Oh.
Yeah, he's my friend.
Just wondering if he's maybe a SPECIAL friend.
Walter...
UGH.
What?
Sixth grade is romance central!
Ahem, not for everyone!
Well, you went to a girls' school!
What's Jen's excuse?
She doesn't need an excuse!
Bye.

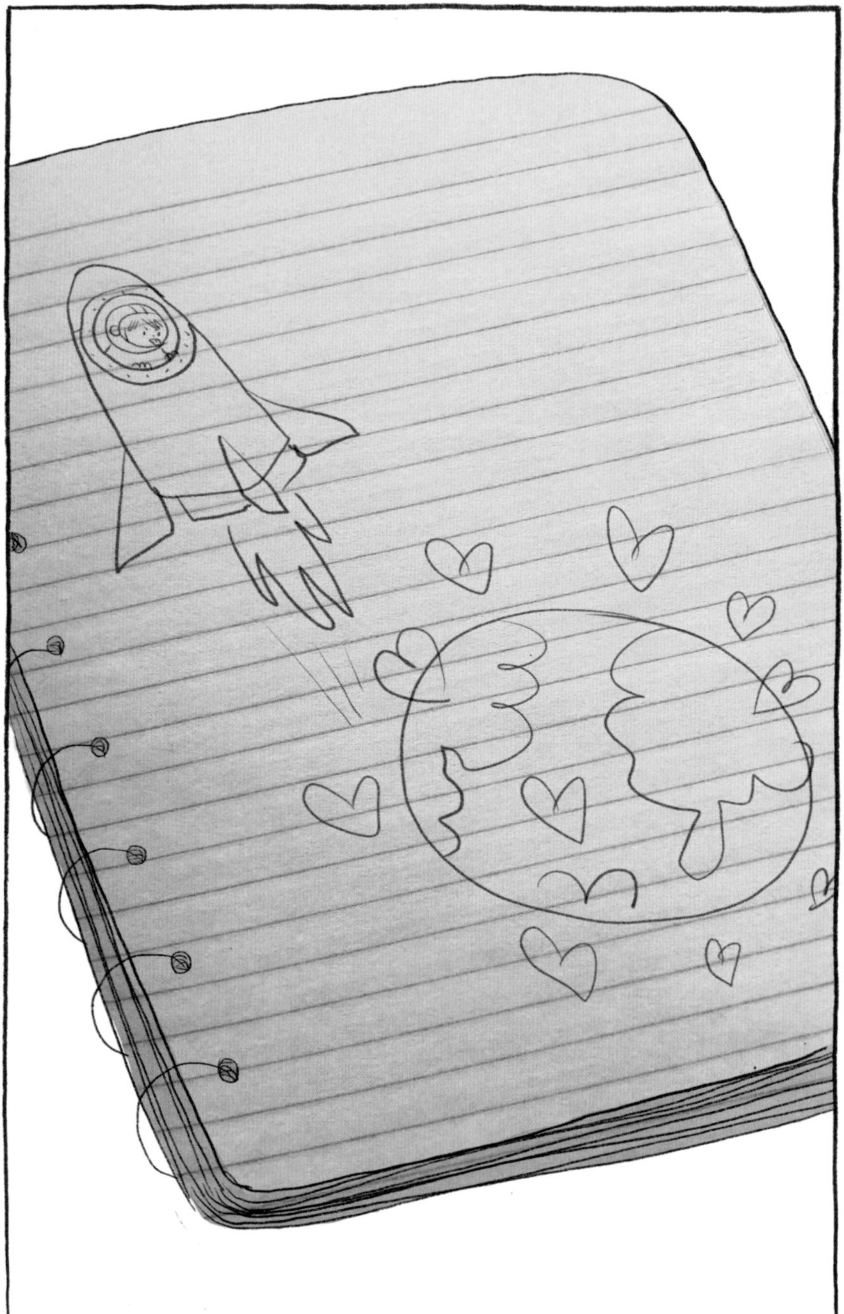

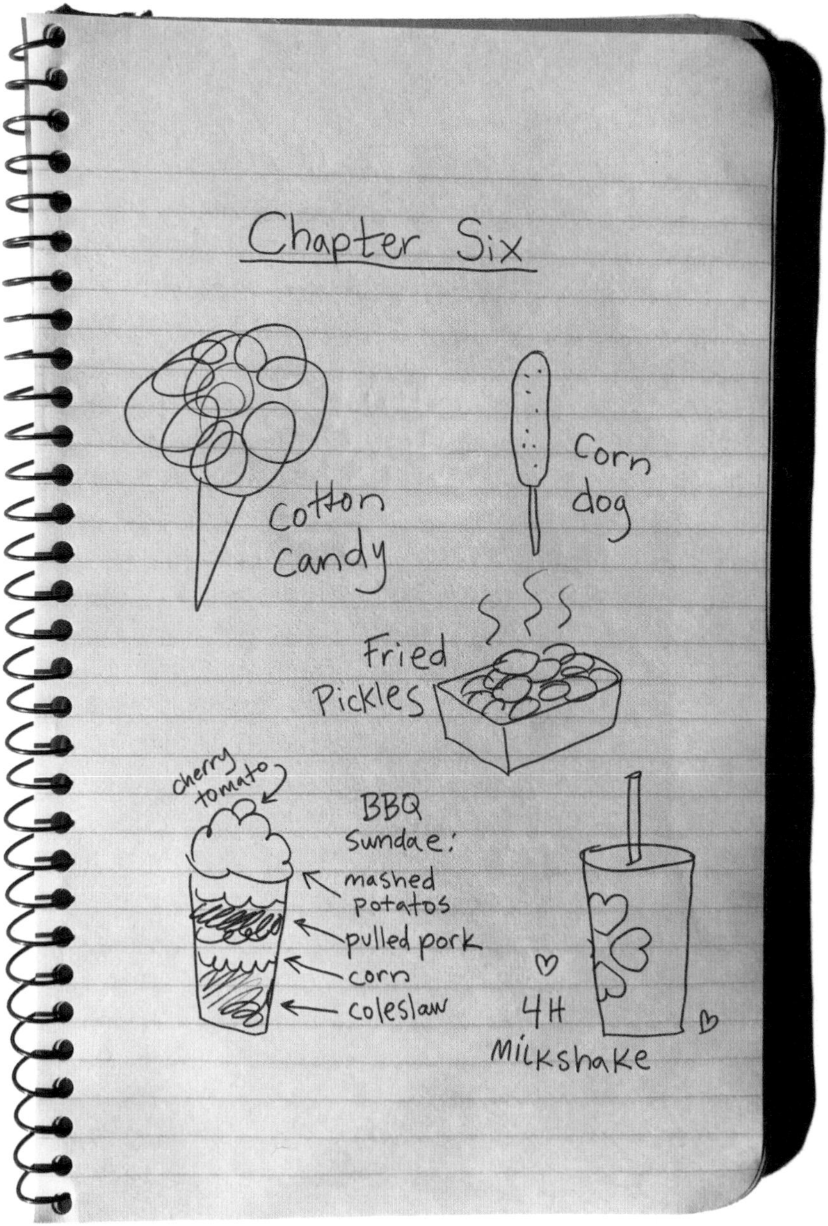
Chapter Six
cotton candy
corn dog
Fried Pickles
cherry tomato
BBQ Sundae:
mashed potatos
pulled pork
corn
coleslaw
4H Milkshake

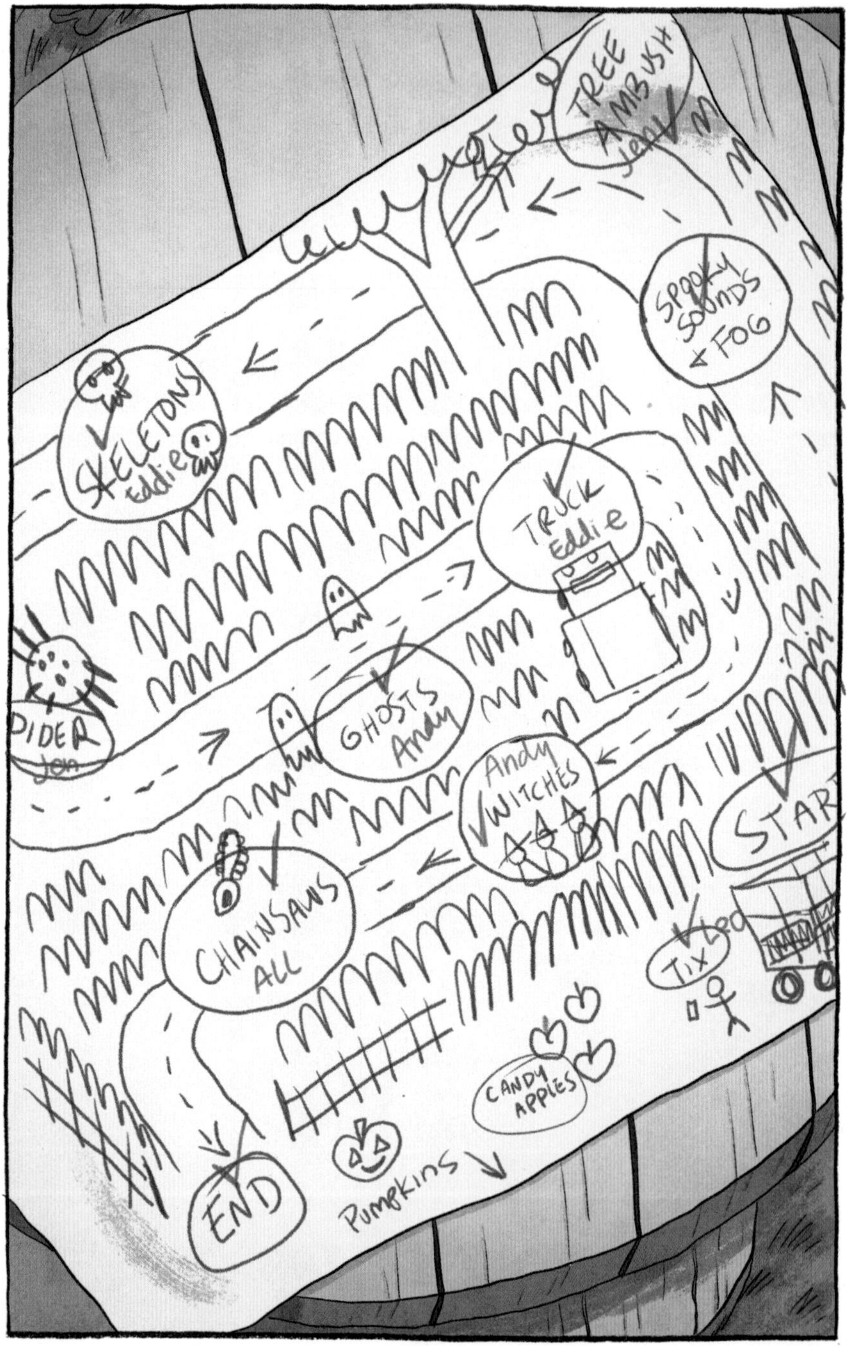
TREE AMBUSH Jen
SPOOKY SOUNDS & FOG
SKELETONS Eddie
TRUCK Eddie
PIDER Jen
GHOSTS Andy
Andy WITCHES
START
CHAINSAWS ALL
TIX Leo
CANDY APPLES
END
PUMPKINS

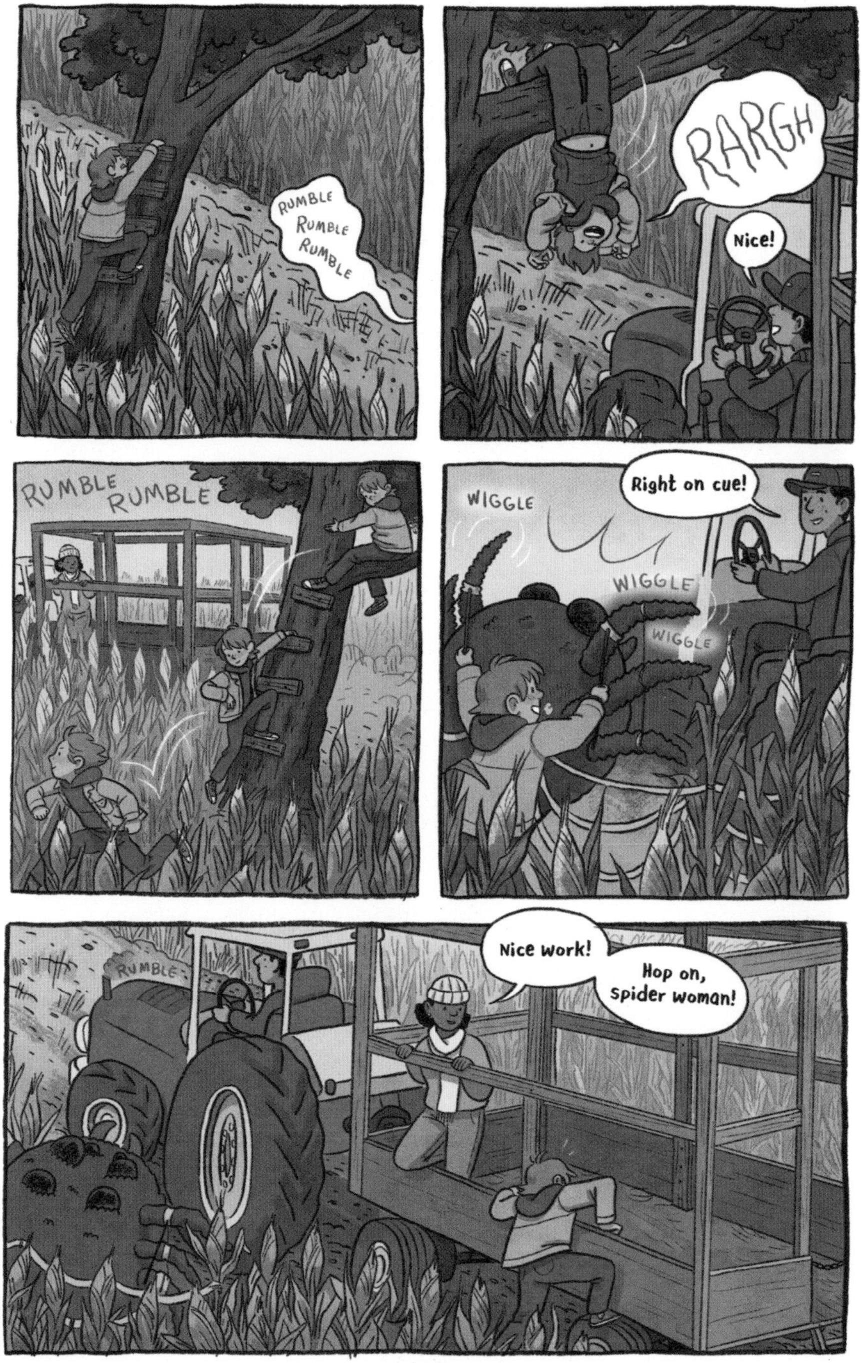
RUMBLE
RUMBLE
RUMBLE
RARGH
Nice!
RUMBLE
RUMBLE
WIGGLE
Right on cue!
WIGGLE
WIGGLE
RUMBLE
Nice work!
Hop on,
spider woman!

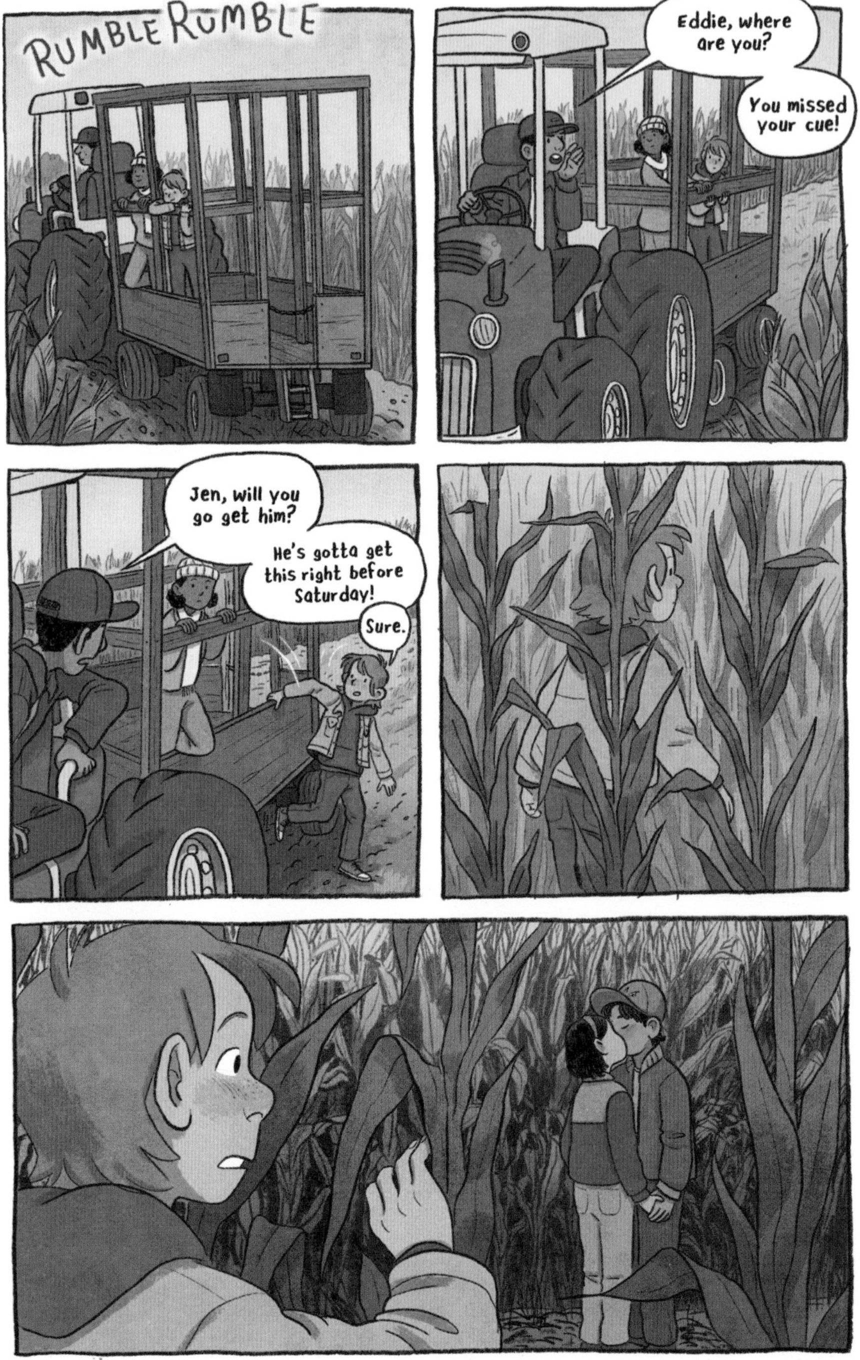
RUMBLE RUMBLE
Eddie, where are you?
You missed your cue!
Jen, will you go get him?
He's gotta get this right before Saturday!
Sure.

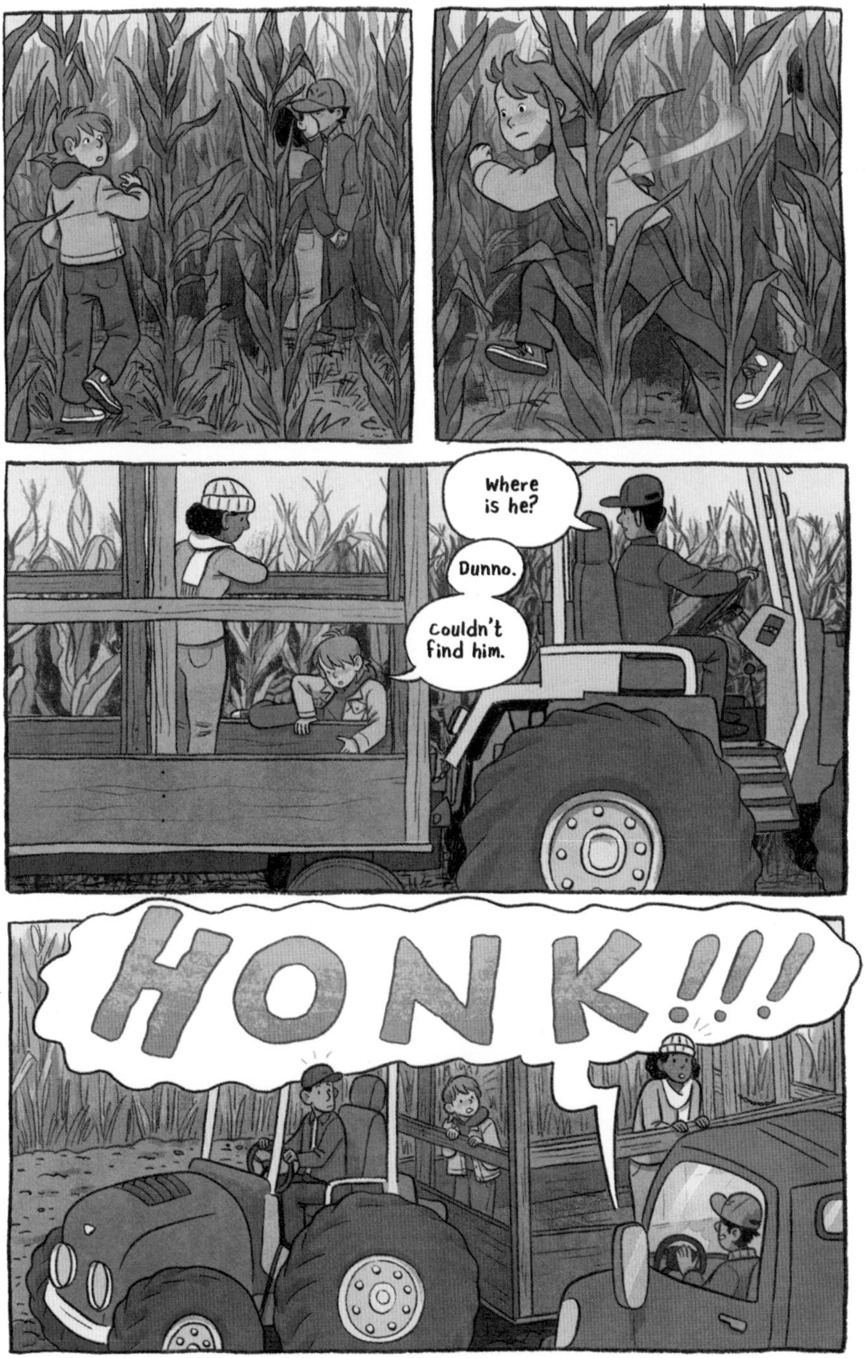
Where is he?
Dunno.
Couldn't find him.
HONK!!!

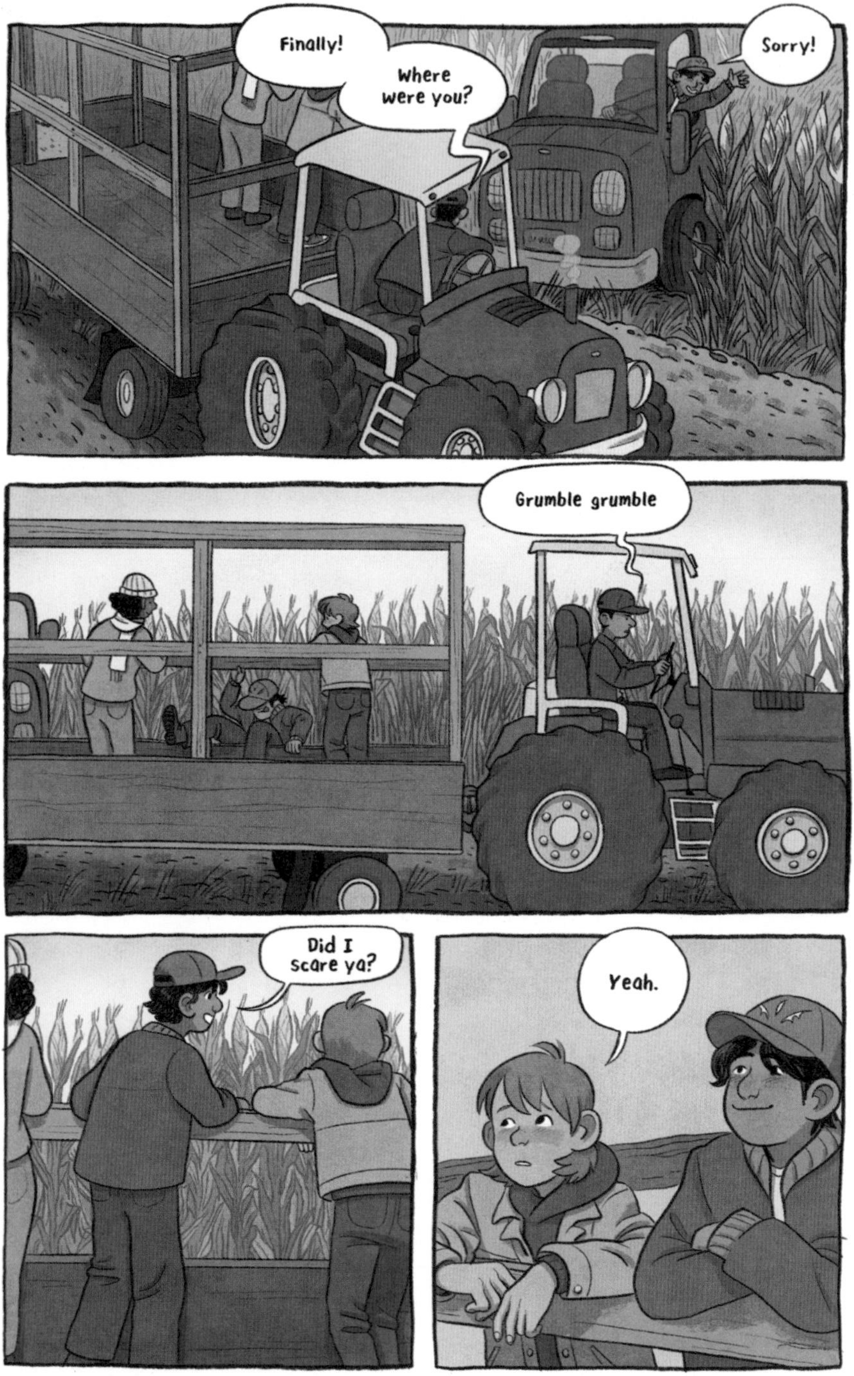
Finally!
Where were you?
Sorry!
Grumble grumble
Did I scare ya?
Yeah.

130

131

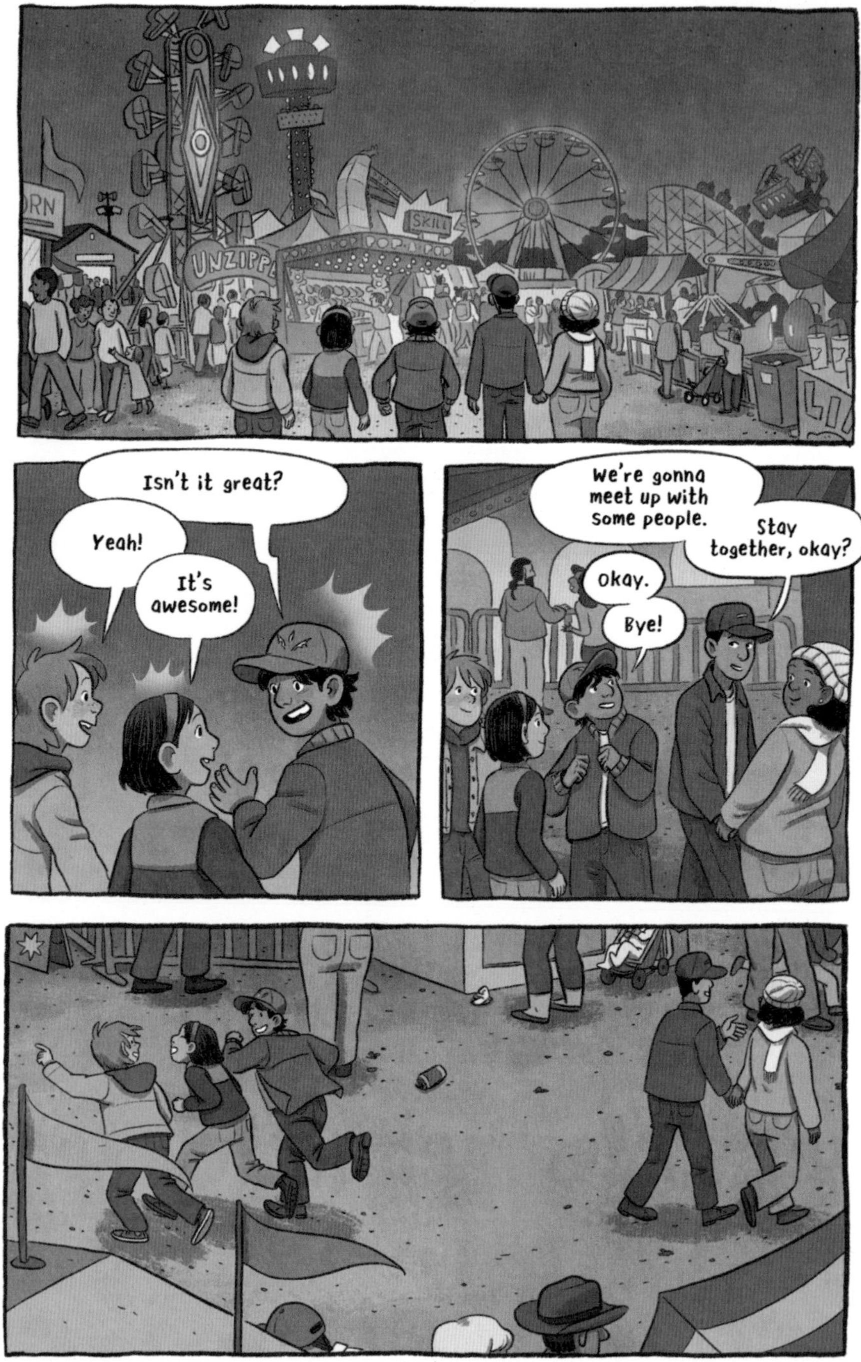
SKILL
Isn't it great?
Yeah!
It's awesome!
We're gonna meet up with some people.
Stay together, okay?
Okay.
Bye!

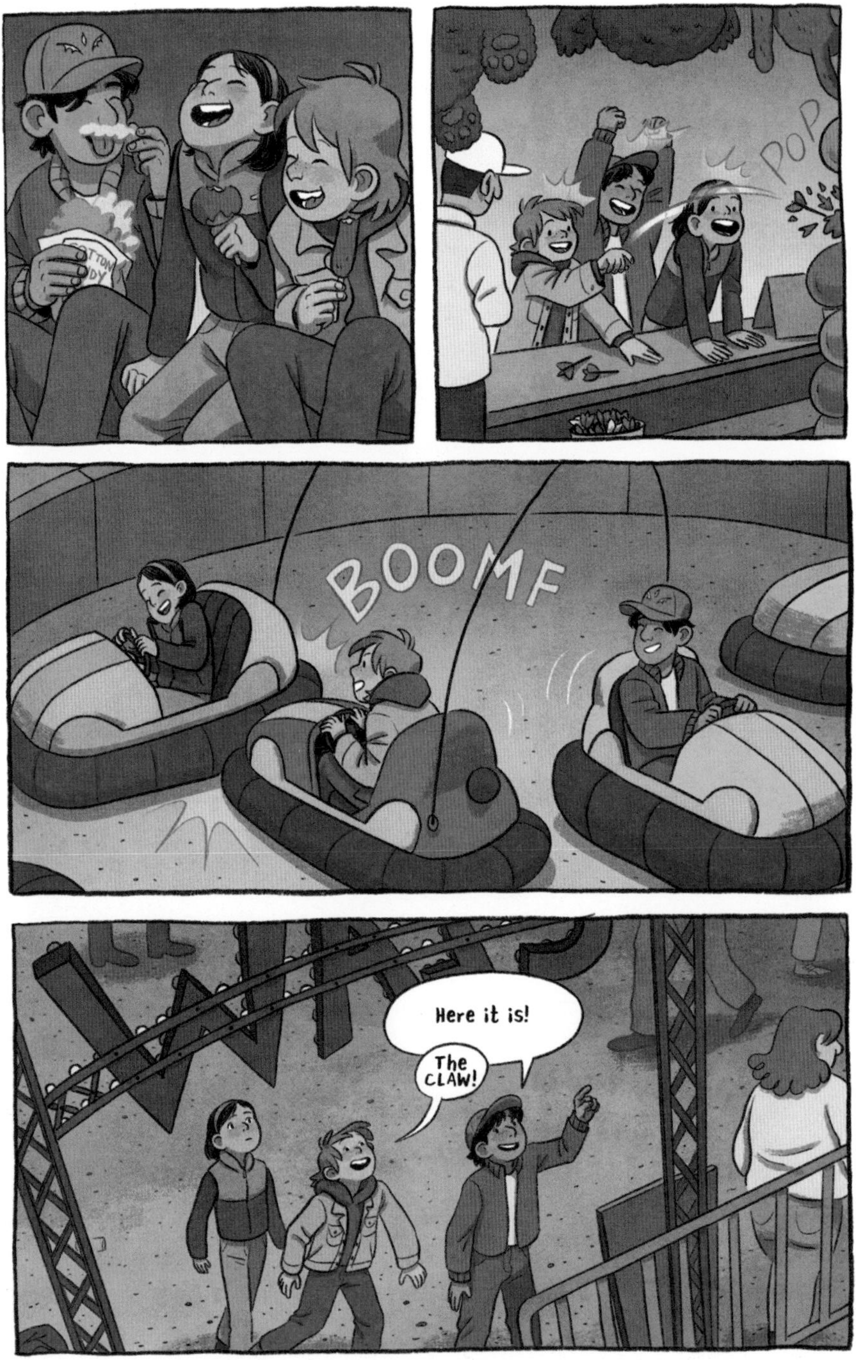
POP
BOOMF
Here it is!
The CLAW!

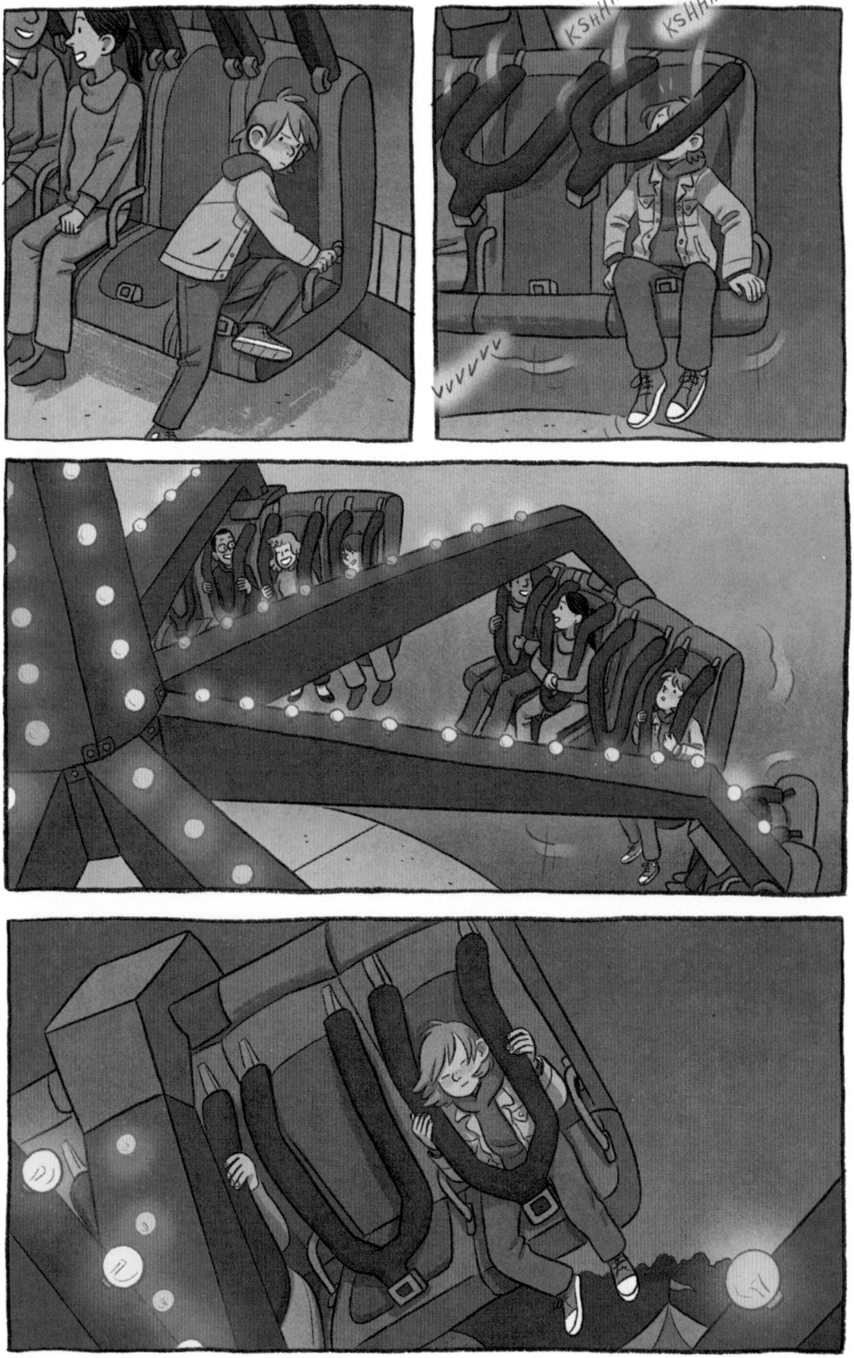
KSHHH
KSHHH
VVVVVV

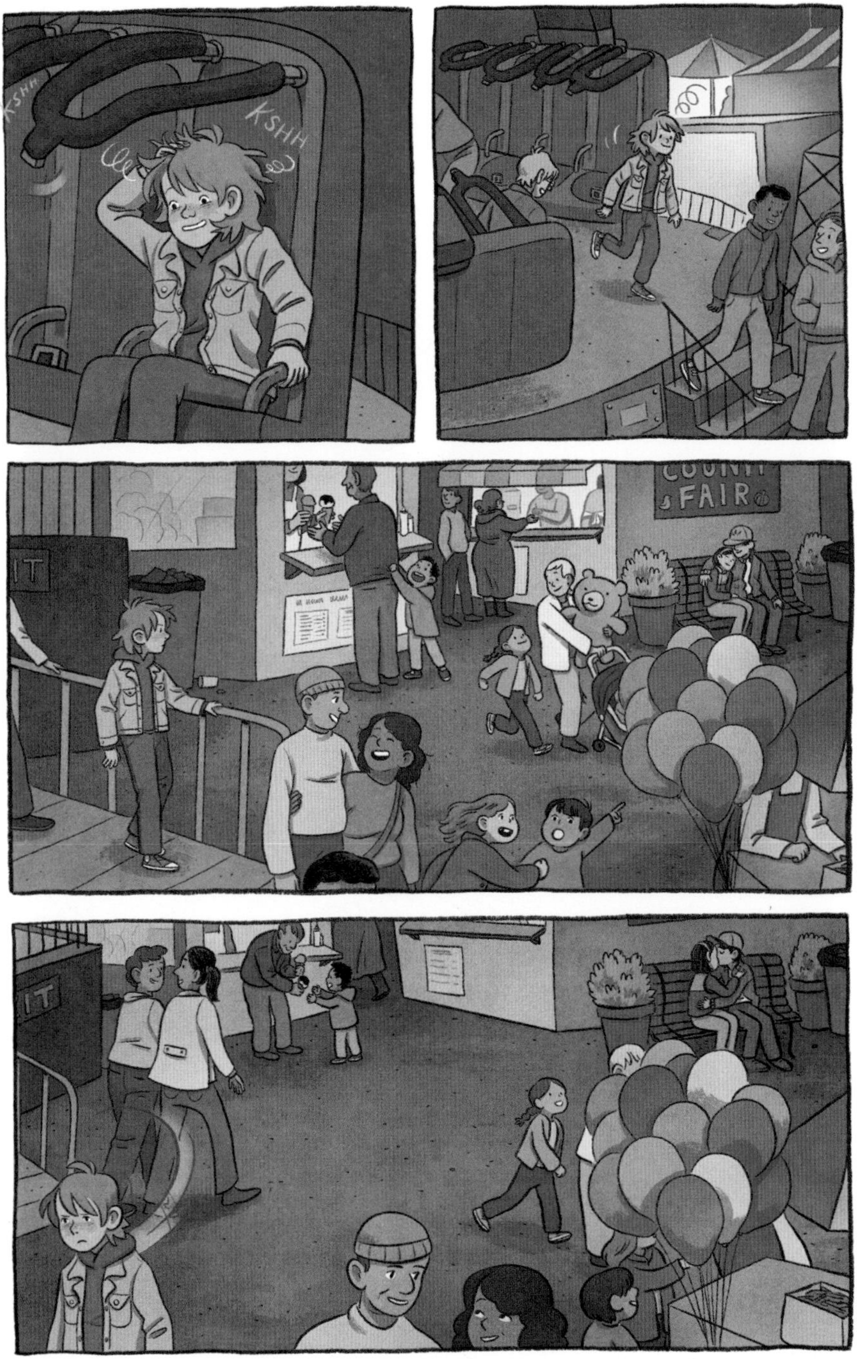
KSHH
KSHH
FAIR

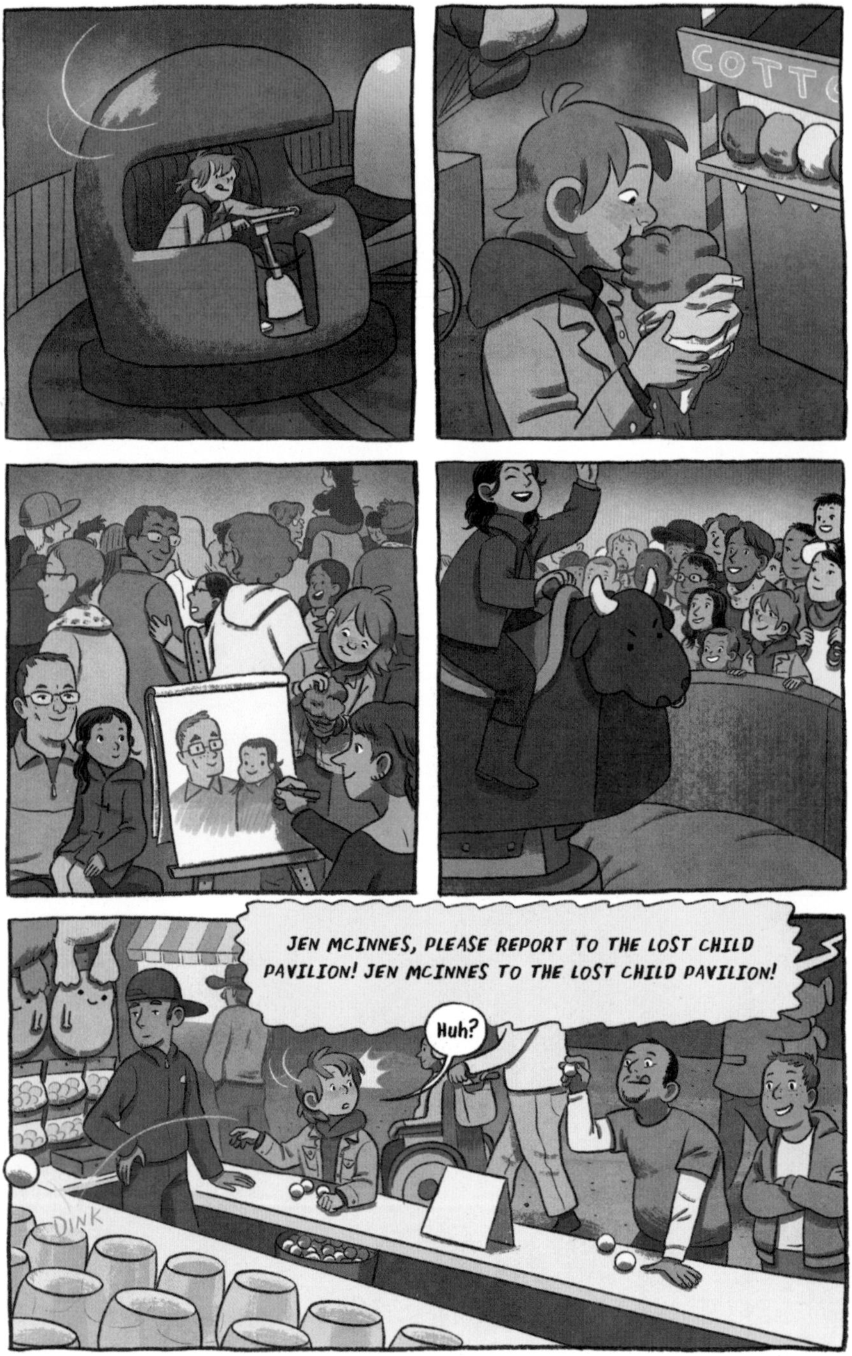
COTT
JEN MCINNES, PLEASE REPORT TO THE LOST CHILD PAVILION! JEN MCINNES TO THE LOST CHILD PAVILION!
Huh?
DINK

139

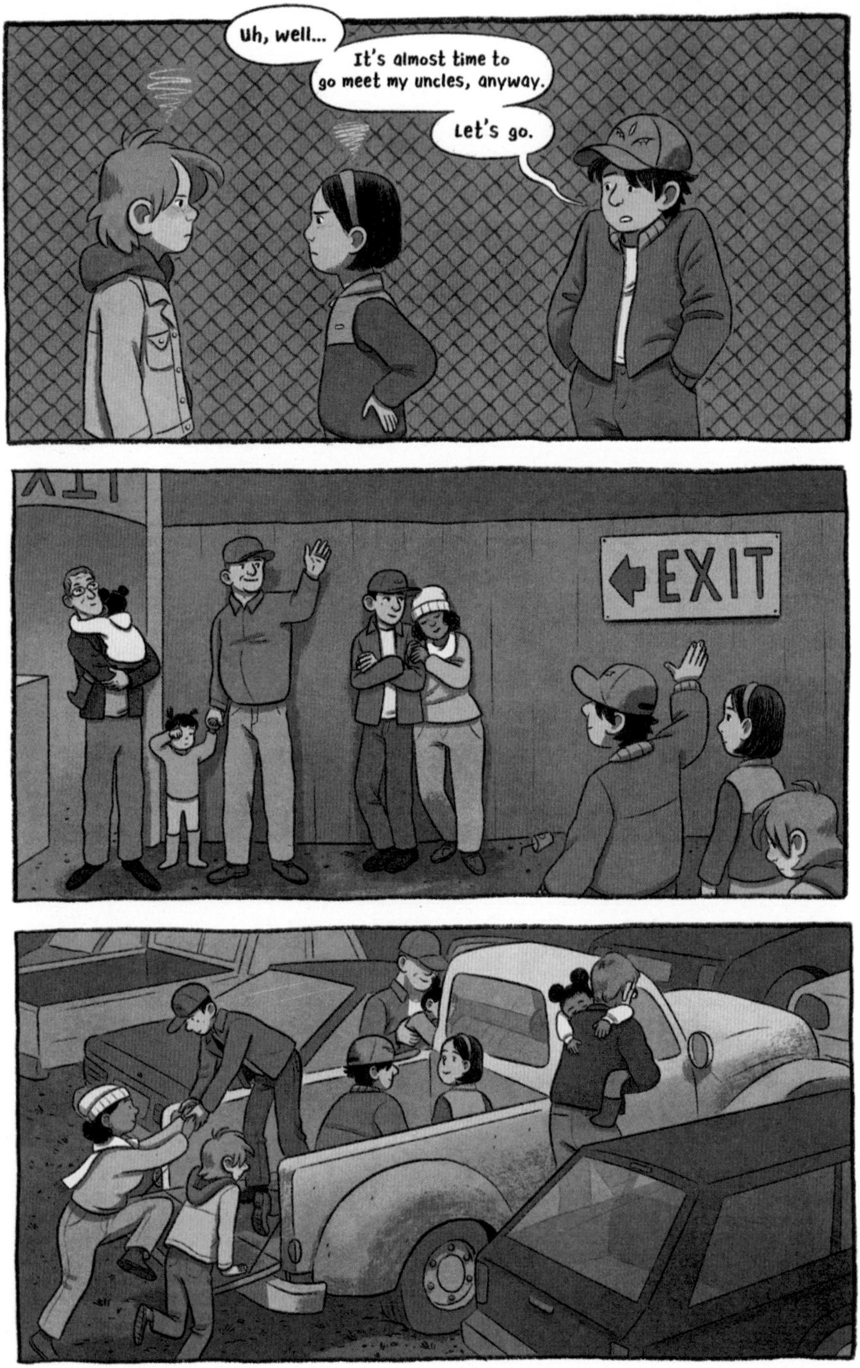
Uh, well...
It's almost time to go meet my uncles, anyway.
Let's go.
EXIT

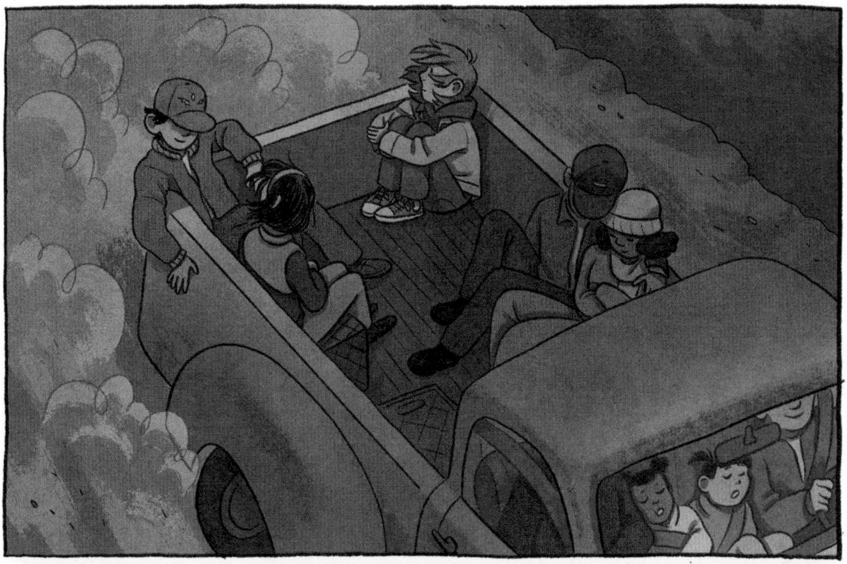

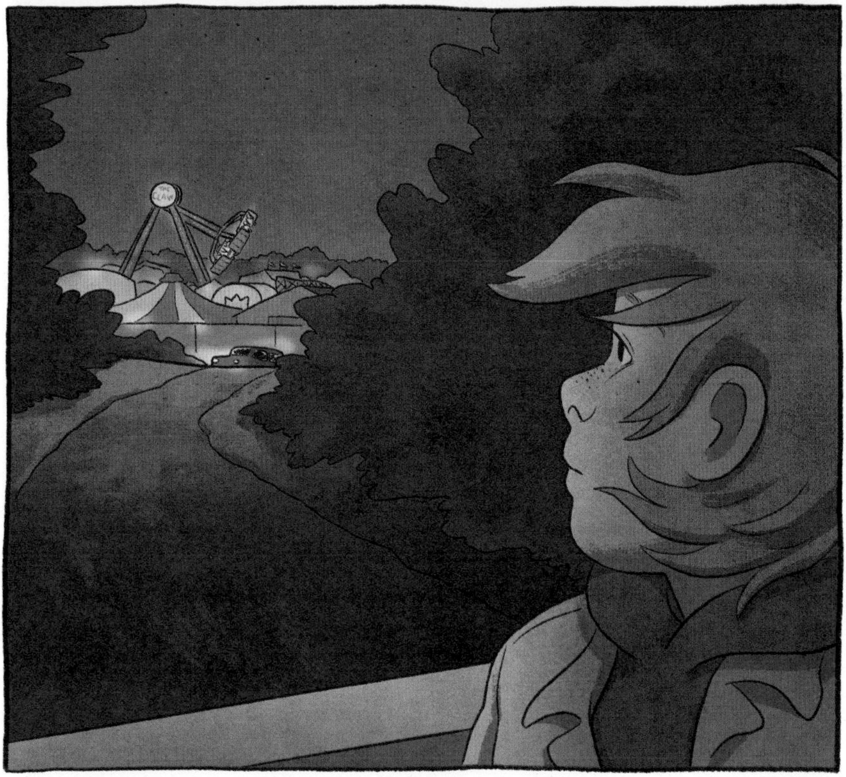
THE CLAW

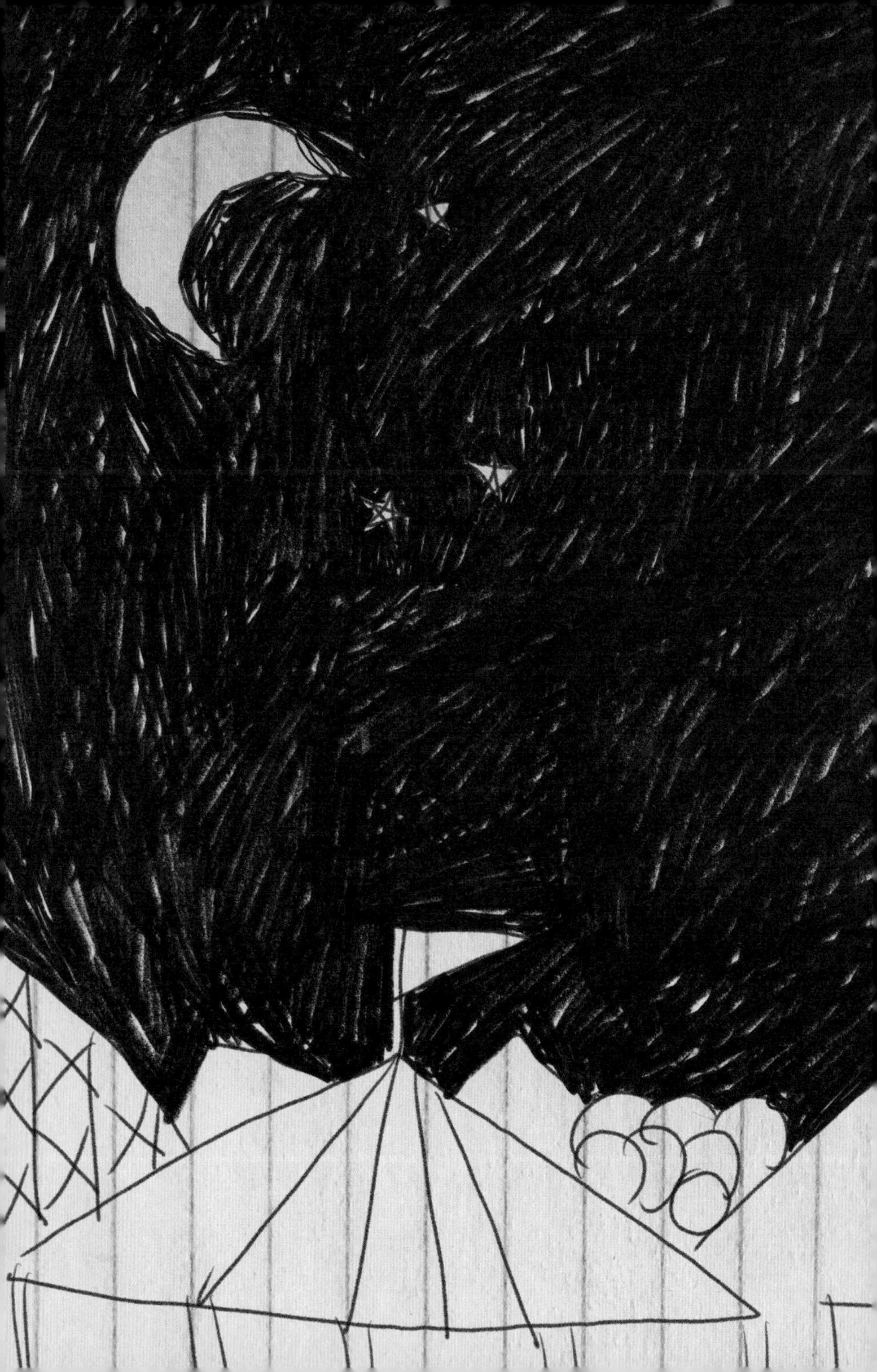

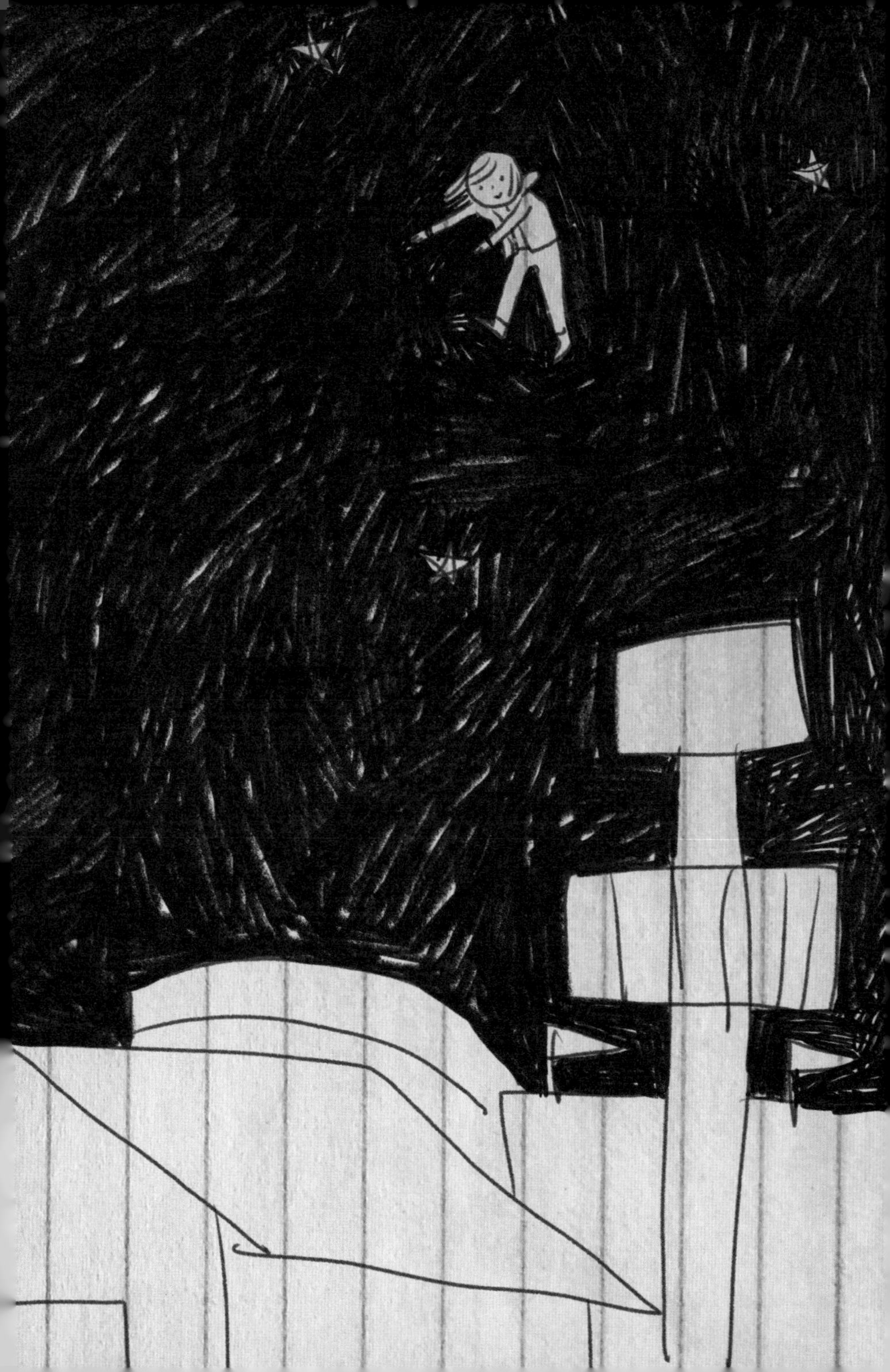

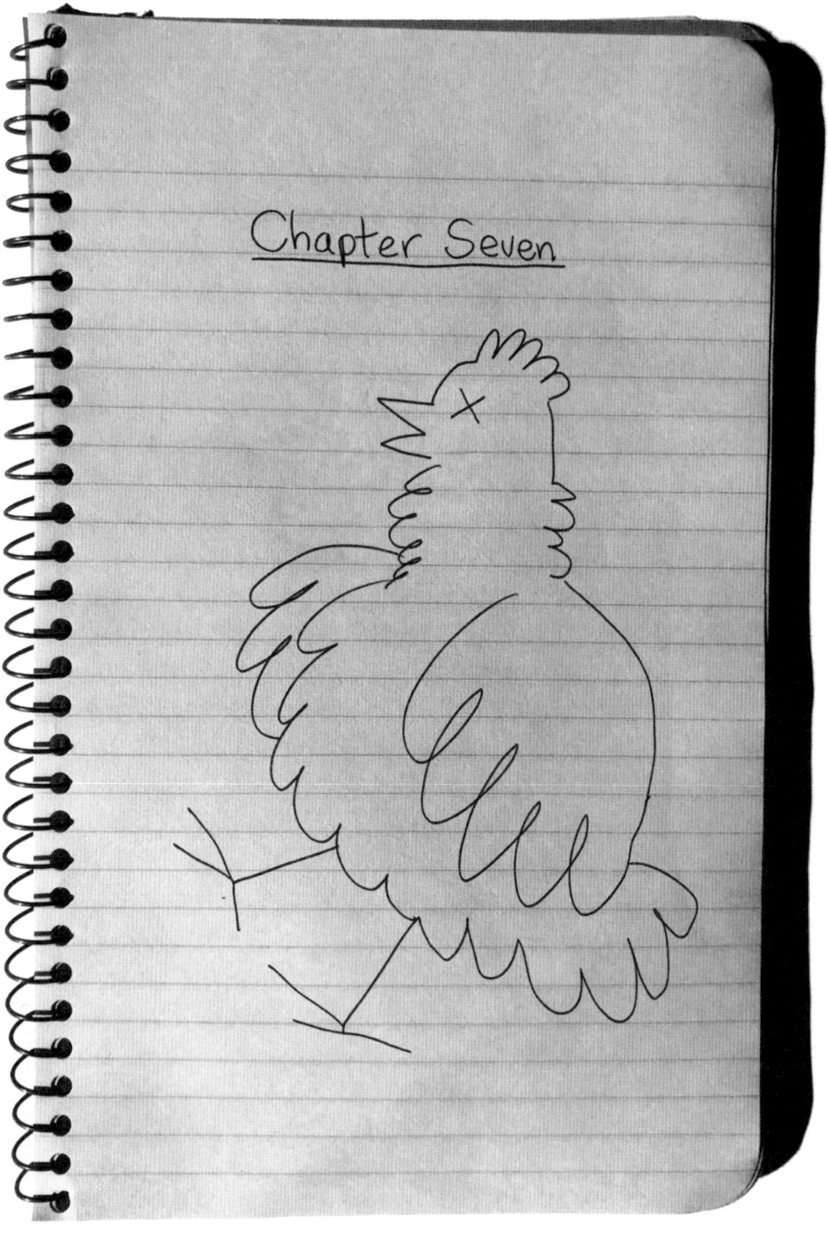
Chapter Seven

147

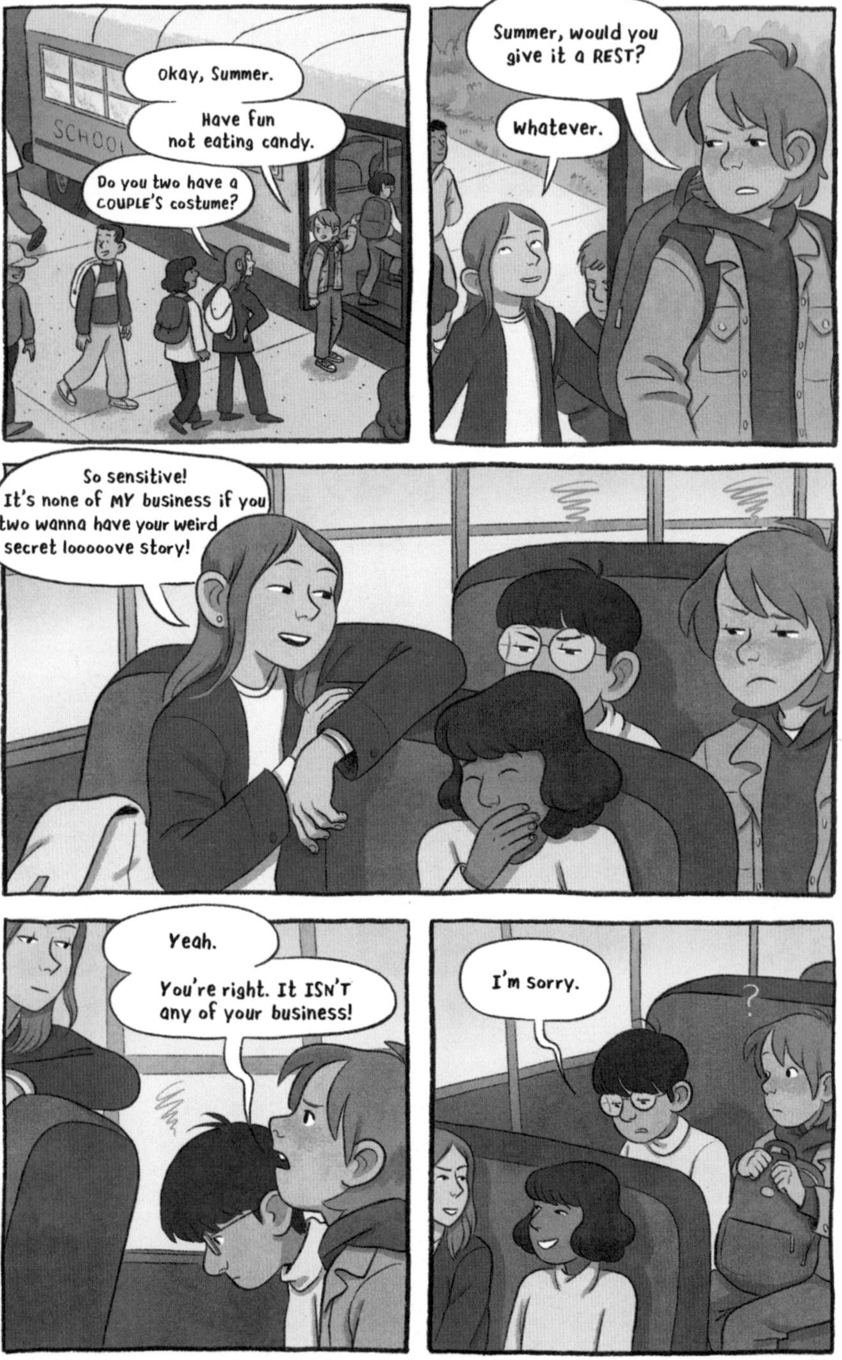
Okay, Summer.
Have fun not eating candy.
Do you two have a COUPLE'S costume?
SCHOOL
Summer, would you give it a REST?
Whatever.
So sensitive! It's none of MY business if you two wanna have your weird secret looooove story!
Yeah.
You're right. It ISN'T any of your business!
I'm sorry.
?

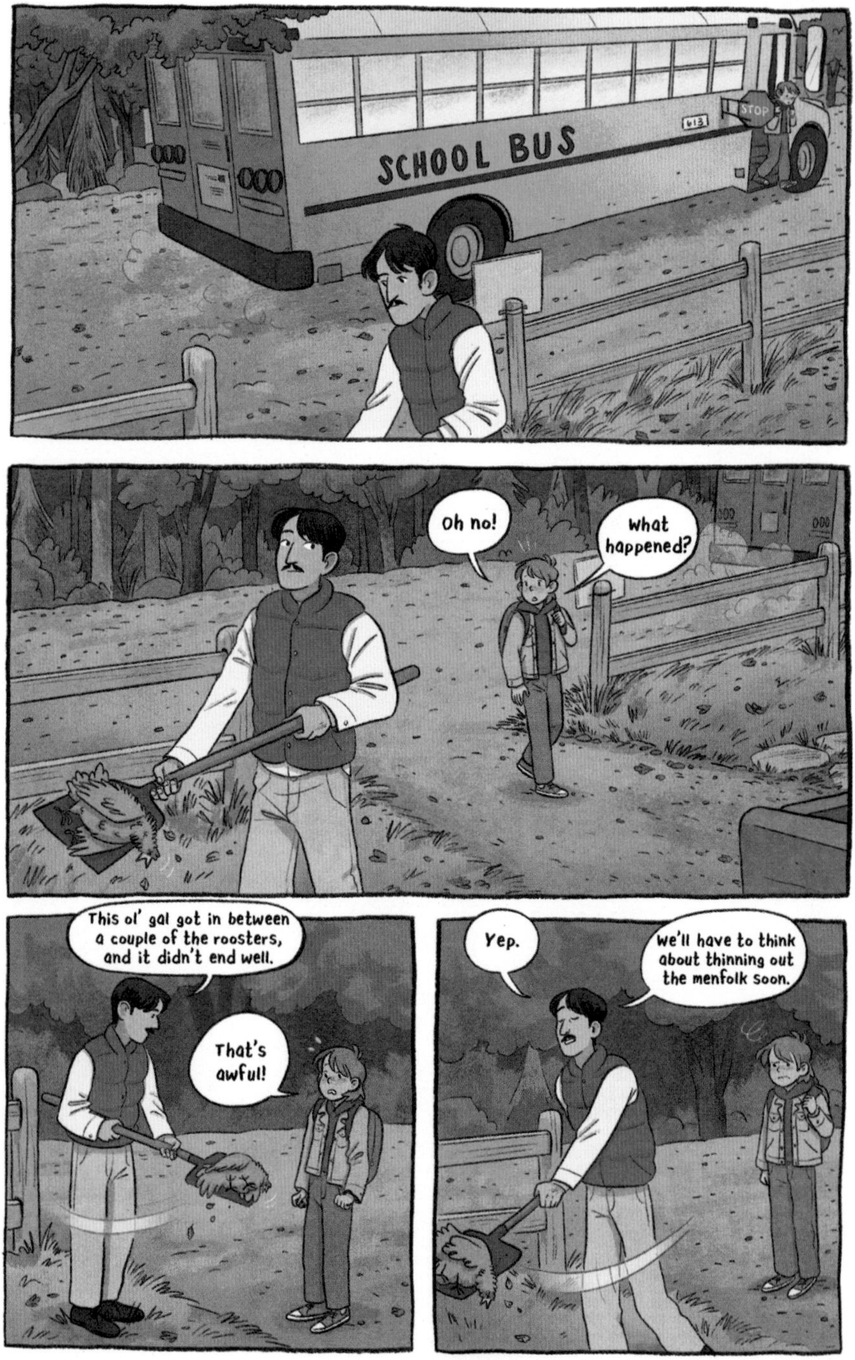
SCHOOL BUS
STOP
Oh no!
What happened?
This ol' gal got in between a couple of the roosters, and it didn't end well.
That's awful!
Yep.
We'll have to think about thinning out the menfolk soon.

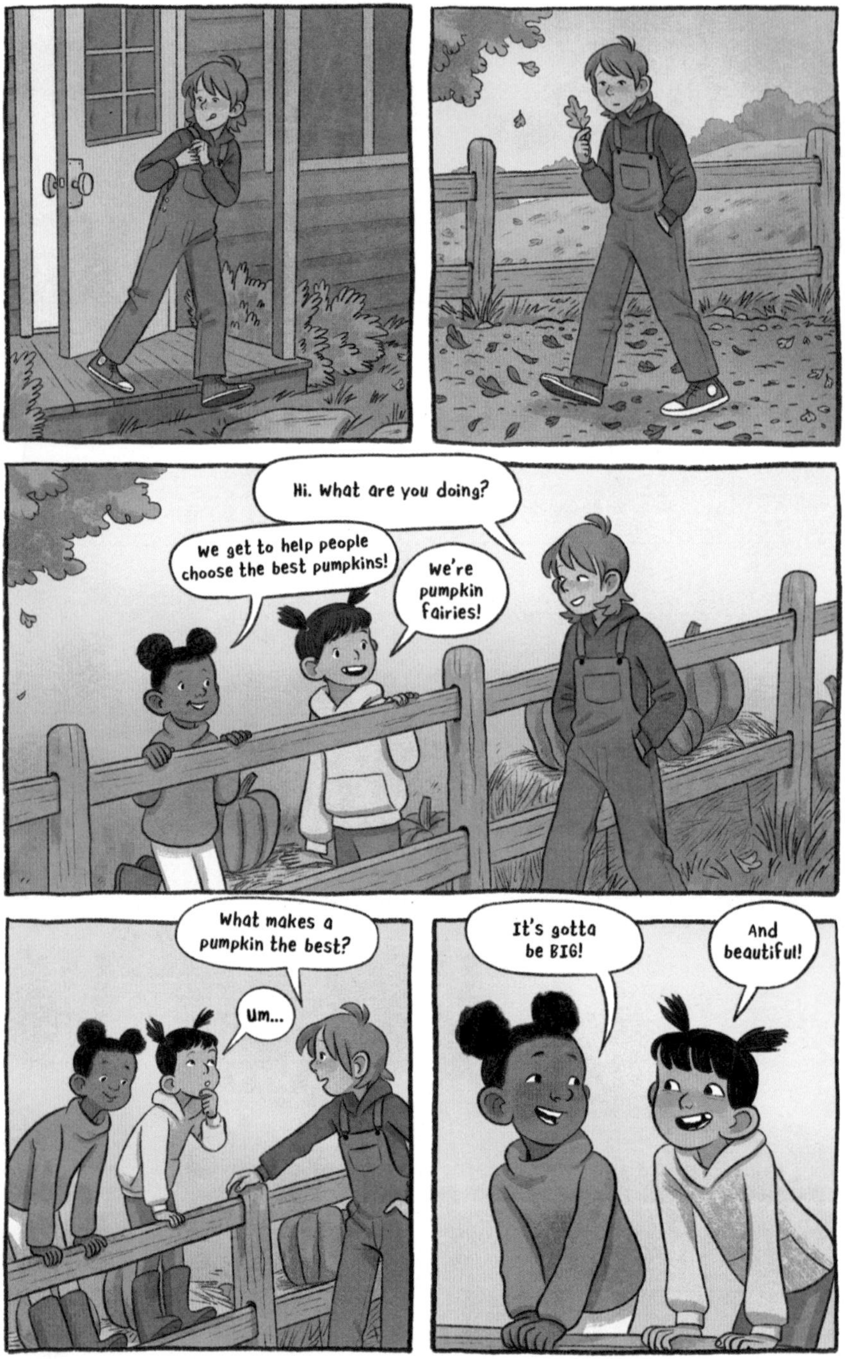

Hi. What are you doing?
We get to help people choose the best pumpkins!
We're pumpkin fairies!
What makes a pumpkin the best?
Um...
It's gotta be BIG!
And beautiful!

155

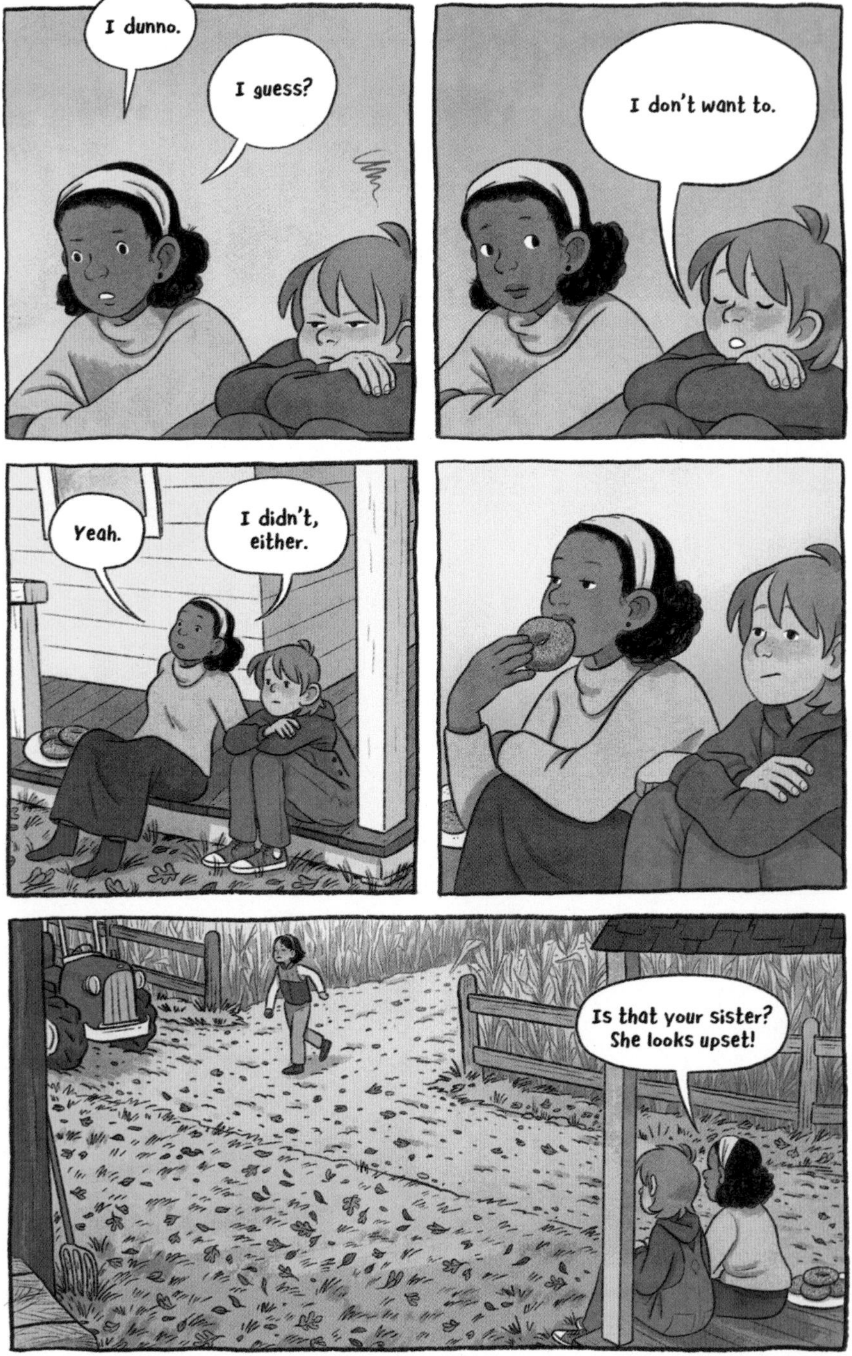
I dunno.
I guess?
I don't want to.
Yeah.
I didn't, either.
Is that your sister? She looks upset!

159

161

162

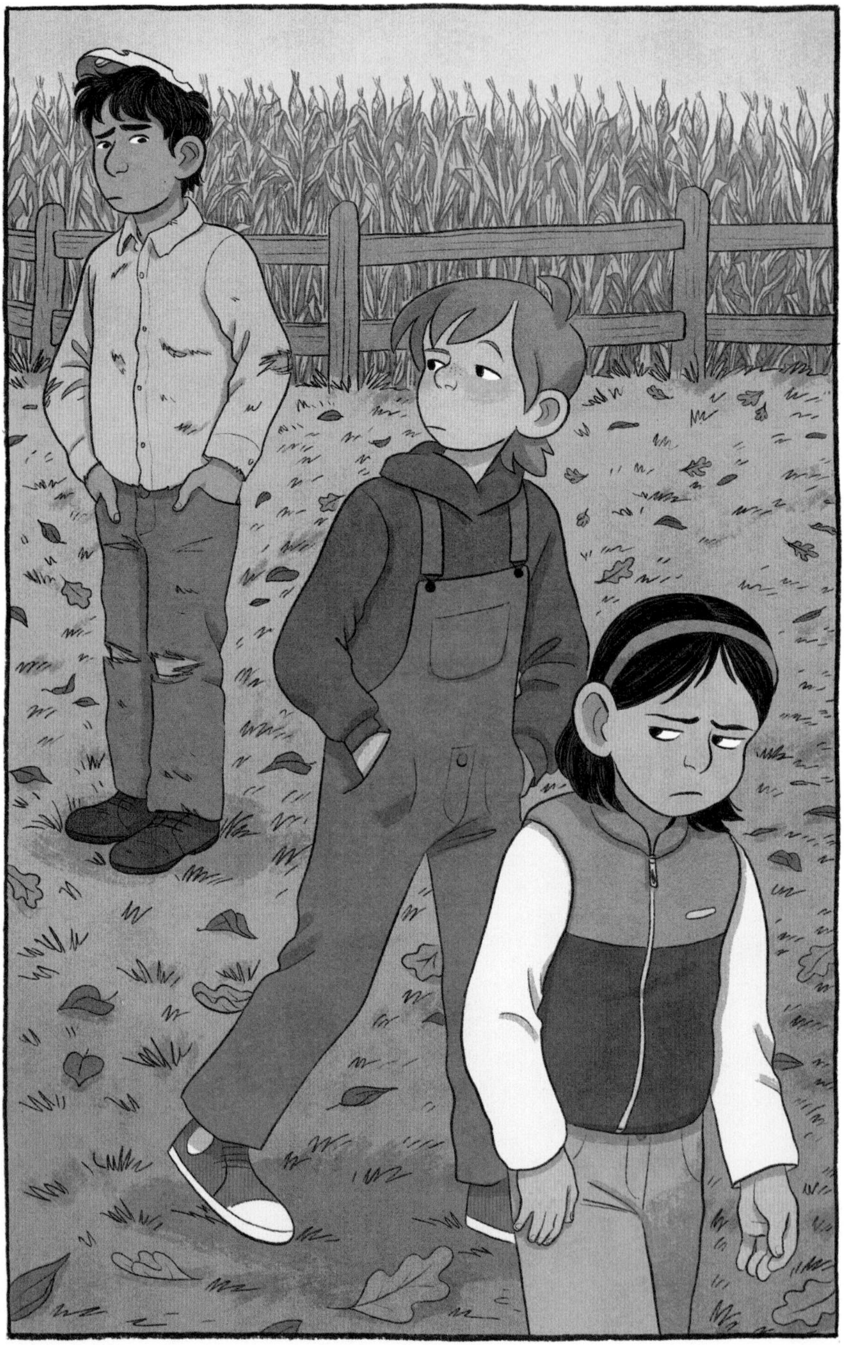

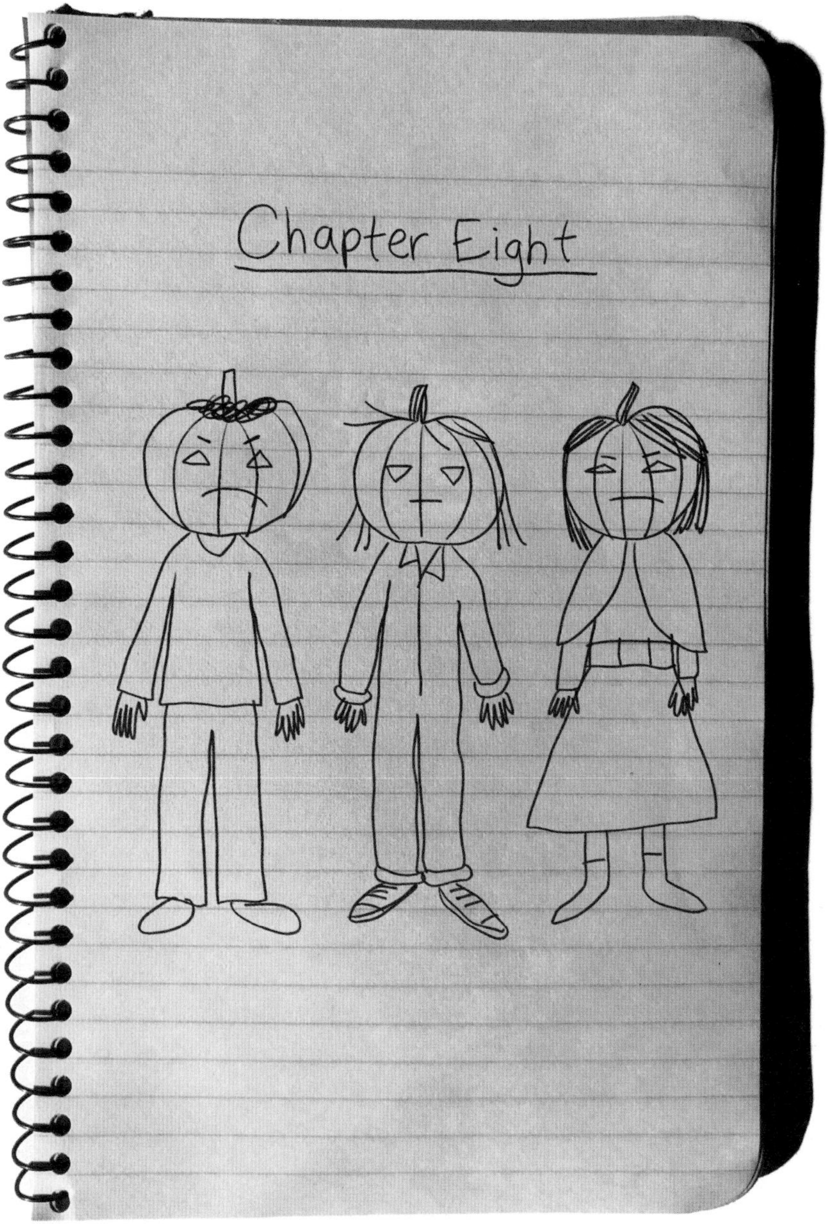
Chapter Eight

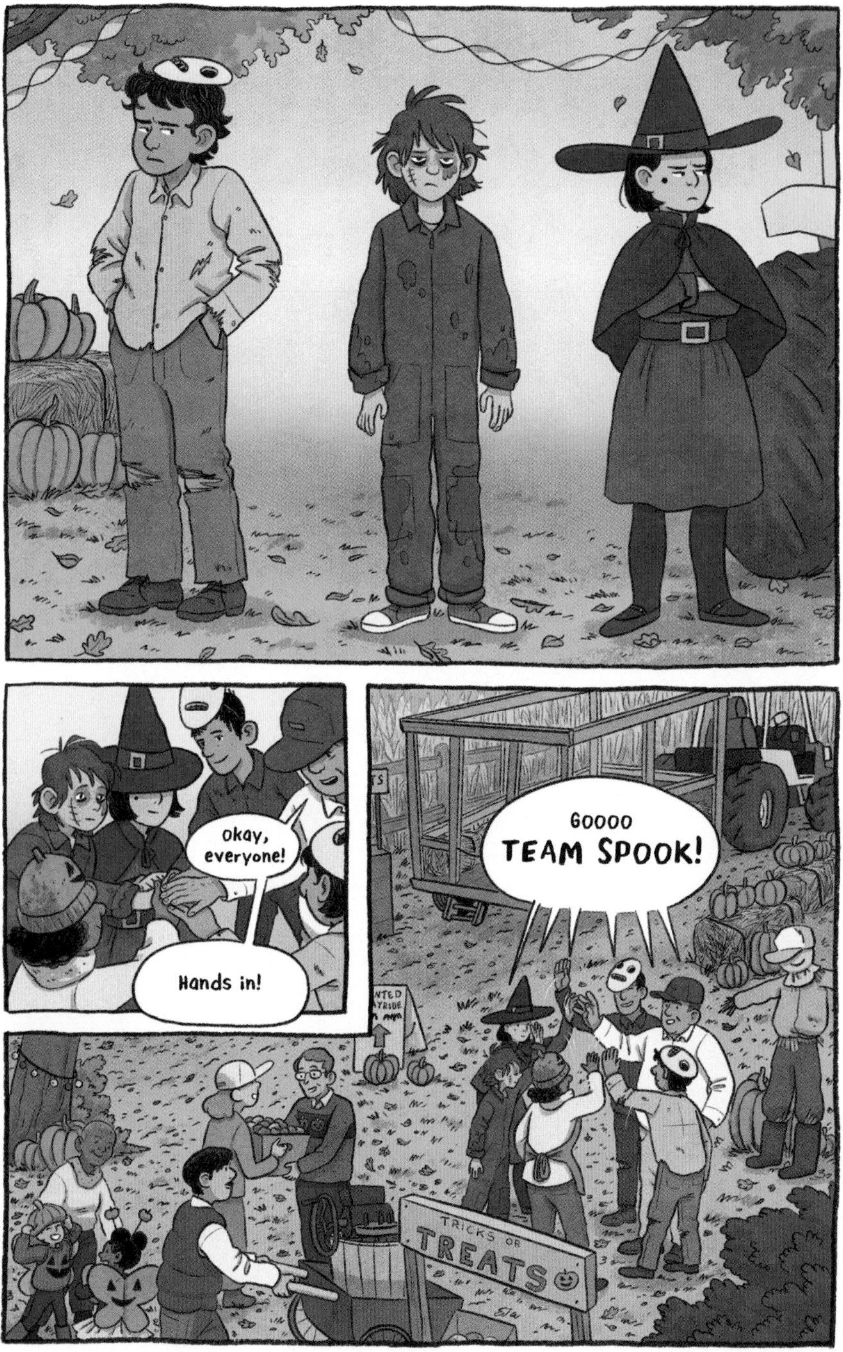
Okay, everyone!
Hands in!
GOOOO TEAM SPOOK!
TRICKS OR TREATS

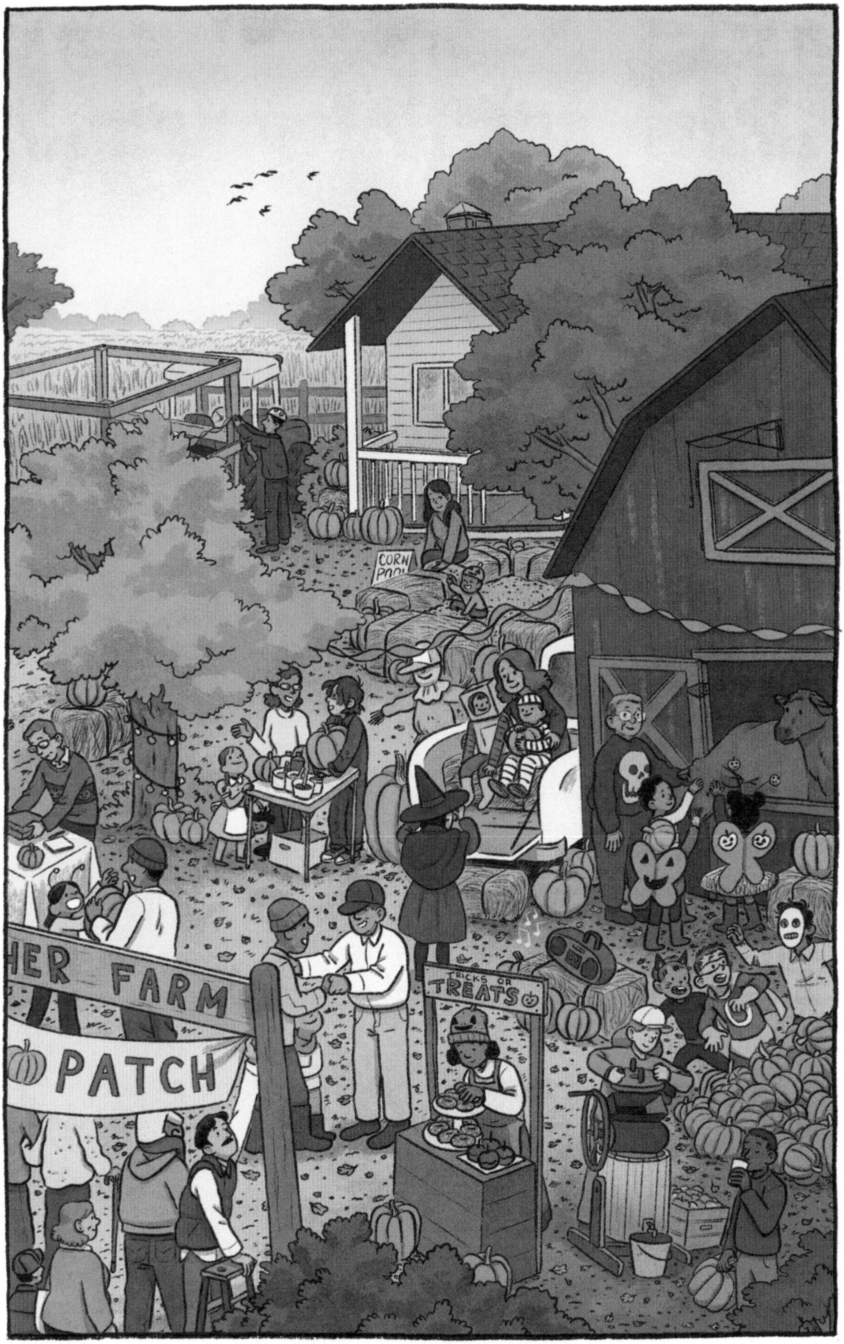
CORN
HER FARM
PATCH
TRICKS OR
TREATS

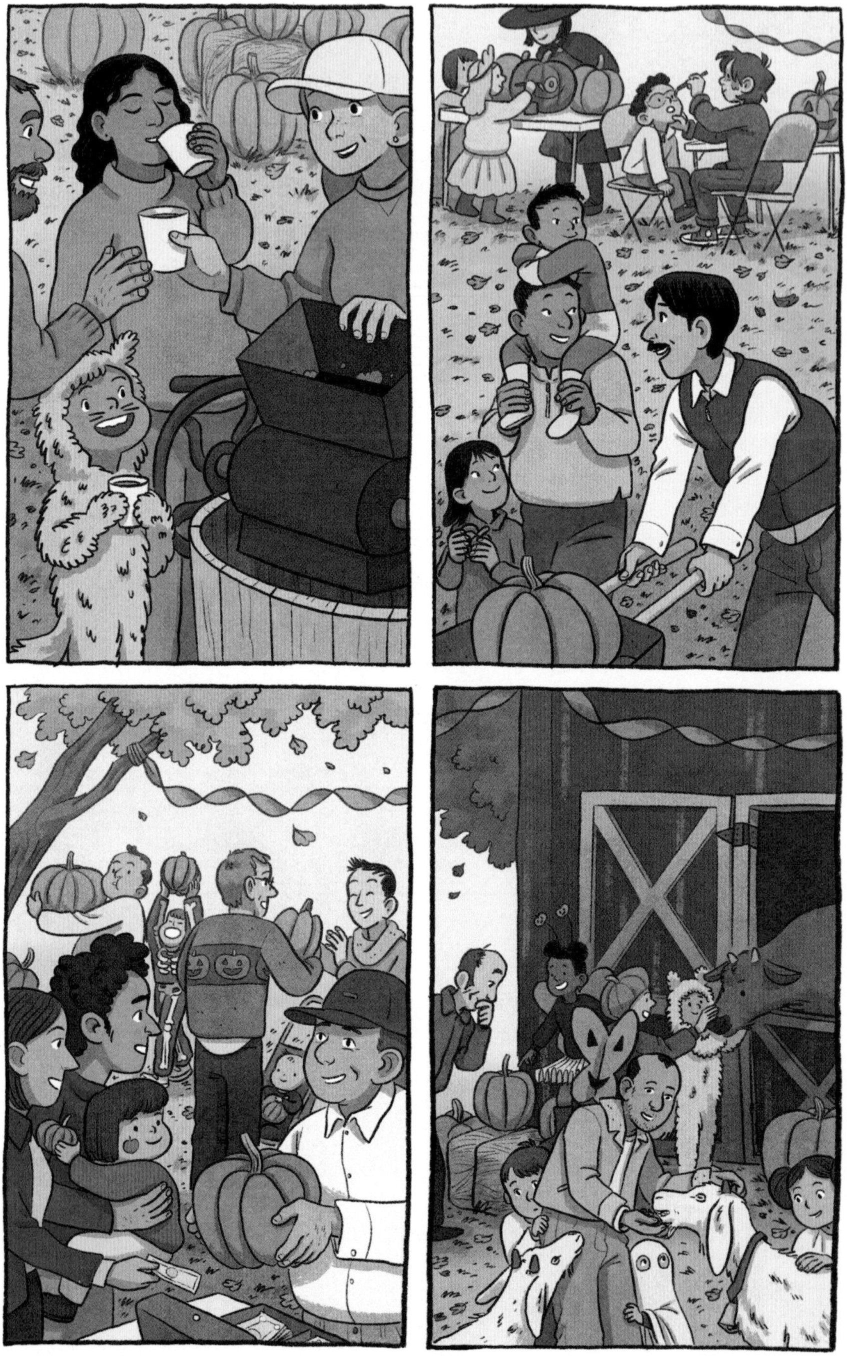

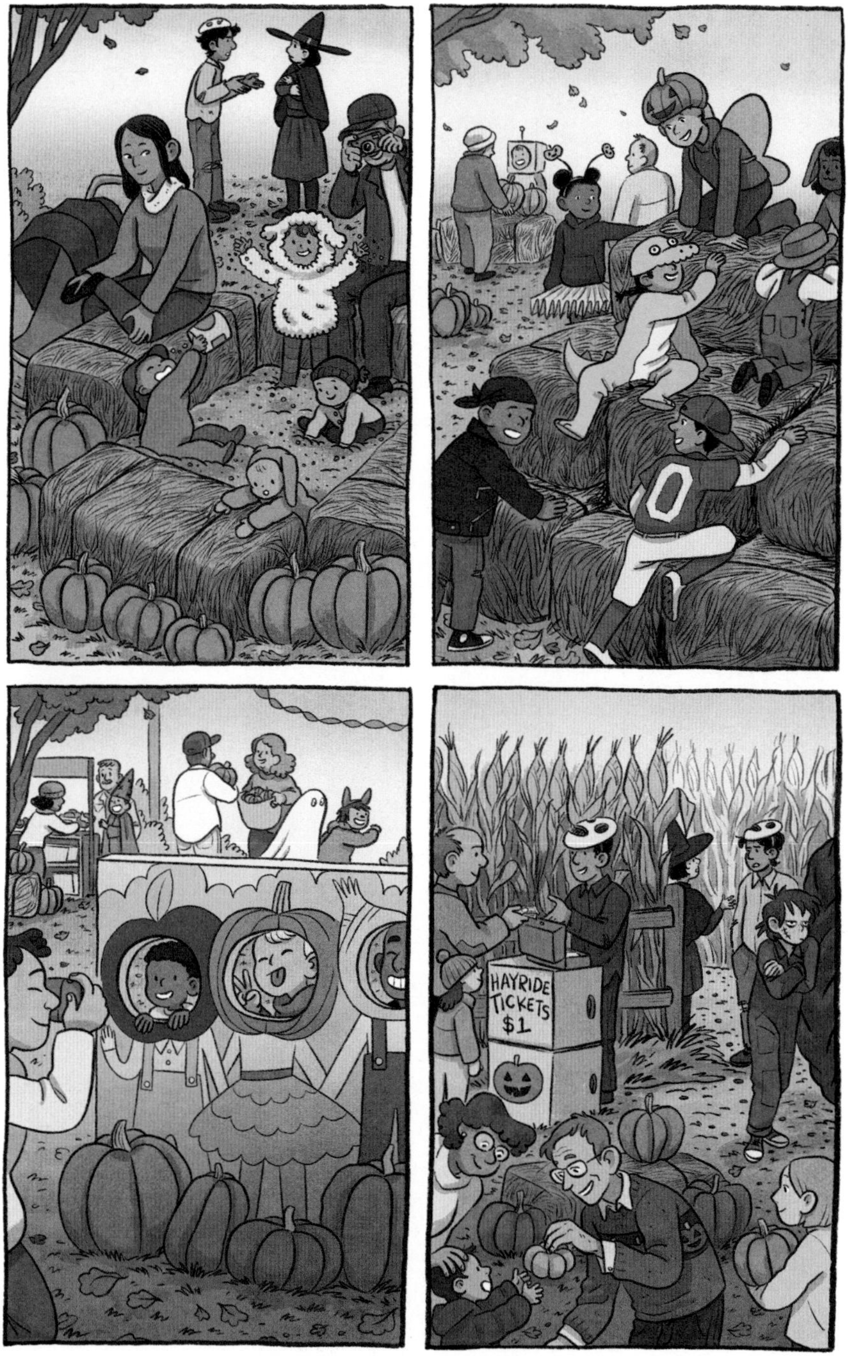
HAYRIDE TICKETS $1

172

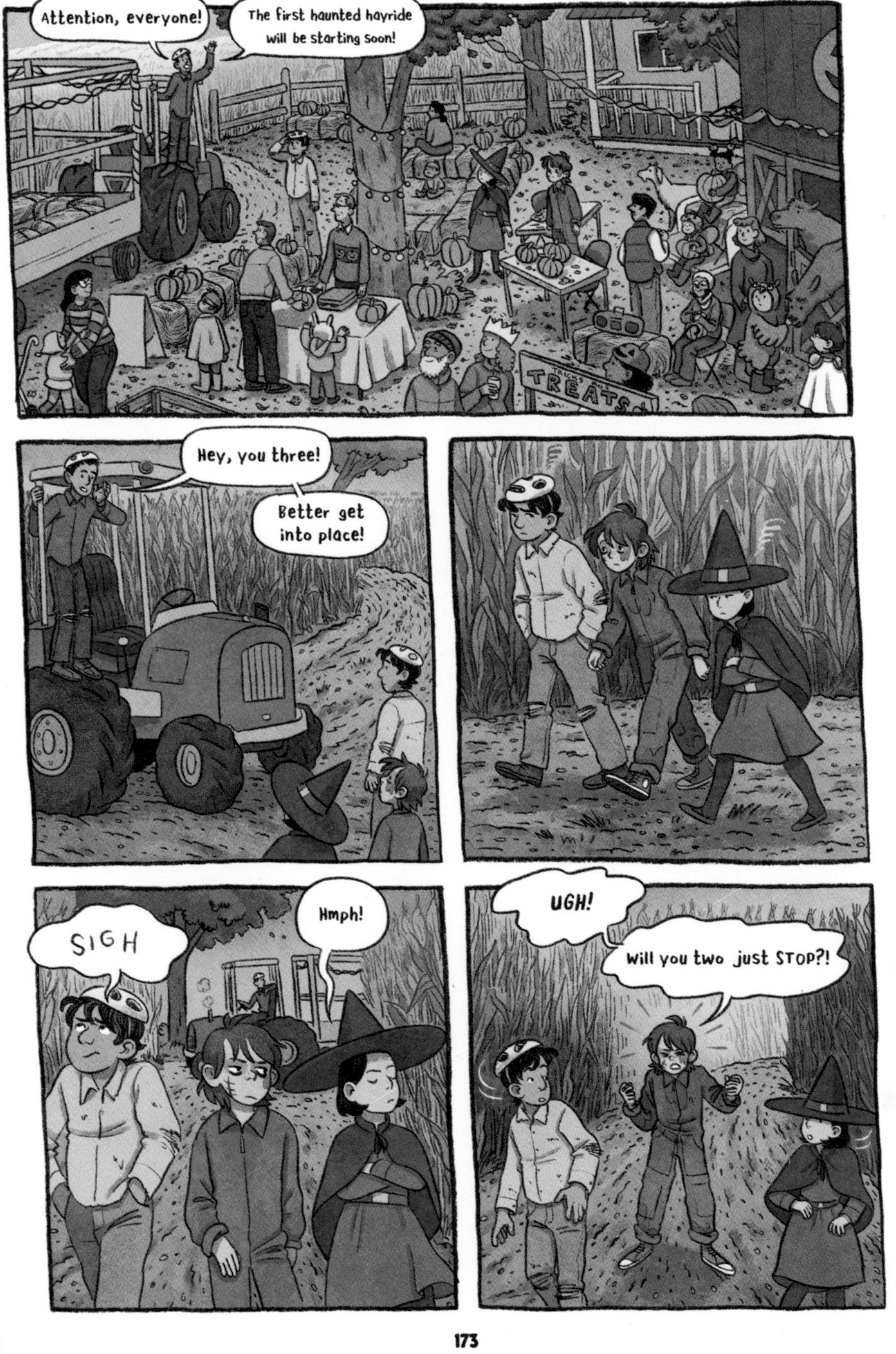
Attention, everyone!
The first haunted hayride will be starting soon!
TREATS
Hey, you three!
Better get into place!
SIGH
Hmph!
UGH!
Will you two just STOP?!

175

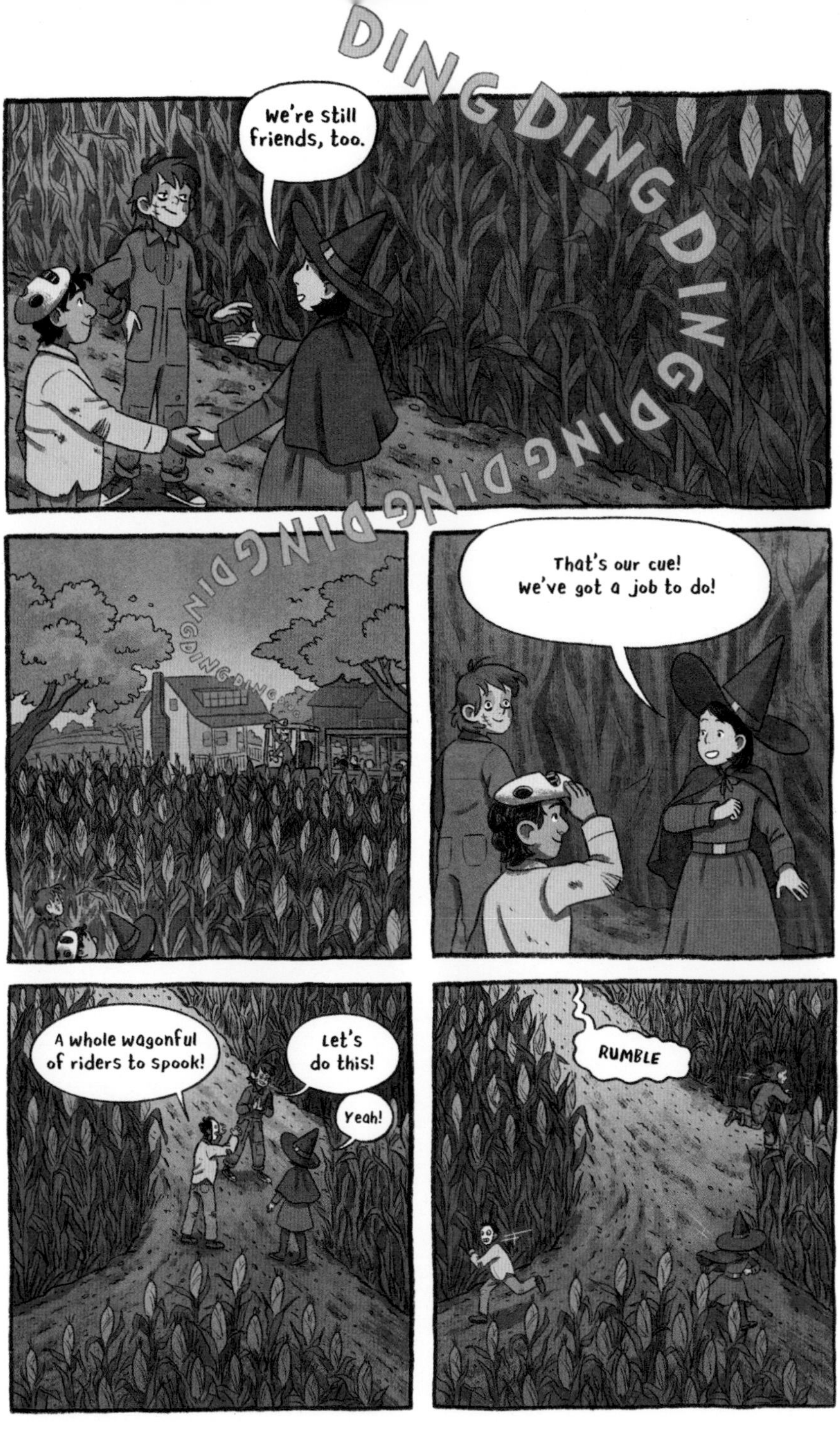
DING DING DING DING DING DING
We're still friends, too.
DING DING DING DING DING
That's our cue! We've got a job to do!
A whole wagonful of riders to spook!
Let's do this!
Yeah!
RUMBLE

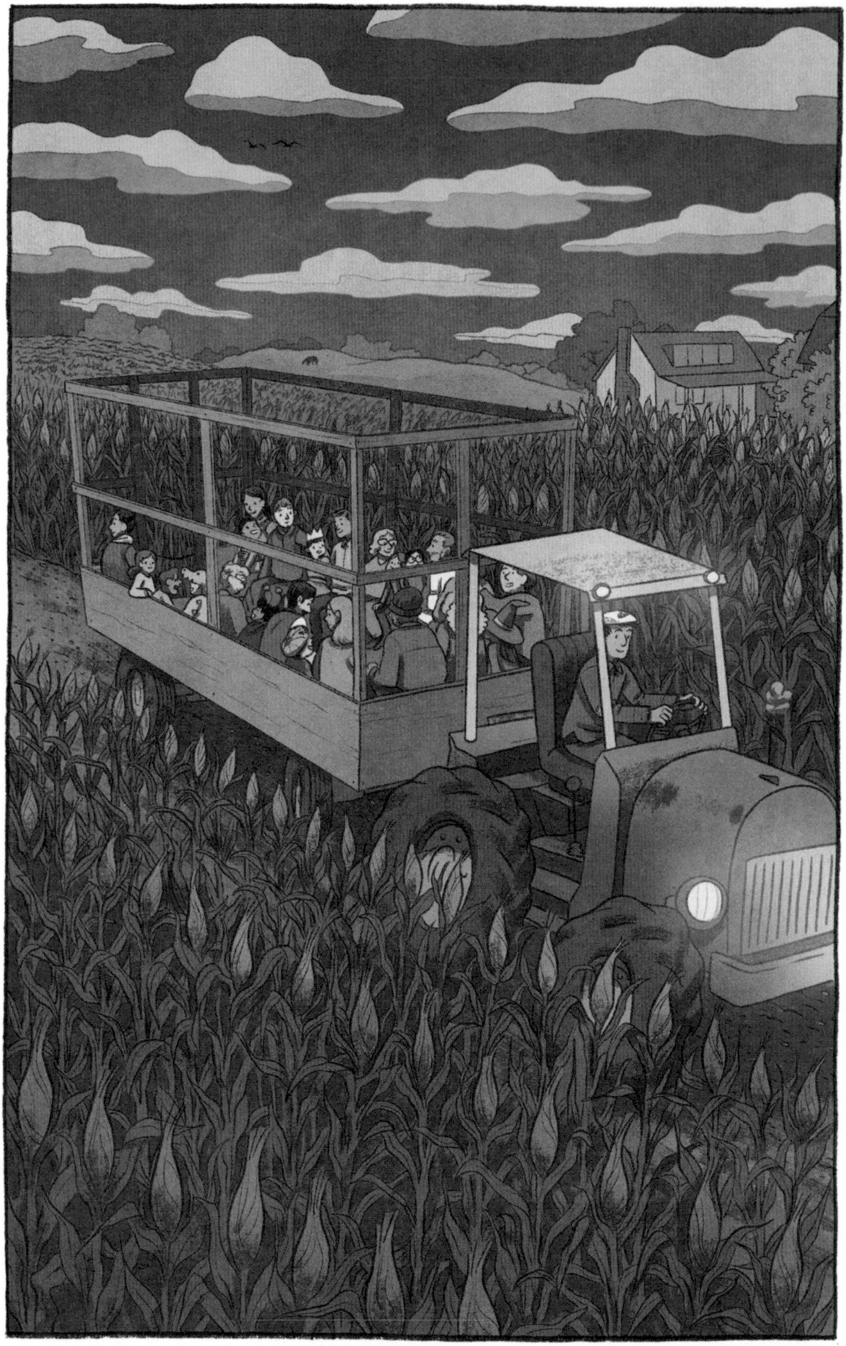

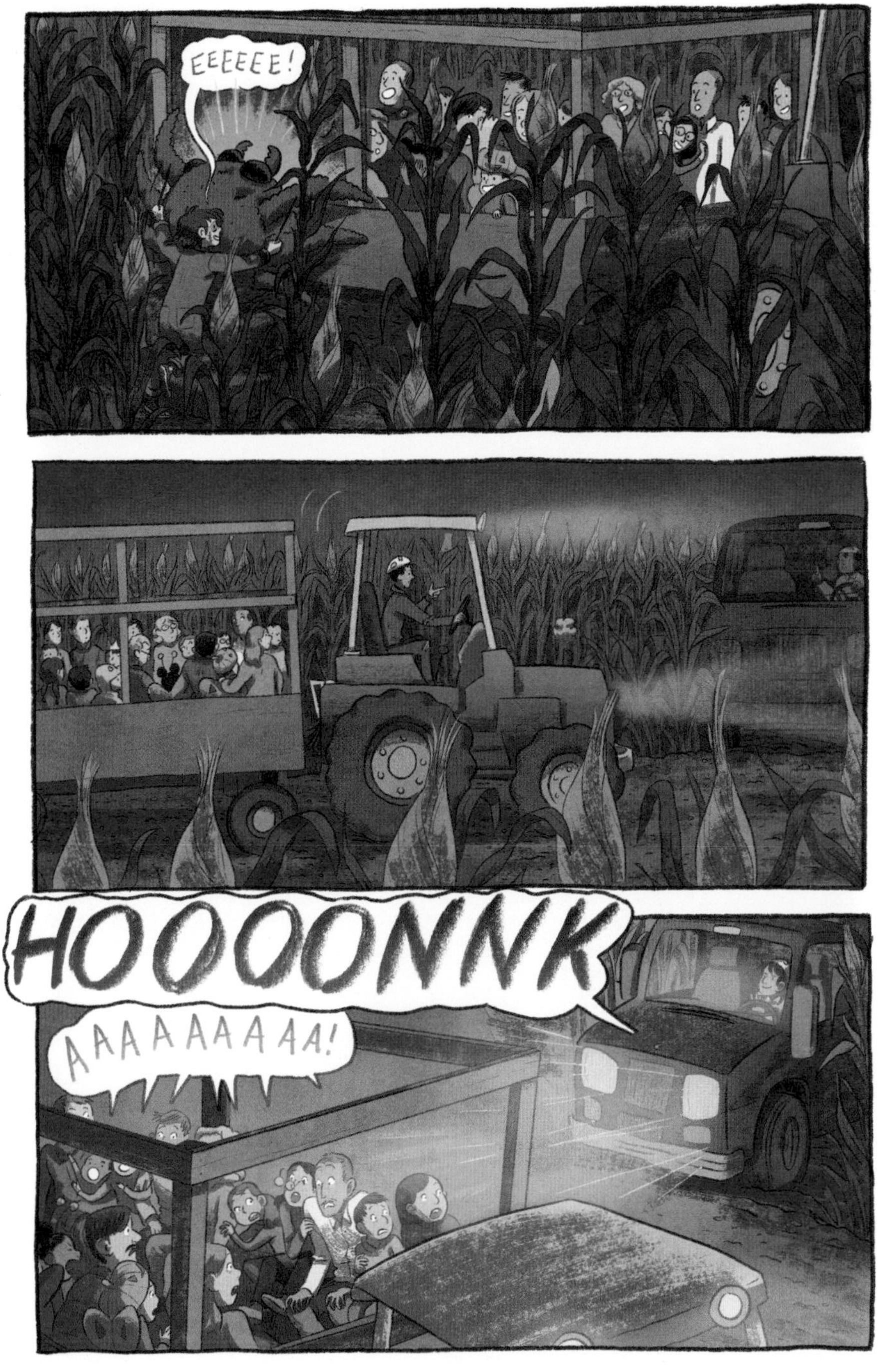
EEEEEE!
HOOOONNK
AAAAAAAAA!

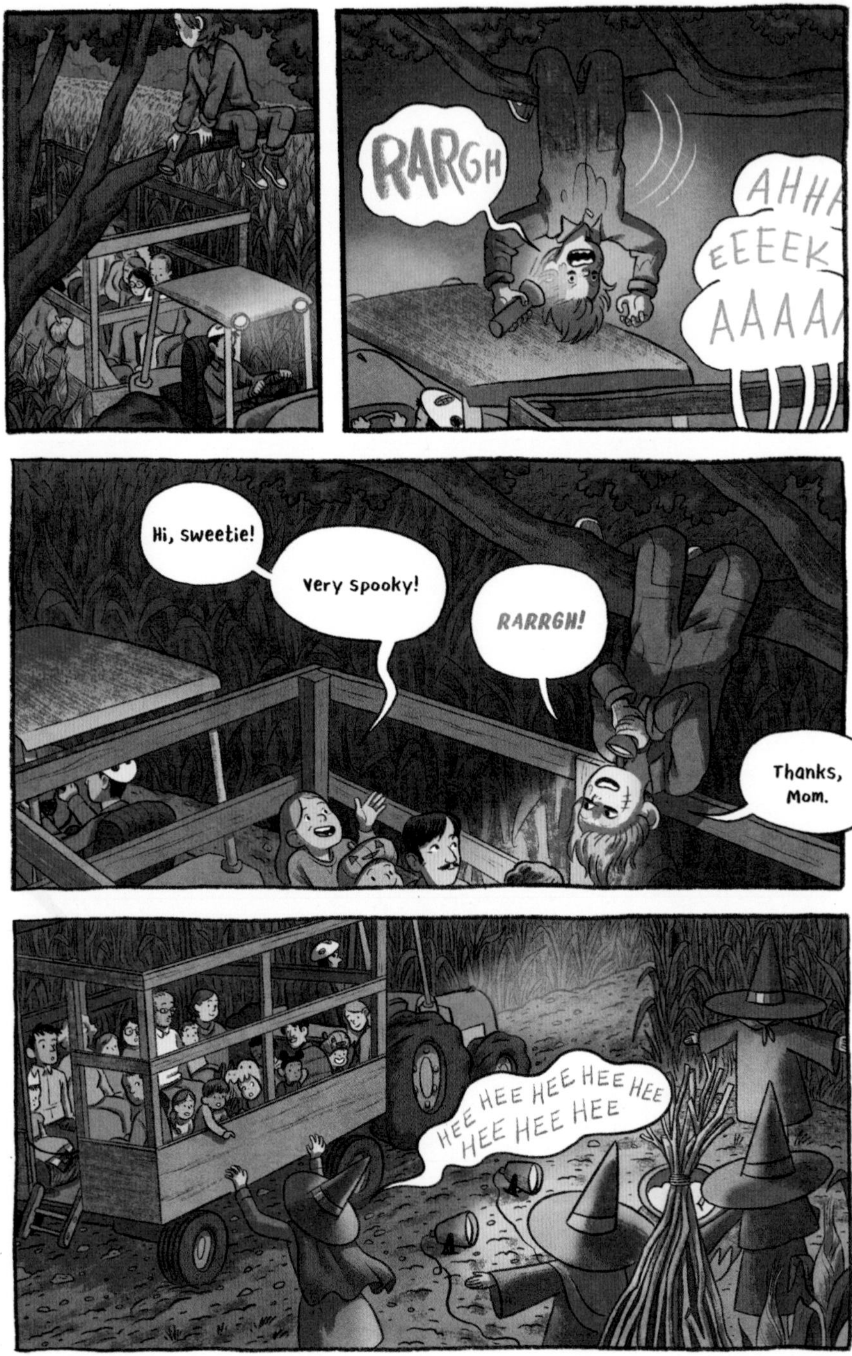
RARGH
AHHH
EEEEK
AAAA
Hi, sweetie!
Very spooky!
RARRGH!
Thanks, Mom.
HEE HEE HEE HEE HEE
HEE HEE HEE

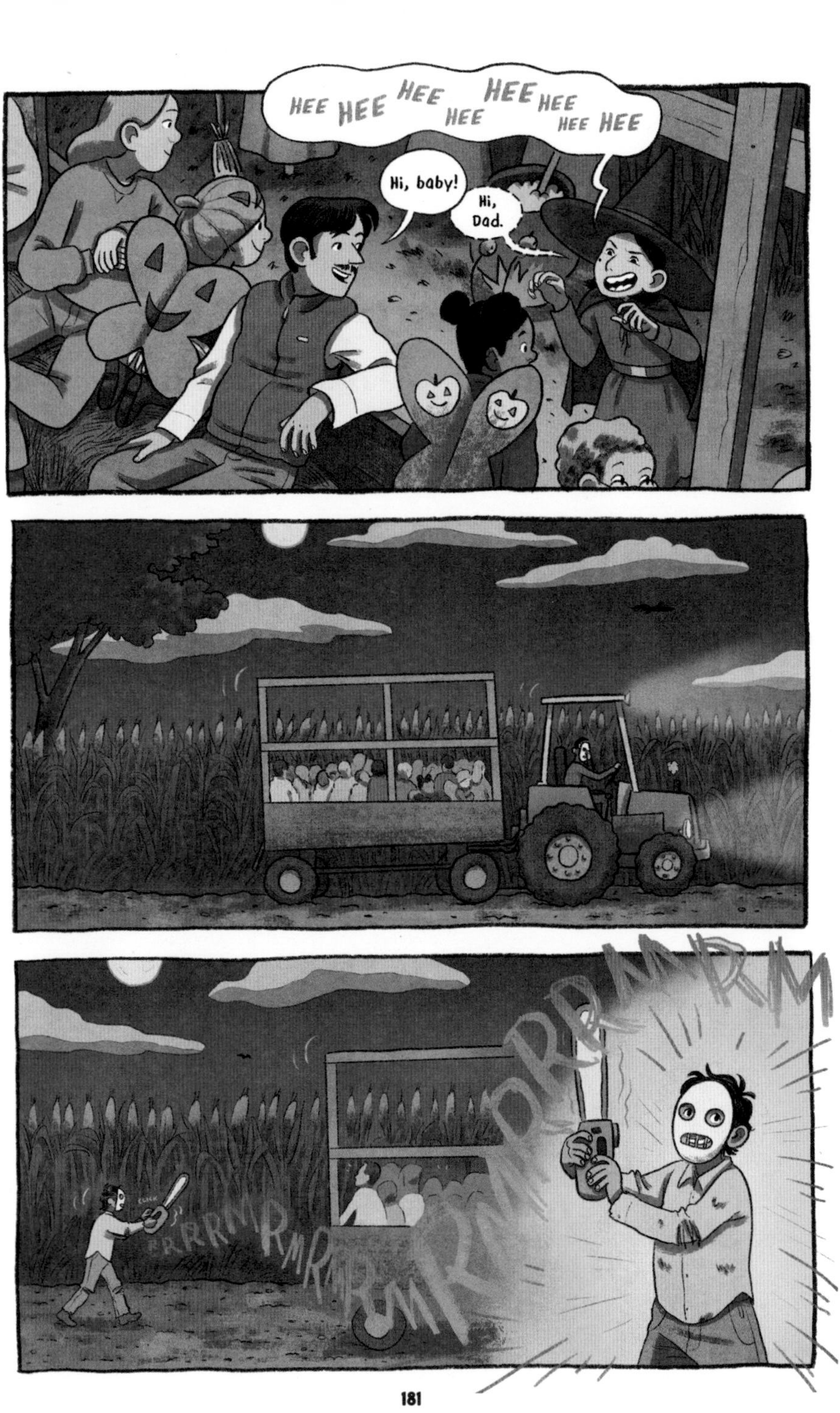
HEE HEE HEE HEE HEE HEE HEE HEE
Hi, baby!
Hi, Dad.

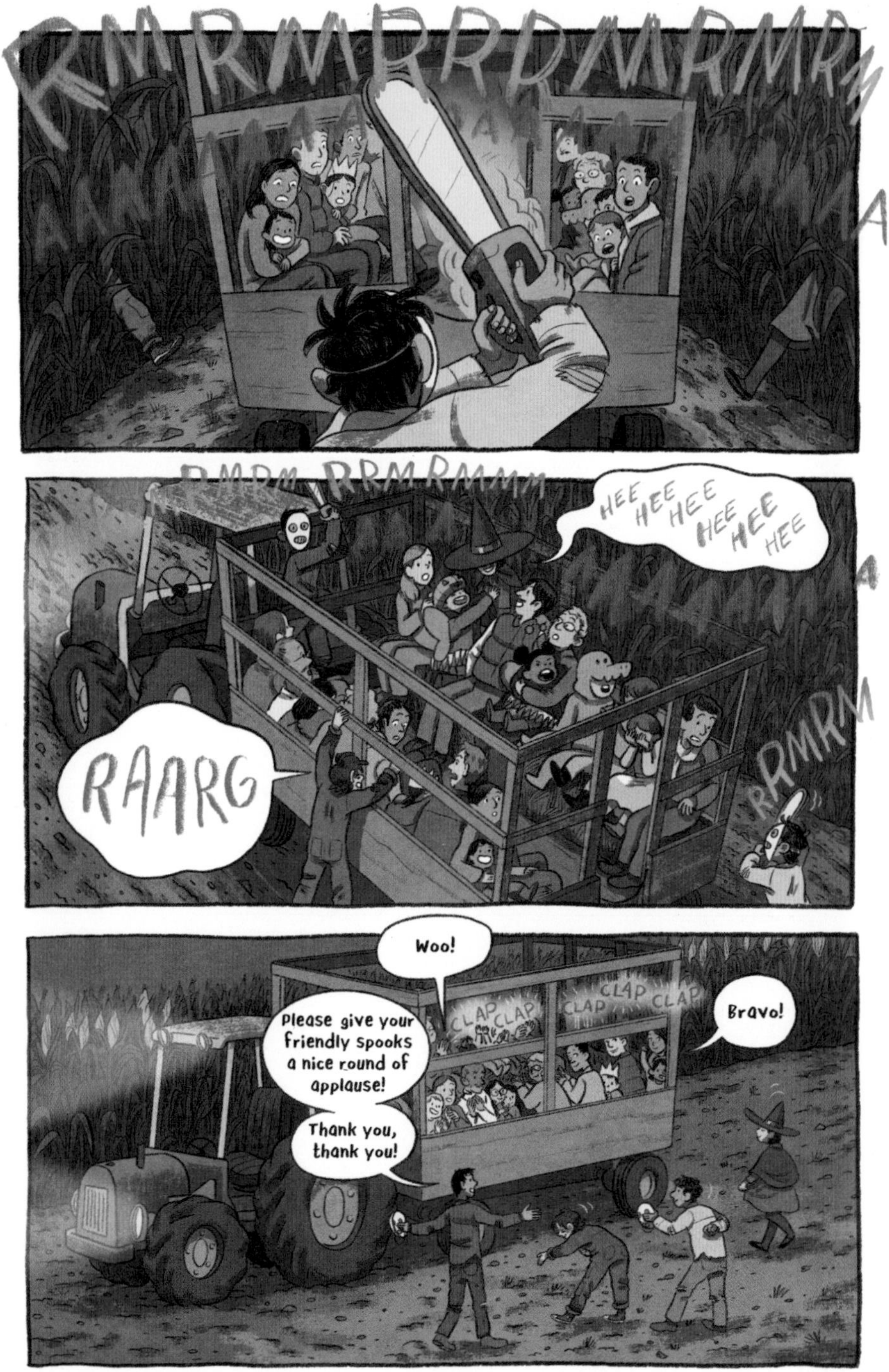
HEE HEE HEE HEE HEE HEE
RAARG
RRMRM
Woo!
CLAP CLAP CLAP CLAP CLAP
Please give your friendly spooks a nice round of applause!
Bravo!
Thank you, thank you!

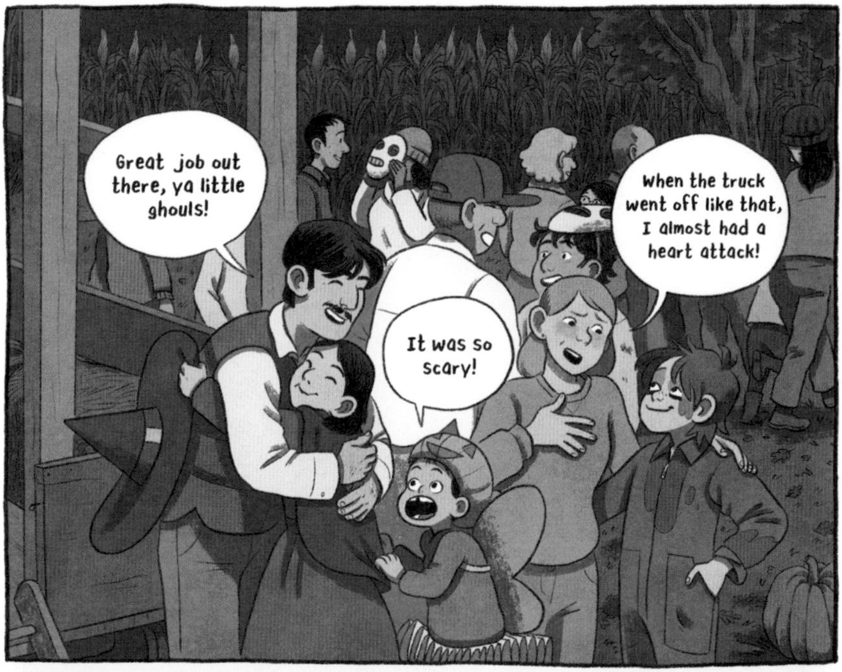
Great job out there, ya little ghouls!
It was so scary!
When the truck went off like that, I almost had a heart attack!

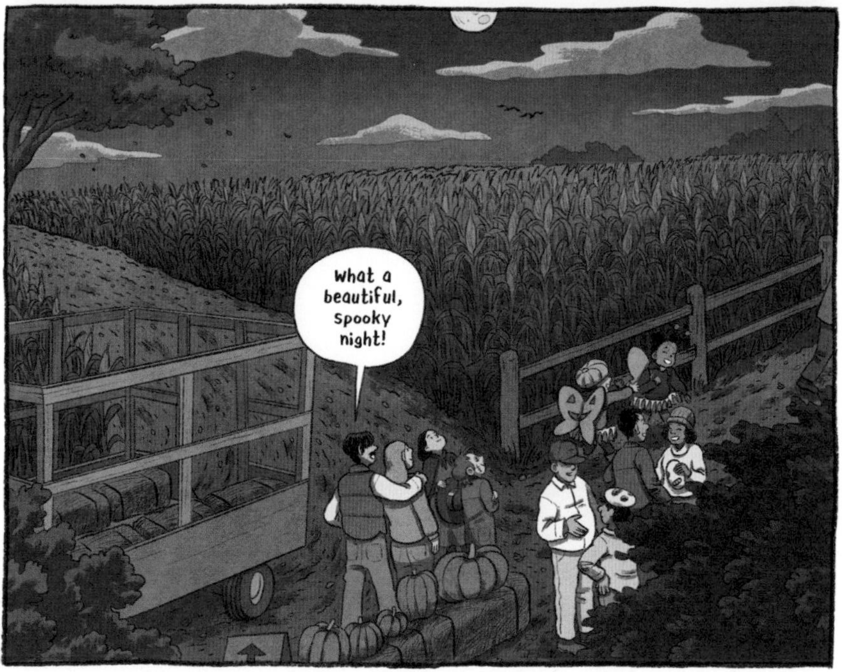
What a beautiful, spooky night!

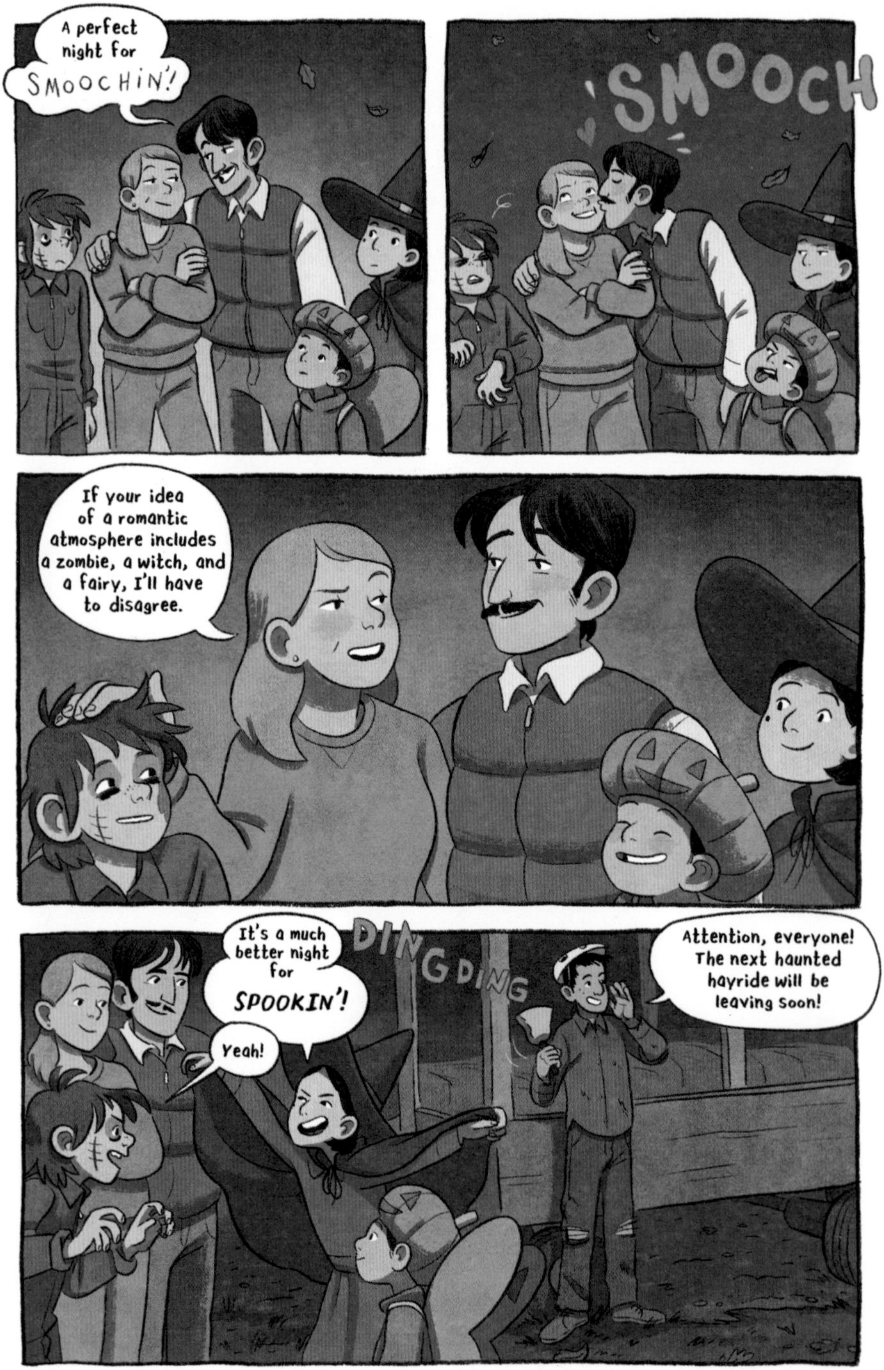
A perfect night for SMOOCHIN'!
SMOOCH
If your idea of a romantic atmosphere includes a zombie, a witch, and a fairy, I'll have to disagree.
It's a much better night for SPOOKIN'!
Yeah!
DING DING
Attention, everyone! The next haunted hayride will be leaving soon!

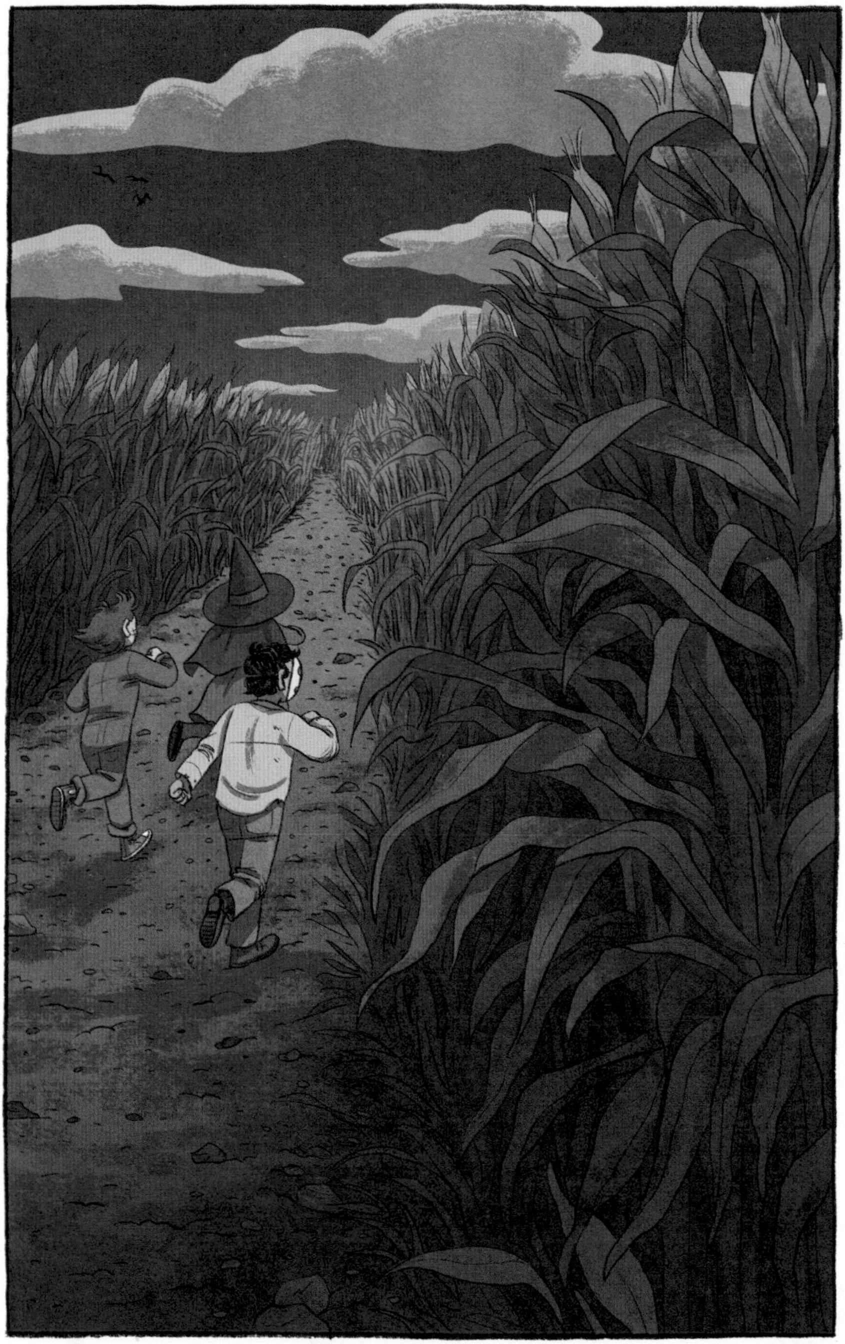

186

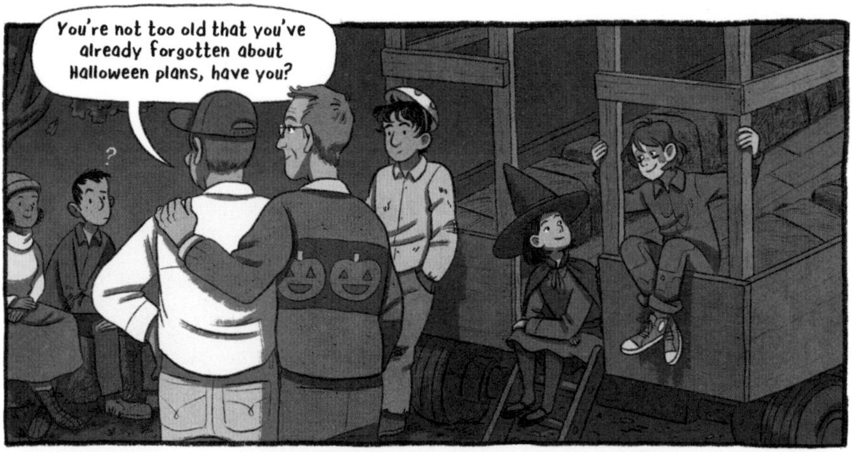
You're not too old that you've already forgotten about Halloween plans, have you?
?

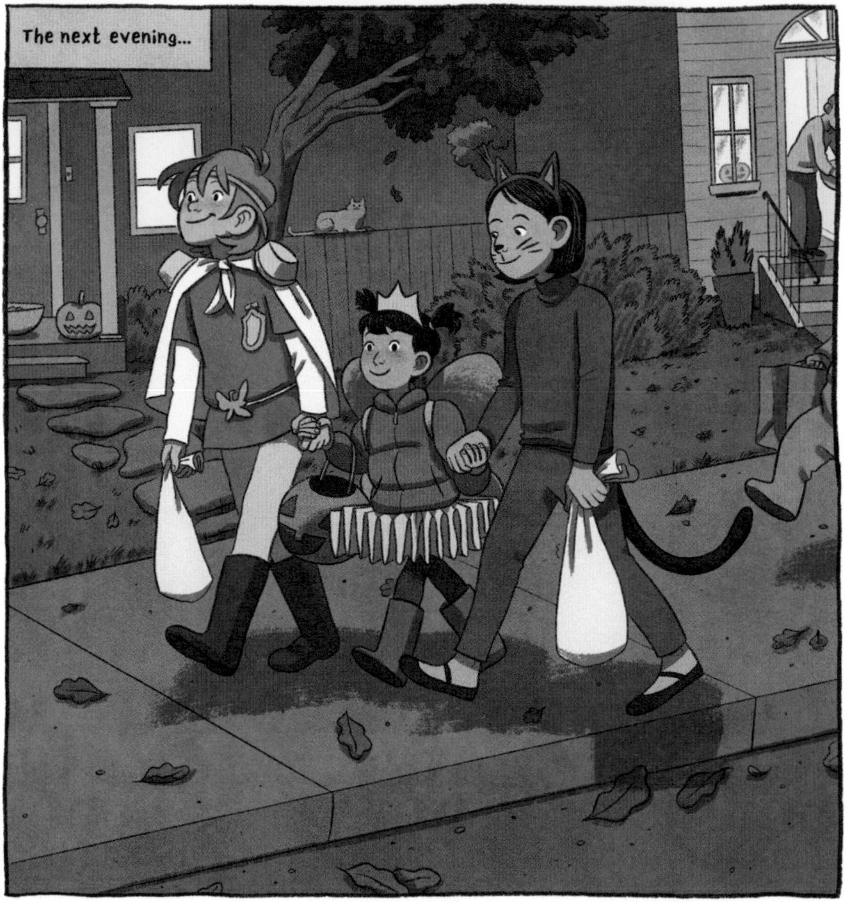
The next evening...

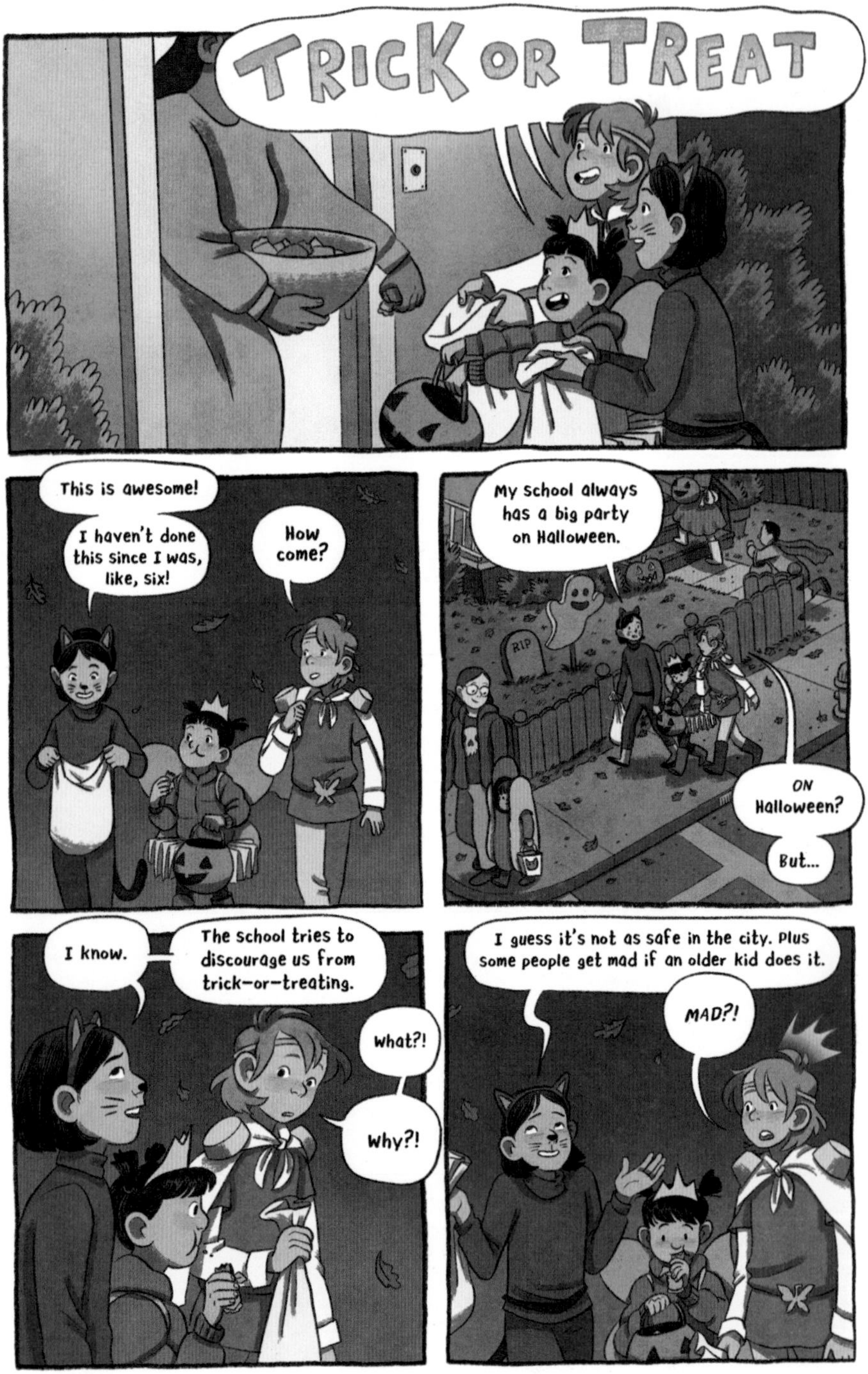
TRICK OR TREAT
This is awesome!
I haven't done this since I was, like, six!
How come?
My school always has a big party on Halloween.
RIP
ON Halloween?
But...
I know.
The school tries to discourage us from trick-or-treating.
What?!
Why?!
I guess it's not as safe in the city. Plus some people get mad if an older kid does it.
MAD?!

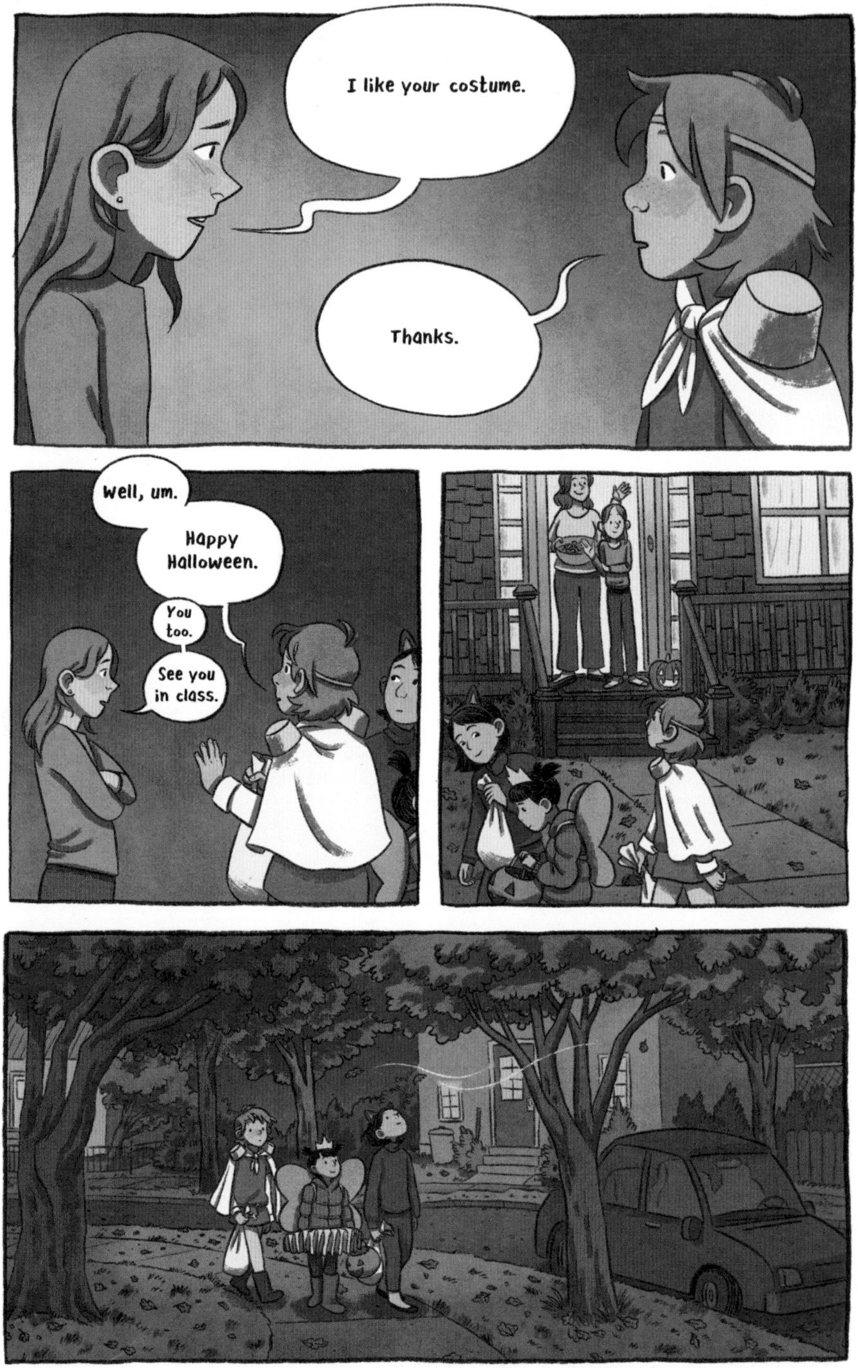
I like your costume.
Thanks.
Well, um.
Happy Halloween.
You too.
See you in class.

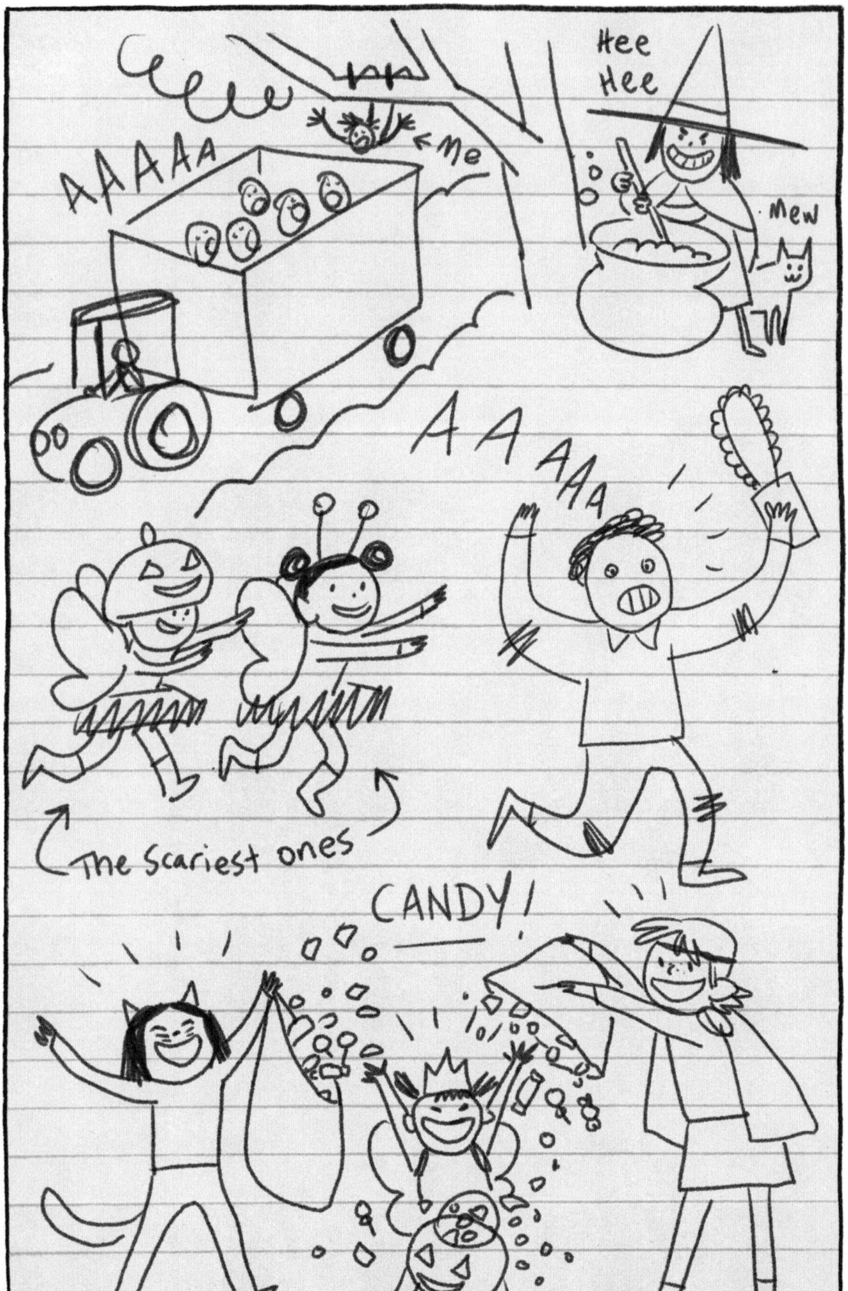
AAAAA
Me
Hee Hee
Mew
AAAAAA
The Scariest ones
CANDY!

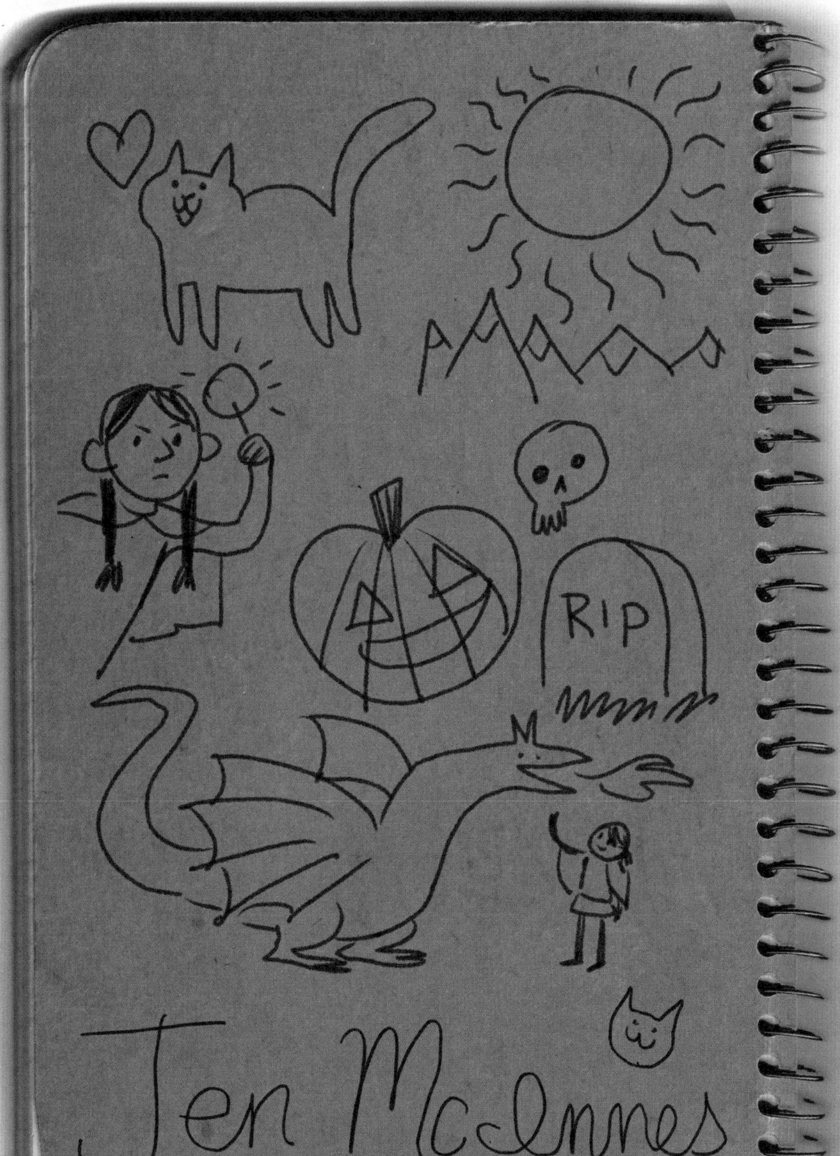
RIP
Jen McInnes

A note from the author/artist:
me

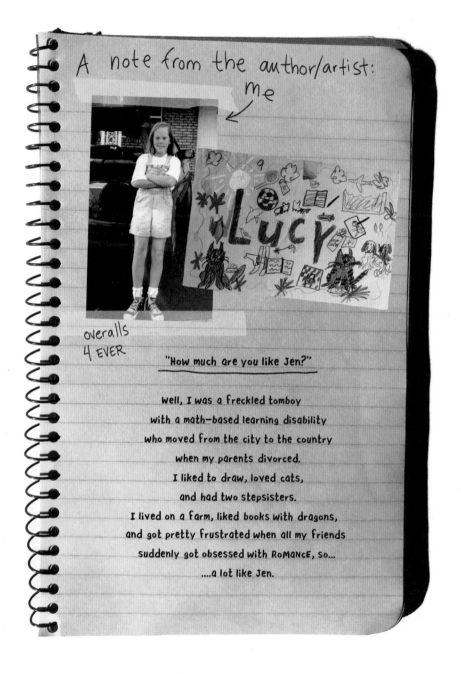

overalls
4 EVER

"How much are you like Jen?"

Well, I was a freckled tomboy
with a math-based learning disability
who moved from the city to the country
when my parents divorced.
I liked to draw, loved cats,
and had two stepsisters.
I lived on a farm, liked books with dragons,
and got pretty frustrated when all my friends
suddenly got obsessed with ROMANCE, so...
.....a lot like Jen.

"What do you or Jen have against romance?"

Not a thing! But it bugged me when my friendships suddenly became more complicated because of it. It took me a while to figure out, but, like everything, I learned that everyone has their own way of experiencing love and dating and that it shouldn't get in the way of friendships.

"Are haunted hayrides a real thing?"

Yes! If you've never had the pleasure of having your pants scared off on a slow-moving wagon of hay, I recommend it. Check out some farms near you in the fall, and be sure to eat a cider doughnut!

our neighbor's hayride ↓ (not haunted in 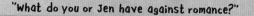 photo)

"YAY, SCHOOL."
FACE
← cool socks

Li'l Stinker

Same Ol' Stinker

Thank you to my kind and inspiring readers, for letting me connect to you through these stories.

And also to the people in this world who give kids dragon books and cider doughnuts.

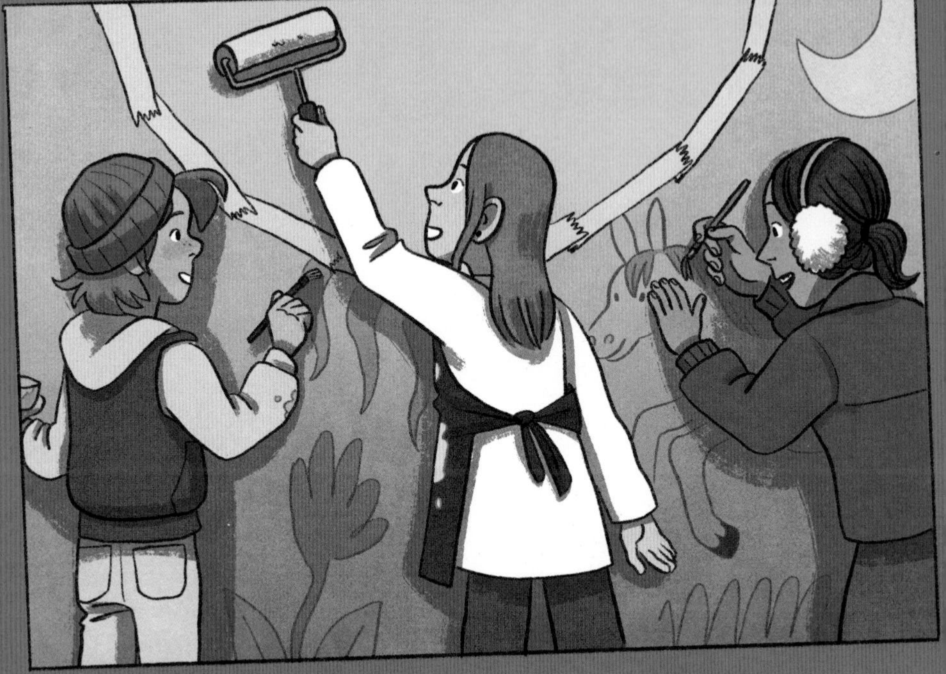

Family isn't the only thing growing on Peapod Farm!

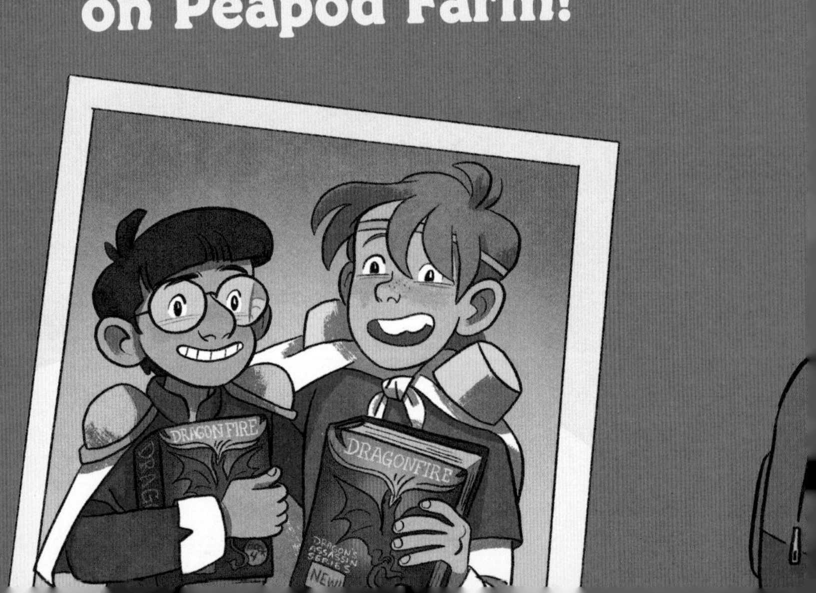
DRAGON FIRE
DRAGONFIRE
DRAGON'S ASSASSIN SERIES

Jen's adventures will continue, with all-new friends and the same old stepsisters!

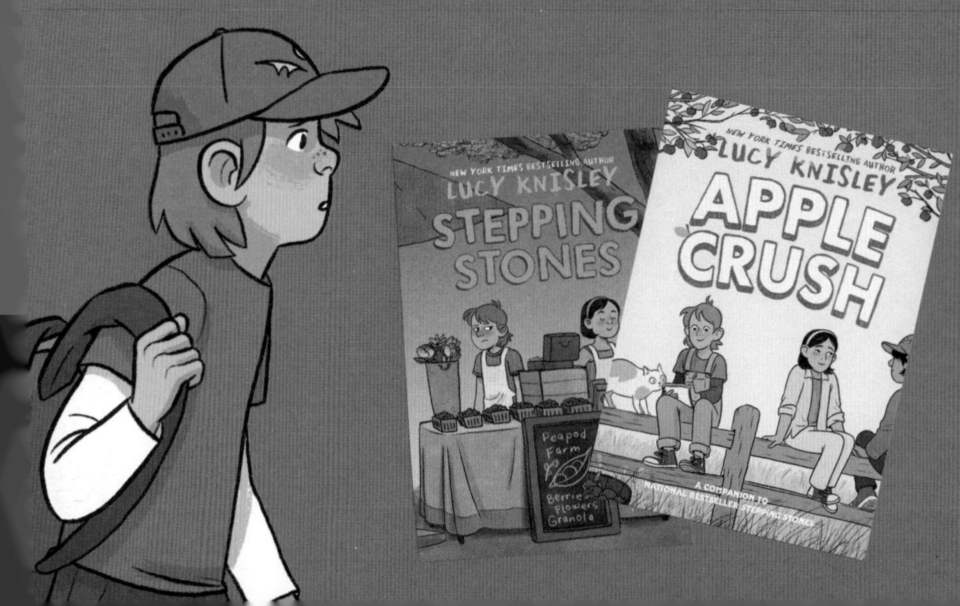
NEW YORK TIMES BESTSELLING AUTHOR
LUCY KNISLEY
STEPPING STONES
Peapod Farm
Berries
Flowers
Granola
NEW YORK TIMES BESTSELLING AUTHOR
LUCY KNISLEY
APPLE CRUSH
A COMPANION TO NATIONAL BESTSELLER STEPPING STONES

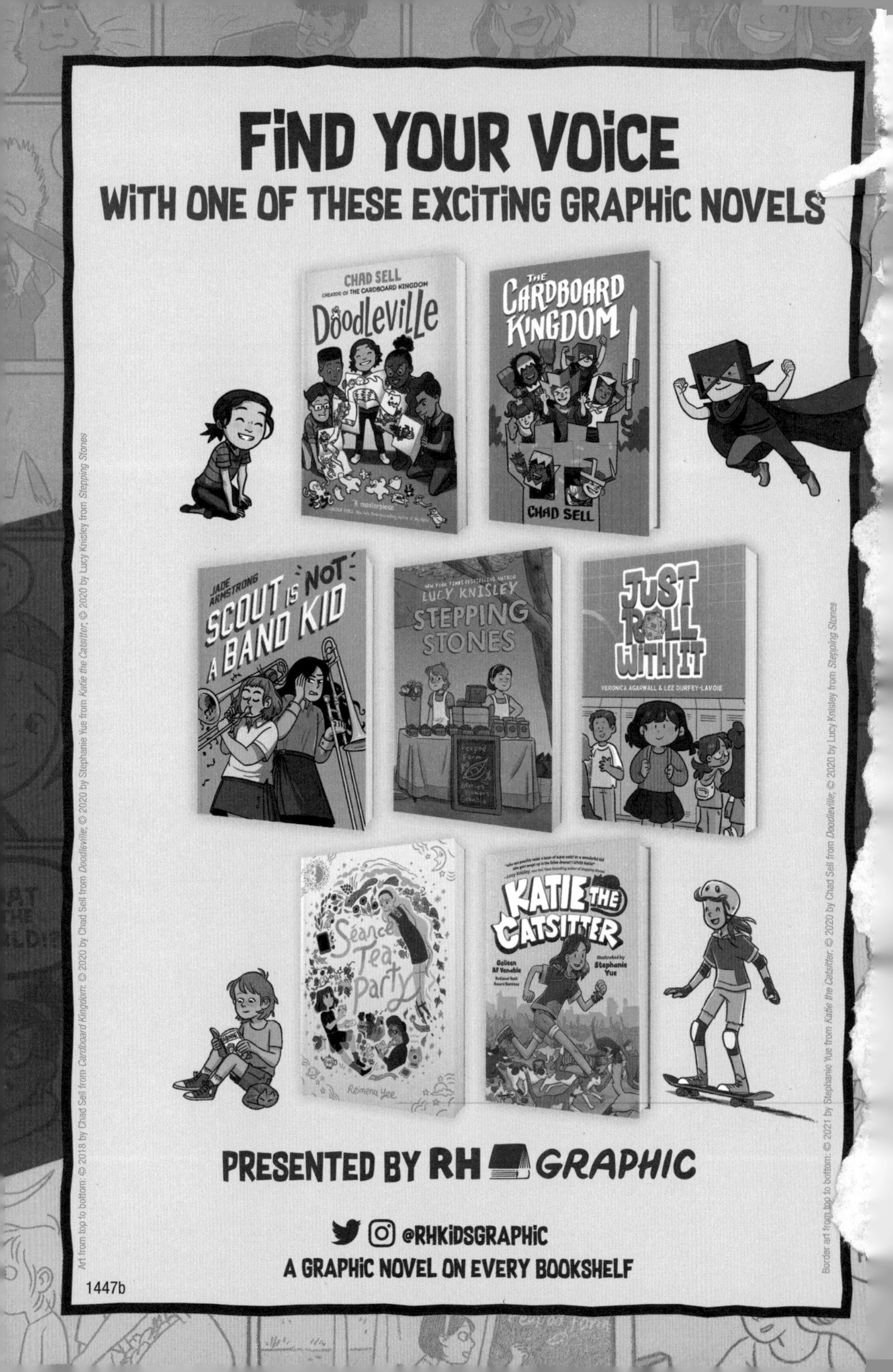
FIND YOUR VOICE
WITH ONE OF THESE EXCITING GRAPHIC NOVELS
CHAD SELL
CREATOR OF THE CARDBOARD KINGDOM
Doodleville
"A masterpiece."
THE CARDBOARD KINGDOM
CHAD SELL
JADE ARMSTRONG
SCOUT IS NOT A BAND KID
NEW YORK TIMES BESTSELLING AUTHOR
LUCY KNISLEY
STEPPING STONES
JUST ROLL WITH IT
VERONICA AGARWALL & LEE DURFEY-LAVOIE
Séance Tea Party
Reimena Yee
KATIE THE CATSITTER
Colleen AF Venable
Illustrated by Stephanie Yue
PRESENTED BY RH GRAPHIC
@RHKIDSGRAPHIC
A GRAPHIC NOVEL ON EVERY BOOKSHELF
1447b
Art from top to bottom: © 2018 by Chad Sell from Cardboard Kingdom; © 2020 by Chad Sell from Doodleville; © 2020 by Stephanie Yue from Katie the Catsitter; © 2020 by Lucy Knisley from Stepping Stones
Border art from top to bottom: © 2021 by Stephanie Yue from Katie the Catsitter; © 2020 by Chad Sell from Doodleville; © 2020 by Lucy Knisley from Stepping Stones